ELIZABETH STEPHENS

LORD OF POPULATION

POPULATION SERIES: BOOK ONE

Table of Contents

Rules for the World After	1
Chapter One	1
Chapter Two	19
Chapter Three	33
Chapter Four	60
Chapter Five	82
Chapter Six	119
Chapter Seven	146
Chapter Eight	180
Chapter Nine	221
Chapter Ten	230
Chapter Eleven	253
Chapter Twelve	283
Chapter Thirteen	299
Chapter Fourteen	326
Chapter Fifteen	344
Chapter Sixteen	351
Chapter Seventeen	369
Chapter Eighteen	385
Chapter Nineteen	400
Chapter Twenty	409
Chapter Twenty-One	429
Chapter Twenty-Two	452
Chapter Twenty-Three	462
Chapter Twenty-Four	467
Chapter Twenty-Five	478
Chapter Twenty-Six	494
Chapter Twenty-Seven	501
Chapter Twenty-Eight	522
Chapter Twenty-Nine	525
Chapter Thirty	534
Rule for the World After	539
All books by Elizabeth	562

To Abel and Kane.
I will never give up on you.

E.S.

Rules for the World After

Rule 1
never hope

Rule 2
pack light

Rule 3
don't get personal

Rule 4
the bigger the badder

Rule 5
run

Rule 6
always trust your gut

Rule 7
never drop your weapon

Rule 8
don't help strangers

Rule 9
no talking in the grey

Rule 10
don't start a fight you can't win

Rule 11
double tap

Rule 12
don't talk to the Others

Chapter One

I lay there at the edge of the bed, closest to the door knowing that it's also the closest spot to danger. A small body warms my left side and I glance over to see Ashlyn's heart-shaped face press against my upper arm while her wandering left hand grips the outside of her mother's coat. She's drooling on me a little and I smile before tucking her silvery blonde hair back behind her ear.

Her hat's come off too, and I carefully slide it back on without waking her. I worry that she'll catch pneumonia, but I'm thankful that at least tonight we found an apartment building to crash in.

The night before we'd been on the streets. Food had been scarce, and the wind had been bitter and brutally cold. So I'm happy for the floor beneath our backs and walls to keep the wind from freezing little Ashlyn to death.

She sighs when I pull the blankets all the way up to her nose and I see that she's sleeping soundly, like the dead. I'm momentarily envious, because I don't really sleep at all anymore. And though I'd like to say that it's the gunfire raging in the neighborhood or the lonely screams, both of these are constants in my life and ceased scaring me years ago.

Realizing that I'm not getting any more sleep, I get up and go to the window. Careful not to remove the boards that cover it, I lift just one about half-an-inch and peer out at the cityscape before me, stretching up and out to meet that distant horizon. Around us are mostly low buildings, most of which are half-caved, their brick sides and concrete foundations reaching up from the ground like crippled hands clawing their way out of the pavement. It's not a city, per se, but it's still the largest town we've dared venture to in the better part of a year.

Rule number four: the bigger, the badder.

Big cities are for the Others, while smaller cities belong to the gangs. And though we'd been happy a few nights ago to find a village too far from a real city to be a real concern, I still know that even in the outliers, a guarantee of safety is only fool's gold.

That's why my first rule for survival in the World After is never to hope.

My breath fogs the murky windowpane and I use my sleeve to clear it. The sky is an ominous purple — even though it's daybreak — but I'm happy that it isn't that awful charcoal-grey-slashed-with-ink-blots-of-violent-orange that usually persists throughout most days. Most nights too. Like the sky itself is bleeding.

The buildings that abut ours are low and ruined. I can see the burn scars on the restaurant across from our temporary shelter and shudder, wondering when the last attack happened on this town. But still, even these broken and bruised buildings seem like skyscrapers after living in the forests for so long. It had been my idea to leave civilization two years ago and move to the forests, but in winter we hadn't been prepared. We still aren't.

Twelve years later and we still continue to cling to memories of the World Before. I know better. It's thinking like this — remembering foreign concepts of family and friendship and allegiance and trust — that gets us into trouble. Or killed.

Becks is one of the rare dreamers still breathing and it had been her idea six weeks ago to try some of the smaller towns and see if we couldn't make it through to March. I hadn't wanted to leave at first, but when Ashlyn got sick we didn't have much of a choice. Medicine is gold, and we haven't had any for over a year. Maybe longer.

I glance back at Becks on the bed, curled around her daughter. Becks is long and lean and might have made an exceptional model if she'd been given the chance. Ashlyn has much more of her dad in her – hard lines in a square face – except for her hair, which is just as bright as her mom's. So blonde it's nearly white. Her little round nose contrasts brilliantly against her whitewashed coloring. It is, as always, bright red.

I smile down at the girls. My girls. Not by blood or anything, but they're all I've got left. I know I'll have to wake them soon, but to give them a few more moments of peace I head to the bathroom only to be startled by a shocking discovery: warm water. Well, nearly warm. I still let out an exalted whoop that has Becks and Ashlyn both running. They charge around the corner, Becks with a knife in hand. She sets it down on the countertop when she sees me smiling.

"Feel," I tell them, laughing out loud. I can't remember the last time I took a warm shower, but I don't know how long it'll last. "Quick. Ashlyn, you go first."

Ashlyn's glossy brown eyes grow round and within a second Becks has her stripped down to her birthday suit. Naked, I see how thin Ashlyn has gotten. She's all elbows and knees and pale freckled skin as she awkwardly grows into her body.

Still as clumsy as a newborn calf, she slips when she gets into the tub and splashes water over me. We all laugh. Becks showers second and though the water is cold by the time that it's my turn, it's at least not freezing. Knowing I won't get another chance like this, I wash my hair anyway. It's been weeks.

Slipping back into our dirty clothes, we raid the kitchen again, hoping to catch anything we might have missed in the darkness of the night before. We obviously aren't the first ones to have had this idea because the only thing we find is dog food, and even that's stale.

We huddle in the kitchen anyway and Becks and I watch Ashlyn crawl around on all fours even though she can barely move in all her layers. She barks periodically and lifts her head up to ask for pats and treats. Her tongue rolls out of her mouth and fleetingly I think that she might have been a great actress if the world that I grew up in hadn't ended 12 years ago. Quietly, Becks and I laugh and eat our kibbles without complaining.

"Do we have to leave?" Ashlyn whines as we step cautiously out of the apartment and into the hall. It's packed with stuff. The stuff that people abandoned in their haste to leave. Suitcases are spread out across the staircase and I imagine that they're the martyrs whose deaths mean that the owners are still living.

After all, if they abandoned their stuff it only goes to show that they followed rule two: pack light.

Heading down to the second story, I gingerly pick through what's been left behind. Finding a single ski glove, still in good condition, I offer it to Becks. She holds up her hands and shakes her head once. "You take it."

I lift my palms to show her the pair that I'm wearing, which doesn't make a convincing case as they're cotton, fingerless, and stained in what I hope is dirt and not shit or blood.

"They're fine," I mumble in response to her glare.

"Seriously?" Her voice is incredulous and bordering on mad. She stuffs her white-blonde hair beneath her hat and narrows her eyes at me in a way that is either supposed to be threatening or condemning, but she's never been a master of either emotion. I laugh.

"You have to stop being so selfless," she says. "One of these days it's going to get you killed."

I know that, but I roll my eyes and say instead, "Have we met? I'm a brilliant, beautiful jujitsu warrior princess. I'm not going anywhere."

I stick my tongue out at her and she hits me with the floppy side of the glove, but takes it nonetheless. She tosses the cotton glove she'd been wearing into one of the discarded suitcases, which opens up at her like a great green mouth. I try not to think about the blood spray splashed across the jade lining or the dead guy we found last night in the apartment below this one...

Our packs are too full, so we load one of the empty suitcases we find with all of our non-essentials. This way we can drop it without thinking if we need to run. Ashlyn complains as we work.

"Can we come back tomorrow?" She begs, knowing the answer already. "I don't want to go out into the grey."

Ashlyn calls the world The Grey because of how low the clouds hang. Fitting, I always thought. Her mother shushes her gently and takes her hand. "No more talking now. What's rule number nine?"

Ashlyn manages to look hilarious with a frown twisting up all that's visible of her little face beneath her scarf, hood, earmuffs and hat. I swear if Becks could have layered more stuff over the child without suffocating her, she would have.

Ashlyn pouts, "No talking in the grey." You never know who might be listening.

"Good girl." Becks kisses Ashlyn's forehead and Ashlyn releases a begrudging grin.

She looks at me and I smile back encouragingly. "You made a very convincing puppy this morning," I say. "You know what else puppies are good at?"

"What?" Her eyes glow as she looks up at me and locks her small fingers with mine.

I duck my head so that we're nearly eye level and whisper, "Sniffing out food. Do you think you can do that?"

She nods excitedly, mahogany eyes large and wet and full of a childhood wonder that feels so alien in this ruined place. Then she barks.

I laugh. "Do you want to pick the next place then?"

She bounces on the balls of her feet, crashes into Becks and nearly knocks the pack off of her back. "Yeah!"

"When you sniff out one that looks good, you point, okay?"

She nods again and opens her mouth, but I lift a finger and touch it to my lips.

Ashlyn beams when I pull her hat down to cover her eyes and I struggle not to laugh when her big, cumbersome mittens shove it up enough so she can see. But the moment doesn't last long.

We sober quickly and look to Becks who cocks her head towards the front door. I take the suitcase in my right hand and continue to grip Ashlyn fiercely in the other. Then I nod once in the affirmative.

Becks's typically creamy face turns sheet-white as she takes the lumpy bronze doorknob between her gloved fingers. With her other hand, she slips her favorite knife into her back pocket. It's also her only knife. Our only knife. I try not to think about that as Becks opens the door and biting air invades the musty, musky space around us that smells only of the dead man in the room at the end of the hall.

I take Ashylyn's hand fiercely in mine and hold my breath in my lungs. Becks takes that first step out onto the stoop of the apartment building, entering the grey.

Then we run.

We move freaking *fast*, keeping low and close to the buildings on our right, eyes scanning left, out towards the street. Parked cars litter the roads like the discarded toys of children. We managed to get one running once, but that was back before when we'd been thirteen. Unlucky thirteen. Now we're just three. Just us.

Six blocks zip by and I can hear Ashlyn breathing hard at my side. I know she's underfed and overheating in her many layers, but we can't afford to lose one single article.

It's a bitter November, made all the more miserable by the grey hanging low over our heads. It's that grey that really gets to me. Beneath it, the air is damp and wet and suffocating. It smells like sulfur too, and human waste.

And somehow, despite the humidity, I can feel my dry lips cracking and my eyes watering even though we've only been outside a few minutes. I'm sweating too, in defiance of the outside chill and even though I've got on fewer clothes than Ashlyn does. Far fewer, and in much, much worse condition.

My tattered jeans once belonged to a man and now drag across the ground as I run. I nearly trip over their hem when Becks lifts a hand and swerves dramatically to the left, into the road. She beckons us forward and we zigzag behind the safety of overturned cars. Even though it makes me feel exposed, I don't question her, particularly when I register the source of the smell.

I shield Ashlyn's face from the sight while I take a closer look at the pile of carcasses that slump against one another in the opening of a small apartment building that looks a lot like the one we just abandoned. Two men, a boy, and two little girls.

One of the men has his arms draped over the bodies of the girls in a way that suggests he'd been trying to protect them. They're twins and still holding hands despite the shrapnel scarring their chests in shades of crimson and burgundy.

One of them is missing her dress and I look down at Ashlyn. She's about their age. I feel my stomach drop in nervous anticipation, but not because I'm sad for the family. God no. I'm worried about what killed them, when, and how.

Gangs, most likely, but I also know that gangs aren't the worst things out there…

I cast my wary gaze around at the empty storefronts, expecting to see human bodies switching back and forth, but so far I only see shadows. And I'm so focused on the opposite side of the street and the graveyard of vehicles surrounding us that I don't immediately notice when Becks comes to an unnatural and abrupt stop.

The rough fabric of her shirt grates my cheek and my nose tingles when it collides directly with Beck's shoulder. I use my hands to brace myself and even little Ashlyn helps pull me back.

A moment later, I'm on my knees, crouching behind a parked SUV. I drag Ashlyn down by my side reflexively. We've come to a stop at a T-intersection, which looked like the last resting place for quite a few souls.

The car shielding us is one of the few that's still intact. The other vehicles involved in the wreck have been incinerated, stripped, and smashed to pieces. Aside from the SUV and a metro bus a little ways off, very few are recognizable.

She reminds me of a meerkat as she stands stiff and tall and peers through the car's back window. She's a better scout than I am, largely because I lost hearing in my left ear during the first attack, eleven years ago. A year after the Fall — the day the Others came and the sky ripped open.

I was ten back then and my mom and dad were still alive. Becks's parents too, though she'd been older and we hadn't really been friends. Our compound had been the biggest human community left on the East Coast before gang violence fractured our city. And whatever the Others hadn't taken, gang warfare destroyed.

I still remember that first attack vividly and sometimes, when I close my eyes, I can even smell raining sulfur and feel the heat from the fires and hear the sound of gunshots ringing and shells hitting the ground around me even though I can't hear anything out of my left ear anymore.

Ashlyn tugs on Becks's pant leg but she doesn't move. Instead she gasps and I hear it only after Becks's has already kicked it into high gear: the sound of feet pounding over pavement.

Without a word, Becks wrenches open the backdoor to the SUV in front of us and throws Ashlyn inside. I climb in after her, wondering why we've chosen not to run as more than thirty people charge down the street towards us, but it's too late to question her now. I toss our stuff onto the floor of the backseat and slam the door closed behind me while Becks feverishly tries to lower one of the backseats so she can get into the trunk.

I'm not sure why. Until she says, "Ashlyn, get in the trunk, okay? They must have seen us, but maybe…maybe they didn't see you. You can still make it. Get into the trunk. Hide and wait for them to leave. You remember everything that aunt and mommy taught you, right? You can still make it. They can't…they can't have seen her…"

Tears gloss Ashlyn's bright eyes. Glorious eyes. The same eyes her father had. I hate to see them there and my voice is harsher than it needs to be as I snap, "Becks, we're not dead yet. And…"

I feel my face twist up in confusion as I try to process what I'm seeing on the road. The thirty or so people tearing down the street towards us they…they aren't stopping.

"I don't *think* they saw us," I hazard.

Becks quiets. I feel the warmth of her cheek against mine as she peers over my shoulder out of the cracked window. Ashlyn sits tucked in the crammed space behind me. She takes my fingers in her gloved hands and I fleetingly recognize that she's wearing the glove I gave Becks earlier.

It's Ashlyn that whispers, "They're afraid."

I feel my eyes widen. She's right. I edge forward, so close to the window that my breath fogs the glass. "These aren't gangs," I say, rubbing the fog away with the flat of my fist. "They're scavengers. They're like us."

An older woman and a slightly younger man move ahead of the pack down the street in our direction. Tears stream through the dirt on their faces and the woman clutches at her chest when the man swings a hard right. He pulls her into an abandoned corner store and I lose sight of them as the larger group of scavengers rushes up to meet us.

But…they don't stop. They keep going. They filter around the car like river water around rocks and disappear into the storefronts lining the street, breaking windows and tearing skin and clothes to claw their way inside. And as they run, I'm reminded of something my father once told me about the behavioral patterns of rats — an invasive species, they only migrate in herds when there's a larger predator driving them out.

I throw open the door and grab Ashlyn by the scruff of her collar. "Move!" I drag Ashlyn out of the SUV, but Becks must have already come to the same conclusion I had because she's two steps ahead, with all of our stuff loaded onto her shoulders. She's halfway down the road now.

The street is desolate and eerily quiet and if I hadn't seen so many people sprinting by us seconds before I might have believed that we were alone. The grey above seems to have descended. It's as dense as a wall and I can't see more than thirty feet past the intersection. Becks calls my name and I run when she does, sprinting to keep up. I'm half dragging Ashlyn, and I can hear her panting so heavily at my side that I imagine we're heard by every other scavenger on the block.

Becks dives left around the next corner and looks up to make sure we're following. I throw myself into the alley after her and, as I land, I clamp a hand over Ashlyn's mouth. On my belly, I can feel the chill of the asphalt seeping into my clothes, but I don't dare move.

"They're here," Becks whispers, "The Others…"

Not a second later, a body flies into the T-junction, impaling the black SUV we'd just used for cover. I jump. Becks winces. Ashlyn gasps. I look down and try to shush her, and see that she's lost her hat in the maelstrom. I smooth down her silken hair and hold her close to my chest. Turning around, I look to see if we might make a break for it, but the alleyway behind me is a dead end.

Shock numbs me and I clench my jaw together so hard it hurts. I'm angry with Becks for bringing me to a city and furious with myself for not standing up to her and more than anything I'm disastrously confused.

I don't understand how or why the Others would be roaming this far from their territories. And finally, I capitulate because in this confusion, I also recognize that there's nothing I can do. As I turn back to the scene it's with the bleak knowledge that we will have to wait and watch this destructive finality.

That, and make sure we stick to the rules.

A body darts into the street after the first. He's also one of them. If I hadn't been able to tell by the fact that nothing besides the Others could have uprooted and dispersed a pack of scavengers as large as that, I can see it in his imposing size and stature as moves towards the SUV and the even larger, non-human body that decorates it. Strangely enough, that body is still moving.

Despite having smashed the SUV nearly in two, the Other wrenches one shoulder out from the crater he's created, then the other, then drops to the asphalt, unharmed. As I take him in, I swallow hard and close my eyes for longer than a blink.

Turns out the Others are every bit as intimidating-looking as I've heard from the stories. Even though he's human-shaped, he's breaching seven feet tall. He's *shirtless* out here even though I'm freezing my tits off, but who cares about the weather when your pectorals burn with an orange glow and steam rises from your skin? I haven't seen one of them with a chest like this before — broad, richly layered in heavy muscle, and burning like a goddamn torch.

The one with the golden chest turns to face his adversary — someone I can't see from around the brick building to my right. I can just see him. And I don't let him leave my sight.

He steps around what's left of the SUV and places his hands against its crumpled trunk. Leaning his weight forward, he gives it a little push and the entire car hurtles across the short space to obliterate the man he's up against.

My lips part in shock and horror. He moves the car like it weighs absolutely nothing. Like he shouldn't already be dead. How could we humans have ever thought we stood a chance?

A swift shot of relief hits me as I catch the stagger in his next step. I smell the blood next. Sulfuric and tangy, like a ripe rotten corpse. When he twists, I can see that it weeps down his entire right side so that I can't actually tell *where* he's been injured, but I know he *has* been injured. It's the only thing to cut some of the bite out of the fear rattling around in my chest and I know that this might be the best shot we get to make a break for it.

I lean into Becks's ear and start to tell her as much, but before I can even slide my knee underneath me, she shoves me down onto the concrete. Hard. In the same breath, six more Others move out to meet the first.

The Others gliding out into the T-intersection are varying shapes, colors, and sizes, but what does remain consistent is that they're all shirtless, they're all huge, and not one of them is lit up like a human night light, like the first. And when the six move into the intersection they approach the loner cautiously, even though he's injured and outnumbered.

Their hesitation is only mirrored by the loner's confidence as he stands up straight and squares up against them. Almost as if in defiance. He wipes his arm across his face, smearing a thick layer of blood across it too difficult to see through. But even though I can't make out his face, I know that he's challenging them.

Injured and outnumbered? So, he's also insane.

One of the Others says something to the loner in a language I don't understand and the loner responds in a laugh that is full of everything but humor. It's a hateful laugh that reaches up to fill the fallen sky and I grit my teeth while Ashlyn shakes beneath me. I lay my palm over her eyes. I know what's coming.

The loner barks out a sentence in that same cryptic language, then releases a roar — no, a battle cry. His voice is a snarl layered atop another snarl and is full of blistering violence. And as I keep Ashlyn clenched beneath me fiercely with my hand pressed over her eyes, I watch the scene, as if hypnotized.

Even though the loner is injured and outnumbered and not even as big as some of the Others he's up against, part of me is rooting for him. But I know that no matter how hard I cheer, the loner is going to die here fighting for his life in this shitty intersection on this shitty road in this shitty town, because that's when I see the gun.

The largest of the Others steps forward wielding an enormous gun I hadn't noticed before. Without warning, this giant fires half a dozen rounds into the loner's chest, and when he still doesn't fall, all six of the Others move forward as one and descend on him.

The ensuing fight is a blur. The loner manages to get a few good hits in, and then I hear a slicing sound and half of his attackers jump back. He's holding a sword. Serrated on both sides, it looks deadly sharp, even in the fading light. It's a good sized sword — about three feet in length — like the kind I used to train with back in our old camp. On me, a long sword, on him, dagger *plus*. But he knows how to use it.

He twists around one of the burned cars, blade moving as swiftly as smoke in the dark. He arcs his sword high, then brings it down, taking one of the Others apart in two pieces, head severed from his neck.

Angry cries fill the night and another shot is fired. The loner snarls and staggers to one knee as he takes another bullet to the chest, but somehow it doesn't keep him grounded — what is that now, eight bullets *directly* to the torso?

Instead, he lifts his blade and points it directly at the giant holding the gun. His arm doesn't waver and when one of the six — now five — comes towards him, he rips into the space and takes off a leg at the knee and an arm at the elbow.

The giant fires again. This time, at the loner's sword hand. The blade flies from his fingertips, clattering noisily to the ground beneath him. When the loner turns to reach for it, the giant moves in quickly. He takes the loner by the right arm and leg, lifts him over his head and throws his body down the street. The loner crashes onto the roof of an abandoned bus — not six paces away from us — and the empty husk of that crap wagon craters around him as if made of tin, rather than steel.

Ashlyn squeals beneath me. I grip her mouth so hard I'm sure I'll bruise her, but I don't soften my hold. Instead, I watch the loner roll onto his side and drop off the hood of the car. He lands lithely on all fours in the shadow of the bus, looking like a shadow himself. Also, like a ghost. And for a few seconds he just breathes. Then his fists clench, his shoulders roll back, his bullet-studded muscles swell and his bowed head snaps up. He looks directly at me.

Every nerve in my body triggers and I seize. At my side, I hear Becks gasp. I can't even breathe. He holds my eye-line for just a second before flicking his gaze away from my face and back out towards the street. Rising up onto his feet, he takes slow, uneven steps around the bus to face his remaining adversaries.

Meanwhile, my brain is all scrambled and I don't track the rest of the fight. I come-to near the end, right after the loner punches his hand through the fabric of one guy's stomach, rips out a fistful of intestines, and then is subdued by the three Others still standing.

"Where is it?" The giant roars as he looms over the loner, a single foot planted in the center of the loner's glowing chest.

I don't mean to, but I can't help it. Even though my heartbeat pounds like a nervous finger pressed to the trigger of an AK, I have to know what's happening. I edge closer to the mouth of the alley and see that Becks has done the same.

I lay as close to the ground as possible. Bodies still block my view, but I can make out the Others propping the loner's knees up on cinderblocks. It takes all of them to do so as he roars and thrashes, sounding every bit the animal that I know the Others to be, even if he is defeated. And I know he is defeated.

"Mathos," says the giant, lifting one hand from the loner's soon-to-be corpse. A shorter, but broader one of his comrades hobbles up to stand and hands the giant a sledgehammer.

Between moving feet, I catch a glimpse of the loner's face and see that he's breathing out hard between clenched teeth. Bloody spittle flies from his lips, but even as the giant brings his hammer down onto the loner's shins, shattering every bone again and again, the loner doesn't scream.

He releases a pained hiss and turns his face away from the wreckage towards the alley where we're hiding. For the second time, he meets my gaze, but this time he holds it, and in this dark world of shadows and monsters, I can see nothing else. Just a glimpse of pain. And then a greater resilience. It makes me believe I could do anything. But only for that second. Because as they shatter his other leg, the loner's features twist in and out of anguish and he roars angrily against the pavement. Defeated. Lost.

The giant takes the hammer and brings it down in a heavy arc against the loner's chest, silencing his rage and severing the hold his gaze has on me. And the sound it makes.

Heavens…the sound it makes…Like a bag of eggs slammed against the pavement. It's sickening and just plain gross.

"Where is it?" The giant says, voice loud enough to touch the grey above us. The loner doesn't answer and I cringe as the giant smashes the loner's chest again and again and again. Mercilessly.

I'd always known the Others to be dangerous, blood-thirsty things, but I'd never known them to show such brutality against their own kind. Then again, what *did* I know? What *do* I know? This is the closest to an Other I've been in my whole life.

The loner spits up mouthfuls of blood as the giant impales him one last time. He dies and I wish him a safe trip to Valhalla, because that's where we all end up, isn't it? Becks's family, mine, and despite how hard I try and stop the inevitable, it'll be us someday too. We all die in violence.

The giant screams and the sound is pure frustration. Which doesn't make sense. He won, didn't he? Even more furious than he had been before, the giant throws his hammer so far down the street it disappears and I can no longer see it.

I'm sure that there are already scavengers racing down the block to get it. That's only if they aren't too afraid. And that's a big *if*.

Somehow I can feel the human presence lurking in the buildings lining this road, likely watching the scene and waiting for their time. The moment the Others leave, there's going to be chaos with different scavengers vying over the loner's body parts.

Some cults believe that their blood contains mystical powers. Some think that you can *become* one of them if you eat their hearts whole. But most are just starving and any meat is worth eating, even if it smells sulfurous and rotten. Like a corpse. Like a long. dead. corpse.

Lying there, I can understand the conflicting temptations. My belly is empty and has been for years.

I'm cold, but so close to the loner's corpse now that I can nearly taste his heat.

And that conflict…it fills me with both rapture and revulsion.

The giant kicks the loner in the face one last time before shouting more incomprehensible words to his clan. They gather their broken and severed limbs and stagger back down the street, heading in the direction they came from.

I see a fourth member of the pack lift himself up from the ground and gather up fistfuls of his own intestines. They glisten slick in the dusky light.

As he stumbles after the giant, he tries to shove the red tubes — so dark they appear nearly black — back into the gaping hole below his chest while I try not to puke up all the dog food I ate this morning. It crawls up the back of my throat in acidic heat, but we don't have much more of it, so I gulp it down with force and ignore the way my chest trembles when I do.

The loner is dead and I know that we need to move quickly down the road before the carnage begins…

But I see it, then. Just a glimmer of steel, a promise of protection. It's hiding in the shadows of the metro bus. I'm up on my feet, gesturing for Ashlyn and Becks to stay put. My breath is hot on my lips as I take off at a run. Becks calls out for me to stop, but I'm too quick, too impatient, too impulsive.

At the bus, I shove the length of my arm beneath a jagged beam, scraping my cheek against cold metal as I fight to push aside bits of shattered glass and concrete pebbles until finally, I feel a smooth weight against my fingertips.

It's heavier than it looks, like the weight of a full backpack all by itself. But still, I drag the sword out from beneath the wreckage and when I hold it up, I catch my reflection in the blade. Even though my brown skin is covered in dirt and my short black hair is sticking out in a thousand directions, I'm smiling. It feels like the first win I've had in a really long time. Years, maybe.

I stand. The street is still empty and this surprises me. Turning a full circle, I keep the blade elevated. Yeah, it's heavy, but not as heavy as Ashlyn. I can manage it.

I throw the sword up into the air and catch it by the hilt, testing its weight against my palm, finding equilibrium. I swing it around in a full circle and that's when it happens. In that split instant when I linger.

Becks screams, "No!" And her voice is pure tragedy.

Chapter Two

I hurtle towards the mouth of the alley, stumbling only once while Becks's voice rings in my ears. In my one good ear.

When I reach her, I'm perfectly balanced, ready for the attack and deadly calm. I come around the mouth of the alley and in the dim light, I make out several shapes standing on top of the low, crumbling walls surrounding us.

"Becks," I shout, "run!" But she doesn't. She can't.

Standing on top of the wall at the end of the alleyway, the giant is holding Ashlyn between his arms, body curved around her much, much smaller one, his meaty fist clutching her throat.

I know that I'm going to die — to reach that illusive Valhalla Beck's dad was always prattling on about — but I'm damn sure going alone. Ashlyn and Becks are staying here. They aren't coming with me. This is a solo, one-way journey.

Pebbles from the pavement scrape against my threadbare soles as I lurch forward, catching Becks by the hair just as she charges forward too.

Her hair is soft and tangled and she releases a strangled moan as I drag her to the ground behind me and edge my body between her and the Others, swiftly breaking rule number five — run.

I manage to stick to rule number one though — never hope — because I definitely don't.

I take a step forward and the Others look between one another and laugh, but I use that to my advantage. Becks's dad trained me to a use a sword, but I don't want them to know that. Surprise may be the only advantage I have.

Shifting my grip on the sword, I hold it like I would a baseball bat. The giant smiles when he looks at me. He has thin lips on a mean face that's a slightly darker brown than mine is and covered in cruel scars.

A black eyepatch shrouds his left eye in mystery while his right watches Ashlyn with wickedness and curiosity. My stomach muscles clench at the sight of him watching her and her watching me. Her big brown eyes are glossy, needing me, but she doesn't cry. She stands tall and tough, with her shoulders back and her fists clenched at her sides. Truly, her mother's daughter.

"Two women and a girl traveling alone," says the giant listlessly.

I don't answer him, but instead watch how the shadows shift above me. Even if I can take out one of them, I know I can't take out four. Even injured ones. I think about the loner I left to die and wonder if this is some sick god's retribution for not intervening in his fate. I had been rooting for him, after all…

The giant cocks his head as if he wonders what I'm thinking. My expression hardens against the invasion and for too long we simply watch each other, waiting…

"You mean to fight me for the girl?" he says, lifting one eyebrow and one edge of his mouth.

I feel heat rise in my cheeks, but I nod. Fight for the girl? The hell I will. I'll kill for the girl. Die if I have to.

He lowers into a crouch, fingers cupping the edge of the rust-gilded gutter lightly, as if Ashlyn isn't a half step away from falling. She issues a tight gasp that makes me clench and the giant, seeing it, smiles.

"You mean to die for her?" he says.

"Just take me instead."

He looks down at Ashlyn fondly, shaking in his grip. She doesn't even make up a quarter of his entire size. I'm probably about half his height, at a constantly shrinking one-hundred-some-odd pound, five foot five.

"I've got more blood in me," I tell him, hoping this argument may sway him. "She's just a little girl."

"I like little girls," he replies, running his fingers through Ashlyn's blonde hair in a way that makes my blood boil. "The taste is far sweeter tainted by such innocence. But I do like your ferocity. Perhaps…" I clench my jaw, hoping vainly that the promise of more blood will sweeten the pot, but he frowns. "However, too much ferocity can be a problem." And without another word, he takes one long step back, bringing Ashlyn with him and sending the bit of wall she'd been standing on, crumbling at our feet.

Becks shrieks, like she's being gutted. Meanwhile, the giant whistles and he and the Other who'd actually been gutted leap down off of the other side of the rooftop, disappearing from view and taking Ashlyn with them.

"Finish them," I hear the giant's now distant voice tell the two Others who remain, "quickly."

My heart is pounding as I hold Becks back, shoving her off of me. Grief is clouding her judgement, her thought process. Not that it matters much. She's not a fighter. She's bad with tough decisions and worse with blood. That's where I step in. She may be the arm, but I'm the axe.

I level my blade, turn my body to the side and throw myself at the first of the Others just as he jumps off of the roof and before he's got both feet planted on the ground.

Surprise lights up his face as I barrel into him, throwing my full body weight behind my first strike. I nick his arm, but before I can take it clean off he moves out from beneath me, faster than I could have imagined.

He lunges towards me with a grunt and swings his hand against the side of my face, clipping me with a force that I manage to displace only because he hits me with an open palm. Out of the corner of my eye, I see Becks backed into a corner with only a short dagger to defender herself with.

I drop to my knees and spin under the arm of the Other reaching for me. As I move, I slice the back of his ankle, severing the tendons smoothly. He cries out and collapses onto his knees and even though the rule book says to finish him off, I can't help but be distracted by Becks just behind me.

I marshal my fear and check my breath. Like my hands, both are steady as I bring the heavy sword around with ease and stab the Other closing in on Becks right between the shoulder blades, narrowly missing his spine.

Three feet from Becks, he lurches away from her and flails wildly. But like a clever drunk, he manages to right himself at the last second, the sword still stuck in his back.

I jump out of his path, but he sees where I'll land just as I do and punches me in the stomach, knocking the breath clean out of me. My lungs sear, but before I'm given too long to dwell on the fire spiderwebbing through my chest, the back of his hand meets my cheek.

He's wearing rings, at least one, and I feel the cool kiss of air against whatever wound he's opened on my face just before a crimson film glosses my vision. I blink up to see his pretty pink form lunging towards me. I also spot Becks right behind him. About to do something stupid.

Like try for me.

Like die for me.

I lift up one arm, fingers curled like desperate claws. "No, Becks," I scream!

She reaches for the blade in his back, but she's too slow and he's far, far too fast. He whirls towards her, grabs her by the throat and tosses her into the right wall, as if she were nothing more than a wad of tissue paper. Her head hits the brick and makes a soft cracking sound before bouncing off and landing on the pavement below, along with the rest of her. She lands at an awkward angle. A horrible angle. One that makes it look like her head isn't connected to her body by anything at all.

The rage I'd been able to check up to now bursts in my chest and I am not the same person I was. I see Becks's knife lying on the ground and I scream as I lunge for it, and I'm still screaming when I throw it.

Maybe it's luck or God or both, but the short dagger plunges hilt-deep into the eye socket of the Other who threw Becks. He canters back and I'm still screeching something terrible as realizations and panic and fear rush over me in alternating waves, drowning me. Smothering me to death.

And they don't care. God doesn't care. Nothing fucking cares. Because there is no Heaven. There is no Valhalla. There is only this purgatory the Others brought with them and us wretches too stupid to lay down and die eleven years ago when the sun went dark and took God with it.

I blink, coming back down from somewhere I wish I could have stayed at the sound of the Other babbling something incoherent. Something pained. He lurches away from me, stumbling over Beck's body into the brick wall decorated with her blood and brain matter.

And as he turns to try to claw his way up, I lunge forward and wrap my hands around the sword in his back. I withdraw it with violence, severing all the muscles left of his spine in one single motion, and then I stab him again and again and he falls to the ground alongside his skinnier comrade who looks up at me in disbelief and horror. Like *I'm* the monstrous among them.

Before I can move onto him next, the survivor scrambles towards the mouth of the alley, clutching the brick walls for support because his Achilles tendons still haven't healed yet. So, I sate my remaining bloodlust by hacking the sonofabitch who killed Becks into itty bitty pieces, making sure to sever his spinal column and remove his head from his neck, which as far as I know is the only one sure way to kill them.

But I can't stop there, and I don't stop there. I scream and scream and slice and scream and when I look down to see what I've done, I count no less than five limbs, though the only recognizable one is his blood soaked skull. By now the shock has set in and the adrenaline's gone. My sword clatters to the ground noisily and I drop to my knees beside Becks's body, which isn't moving anymore.

"Becks?" I say, but she doesn't answer. She's lying face down and I'm afraid to move her, but I know I'll have to. I mean, it's not like I can call an ambulance. It's not like I can call anyone. I take her by the back of the neck and turn her over. Her eyes are wide and there's blood staining her pale lips. Her neck is bent to the left at an unnatural angle and her limbs are splayed so that from above, she looks like a broken swastika. There is a bulge in the center of her throat and I remember the medical advice Becks's father had once given me. I need to perform a tracheotomy.

I grab the sword from the ground and I tip it towards her clavicle but just as I do, she blinks. "Becks?" I don't sound like myself at all. I sound weak. She shakes her head in these small, desperate motions and tries to speak, but coughs up a lung full of blood.

"Becks, please," I say, as if it's her fault. It's mine. I should have gone back for them sooner. I shouldn't have gone for the sword. I should have made them stay in the forest six weeks ago…

"Rebecca," I whisper.

"Go…go…" She stammers, pints of scarlet flowing from her mouth with each word, bright red ribbons, "Ash…"

"I'll find her." I lick my lips, clear my throat and repeat, "I'll find her, I promise. If it's the last thing I do, I will find her and I will bring her back and we'll live like nomads forever in the forest and nothing bad will ever happen to her."

And I mean it, even though every word I've said goes in blatant contradiction to my first rule. Don't hope.

How can I when there's no way I'll be able to find her and even if I do, there's no way she'll still be alive when I do and if she's still alive, there's no chance that she'll want to be. I don't want to know what the giant, that horrible cyclops, has in store for her.

But I've got no other choice. It's either go after her, or lie to a dying mother.

"I'll get her back," I say gently while Beck's eyes cross and her whole body seizes.

My entire purpose for living was to keep Ashlyn safe and Becks still breathing and in one fell swoop, I failed them both. I've lost my girls and my purpose. After the last member of my family died six years ago, I'd figured I was sort of expendable. Now, I realize I'm not even that. I'm just a ghost.

Becks chokes on one last breath and dies with her eyes open. Her hair is soft against the back of her head, made softer by the blood lubricating each strand, dying them pink. She'd found a box dye once in a supermarket that hadn't been too badly raided and dyed her hair purple, just for fun. Ashlyn had laughed for days.

I don't cry even though I feel my eyes and the back of my throat light up in blistering heat. Pain razes its way up from my belly, tearing through my chest before finally passing into my throat. I unleash it in one bellowing scream.

I scream long and loud and hope that all the scavengers still in the area hear it. I hope they hear the anger. I hope they hear the rage and they fear it and flee. Because when it's all over I'm still just stuck in a dark alley with the smell of sulfur and my best friend's blood covering most of me. Her lifeless grey eyes mirror the starless sky above us. And as I close them, I box out the grief threatening to ruin me.

With nowhere to bury her body and no time for anything elaborate — no, not elaborate, but honorable — I drag her into the back of the alley.

I take bricks and rubble and rocks and stones and I pile them over her, covering her face last, then I gather the sword and her pack and step out into the T-intersection with my chin level. I feel nothing. Nothing but resolve. Perhaps it's because of a promise that rips through my meticulously compiled rule book. A promise made to a dying mother.

I think about this promise as I crouch down onto one knee in the shadows of the metro bus. There, in the carcass of the overturned vehicle, I find Ashlyn's hat. I pull the patch of green from the rubble where it's caught between two bits of melted metal and wonder how it got there.

It snags on an exposed beam, and I tear a hole it in on accident. My face twists. I hold it to my nose. It still smells like her, and also like Becks. A little bit like me. I tuck Ashlyn's hat into my pocket and as I do, I betray half the rules in my book, simultaneously.

As I walk around the SUV, I focus on cutting through the fabric of my pack so that I can stow and retrieve my newest weapon with ease. Then I find the suitcase I'd long since discarded and try and consolidate that and Becks's pack into my own. I'm not able to carry much of it, and I remember that I'd stowed my canteen in Ashlyn's pack earlier.

I sweep my gaze around the blood-embellished darkness, but I can't find it. She must still have it with her. I start to think about where she is and immediately have to stop myself. Because all I can picture is her pale little body in the arms of the cyclops, her eyes as lifeless as her mother's.

I kick aside one of the Others's corpses that the loner left behind and move away from the intersection mechanically, like I'm not afraid. In a sense, I guess I'm not anymore. What have I got left besides a mean right hook and a promise? The answer is nothing at all.

I can hear a subtle scurrying, like rats, in the darkened doorways of the vacant buildings lining the street. Hollow shells that only serve as a painful reminder of the bustling life that existed just over a decade ago. Scavengers, but they don't show their faces. They remain in the shadows because they fear me. *I* would fear me. There aren't many scavengers that could take on one of the Others and live, let alone kill it, making me the most dangerous thing on the road at the moment.

I walk like that's true and pull off my outer coat. It's saturated with fiery crimson that smells so strongly of rotting eggs and piss that I start to feel light-headed. I pretend not to notice the bitter chill sweeping in through the holes in my men's tee shirt and jeans as I shoulder my pack and step into the center of the T-intersection, where all this senseless carnage began.

I stare in the direction that the cyclops went, but the grey is too thick to see more than two streets over. The grey presses in on me, heightening this new sensation of loneliness. It's invasive, more threatening than a blade. Humans weren't made to travel solo. I never wanted to travel solo. I kind of always thought, if I made it this far — to be the last one left of my pack — that I'd just...give up.

But I can't.

I made a promise.

I take a step to meet the grey and as my mind starts constructing the rudimentary outline of a very poor plan, I hear a cough.

Confused, I withdraw the sword from my pack and look around, frowning when I see nothing. Maybe my half-hearing? Maybe my imagination? Maybe my fear and adrenaline and shock? It could be all of those things, but I'm not in the business of being sucker-punched in the back, so I take a slow turn and then a tentative step towards the SUV —

what's left of it — in the blood-basted intersection, where the sulfur smell and the metallic blood lies thickest.

I freeze when I hear it again. A few seconds later, there's a short grunt followed by a cough that's too close to have been emitted by one of the scavengers lurking in the bombed-out storefronts. In fact, it's so close that I dare to believe for just an instant, something utterly unbelievable...

Caution tells me to press forward, but curiosity has me moving closer to the bus, the SUV and the Other lying between them. Well, what used to be an SUV, what used to be a bus, and what used to be an Other. None of them are recognizable, the loner least of all.

His face is mangled — nose bashed into his skull, lips sliced and bloodied, cheekbones shifting out of place beneath closed lids — and what was once black? hair stands up away from his face in matted chunks. His body didn't fare any better.

There isn't a single piece of him that isn't covered in that pungent, sickly red. His chest is concave, pockets of blood oozing out from beneath the patches of his tee shirt like little geysers, making it impossible for me to tell if he's still glowing.

His arms twist out from his sides like gnarling tree limbs while his shattered legs lay flaccidly atop grey ash that had at one point been cinderblocks. Now, they're just dust. I know that he can't be alive, but precaution keeps my sword angled down towards his neck, because despite the fact that there's not a chance in this galaxy or the next that he'll somehow muster the strength to attack me, my heart still hammers anxiously in my chest.

I see something glittering amidst the pools of sulfurous blood. Near his mouth, a shard of steel stretches up to meet his parted lips. I want to take it before the riff raff come and dismember what's left of him so I kick his foot once, just to be sure.

When nothing happens, I squat down and flick through the blood and teeth and chunks of whatever else he's thrown up. Finally my fingers close in around a slippery silver object. A hard object.

I wipe it off on my blood spattered jeans and tilt it towards the limited light shining down from the grey above me. It's a key. One of the big, old fashioned ones. A skeleton key. I scratch my head, understanding only that the key must be something important for him to have swallowed it. I think back to what the giant had shouted at him, and it's clear he'd been looking for something. Was this it?

I see no reason to leave the key behind even though I've got no clue what it's for, so I put away my sword, tuck the key into the side pocket of my pack and stand.

I take a step back towards the grey, but the instant my left foot touches down onto pavement, a vice clamps around it and I stagger.

Spinning, I rip the sword from my pack so fiercely I nearly shred it in two. I point the tip of the blade down, but the dead guy that has a hold of me doesn't react. Through the blood and the abrasions, I see that his lips are curled up in an expression that I recognize, but that makes my adrenaline rush in worry and confusion.

This dead guy is…he's smiling at me.

He says something that I can't make out, coughs, coughs some more, then coughs again. "That doesn't belong to you," he eventually croaks.

My jaw falls slack and for a moment the tumult of thoughts that so viciously assault my mind are silenced. "What?" I manage to stammer, sounding like an idiot.

I yank my foot back but his broad, flat hand is unyielding. He grits his teeth and I can tell that it causes him great pain to hold onto me, but he holds me nonetheless. How is he alive? And more importantly, how is this dead guy stronger than me?

"You have." He pauses, coughs, then says, "You have what is mine, human." He spits this last word out disdainfully and the little sympathy that I once had for him when he was just a lonely loner with a glowing chest against a cyclops and his band of goons, evaporates.

I tip my blade down to the inside of his arm and press just hard enough for blood to well in the crook of his elbow. He releases a feral roar, but I can feel the pressure of his fingertips around my ankle relax ever so slightly. He scratches me as I pull away from him and I feel that he has drawn blood. And then I'm *sure* of it when he reaches his fingers up to his mouth and tastes them.

I shudder. "It's not yours anymore, demon." I try and mimic his tone, but fall short. Instead, I'm vaguely aware that some of the scavengers have crept from their hiding places. I look up and see a soot-colored face disappear behind the safety of an overturned car. I shudder again as I think about what's in store for him.

Meanwhile, he doesn't seem so concerned. Instead he just blinks up at me with one good eye, given that the other is swollen shut. His lips are tensed together into a thin bloody line, but he holds my gaze intrepidly.

Part of me almost wants to give the key over to him. But I don't. If this key is important, then perhaps I can use it to leverage Ashlyn's release. Plus, it's not like he really needs it. I know that he must know that we both know that he won't last the night. He coughs again, as if to prove my point, and blood spills down his chin in reckless abandon.

A sound catches my attention and when I look up this time, I see the faces of two men watching me from a second story window missing the pane in the apartment building across the street. They don't move away from the window until I glare, which makes me think that perhaps, having seen me, they're willing to chance death in order to get to him. I cringe.

I wonder if he'll still be alive when they start eating him.

Rule number eight sits heavy in my chest. Never help strangers.

But even though he *is* a stranger, *and* an Other, *and* scum, *and* probably deserves to die, I keep thinking about the way he fought that giant and those other bastards. I keep thinking about the way he looked at me when he collapsed onto his knees off of the bus, and then again when he held my gaze when he was being tortured. Something tells me that if he could have moved, he might have made a good ally in the fight to save Becks and rescue Ashlyn.

Or maybe I'm just tired of hearing things screaming.

But whatever the case, I've seen enough death for the night, and even if he dies — which he will — I'm not going to let the cannibals have at him. I'm not going to let his screams haunt me through the night.

I lift my blade over my head and bring it down so that everyone on the street can hear the ringing of metal against pavement. "Fuck you scavengers!" No one is close enough yet to see that I've missed his head by inches.

"He's mine you sacks of shit," I shout, and when I bend down close enough to feel the pressure of his gaze on my face and see his widening eyes — *they're green, his eyes* — I grab a fistful of rubble, drenched in his blood, and lift it over my head.

I toss my hair back and disgustingly, let a few droplets of his blood shower my chin and chest. I want them to think that I'm drinking him, even though I'd never let an ounce of that toxic, fetid blood touch my lips. The smell of it alone is deterrent enough.

I make a great show of stowing my blade and dragging his limp body across the ground to the nearest building. He's heavier than lead and I handle him gracelessly because it's the only way I can move him at all as I kick open the flimsy wooden door and wade into the shadows.

Even though it's dark inside, I can see well enough to know that the place has been looted too many times to count.

There's nothing left that a person could have carried out, and there's no smell but dust. Something old. Stale, but clean. Stolen, but forgotten.

This clearly used to be some kind of cafe or coffee shop — I can tell by the busted chalkboards against the back wall, the faux-wooden counter in the middle of the small space and the refrigerator by the front door where I'm standing.

After getting the dead guy past it, I heave my weight into the side of the fridge and let it slam down with glorious thunder. On its side, it successfully blocks the bottom half of the door, which is badly rotted. I just hope it'll be enough of a deterrent. He just needs a little more time to lose a little more blood and die in peace. Then the vultures can have at him.

Luckily the windows are all boarded up and seem more or less secure, so I don't bother with those and instead, drag what's left of the dead creature around the far side of the counter. I drop his arms and his head hits the fallen cash register with a sharp clang and a dull thud.

He releases a groan that startles me so much I jump. Our eyes meet and I don't like the look he gives me, that baiting condescension and impish curiosity, so I don't give myself time to think about the rules I've just broken or why I've broken them.

Instead, I scramble over the counter to the street-facing wall and wriggle through a high window, keeping my pack close.

Once my feet hit the pavement, I take off down the road at a sprint and I don't stop running until I can no longer feel the creeping chill of the night air numbing me. I run until I burn, inside and out.

Chapter Three

I stumble upon a row of townhouses, which makes me clench my teeth together so hard I can feel little lances shoot into my brain.

Townhouses mean towns. Towns mean gangs. Rule number four says to steer clear of them, but darkness is falling around me fast and I haven't eaten anything but dog food all day. I'm going to have to chance it.

The buildings are bunched together like bodies huddled, bracing against an impending storm. They don't reveal much. Faded brick faces are dotted with destroyed windows that are black and empty, like blind eyes. I don't get a good feeling when I look up at the townhomes, wondering what manner of rich people lived here in the World Before and more importantly, who lives here now.

Rule number six: always trust your gut.

Or in my case, trust *Becks's* gut. But Becks isn't here and I'm too hungry and my adrenaline is crashing over me in a way that's starting to feel dangerous. I need to get inside and close my eyes. Even if only for a little while. And it will have to be a little while, because I can't let too much distance get between me and the Others I'm hunting.

I climb the stairs to the first of the townhouses, remembering what my mother once told me about toilets. The first toilet is your safest bet because most people skip it, thinking that everyone else has used it. I hope she's right. And that this analogy also extends beyond the crapper.

A huge X painted inside of a circle covers the wooden door. It's a gang sign. One that I've seen before. It's drawn in red paint that drips down the rotten doorframe to meet the concrete stoop in front of it. Scarlet seeps into the doormat, which at one point read HELLO, but the O has been painted over.

I withdraw my sword instinctively, as if the act has already become perfunctory after just a few hours. Then I kick open the crumbling door. It gives easily and in my experience, that's a good sign. Nobody with half a brain would set up camp, then leave the front door unbarred and open.

I flash the light in my left hand across the entryway. Even though it's dangerous to use a flashlight at night, I'm betting against finding anything scarier than I am inside. No big deal. Just betting my life.

Everything's quiet. Blessedly.

Almost directly in front of the front door is a set of stairs rising up. Moving around them, I find the kitchen a short ways after. The cupboards and drawers are all open but gods be good, I manage to find a few packets of unopened ramen in the bottom of one walk-in pantry. Next, I check under the sink to see if there's anything left in the garbage. It's there that I find the Mecca of all finds — a half full jar of only somewhat spoiled peanut butter.

"Becks," I say, turning to show her what I've found, "can you believe…"

Finding only darkness, I have to remind myself that I'm alone. Ashlyn's taken. Becks is gone. Alone, taken, gone. Alone…

After I finish checking the rest of the house and committing the location of each available exit to memory, I take the porcelain figurines from an untouched china cabinet and place them before each window and door — they might not hurt anyone trying to get in, but they're large enough that they'll make noise when they shatter.

Finally, I trudge upstairs to find an empty bedroom. Claiming the smallest of the three, I close the door behind me and lock it, placing a chair beneath the handle for added measure. Then I fall onto the bed, take three licks of peanut butter, crawl under the mold-scented covers and pass out.

I'm not asleep for more than an hour. Maybe two. But I wake to the sound of shattering glass — no, not glass. Porcelain.

A door opens somewhere on the first floor and as I slide off of the bed in a pile of blankets and sheets, I'm wide awake and listening hard for the sounds of gangs and scavengers. I hope for the latter.

I don't hear anything for the first moment, then I slowly begin to make out the steady metronome of footsteps on the staircase.

Whoever it is, is clomping loudly and I immediately assess that the intruder is both male and alone. A woman wouldn't walk with a gait that heavy. She wouldn't be so stupid in a world full of lawlessness and perverts. Or so bold.

As quietly as I can, I slide across the floor to the window and rip open the blinds, letting in a pale, silvery light. I wonder if the moon is full behind the grey, shining away in a cloud-filled world that's empty and beautiful.

From below, the grey is a stagnant, oppressive thing. It doesn't even move for the wind, making me think hard about the last time I even saw the sky, a familiar constellation, or the glimmer of even a single star... I must have been a kid. Maybe I don't even remember anymore, what those things are...

The footsteps pound harder, coming closer, and I quickly shuffle across the floor and tuck myself into the darkest corner of the room — right up against the head of the bed, on the side closest to the door. This way I'll be able to see the intruder before he sees me and ideally, cut him to pieces before he crosses the threshold. That's *if* he even decides to open the door. After all, once he finds out that it's locked and barred he may assume that I'm not alone, or that I'm the greater threat.

As I make mental bets with myself over whether or not he'll fight or run, I pull my sword out from underneath the bed and hold it in a firm, fierce grip. My mouth is dry and my muscles are tense.

The footsteps come to a stop just on the other side of the wall. If not for that wall, the intruder would've been no more than four feet from me.

Fight or run? Which will it be?

How 'bout neither. Because to my shock and chagrin, a momentary pause is followed by a gentle knock on the back of the bedroom door.

"Hello?" The voice is low, slightly carnivorous, fully condescending, masked by the thinnest veneer of pain and completely recognizable.

This can't be happening.

But when the bronze doorknob jiggles, I know that I'm not dreaming. I jump, more skittish now than ever — and with reason. It's not often that I'm greeted in the night by the gentle rapping of a dead man against my door.

The doorknob rubs dully against the back of the chair. "Don't you dare," I say, trying to keep my voice even as the wall and door split to reveal a three inch sliver of darkness.

I can just barely make out his face among the shadows, and from what I can see, some patches of it are gleaming brighter and bloodier than others. How is he still standing!

The handle abruptly stops grinding against the back of the chair and though I can't see his eyes, I still get the impression that he's looking directly at me. Alright. I'll just say it. I'm beyond rattled. I'm freaked the frick out. How in the frick can this guy see in the dark? Maybe he can't. Maybe I'm just being paranoid...

"I see you," he says, silencing that last thought.

His words are punctuated by the creaking of the floorboards as he inches across them, pressing himself closer and closer to me.

I open my lips as if to respond, but the cold invades my mouth. I shiver all over.

"Little human, you have something that is *mine*."

Little? Who's he calling little? And while that is definitely *not* the most important thing to tell him, naturally, I do. "Little? I killed one of your kind. Would have been two if I'd bothered to cut your head off in the road."

"Ha," he says in a theatrical way that's utterly condescending. "It was your own human folly that you did not. Now I've returned and I want what it is that you have taken from me."

I don't know what to do. There's no reason that I shouldn't just go find what he wants and slide it across the floor to him. But the thought of maybe even possibly being able to trade that slippery piece of silver for Ashlyn's life keeps me from it.

"I'll give you what you want. But you have to do something for me in return."

Silence. And then, "What?" His voice is dangerously even. It betrays absolutely no emotion this time.

"You can have your stuff back, but at a price."

"Name your terms."

"My sister."

"Sister?" He scoffs. "She looked nothing like you." And I notice that he pointedly uses the past tense of the verb.

My brows pull together and heat rips down my back. I stammer, "Do we have a deal?"

"Do I look like I have a little girl somewhere on my person?" He growls, "I forget that you humans have such poor eyesight. Let me assure you that I do not."

"Well, your friends took her. You know where they're going. You must know where she is," I say firmly, though I can think of about a dozen reasons why he wouldn't and about a hundred reasons more why he wouldn't tell me even if he did.

"Did they look like my friends?" Something vicious simmers through his speech. Something lethal.

Sweat surfaces on my hairline and between my shoulder blades, chilling me even through my many layers. "Tell me and you'll get your sword back."

"You and I both know that I'm not here for the sword."

"Tell me where my sister is and you'll get your sword back. Help me find her, and I'll give you back your key."

The silence stands between us like a bridge neither of us is ready to cross. It's toxic, effecting everything with a definite doom and gloom. The door flexes around the chair and I hear the sound of it straining. Splinters of wood and chipping lacquer flake off onto the floor.

"That I ask is a courtesy your brutish human mind likely does not understand. So let me make this clear for you now. I will only ask once more. Give me the key."

"I'm not afraid of you." I try to pitch my voice loud and strong, but it just comes out warbly and scratchy. "I killed one of your kind tonight…"

"Congratulations!" He raises his voice and barks out a sharp laugh. "But an animal that defends itself is still just an animal and I will have what is mine."

"You owe me! I saved your life."

"Saved my life?" I imagine that if I could see him clearly now I'd be infinitely more afraid. "Dragging me into pile of garbage is your rendition of a rescue attempt?" He seems genuinely confused and somehow that confusion hurts me.

Saving his life is pretty much the only decent thing I've done for a stranger, possibly in forever. I broke rule number eight for him.

I frown. "I could have let you get picked apart by the scavengers. I saved your life and you know it. Without me, you'd have been eaten or tortured or worse."

"I'm a tough chew to swallow," he whispers. "You underestimate me."

I know that, but I don't cop to it. Instead I surge up onto my feet and brandish my sword. Well, his sword. I mean, unless I kill him, then it'll be my sword. And if he kills me then, well, things like ownership won't matter.

But that won't happen. It can't.

She needs me too much.

A delicious calm settles over my bones and when I speak next, my voice belies that fresh determination. "Maybe you're the one underestimating me. I'll do whatever I have to in order to get my sister back and if you don't tell me what you know about where they've taken her, God help me I'll…"

Before I can finish spewing out my empty threat, the door flies open with one swift jerk and the chair beneath it snaps into pieces. The loner moves into the room and he. is. huge.

He towers over me by a solid foot-and-a-half but I don't find him frightening until the moonlight washes over his flesh and illuminates the destruction that's been waged over his form. He's draped in violence and for the life of me, I can't understand how he's still standing. Still breathing. Still glowing.

Burgundy bathes his face and covers his arms from shoulder to wrist. His legs are only halfway healed leaving bits of bloody bone protruding from his skin in a way that makes my stomach pitch.

Crimson smears decorate his chest and frame gaping bullet holes, but underneath all this I see the very faint pulse of a gentle orange glow. It's hypnotizing, that aura, but I'm distracted from it when the loner lunges across the room towards me.

He's quick as a cobra and I just manage to avoid him by rolling backwards over the bed, putting its width between us. I feint to the left, then duck right, keeping the sword angled towards him as I charge.

He's clever, and surprisingly quick for someone his size. He moves out from beneath the arc of my sword at the very last second and as I continue charging in his direction, he kicks open the bedroom door and pushes the back of my head so that I'm propelled out into the hall. Oh shit…

I career towards the staircase. My left cheek, which is already injured, screams in pain when my face connects with the banister. I might have lost an eye had the sword not lodged itself hilt-deep into the drywall and done its work in keeping me upright.

I hear him loom up behind me as I collapse onto my knees. I know I don't have much time, but the serrated edges of the sword are caught on the wall studs and I can't extract it.

Cold touches my ankle and I look back to see that my right leg is caught between his black, steel-toed boots. I'm flat on my stomach and though I don't have many options, I can see through his tattered black pants and I remember what the Others did to his legs earlier…

I crush my left heel into his shin and when I hear a sharp crackling sound, like bubble wrap exploding, my stomach heaves again. Half out of ick, the rest out of panic. If he survives this, he's going to be pissed.

And there's very little chance he's not going to survive this. I'm one *little* human trying to succeed where half a dozen Others failed.

My eyes blink closed just a moment longer than they should, but when I'm not immediately decapitated and he releases a pained roar, I move.

The weight of his massive form crashes towards me and I just barely manage to scramble out from under him, down the steps, in time to avoid being crushed completely.

He slinks onto his side and maybe it's recklessness or just pure, pent-up rage, but I advance on him while he's down and I hit him as hard as I can in the mouth. I'm pretty sure the punch hurts me more than it does him, but I'm still vindicated when I watch him swab the inside of his cheek with two fingers and pull them back, stained in blood.

Again, I wait for his wrath to descend on me like something biblical, but again, I'm disappointed. This time, by his smile. My stomach pitches again, this time a little differently. Like I'm made sick to my stomach by his smile and at the same time, strangely soothed by it.

I expect him to be furious. I expect him to pull my head off my neck like a cork out of a bottle. Will it make the same popping sound?

I don't expect him to smile at me from my position a few stairs below him, or look so surprised. The good kind of surprised.

"You are...unexpected," he says finally, so softly I'm not even sure he's speaking to me.

I think about asking him what he means, but it's not relevant. "Tell me where he's taken her." I stare at him from over the tops of my fists, even though he doesn't look like he's up for a fight and I'm definitely not up for a fight.

My bones hurt. Everything hurts. My cheek is fiery hot and simultaneously cold and a stitch in my right side is screaming at me. The fingers of my right hand tingle and my cheek aches.

He rolls his eyes and eases up against the wall into a sitting position, using the sword as an armrest. His shoulders deflate but he's not deflated. He looks more rugged, if anything.

"She's long dead."

Rule number one dictates that I believe him, but I don't know what to do with the rule book right now. Not when Ashlyn is missing.

"I don't believe you, and I don't give a shit. I want to know for sure."

"Selflessness will only get you killed in this world," he sighs, repeating the words Becks said to me not a day earlier, making me blink.

"I know that," I whisper.

Even in the non-light, his eyes glimmer. "You fight hard for someone who wants to die."

Emotion blisters my throat, lodging in it like a knife. With each word, it opens new wounds. And I hate him for his callousness. For his honesty. Just lie to me, baby, I think, remembering lyrics to a song Becks sang to me once. A song I'll never know because there's no music anymore in this world.

"*Wants* to die? Without my family, I'm already dead. The way I see it, I've got nothing left to lose. So tell me now, you alien zombie ass hole, where. is. Ashlyn?"

He cocks his head and for a second I think he's really considering telling me where she is, then his eyes look past me, becoming distant.

"I'd prepare yourself. It looks like we're about to have guests."

I don't hear anything myself and even though I don't trust him, I at least trust his hearing. I curse under my breath and reach for the sword even though it's closer to him than I care to be.

I grunt as I pull, but nothing happens. Grunting louder, pulling harder, I'm still not making much progress until I feel his rough hand close over mine. I hold my breath, preparing to defend myself, but when I glance at his face I see that he's watching me and though I can't name the emotion I see in his dark eyes, it's not murderous. A little creepy crawly, but not murderous.

For now.

He gives the sword one swift jerk and hands it back to me.

I don't know what to say, so I stand over him and mutter, "Just try and look dead or something."

He closes his eyes and lies back on the floor with a groan. "Shouldn't be too difficult."

I have half a mind to laugh at his calm, especially given that he's mortally injured and in enemy territory, but I'm distracted from the compulsion by distant hollering.

"Gangs," I whisper, gritting my teeth. "Frick."

"Gang," he corrects, "just one."

I look down at him. His eyes are closed and a slash of moonlight cuts across his blood-covered chest to reveal no less than half a dozen gaping, bloody mounds. Bullet holes that haven't closed up yet. Other than that, he's got the body of a regular human guy. Well, minus the fact that he's ripped beyond belief and also *glowing*.

The moonlight helps disguise what is very definitely a faint orange light emanating from the space over his heart. I watch it for a moment and notice that it seems to pulse at a slow, but steady metronome. I tilt my head to the left and watch the way the light flares and dies then flares again. It fascinates me for longer than it should. Also because it's warm. His entire chest emits a faint heat that I find intoxicating.

"Yes?" He catches me watching him, so I straighten up quickly. Too quickly.

I look away from him and am fleetingly thankful for the darkness, which I hope disguises the heat in my face. He's the enemy and I'm standing here ogling him when I should be running him through when his own blade.

"Can you hear them from here?" I ask, forcing myself not to rise to the condescension in his tone.

He tilts his head to the left, as if he's considering lying to me, then in the end decides against it. "Yes."

"How many are there?"

He pauses, as if to think. "Seven, maybe eight."

"Any women?"

"No."

My face flushes. My voice breaks. "Great."

"You need not fear, little human," he says, voice dropping an octave, so low I'm reminded abruptly that he's not one of us, because that's not a human pitch. "I will not allow them to dishonor or defile you. Kill you, perhaps, but dishonor you, no."

"Well, that's comforting," I mutter. The funny thing, is that it is.

He cocks his head towards the room at the end of the hall. "You'd best be going." And just as he says that, I hear the unmistakable crunch of porcelain on the first floor.

An excited voice calls into the space, "Johnny, I'm home."

I creep into the bedroom at the end of the hall and peer out of the door, which I leave slightly ajar so as to seem less suspicious. It doesn't take long for the gang to find the loner, lying there on his back 'dead,' for our purposes.

They ooh and ahh over him and I feel myself tense up, even though I shouldn't. Isn't it a good thing that they take their time killing him? The more time they take with him, the more time I have to run.

Behind me, shards of glass frame the space where a window once was. It looks like a big, open mouth, and allows in gusts of frigid air. Outside in the distance, it looks like snow.

I hate snow. I hate it more than anything.

Except for Others.

And gangs.

And other scavengers.

And spoiled food.

And dirty clothes.

And cold water.

And bad water.

And the grey.

Fine. Maybe snow is okay.

"Hey, AK, check him out. Damn, how many times do you think they shot him?"

"Who's they, idiot?"

"Whoever they are, they better be long gone or I'm gonna bust 'em up."

"Can't be too far. Look at him. He's still warm."

I wonder if I'll get lucky and they'll leave, thinking that the house has either already been raided, or that it's haunted by something more dangerous than they are. But then I remember that there's no such thing as luck when they casually step over his corpse and move into the bedroom I'd once occupied.

"Hey guys, there's a bunch of stuff in here. *Girl* stuff," one of them shouts. I feel my stomach clench.

Someone lets out a loud whoop and a guttural voice says, "Come out, kitty, kitty."

I slink behind the door when the shadow of a man starts moving towards me down the hall. With my sword held upright, I'm so alert I can practically feel as his fingers graze the doorknob.

"Here kitty, kitty…"

I remain planted behind the door and watch his back as he moves into the room and creeps towards the open window.

"Hey guys, I think she might have run off. Let's go after her and see if we can't make her feel at home." He's still laughing as he pivots to face the door and me, standing behind it. Our eyes meet. Shock fills his. His mouth opens and he starts to grin, but another voice cuts in, like a guillotine, between us.

"Brent!" A voice in the hall screams, suspending the chaos for just one more second, "This guy ain't no guy! He's one of them. He's fucking one of the Others and he's fucking alive!"

A scream in the hallway pulls the man's attention away from me and I use his hesitation to slaughter him. I step out from behind the door and swing my heavy sword. It's heavier than anything I've ever used before and my armpits scream as I lift it high above my head…and then bring it down.

I find his neck by some miracle and hack through half of it in one stroke. Hot blood slashes over me and I feel myself respond to it. To the tinny sound of metal meeting bone. To the thud of the body hitting the floor. To the heat of his life-force as it slashes across my chest and face. *It's so warm.*

A momentary thought hurts me as it comes and leaves again just as quickly. I'm a savage. Just savage enough to survive this place. And that's why Becks is dead and I'm still breathing.

Footsteps thunder down the hall while others thunder up — or maybe down — the stairs. I dive for the window just as two bodies burst into the room behind me. One of them shrieks when they spot their dead friend's head separated from his body — *mostly* separated — while the other one charges me, cursing as he runs.

I'm quicker though, and pain digs its greedy claws into my palms and knees when I shred myself on the glass opening of the shattered window and pull myself out. As I dangle by my bloody fingers, my feet hovering some indeterminate distance off of the ground, I calculate how many bandages I'll have to use and how many will be left by morning. Then I remember that the first aid kit is in Ashlyn's pack. As I drop onto the grass one story below, I pray to God — any god, *all the gods* — that she won't need to use it.

My arms pump awkwardly underneath all my clothes as I sprint back around to the front of the building. From the open doorway, I hear a pained shout and a roar, a body gasping for breath, and then a sharp hiss. I'm not sure whose is what's until I surge into the entryway and glance up the staircase to see a man standing over the loner wielding a long, slender blade.

He stabs the loner's arm while the loner drags a second man to his knees. A third already lies dead on the staircase, his throat spread wide open. A fourth closes in on the loner. With what looks like impossible strength, the loner heaves his mutilated torso off the floor, grabs the offending kicker by the shin and drags him to the ground all while the other assailants continue to stab and punch him relentlessly.

The loner grits his teeth, looks away from his attackers and speak to *me*. "Run," he says.

Of course I should be running, but as I charge up the stairs and swing my sword around, it occurs to me that the loner might have meant 'run *away*'.

I cut into the stabby guy right at his waist and he folds over my sword like a big, meat taco. Then the loner says something, I think to me, but I'm facing the wrong way and his words come out all muted and warbled.

Then I turn on the landing to see a youngish looking guy pointing an old-fashioned gun at me. My heart stops. The man's hands are shaking. I killed his friends. He was the one screaming about the guy I dismembered in the other room and here I am, having done it again.

BOOM. BOOM.

The sound of the gun going off makes my heart stop beating. I'm dead. Well, I had a pretty shit run. I failed Ashlyn and Becks and everyone.

I press my hands to my stomach, waiting to feel the familiar heat of blood — only this time, my own — but instead, I just feel the heat of the sword trapped in my fist and against the outside of my knuckles, the cold chill of my stolen clothes.

The loner is standing in front of me. He's standing in front of me and now he's cantering to the side. He releases a pained moan as he hits the wall hard. I swallow. The loner just took two bullets for me. But why?

The guy standing on the other side of the loner holding the gun is staring at me with a mirrored shock and for a moment, and in a very small way, I feel *kindred* to him. It should be the two of us fighting against the Other.

But it's not.

He starts to lift his gun and I switch under the loner's arm, armed with the knowledge that a knife is more dangerous than a gun within twenty-one feet. To prove it, I cut the guy with the gun down in two easy strikes, splitting open his face and then his stomach.

Breathing hard, I shake my head, trying to rid myself of the image of the gun in that guy's now limp hand. He'd been aiming for me, but the loner shielded me and we're mortal enemies and I stole from him and he tried to fight me and I definitely still plan on extorting him. It just doesn't make sense.

Shattering my thoughts — fortunately — a body barrels through the bathroom door — unfortunately — landing directly in front of me. I shout when a heavy arm clips me across the throat.

An emaciated man with a mouthful of rotten teeth slams my body into the wall hard, the square edges of a picture frame digging into my spine the harder he presses. I wonder distractedly if it's a family photo.

I drop my sword in direct violation of rule number seven: Never drop your weapon.

I quickly flit through a list of ways to incapacitate an unarmed attacker that a woman in our old camp taught me. Deciding on one, I bring the heel of my hand up to meet the man's nose and hit him hard enough that some of the pieces *should* shoot back into his brain, if I did it right, anyway.

He screams bloody murder and the sound plus the smell of him plus the fact that I'm lightheaded from how hard he squeezes prevents me from keeping upright when he drops me.

My knees give out as my feet hit the floor and when I'm down, he kicks me. I curl up defensively and wrap my arms around my head as I ready myself for the next blows, but instead of hearing the sound of my own bones breaking under the strain, I hear a strange gurgling.

Untucking my head, I look up at the loner standing in front of me with the guy's head trapped in one fist. His mouth is pressed to the man's throat and I don't need to be told what's happening.

He's *drinking* him. Like an orange juice box. Extra pulp.

As the last of his limbs stop twitching, the loner tilts the dead guy's open-gash-of-a-neck towards me and says dryly, "Care for a drink?"

The man tumbles from his grip, falling to the floor with a thud. I'm vaguely aware that there are still two gang members standing at the top of the stairs watching us, but I'm frozen for good.

I've seen people killed in all kinds of unusual ways, but I've never seen anybody eat anybody. I know there are gangs of cannibals who do that, but I've never come across one. Obviously.

The loner turns to the remaining humans and smiles to show all of his red-tipped teeth.

"Come," he says to them, "just a little closer. I'm still hungry." He beckons them forward with a sultry wave of his finger and the two don't need more encouragement.

They run — more like *fall* — down the stairs and when they reach the front door and bound through it, I hear one of them shriek.

My stomach twists. That peanut butter I ate is no longer sitting quite right. My straining eyelids are wrenched open so wide they start to hurt and my feet propel me backwards against the wall, as far away from him as I can get.

He asks me a question, but it sounds like white noise right now. I keep looking between his mouth and the dead man's open throat, wondering what in the hell had propelled me to challenge this blood-thirsty lunatic in the first place. More than that, I wonder why I'm not lying next to the dead man, bloodless just like him.

"Hello," he says angrily, eyebrows twisting down towards his sharp, straight nose as he glares.

He kicks my foot and I jump, startled. "Wh…what?"

"What is your name?"

Rule number three — don't get personal. Even a name is personal to me.

Feeling heat rush up the back of my neck, I blurt out, "What's yours?"

He wrinkles his forehead, but still says, "Cain."

"Cain?" I repeat, thinking that a name from the Bible is a pretty weird name for an alien from another galaxy. "Like Cain and Abel?"

"K-A-N-E." Kane spells out his name with his fingertip and even when he drops his hand, I still see the word hanging suspended, its ghostly form glimmering. "Who is this Abel?"

"I…I think it was his brother. They killed each other, or something."

"Why are these people I would know? You humans kill each other all of the time." I frown and open my mouth to retaliate, but he cuts in. "I don't want to hear your opinions on your own kind after one of them tried to shoot you."

He gives me a pointed stare. I want to ask him why he did it, but I'm not sure I want the answer. Instead, I hear myself whisper words I never thought I would…not to one of the Others. "Thank you."

His face softens. It happens so suddenly, I'm thrown off by it. It makes him look less like a genocidal maniac and more like an Adonis. "I was returning the favor. You should have run away. I would have dispatched our attackers on my own."

"They were hurting you," I say, totally against my own volition. Why am I telling him this?

His face softens further, then all at once he shakes his head. "I asked for your name."

"Nothing…I don't have a name." What? I couldn't think of a fake name? Well done, moron. Well done…

He rolls his eyes, then sighs, "I see taking two bullets for you has not earned me the privilege of something to call you by."

"You said that taking the bullets was returning the favor. I don't owe you more than that." I don't owe him anything at all. "Plus, I saved you back on the street when I pulled you into that building." He opens his mouth as if to argue, but I say quickly, "So really *you* still owe *me*."

He releases an exasperated grunt that has me smiling, of all things. "In all my many years, I have not encountered a human so frustrating. If you will give me nothing to call you, then I will have to call you nothing."

"That's fine with me."

"Nothing," he says again, "are you all right?"

I'm not sure, but I nod anyways.

"You're a poor liar, but as I can't smell any blood on you and you don't appear any more disoriented than you humans usually do, I'll assume you are correct enough in your assessment."

"How can you smell my blood at all with that nasty milk mustache you're wearing?"

"I don't have a mustache, let alone one made out of milk." He frowns and, covered in blood as he is, looks like he was catapulted straight out of hell. If I hadn't seen the ships falling from the sky with my own eyes, I'd be sure that the religious communities around the world got it right. He is one hundred percent demon.

My jaw works. "I just mean the blood on your face. You look like shit."

As he leans against the wall I watch his face switch in and out of discomfort. He favors his left leg, even while sitting, and I have the strangest feeling that I should be guilty knowing that I caused that when I kicked him — or at least *exacerbated* it. Hell, I even am a little.

"Have you seen how you look, human?"

"I know I look like shit, but luckily, I don't have to look at me."

He frowns even harder, face losing all of its softness as it becomes impossibly severe. It's like God took out a ruler when creating this guy, and decided to make him at exclusively hard angles.

He says, "You're taking this with a surprising amount of humor."

"Taking what?"

"Killing."

I balk at that. "Are you kidding? In Population, this is considered a good day."

His gaze focuses a little harder on my face. My eyes, my nose, moving down my cheeks to meet my mouth. He lingers, but only for a second before widening his gaze to take in my hair, and then the rest of me. He must not like what he sees because he opens his mouth like he'll say something — probably an insult — then changes his mind.

With what looks like enormous effort and about a thousand CCs of pain injected straight to his everything, Kane rises to stand. He wobbles, looks like he'll fall... I start to reach for him, but he waves me off.

"Do you know why it's called Population?"

"You mean the human parts of the world?"

He nods, albeit reluctantly.

"I don't know why," I say with a shrug. "Could just as easily call it The Rest or The Grave or The Grand Ole Garbage Dump, but I guess because it's got people in it, Population is what they went with."

"They is *we*. It is a Heztoichen term. When we first landed, in each city we arrived in, we saw signs. They all said Population followed by a number. We did not speak your languages then and thought Population was the name of this place, not the term used to describe a city's occupancy."

I don't mean to be as surprised as I am, or as disappointed, but it irks me that the name of the only thing we humans have left isn't one that even belongs to us.

Out of the corner of my mouth, I spit, "You should have just called it Nothing." Just like the moniker he has for me. It fits. "That's what you left us with. There's nothing out here worth anything. Nothing worth saving."

His voice echoes through the dead hallway a little harder as he says, "Then how does that explain that I just saved you?"

Heat crawls up my neck into my jaw, making it sing. I glare up at him, meeting his gaze and finding it, in a word, obliterating. As a girl whose middle name is self-preservation, I have a hard time not looking away.

"Because you saved me doesn't mean I'm worth saving."

He snorts in a way that should be unattractive but annoyingly, isn't and gives me one last look over, this sweep much more invasive than the last, and much, much colder. I tell myself to stay still under the interminable way he stares, but can't. The second I move, something flares in his gaze. His lip curls up cruelly.

"Perhaps not."

Not bothering to shut the bathroom door all the way, I see movement and then eventually, the sticky sound of wet fabric slapping onto the tiles — *bloody* fabric. I catch sight of an errant heel, a flash of an elbow, the curved shape of a bare ass…

I close my eyes, rather than move away, feeling an irrational confidence in his presence, even as the shower's rusted pipes scream into action and I'm sure we can be heard ten townhouses away.

When he steps out of the bathroom wrapped in only a towel, I slide past him, avoiding his gaze at all costs. In fact, I try not to look at him altogether. But I can still *feel* him. His heat reaches out like tentacles to stroke my face, almost lovingly. Somehow, with the day I've had, it makes me want to cry.

But I don't cry. Population doesn't spit out people who cry at the hint of affection.

Population births people into the world who don't even understand its definition.

My eyes, which I hadn't realized were closed, open and I catch sight of a rippling abdomen, a muscled chest, inky black hair dripping in front of bright eyes. They're green, his eyes. Green.

"Nothing, what are you doing?" He's watching me with a puzzled look and I realize that I'm just standing there absorbing his heat like a freaking weirdo.

"Uhm. I…" I don't bother finishing my sentence, but slide into the bathroom and shut the door between us.

Looking up at myself in the mirror, I do look like shit.

My curly hair, which I chopped off about a month ago in the hopes that it'd make me look more like a man sticks straight out from the left side of my head, cemented there in sweat and blood.

Grit covers my face and when I smear it with my sleeve, I wish I hadn't because there are bruises there layered beneath two rather gnarly looking abrasions that glisten cherry pink atop a green color that looks like vomit.

I sigh and start to take off my clothes, which is a physically painful feat. Moans, gasps, and curses — mostly curses — escape my lips until I'm down to the outfit I was born with. Then I see the results of the past hours. Or is it days? Years? Eleven of them?

I'm blotchy with indigo spots, new blue bruises and older ones, which are jaundiced and yellowing. I cringe when I pull glass bits from my hands and knees, knowing that I'll have to just let my cuts bleed and hope they don't get infected. Scrapes and shallow wounds cover most of me.

More than that though, I'm startled by how scary thin I look in the mirror's gaze. My wide pelvic bones jut out from my skin precariously, like a skeleton covered in a threadbare brown sheet. Even my color, which usually glows bright brown as a result of mixed black and Cherokee heritage, is weak and sallow. More grey than anything.

My eyes are still the same dark blue they've always been, but they look both sad and angry, even to me. I turn away from the sight of my own face, thinking that I look... diminished. I don't feel it somehow, but I look it.

The broken window lets in small tufts of air, carrying frost on the breeze. I've got goosebumps covering every inch of my skin. My nipples pebble like hard diamonds, ready to cut glass. My toes curl against the icy tiles on the floor.

I'm shaking already and that's before stepping into the shower, and after I get out? I'm broken. I only stand under that deadly stream for a minute, maybe less, and only because I know I need to clean out my cuts, however, the full body nausea and dizziness that grips me when I step back out of the shower onto the tiles is enough to make me wish for sepsis.

There's a rumpled pile of towels in one corner, and even though there's a distinctly moldy smell wafting from them, I pluck the biggest, least smelly one from the top and delicately drape it over my shoulders.

My wet hair crystallizes and my fingers seize up when I try to dry it, so little torturous drips trickle down the sides of my neck and over my collarbones.

I lose feeling in my toes as I plod softly down the hall, going crosseyed in my attempts to avoid the broken glass and red and black blood covering everything.

Also, all the dead bodies.

I peek into the first bedroom and see Kane already facedown on top of the bed. Even though it's practically snowing in here and he's in just a damp towel that's slipping off of his ass — his *ridiculously* muscular ass — he seems to be sleeping soundly.

I can't remember the last time I slept like that — without worry — and I roll my eyes as my stomach fills with a renewed rush of resentment. Then I continue to the bedroom at the end of the hall.

This room is even colder — maybe because of the decapitated corpse I left here earlier, or maybe only because Kane and his stupid glowing radiator chest isn't also in it.

I shuffle to the left and feel my way through the dark towards the closet, then I rip open the doors and drag all of the clothes out onto the floor, into one little patch of…light? I can't really call it that. It's just the light*er* glow right under the shattered open window that's still tagged with bits of my coat and skin.

I'm looking for underwear, maybe even a bra, and a shirt and pants small enough to fit me. This was clearly a teenage boy's bedroom in the World Before, so I'm not optimistic about the bra. If it hadn't been made clear by the posters of half-dressed women on the walls, interspersed with football legends I can't name, the wardrobe selection confirms my suspicions.

A gust of cold air billows into the room, bringing a few tendrils of snow with it. I'm suddenly unsure whether or not the shower was worth it. Will I even last the night? Will I see tomorrow morning?

My arms are completely numb and my hands refuse to cooperate with me. The sheet on my back hugs my shoulders like the cool fingers of death. I can hear my teeth clacking together as I bend over and fight not to succumb to it.

It would be so easy just to let the exhaustion and lethargy set in and go to sleep…

And I'm so tired of this.

The fighting.

The pain.

The grey.

The cold.

The loneliness.

The goddamn suffering.

The sheet rips off of me, hard and fast enough to hurt, like tearing flesh. In its place comes a sudden blanketing heat at my back, shocking my system and sending my nerves scattering. I gulp as the heat gets stronger, molding itself to my spine.

Did I die that quick? Is this hell? Because it feels *damn* good.

And then my senses settle. I've never been the smart one, but I've never been superstitious either. This isn't death. This may be the harbinger of death, but it isn't death…

It's a radiator. The alien kind.

Heavy hands wrap a thick blanket around me like a bandage. Between that and the unmistakable presence of his radiator chest, I release a small sigh.

Though I hear Kane's soft, snobby laughter in my ear, it's hard to care. The warmth is everything.

"I can hear your teeth chattering from the other room," he whispers against my cheek.

Large fingers tuck my hair behind my ear, then slip around my neck, making it easier to breathe and more difficult at the same time.

I don't think anyone's ever touched me this intimately, and though I should care that it's one of the Others, I don't. I just watched him tear the throat out of a human man with his teeth, but I don't care about that either. If he wants my throat now, he can have it. I can't fight him. In the meantime, I'll take his heat until he's decided he's had enough of being pawed at by a human. Because that's exactly what I'm doing.

I awkwardly shuffle around on my knees, only to feel my legs pulled entirely out from beneath me as I'm repositioned on his lap. I hiss as my toes wriggle against the open air. Before, they were meat popsicles, but now that they've actually got sensation, they hurt.

He reaches down the length of my body and captures them in one hand, while his other wraps around the blanket tighter around me and holds me close. I press my palms directly to his chest and fail at doing what I succeeded at earlier — avoiding looking at his face. I glance at it a couple times.

His wounds have healed up entirely to reveal an unblemished face. An *attractive* unblemished face. Damn him.

He's got hard cheekbones and hollow cheeks and long, inky black lashes and bright, bright green eyes. The one on the right's got a starburst of orange in it. It's an imperfection I find troubling. It's so…human.

"What are you thinking?" He tilts his head to the side, kind of like I remember this dog doing once, but that was years ago, so I'm probably remembering it wrong. Unless they're roasting over spits, I don't see dogs anymore.

"Nothing." My voice is ragged. I look away from him quickly, but I don't try to move.

We must make an odd sight, sitting in the middle of the floor, a human and an alien wrapped around each other, a corpse freezing casually close by.

His large pointer finger slips under my chin and tilts my head back, back, back, until he can look into my eyes. "You are a terrible liar."

My fingers tense over his pecs and I blurt out too quickly to sensor myself, "The bullets. Where'd they go?"

There are some pocked bits of skin, but no bullet holes. I stroke one with just the tip of my finger, winning absolutely no reaction from him.

"My body rejects them."

"What does that mean?"

"It means my body pushes them out."

Right. Like that's normal. "Oh," I say, because I can't think of anything else.

Just then, a gust of chilly air careens in through the window like a wrecking ball and smashes into me. My teeth start chattering again, despite his heat.

I open my mouth to make what was sure to be a pretty terrible joke about it, but before I can say anything, he gathers me up silently and carries me to the other bedroom. I'm speechless as he places me gently on the bed beneath a second set of covers and I can't help but smile when I notice that he's wearing a set of basketball shorts that are definitely too small for him.

Then he crawls beneath the covers beside me and curves his body around mine so that I'm tucked neatly against his chest. And I want to be embarrassed, or afraid, or nervous, but I'm none of those things. The heat is overwhelming and my eyes close instantly as I prepare to take a swift journey to a faraway place.

I'm nearly asleep when I feel his breath on my ear. It's warm, like everything else about him. "What is your name?" His voice is as gentle as a dream and if I weren't such a light sleeper, this might have been a clever trick.

"Abel," I say. My lips curl up into a smile, relishing the lie as I exhale it.

He laughs lightly, but doesn't question it. Instead, he asks me, "Aren't you afraid?"

"If you were going to kill me, you'da done it."

"What if I'm still deciding?"

"Then you don't need me for that. Goodnight, Kane."

He laughs quietly, "Goodnight, Abel."

Chapter Four

I don't remember falling asleep, but I remember my dreams.

I dream about the apocalypse, which isn't weird. I've dreamt about the day the Others came before. Only those aren't really dreams, are they? They're memories, and I usually wake from them shivering and afraid. Strangely, this is the same dream as all the other ones, only it's good.

It starts with the Fall, the day the sky fissioned in shades of lavender and gold, and instead of being totally terrified when hundreds and thousands of comets plummet through the opening left behind like a great, raw wound in the face of God, I manage to find the entire scene beautiful. Holy.

In the World Before, it hadn't taken us long to figure out that those comets were, in fact, people-like beings traveling in cocoon-like pods. The Others' spaceships, if you can call them that, hadn't been much more technologically advanced than what we could come up with here on Earth and at least ten percent of the pods that had made the voyage were incinerated in our atmosphere. It was their physical dominion over us that led them to the seat of power at the top of the food chain. That, and the fact that they struck first when they bombed Tokyo, Lagos, Hong Kong and London.

For the first year, we thought that we were safe in the Americas. Then, as if to correct the misconception, they came for Moscow, Rio, Cairo and New York. They carved up the world and divided it between themselves in ways that never made much sense to us humans.

They split North and Central America in two, but left the middle of the US and the entirety of South America untouched. They took all of Europe and Asia, splitting it horizontally so that some sorry Others got stuck with Siberia, while the others got the biggest cities of Western Europe and Southern Asia.

Africa got split into three big chunks, again, horizontally. Australia got left alone. Not that it mattered. Last report I heard, the Australians had depleted all of their resources and were busy tearing each other apart for what little was left. The Others didn't even have to set foot on Australian soil to destroy it.

But back in the dream world, blood and politics are irrelevant. Because like in most dreams, it doesn't make any sense. Instead of being afraid or scared or panicked, I'm perfectly warm and happily seated at the wheel of a space ship with my father to my right, my mother to my left, and Ashlyn's little hand trapped in mine.

Kane is telling me where to fly and how to do it, and calmly we drift away from what's left of Earth into space, tracing a path to the stars.

It's so quiet out here in the universe…and so cold…

I lurch awake.

The place beside me is freezing and I lurch around like an angry drunk, trying to find my feet and something to defend myself with. I fall, catch myself on the bedside table and knock over a lamp in the process. Beneath my palm, there's a scrap of something dry and crinkly. I hold it in front of my squinting, sleep-blurred eyes and read…

Abel,

I would encourage you not to seek out your fallen sister, but I understand now that the point is moot. The Heztoichen that has taken her is known by the name Memnoch. If she is still alive, you will find her at his estate in the place we call the Diera. Your kind once called this territory Canada, I believe.

Best of luck,
Kane

What. an. ass. hole.

Angrily, I crumple the paper into my palm while the heat in my face and neck and chest blots out the lingering cold.

I want to kick something, but don't want to risk stubbing a toe, or God forbid — breaking one. Quickly, I throw on a boy's long sleeve tee shirt that is ridiculously big on me, and I layer it with some tank tops, shirts, and sweatshirts until I'm nearly ballooning.

I finally find a solid coat and two pairs of warm pants. Then I start to go through my stuff, jettisoning anything I no longer need — three bowls instead of just one, little girl clothing, the plastic duck that Ashlyn sometimes played with...

Rule number two — pack light — may be second-most important, but as I stare down at Ashlyn's hat, I feel a hurt blossom in my chest that I don't understand.

It's just an ugly green hat dotted with holes. It doesn't fit me. I feel hot tears touch the backs of my closed lids when I finally lay it aside and finish going through the rest of my things.

I make an effort not to look back at the hat as I work fastidiously, expecting that a lot of my stuff will be missing since Kane had no equipment, gear, or clothing of his own.

Except, my stuff hasn't been touched. He didn't take anything at all. Not even the items he came for.

The key is still in my pouch where I left it and the sword is where I dropped it the night before. He didn't even take the best prize of all — my rank and delicious peanut butter.

I run the sword under cold water and stuff it into my belt. Then I head out into the grey world alone, leaving the last of Becks's and Ashlyn's stuff behind me, including Ashlyn's ugly little hat that breaks every bit of my heart.

I eat dry ramen as I walk.

I've got a compass, so I head north along the highway. Dilapidated signs mark it as I-5 so I have to imagine that I'm somewhere in what used to be Oregon in the World Before.

Evergreen trees, moss and ivy roll over the highway in parts, and even though the sky is grey and damaged, I pretend like this is just another cloudy day in the Pacific Northwest and the world seems beautiful. Nature has reclaimed the parts of Earth that the Others didn't want, and when I leave the highway that evening and trudge into the forest, I catch a glimpse of something I haven't seen in a *loooooong* time — a rabbit.

It's dark by the time I catch it, but I can't even remember the last time that I ate meat, so it's worth the hunt. It's not a particularly fat rabbit, but my mouth still waters at the sight of its fuzzy, squirming body.

It's almost painful, but I persuade myself to wait until the morning before I kill, skin and roast it. I don't want to attract any unnecessary attention by building a fire at night. Even if it is freezing.

Snow drifts down on the wind, and as I curl up in a hollow at the base of a great oak tree, I can't help but remember Kane's heat. Just the thought of his heat warms me and I find myself drifting to sleep for a few hours, peacefully.

The next morning, I kill and cook the rabbit over a small a fire. As it roasts, I collect the fat drippings in a tin case that had at one point contained Altoids, though I'm sure I've never had one of those before. I can't even imagine what an Altoid even is. Thinking that it's something sweet is what sets my stomach a growlin' and even though I try not to eat more than a few bites, I devour over half of the rabbit before I set the other bits over the embers and smoke them dry.

As the fire dies, I smear the fat drippings over my chapped lips and dry hands, and over all of my cracking, crackling scabs, then I continue north.

Towards fucking Canada.

The next days are boring, especially now that I'm alone. I find myself whispering quietly to the trees only to be disappointed when I get no answers. I start wishing that I had somebody — *anybody* — to talk to, even Kane.

Especially Kane, though that thought hurts to admit even to the trees, who pass no judgment.

I keep picturing the way his face had been angled in the moonlight, so that he looked like some sort of movie star from the old black-and-whites my mom used to watch when I was a kid. Either that, or a stunningly handsome apparition sent to haunt me. And sometimes, I even think he might have been.

Maybe he was just a hallucination borne from the trauma of killing all those people in that townhouse. A way to rationalize my own savagery. Maybe he was just a product of my adrenaline and shock over the loss of Becks and Ashlyn in one instant.

After all, he healed impossibly quickly and was unbelievably strong and above all that, strangely *civil*.

But then I remember the smell of his skin in shades of cinnamon and smoke when all that stinky blood was washed away, and I touch the crumpled letter in my pocket.

Still, days later, I'm embarrassed to think of how long it took me to read it the first time. To be able to read at all is a luxury only those of us who grew up in the World Before are privileged enough to have. Becks is one of the smartest people I know, but even her daughter can only read a little. *Was*, I mean. She was one of the smartest people…

I wake the third day of my journey to see the embers of the morning's fire pleasantly dead, and though I'm colder and more exposed to the elements, I still think of the fight Becks put up to venture to the city. I'm mad at myself for not stopping her.

We could have all made it out here, even Ashlyn. I'm sure her fever would have broken eventually, even without the antibiotics we found at an abandoned pharmacy.

I start arguing with myself aloud, coming up with all these clever things that I should have said as I follow the line of the freeway, careful never to venture too close to it. I'm steeped in such a heated debate with myself that I almost miss it.

It's a small sound, but I know that if it's close enough for me to hear it, it must not be far off. I tilt my right ear up to the wind and cup my hand around it. I take a few more steps and the muffled words reveal themselves. It's a woman's voice, and she's begging for help.

I feel my carefully compiled list of rules slip out of place, like trying to sprint up a broken staircase. Last time I broke rule number eight — don't help strangers — it worked out in my favor.

Kane saved my life. He kept me warm. He made conversation with me — okay, it was heated conversation, but I haven't had a conversation with anybody since Becks and Ashlyn and I've *never* had a conversation that wasn't about death and killing with a stranger before.

Curious and compelled by the fading memory of a blood-soaked alien, I feel edge closer to the freeway than the logical part of my brain knows is safe.

I listen closely from the cover of some wiry bush as she says, "Please! Is anybody there?"

She sounds like she's alone, because I don't hear signs of a struggle. Taking solace in that, I step onto the freeway and scratch out rule eight from the rule book.

The highway is littered with abandoned cars all shoved together in a warped pile of melted and eroded metal. They are beyond recognition and I don't need to see the mass to know though that the crash that happened here was serious. I can tell by the crunching beneath my feet.

Twigs and leaves snap and break and bend, but the dry, brittle bones do not. They linger.

They linger long after the skin has been picked apart by carrion and the flesh below has sloughed away. They linger until the insects have at everything left and eventually, the trees and the plants that thrive now in this cold, grey world, take what's left and use us to grow.

Or the bones are used to make more bones. Bones are valuable weapons out here. If I'd had more time, I'd have picked up a few of them myself, but I'm too enrapt by the sight that greets me.

An older woman with pale, almost translucent skin, and frizzy grey hair stands in the middle of the wreckage with her wrinkled hands on the handlebar of an overturned shopping cart. She's crying from what I can see.

I'm about thirty paces away but she still hasn't registered me, and continues calling out for help. She's gonna wake a world of monsters much worse than me if she doesn't shut up.

I jog towards her and when I'm close enough to be within earshot, I whisper, "Shh, don't scream."

She looks up at me with half-blind eyes. I can see the way they gloss over, pupils dilating unnaturally, and I frown. It seems unlikely that an older woman with eyes like that could have survived this long on her own. I glance around, certain I must have missed something, but I see nothing and no one.

"Are you okay?" I say, moving closer with my arm still outstretched in a non-threatening gesture. I keep a lookout towards the woods, hoping that I'm the only one who's heard her. The fact that no one else has come out of the tree line yet is a relief in itself. I touch her elbow.

Her skin is dry and leathery, like well-worn hide, and thin enough for me to feel her slender bones through. She's shaking like a leaf, and I see the age lines in her skin crease deeply when she tilts her face towards me. I wonder if she can see me at all. She's got this billowy grey hair and a sweet round face that reminds me of my own grandmother, or at least what I think she looked like. It's hard to be sure. Hard to remember anything with absolute certainty.

"Sweet child," she says, reaching her hand up to touch my face. Her cracked, dry fingertips reach my mouth, then trace delicate lines up over my nose. All at once, she shudders.

"Are you alright?" I say, "What's the matter? I heard you calling for help."

She takes several steps away from me and licks her worried lips. "Oh child, sweet child…" Tears come to her eyes then. She weeps.

"What is it? What's wrong?" I touch her shoulder, but she pushes me away and holds her face.

"Just a girl…you're just a girl." She looks around while panic hits me with one crushing blow. "Run," she whispers, "run!"

I spent my time being so terrified of the woods that I didn't realize that the car graveyard surrounding us has actually got a pulse. I take the advice given to me by the kind old booby trap and take off towards the tree line just as the sounds of scraping metal and people moving reaches my ears.

I'm out of the frying pan and among the trees now, but I've always been the muscle — Becks was always the eyes — and I miss the net well-camouflaged by leafy undergrowth. A hard, taut rope snags my ankles and legs then the rest of me and scoops me up.

I fly up, up, up into the treetops. My arms are wedged to my sides so that I can't reach my blade. Not like it would have mattered much. There's a crowd of people now — a larger clan than any I've seen in years — gathered below me, hooting and hollering and pointing. The older woman stands off to the side, alone, withered hands cradling her own face.

The only thing that brings me an iota of comfort at all is that there are women in the crowd. Just a few, and weakly dispersed. They're clustered around a single man standing directly underneath me, about ten feet down, and when I meet his gaze I can tell that he's hungry for more than just the peanut butter in my pack. And in thinking about the peanut butter, I feel momentarily annoyed that I didn't eat the rest of it last night.

Scratchy rope chaps my already chapped skin as I'm lowered into greedy, grappling hands. As soon as I'm freed from the net, my sword and pack are ripped away from me, its contents emptied and dispersed. Two men grab me by each arm and start dragging me away from the highway, deeper into the forest. They hold me too roughly, especially considering I'm not planning on running. Not *now*, duh. And as people crush against me, I can smell how desperately malnourished they are.

Jaundiced eyes stare down at me lecherously as if trying to see through my sweatshirt and I can feel gaunt fingers grope my butt, even through two layers of pants. I'm annoyed. The next guy who makes a grab for my breast gets a swift kick to the gut.

The two holding me seem shocked that I would try to fight back and one of them socks me in the ribs, igniting all the places I got kicked back in that townhouses with a dull ache. I breathe through my teeth to displace the pain and narrow my gaze on the one in front of me, holding his fist up so proudly while his buddies egg him on. He's gonna hit me again? Is that what he thinks? Well this asshat's got another thing coming.

Using the leverage of the guy at my back, I swing both my knees up to my chest, then kick the guy in the sternum hard enough to hear a crack. He flies back and so does the guy behind me. We land in a pile of limbs. Hands grab me and haul me up and I brace myself as I take another light beating.

By the time the fists stop their assault and my body decides it's okay to relax just a little bit, we're so deep in the forest that I can no longer make out the highway we left behind. We're deep enough that the grey darkens the world around me and is illuminated only by lanterns mounted on tree stumps.

It's in the weak light of the electric lamps that I start to notice rope ladders and swinging bridges dangling dozens of feet over my head. I have half a heart to be impressed by the ingenuity, and I think fleetingly of the storybook character my mother had once told me about — some guy called Robin Hood. I told Ashlyn the tale of Robin Hood all the time. It had been one of her favorites.

"Lock her up in jail," a raspy voice calls, and everyone around me erupts into cheers.

It takes me a second to identify the man speaking. When I do, I see it's the one who'd been surrounded by all the women. He's still surrounded by them. There are four. He smiles at me sleazily when my gaze catches his.

Repulsed, I look away, but as my gaze drops down to his chest, it snags on the dog tag he's wearing. It's decorated by an X inside of a circle — the same sign I've seen before and on the townhouse doors. Is *this* that gang? Is he its leader?

I discard the thoughts to focus on my present predicament when I'm dragged into their makeshift version of a prison.

The jail they put me in isn't really a jail, but a shack, and the locks they use aren't really locks, but rope. Still, I manage to be momentarily envious that they even have rope. Becks and I ran out seven years ago, back when she was still a wife and not yet a widow.

I lie on the ground on my side, head bent at a weird angle. Seriously — could they not do better for accommodations? A pillow would go a long way right about now…

Cold from the packed earth seeps in through my clothes as I wait…and wait…and wait…

The man with the gang sign necklace appears in the open doorway flanked by other people — men this time. He orders them to leave. Only the women stay with him. One of them stares at me longer than the others and in a way that's nearly apologetic, but mostly afraid.

She's got pale skin and red hair and looks very young. Too young. She doesn't look a day over fourteen. I look at the girls to her left and comb my gaze over their dirty, unwashed faces, realizing that none of them do.

My gut clenches as I return my gaze to the man. I don't have to wonder what he's doing to them to be disgusted by him all the same.

"You the pedophile running this colony then?"

My ankles are shackled to my hands in front of my body and my hands are shackled to my throat and there isn't much slack between them. I try to kick my legs out, but I don't move very far. Meanwhile, the man with the women watches me.

After about an eternity, he clicks his tongue against the backs of his teeth and shakes his head, but otherwise doesn't manage to look offended enough for me to believe I'm wrong.

"Are you referring to these lovely women?" He looks at them and when he does they all hasten to smile back. Stiff smiles do nothing to hide the anxiety running through all four of them. It has its own pulse.

"These are my wives."

I wait for the punchline that never comes before balking, "Wives? You like little kids because you're not man enough to handle a grown woman?"

He laughs easily, even as a muscle in his forehead ticks. "I believe I might take a fancy to you. Perhaps if you're just lucky enough, you can be one of my wives too."

He takes a step towards me and sweeps his arm back at the girls. "This here's Marmalade, Bon Bon, Sugar, and Candy." He drags the redhead forward by the elbow. "Candy here's my newest wife."

He tucks her hair behind her ear and plants a sloppy kiss on her forehead. He has to bend down to do so, and when he does, he lingers. He licks the side of her face and I cringe, even though she doesn't.

She stands stiff and still and without flinching — brave — even as my eyes are drawn to the lines that decorate the side of her neck. They crisscrossing back and forth, looking red and angry and *painful*, even from here.

My brain shorts for a second as I try to process how she'd have come by marks like those. Memories flit through my head like pages in a book I can't even read.

I swallow a gasp and say accusatorially, "You're one of *them*?"

He grins to show all of his teeth and I note that the ones at the back have definitely been filed. I'm both surprised and not surprised that it took me until now to realize he's one of the Others.

He's not that much bigger than the average human and even though he's probably nearing six feet tall, Kane would have towered over him. He's muscular, but not that muscular. His dirty Rolling Stones tee shirt and army green vest seem to hang off of him awkwardly, clearly having once belonged to someone else fatter than he is. What is an Other doing out here wearing shabby human clothes and eating children? I frown, arriving at no conclusions.

He's not an attractive guy, this freak. He's got frosty pale skin and strawberry hair cropped short so that it sticks out away from his face in every direction. Only his eyes are the least bit disarming, and they are. Well, disarming, not so much, but unsettling, sure. They're black. Not dark brown, but pitch black and flat as a board. I read nothing in those eyes. Nothing but hunger.

I grimace when he lifts Candy's wrist to his mouth where she's got dried blood crusted over more scabs and scars. Dozens of them. *Poor baby...* For a moment, I pray to God that wherever Ashlyn is, she's safe from monsters like this one.

"I am," he says, and he says it with some pride. "But I'm a bit more of an explorer than those pansies. A man can't get what he really needs consorting with all those pricks in the Diera."

My ears perk up at the name even as my eyes slit. "Why? What's in the Diera? Competition?" I challenge.

He twitches dangerously and I know I should be afraid to have hit a nerve, but all I feel is vindication. This guy deserves to bleed, even if I have to take him apart with a needle.

"You know, you've got quite a set of lips on you," he replies. "I wonder if you'd mind if I ripped them clean off."

The girl in his arms — Candy, if that's even her name — tenses and clutches the backs of her arms. As she shoots fretful glances up at the man, I notice that even in this weather, she only wears a thin dress beneath a tattered trench coat.

"If you're not here to torture me, then what are you here for?" I lick my lips and at least have sense enough to fear his answer. I'm not going to be his fifth wife. I'm not as brave as Candy is.

He crouches down onto his haunches before me and I work myself awkwardly into an upright position so that we're nearly at eye level.

"What's your name, human?"

I remember when Kane asked me that question and it's in thinking about Kane that I whisper, "Abel."

"Well, Abel, that all depends," he says, grinning to show a mouth full of yellow teeth. His breath smells like blood and shit as it wafts to me. My stomach lurches.

"Depends on what?" I say, cutting off my air supply to keep myself from retching.

"On whether you behave."

I don't have any more air left, so I keep quiet.

Likely for the best, anyway.

The Other doesn't seem to take pleasure in my silence, because he frowns. "I think I'll leave you in here until you decide to behave properly. It won't take long for me to break you." He rises without another word and stalks from the jail cell, his four *brides* following in his wake.

It's not long before I'm visited by another member of the clan, though this one is clearly human.

"I'm Rick," he says nervously, taking a seat on a short stool in the corner and the room's only piece of furniture.

His pale eyes glance up at me from beneath a pair of broken glasses, but he can't seem to hold my gaze.

"Rick," I answer, clearing my throat and trying to be kind, "I'm Abel."

"Abel what?" He pulls out a Steno notepad and starts scribbling feverishly though I haven't said anything yet.

"What are you doing? Gathering intel?"

He snorts and hiccups and rubs his pudgy, red nose quickly with his free hand. I don't miss the way it shakes.

"Why did they send nervous guy in here to check up on me? Where's the perv?"

Rick's face scrunches up and I realize that he can't be that much older than I am. "Who? Do you mean Drago?"

"Drago, the Other with all the wives?"

"Yeah."

"Then yes."

"Look, I uhh…"

Rick pushes his glasses further up onto his nose with his middle finger. I can see that they've been broken and patched up several times and the left lens still has a chip in it.

When the Others started their attacks on camps and settlements, glasses wearers had been of the first to die, along with anyone that was deaf, blind, old, pregnant, or with a disability. Like the misleading old lady earlier, I can't help but wonder how this shrimpy kid made it this far.

"What?" I snap.

"I have some questions I need to get through..." He flips through his notes for a second, then says, "Have you ever heard of the Hive?"

"Is that what this is? Your little gang with the X-O thingy?"

"That answers my next question," he says, jotting something down.

"So what's the deal with this place? And why the fuck would you guys all follow one of the Others? Do you *all* have serious memory loss? Do you not remember what they did? How things were in the World Before? Before we became animals? Before they made us this way?"

I lean as far forward as my shackles allow. My neck is bound to a metal ring behind me and the rope attached to my feet is short, so that way I can't stretch my legs or lie down comfortably. Even after only a few minutes, I'm squirming restlessly. What ass holes.

Rick seems uncomfortable that I'm engaging him in conversation, and I watch his pale face light up like a cherry tomato. He licks his dry lips and glances up at the skylight — well, the caved-in ceiling — as if the trees might be listening.

"I really can't talk to you about this. Drago has exceptional hearing."

I think about Kane and the way he was able to see me so clearly, even in the dark. "So what does that mean? Is he keeping you here as a prisoner?"

Rick's face blanches. "No. No, we…" And then his eloquence fails him. He stutters, "We…we bartered to get… to get in."

"To get in? Into the gang you mean? Into the Hive?" I say, using the same name he did.

Rick nods, but his eyes grow large and distant. He shrinks back into the wall behind him, becoming a part of it, looking like a shadow. "Being part of the Hive…Drago he…he offers us protection."

"From what?"

"From the other humans. They won't cross one of the Others. And the Others don't seem to care that Drago lives out here with us, so they leave him alone. They leave us alone, so that way we can…you know…grow food, build shelter, stay in one place. So we don't have to start over."

His eyes are touched with sadness. It's a sadness that I can sympathize with. At some point, for me and Becks and Ashlyn, a place like this would have had definite draw.

"So what did you have to barter?" Rick looks down at his hands and I get the idea that he's near tears. I don't know what I've said, or what to say next. And then it hits me.

My eyes narrow. "What did you mean, *we* had to barter?"

"Me and my…my sister. She's…she's one of Drago's wives now."

I don't know how I didn't notice the family resemblance immediately. Pale face, red hair, heart-shaped faces. "You're Candy's older brother," I shout.

I lurch away from the wall as if I might fight him, but the scratchy rope chokes my throat and I'm flung back down to the ground. The flimsy wooden wall rattles and shakes behind me.

"You're a fucking coward. You're her older brother. You're supposed to protect her!" I can't even breathe as a lifetime of memories revisit me that I've fought damn hard to suppress.

Vividly, I catch a flashback of a grocery store six years ago…aisles of rotting fruit, stale chips crunching beneath running feet… I kick my head back into the wall behind me like I might knock the sounds out of my ears and the thoughts out of my head.

Rick tries to stand, but slips. He tries again, straightening and pointing a finger at me that does nothing but make me want to break it. I would have, if I'd been able to reach him.

"You don't know anything. You're a fighter. I'm just a skinny boy with half a brain. Not even half a brain can keep you alive long enough in this world. We couldn't have survived," he chokes on his own breath.

"We *weren't* surviving. I had to do something and I…" But the look of horror and shame that crosses his face then makes me wish I hadn't even asked. "You had a family once, didn't you?"

I tense my lips, but don't answer.

"I thought so."

He turns to leave, but I stop him. "So what happens when Drago decides he doesn't like them anymore? When they get too old?"

His shoulders quiver, just like his knees. And when he speaks his voice is hollow and in it, I hear that he's not even a person anymore. He's the same thing I told Kane I was.

Nothing.

And definitely not worth saving. Him, maybe even less than me.

"He eats them."

Ah. That all?

"So you've resigned her to that fate? You know she won't make it that much longer. What is she, fifteen now? Sixteen max?" He looks at the open door and the trees beyond it, like he's thinking the same thing I once did — that he might use them to escape.

When he continues to refuse to acknowledge my guesses, I spit, "However old she is, I give her a year, maybe two before he finds a replacement."

"Well, at least..." Rick's chest inflates, but his shoulders slump forward, retaliation falling short.

"At least *what*?" I challenge.

And when his eyes touch mine I can see that he hates me, and if I had to guess, it'd be because he's feeling right now something I've never fully felt: resignation. Somewhere along the way, Population chewed him up and spit him out and he just gave up.

But you can never give up. It's not a rule on my list, but I mentally add it. Never give up, not while you're breathing.

I'm about to tell him as much when Rick looks over his shoulder at me. He says, "At least she'll make it longer than you."

He slams the door shut behind him — no matter that it's flimsier than cardboard and I can see through the uneven slats. Still, it's enough to drive me a little crazy now that I can't see outside, unless I'm looking up through the broken roof at the trees in this dark, twilight hour.

Sorry, not the broken roof — the skylight.

Time passes. I'm not sure how much of it. When the next person comes to visit me, the sky up above is about as bleak as my current situation.

Candy enters and sees the rope burns on my neck and bloody rings around my wrists and tries her best to massage them. I thank her, but know it won't do any good. Who knows how many other victims have bled and sweat all over these crusty ropes?

Nope, I accept the rawness without complaining. A feat that's made easier when I see that she's holding a bowl of soup that's shockingly still steaming.

"Your brother told me you guys grow all this food yourselves," I say, trying to make my voice light so as not to scare her.

After all, she is spooning bites of potato soup into my mouth. It scalds my tongue, but I chew through the branding.

The soup is watery and the taste leaves a lot to be desired, but I'm certainly not one to complain about taste after eating off-peanut butter, two packs of dried ramen, and kibbles by the handful.

Though, if I had the choice, I'd gladly trade my soup for more rabbit.

Candy nods. She doesn't talk much and when I mention Drago, she shuts down entirely. Trying to muster some of that elusive foreign emotion Becks would have called 'tact,' I attempt to learn what I can from her without being too harsh. Or a pain in the ass, as Becks would have also put it.

I force myself to smile, though I'm sure it comes out more of a grimace, as I ask, "How is it with the other girls? With Drago's other…wives?"

She pauses, spoon hovering over the bowl as she waits for it to cool. A kindness I don't feel that I deserve.

"Good. They're nice."

"Nice how?"

"Just nice."

It'd be easier getting information out of an oyster.

I smile — grimace — at her again. "Do you ladies do anything around here for fun?"

A small spark lights in her eyes when I say this. Softly, she says, "Sometimes Drago lets us dance. He plays music."

That *is* something. I haven't heard music in a long time. Once Becks found an abandoned iPod that still had juice. We managed to make it last for nearly six weeks by taking turns and only listening to one song every day. Ashlyn listened to *Yellow Submarine* by the Beatles on repeat every other chance she got. Now even *I* know all the words.

"What kind of music?" I prod.

"All kinds. Sometimes hip hop, jazz, classical. Classical is my favorite. Reminds me that there used to be instruments and people who knew how to play them."

She smiles at me and after I swallow the next spoonful, I smile back at her even though her words make me feel a little sad. Who knows how to play instruments anymore? Why would they? It's a wasted talent. Now, coveted skills include all things violent. All things savage.

"Yeah that's um…that does sound nice," I say thickly, meaning it.

Candy brings the spoon to my lips, but as she does, leans in close. This is new. She glances around as if someone might be watching and only after she's confident enough that we won't be overheard does she press her face close to mine and whisper directly into my ear.

"Are you going to be Drago's next wife?" The sensation of her breath on my face, coupled with her words, makes me shiver.

"No."

She exhales, evidently relieved, and doles me up another spoonful. When she doesn't elaborate, I ask her the same question I asked Rick — about what happens to the other women.

"They go away," she whispers, gaze carefully avoiding mine.

I grimace. "Into the ground, you mean?"

She nods, and her pale pink lips tremble. "And Drago only likes to have four wives at a time. When he finds a new one he likes, he kills one of the others."

I can't help it, I have to ask. "Why don't you run? I mean, you're gonna die anyways. Why don't you at least try?"

She looks down at the emptying bowl and says, "Rick." She pauses and for a moment I don't think she'll say more. Then her confession comes all at once, "He'll kill Rick if I run."

He uses their love against them.

I shake my head and say, voice simultaneously accusatory and pleading, "Rick doesn't deserve your sacrifice. He sold you out."

But she cuts me off, voice getting harder than I would have thought possible. "He's my brother. Didn't you have brothers or sisters once? A family you'd have done anything for?"

Meek. Is that what I thought of her? No, there's fire there, trapped beneath layers of resignation. A fire I don't think her brother has.

My tongue tangles with my vocal cords and all my words get lost in the middle. I'm mute as Candy roughly shovels the last few bites of potato soup into my mouth. That's fine, though. I'm suddenly not that hungry.

I want Drago. I want him dead. I want his blood covering my hands, warming me up like Kane's radiator chest once did. I want to punish him for what he's doing to her. She deserves more than this.

Wordlessly, Candy lowers the bowl and starts to stand, but she's just close enough to touch, so I do. She seems startled and afraid when I slide my fingers over hers, but she doesn't pull away from me this time even though she could.

I squeeze her fingers fiercely. "Candy, if you bring me a knife I can get us both out of here."

She doesn't respond. Her brown eyes are wide and afraid. "What about Rick? You don't even think he's worth saving."

"I don't, but I think you are." Despite what I told Kane, I do think she's worth saving.

She's just…good.

"Like you said, Rick is your brother. I had a brother once too and I'd have done anything for him. I understand and I won't let you abandon him." Even if he's already done the same to you.

"I can protect both of you," I say, though I know at the moment it doesn't look like it. "I just need you to bring me a knife. That's all."

She doesn't answer. She doesn't even look at me. Her expression is conflicted, tormented.

But at least tormented is better than defeated.

"We can't give up. Not ever. Candy, please."

Candy gasps and keeps her eyes trained on the places where our fingers touch. Robotically, she recites, "No. I'm happy here. Drago is my husband."

"Candy," I exhale, but she pulls her hands away from mine and pretends not to hear me. She turns and slinks out of the cabin, the soft train of her tattered dress catching dirt as she walks.

Chapter Five

N ight creeps over the camp slowly and even though I can't lay down without serious pain in my neck and even though, sitting up, the rope is rubbing away what little's left of my skin, I manage to doze off into a strange, transient sort of half-sleep. And as I float at the crossroads of wakefulness and wakelessness, I dream of strange things...

Women dressed all in white seated at a long table full of fluffy, fuzzy rabbits...a face among the grey clouds overhead constantly laughing...filed teeth...blood dripping down bare thighs...space ships...syringes...caves full of dead men... trees whispering 'Abel'...Abel...

"Abel."

I realize that something is touching my ass through the slats in the wall behind me before I realize I'm even awake.

I blink rapidly, trying to clear the haze from my eyes and the dreams from my consciousness.

"Abel," comes the voice a second time, like the hard crack of a whip.

"Kane?" I say, and my tone is one of incredulousness. Maybe I'm still sleeping...

Light, impish laughter confirms my reality: Kane is here, just on the other side of my prison wall.

What the hell is he doing here?

"Just checking," he whispers, and he must be close, because I can feel warmth already emanating from behind me, even through the flimsy wooden wall. "I wouldn't want to have freed the wrong prisoner."

The wooden wall bends against my spine and starts to crack. One swift snap and all of a sudden a gust of cold air hits me and I'm left looking up at Kane's head, silhouetted by silver-lined treetops. Even in the dark I can still make out his taunting expression but instead of pissing me off royally, laughter bubbles up to my lips.

He smiles rakishly in response, and I hate the strange softness to his expression, because it's the same one I memorized from before.

That I immortalized.

Because I never wanted to let that memory go.

His fingers brush over my forehead, pulling back some of my curls. He says, "I can't remember the last time anyone looked so pleased to see me."

I'm grinning shamelessly and though I try to squash the expression, my efforts are met with absolutely no success. Quickly rallying, I pitch my voice low and careless. "Don't look so smug. I had a whole escape plan mapped out that you just interfered with."

"Sincerest apologies, ma'am. I'll just slide these boards back into place and let you get on with it." He starts to lift the boards I'm still pinned to — with me on them — and push me back towards the black opening in the side of the jail cell.

I laugh quietly. "No, no. Don't do that. This escape plan will do just fine."

His responding laughter is low and dark and full of mischief as he lowers me onto the damp leaves, then snaps the rope connecting my hands to my neck. Before he does the same to my feet, his eyes sweep up and down my body and as they do, they glisten carnivorously.

"You know, I have half a mind to leave you like this."

Heat fills my face and my chest and my neck. My lips are slack and though I try to counter confidently, my voice is too low and whispery to achieve it. "What would you do with me?"

Oh God, was that an invitation? Was that innuendo? Am I flirting? All questions I can't define, but I see their answers in the way Kane's gaze heats.

"I…just…sorry," I blurt.

He cocks his head to the side and I'm grateful that some of that heat cools. "Why are you apologizing?"

Hell if I know! "Can you…um?" I say dumbly, gesturing to the rope around my ankles.

He quickly frees them and pulls me up onto my feet so quickly that I tumble straight into his chest.

"Sorry," I grunt, struggling to regain my coherency as well as my footing. He holds out his hands and lets me use his arms for balance.

Stable now, I try to pull back only to be arrested by his fingers on either side of my jaw. "You didn't answer my question, and now you're apologizing again." He shakes his head. "It's like you were made to confuse me."

As he speaks, he angles my face up towards his and I'm so stunned he's touching me at all — and *gently* — that I don't resist, even though I should. I also don't respond. Can't respond.

Rule number twelve is the last rule on my list and states, very plainly — don't talk to Others. That includes interacting with them in all its forms. But right now, I've never been touched gently before…not by anyone, really. I touched Ashlyn and gave her pats when she was a puppy, but I never had an affectionate family, even before. So this? This is all new territory for me, and what's more is that I like it.

I can feel rule twelve getting erased, letter-by-letter, the longer he touches me.

His thumbs are rough against my cheeks as he tilts my face first to the left and then to the right. I wonder, as he inspects me, if he's admiring the patchwork of fresh bruises along on my neck and cheeks. Relics of our last encounter, and the encounters I've had since. I note the disparities between his face and mine, and frown. Despite having died three days ago, there isn't a cut, scratch, or bruise on him.

"Now *you're* frowning even though, as you once so cleverly reminded me, you cannot see yourself." He remembers me saying that? "What's wrong?"

"You...don't have any bruises."

"And you have far, far too many bruises." His voice comes out stormy and louder than it was. His fingers tense against my cheeks, prodding wounds. I wince and he lets go of me.

"What happened?" He barks. "Who did this to you?"

"I...why do you care?"

He closes his eyes for longer than a standard blink. "You are infuriating. Can you ever simply answer a question I ask you?"

No. Probably not. "It's not a big deal. I made friends."

Kane's eyes narrow. He looks particularly displeased by that answer. His hands clench at his sides, but when he catches me eyeing them apprehensively, he crosses them over his chest.

"The kind of friends who like hitting women."

I balk, "Hate to break it to you, but most of the friends I make out here are the kind who like hitting women."

A shiver passes over his body. He looks away, off into the distance. "I should never have left you here."

"What?" Excuse me, sir? Have I heard you correctly or am I having a minor stroke?

"I will not make that mistake again," he says instead of offering any kind of answer that makes any kind of sense. He grabs my hand suddenly and starts to move — *fast*.

I lurch along after him, and it's only as we start to move away from the jail that it occurs to me... "How did you find me?"

"Later," he grunts.

"You know, for someone who hates when I avoid questions, you're really catching onto the trend."

He shakes his head and when I catch sight of his profile, I can see him smiling just a little bit.

We quiet and duck low and I let him pull me through Drago's camp, zigzagging behind him in a way that's truly impressive. We don't encounter any guards of any kind. Heck, we don't encounter anyone.

More impressive still is the fact that even though he's as big as a rhino, he's as agile as a mountain cat and makes virtually no noise as we cut through the forest. Meanwhile, I sound like I'm stepping on landmines each step I take. I mean it — every single one.

Over his shoulder, Kane shoots me an annoyed glance, and when he tugs harder on my hand, urging me to keep up, I lose my footing and slide over wet leaves. Unable to maintain my balance, I trip and fall and break what must be the forest's equivalent of bubble wrap.

"Erm...oops."

Kane lets go of my hand so that he can reach up and massages his temples with both. He looks like I'm giving him one hell of a migraine. He's also entirely visible.

The torches beam brightly where we're standing and I feel creepily exposed. And when I hear the scrambling of many feet over damp leaves, I realize that if *I* can hear them, running must have stopped being an option a while ago.

As I lumber ungainly to my feet and brush the leaves off my pants, a voice calls out to us from the darkness. "Well, what have we here?" It's unmistakably Drago. "Trying to make off with my soon-to-be wife, I see."

Kane tenses visibly at my side and his voice is not the same when he speaks. It's darker. "I see you have many others. Taking one shouldn't be a problem."

It takes me a second to see what Kane does already — Candy, tucked into Drago's shadow, and the other three girls just behind her.

Drago smiles as he steps forward into the clearing like an actor moving to center stage for the big number. Torchlight glistens off of his dog tag. He says, "I think that *many* may be a gross exaggeration, my brother. Particularly when you take the true gem, and the only one I haven't tasted yet."

Briefly, I wonder if that's what Kane had been looking for. Bite marks, as well as bruises.

"I've already named her, in fact. Sweets. A perfect addition to my delicious collection."

"Perhaps purchasing her from you would sate your appetite," Kane says, voice about as flat and dry as stale toast even though his face and posture are pure malevolence.

For the first time ever, it makes me feel like I stepped into a fight alongside a Rottweiler. And it feels good. Because I don't know what Kane's got in mind, but I'm not leaving here without Drago's head on a pike. And I'm going to need Kane's help to do it.

"You speak to the man who has everything he wants and wants everything he has. Money and things have little appeal to me. Only beauty." His gaze hovers over mine and I level my shoulders against the invasion, only for Kane to step between us, severing Drago from sight.

Still facing forward, Kane reaches back for me, presses just the tips of his fingers to my chest. In a feral move, he grabs the front of my sweatshirt and wrenches me closer to him, so that I'm nearly hugging him from behind. Confused, my feet drag and I stumble against him.

What is he doing? I'm confused. Because now I can't see Drago at all and Drago can't see me. It's almost like Kane's trying to be some kind of shield. Almost like he's…oh God. Is he protecting me?

My mouth runs dry, my skin gets cold, then abruptly heats. No. *Nononononono.* Monsters like him don't protect humans like me.

But that's exactly what he's doing.

Lightning rushes up the back of my legs and all at once, my knees feel weak. I grab hold of Kane's black tee shirt to keep myself upright and I feel his hand slide down my body to rest on my hip. He gives me a small squeeze.

No. Nonononononono. Emotions. I'm starting to feel them. And emotions are dangerous, bloodthirsty things. The most dangerous things that exist in Population. I close my eyes and focus on slaughtering them all while in front of me, Kane speaks.

"I forgot that after your disgrace, you were exiled out here. You attempted to rape one of your own kind and she fought you off with a knitting needle."

Kane laughs and it's a horrible sound. I wish I could see Drago's face right now, but right now, I've still got my fists balled up in Kane's warm tee shirt.

"I wanted your life, but the Lahve felt that our population had already been too badly ravaged by wars with the humans and the failed arrival that brought so few of us to this planet. I rarely speak against him, but it's clear now that he was wrong. What you are doing here is wrong. Disgusting. Raping the most vulnerable creatures on this planet because you are too weak to fight off a true opponent."

"Stop it…" Drago tries, but Kane speaks over him.

"You are a pathetic shell of a Heztoichen. It's a miracle that your mother died on Sistylea before she had a chance to see the monster her son would become…"

"You dare!"

"I dare? You chose small, slight, female youth to terrorize. To call you male or otherwise is an insult to all creatures of this world. You are not even good enough to be called living. You are nothing. And certainly not something worth saving."

He remembered that too?

"You prey on the weak because you are a coward, and though I might have offered you a chance to walk away tonight alive, that offer has been rescinded." My chest burns with a new sort of fire. One that's *ready*.

"You think you can beat me? I have an army! I'm not alone anymore like I was in your cursed Diera!"

The crack of twigs and the rustle of dried leaves calls my attention away from Drago and when I sweep my gaze around the glade, I flinch. Drago's got us surrounded by men armed with stakes, machetes, knives, pitchforks and at least one gun. But more than their weapons, I'm concerned by their numbers. There must be at least forty of them.

"I'm not alone either. My travel companion and I will tear your desperate village apart."

Wait. Does he mean me? That would mean that he's talking about me like an equal…or nearly.

Creeping emotion, emotion, emotion — *stay back!*

Drago barks out a laugh. "You came all this way to collect one little female. Don't worry, I'll let you watch as I bond with her over and over again."

A muscle shifts in Kane's back and I fight the desire to soothe him. I don't even know how.

"Alone against my human, you would not stand a chance." His human? What now? And wait — he thinks that highly of my fighting that I could take on Drago?

Pride. Emotion. Everything. For just one fragile second in time, suspended, I feel everything.

A muted roar, a lousy insult, then Drago shouts, "Give me back my wife!"

"She's not your wife," Kane's voice rises in a way that makes all the little hairs on the backs of my arms stand on end.

Kane shifts and maybe it's the light tricking me, but his shoulders seem to swell, becoming even broader than they had been before. His chest pulses and emits a faint glow that I can see even through his dark tee shirt.

Wait a second — he wasn't wearing this before. Last I checked, he was filthy and wearing basketball shorts that fit him like tighty whities. Since he left me, where did he go?

"Well, we seem to be at an impasse, my friend," Drago says, abruptly stepping to the left and into my view. "I can't let you leave and you seem unwilling to leave without her."

Kane shakes his head once, definitively. "That I will not do. I also wish to reclaim her things. She has stolen something of mine and I will have it back."

"Oh?" The slight lift to Drago's eyes is enough for me to know exactly where he's taken my pack.

Two men dressed in ratty clothes stand on a wooden platform built into the tree above me. Nailed into the tree trunk are a set of precarious-looking rungs. What fun.

Slowly, I step back from Kane, even as he reaches for me, and start to edge towards them. The thought of my sword in this moment has definite appeal.

"I'm sorry, but what was once yours is now mine. This is your last chance, Notare," Drago says, calling Kane by a name that has no meaning to me. "Leave or live long enough to watch your human suffer."

I freeze. Not because Drago and Kane are suddenly both looking at me, making me feel horribly naked and alone, but because Candy is still standing next to Drago, and she's doing something that's about to change *everything*.

Her haunting gaze is pinned to me and I can't break the hold. Not even when I see the knife glint in her hand. This knife was meant for me, I can feel it in my bones. And when her eyes flicker to Drago, I know exactly what she intends to do with it. Her hesitation turns to hate. Her resignation falls to that fire within. It blazes bright, bright, and brighter still. She takes a half-step towards him.

A man only a few paces to my right stumbles forward into the clearing and points to Candy, babbling. Eyes start to turn. What can I do to stop them? Nothing. No. Nothing has never been an option.

So I do the only thing that comes to me at all. I scream bloody murder.

I scream loud enough to jerk Kane around, his body poised and on the defensive. The human man who'd been about to out Candy looks my way too, and I'm only a few paces from him.

I throw myself at him without hesitation, taking him to the ground. I punch him once in the throat and again in the eye-socket. While he struggles to catch his breath, I relieve him of the rusty weapon he carries — some kind of garden tool — and stab it down into his jugular. Blood sprays like a broken water fountain.

Shouts and screams light up the night. I've got at least twelve armed recruits running towards me but I look past them at Candy just in time to see her shaking arms bring the knife down.

Though her arms are as thin as splinters, the force of her blow is still enough to make Drago cry out. He rips an arm around, hitting her in the cheek, and as she falls back into the shadows I hear a name — Meredith — shouted in a voice that could only be Rick's.

Bodies dance in my way, preventing me from seeing what happens to Candy or Rick or Drago. I look around, finally taking notice of the surprising number of corpses littering the ground around me.

In my absence, Kane has truly taken over.

About ten paces away from me, he has a man by the hair. He punches another in the face so hard that his hand breaks through all of the man's teeth and flies through the back of his head.

He shakes the man loose and swings the first over his head, using the man's limp body like some great big mace, taking out three others. He stands in the center of the glade like a god amongst insects and for a second, I just sit there and gawk.

"Abel," he shouts through the commotion, without looking up to see that I'm there. "Get the key."

I don't hesitate. Snatching up the spade, I leap falling bodies and dodge the hands that reach for me. Tree bark flakes off beneath my fingers, but I dig my nails and toes into it and climb.

The tree is cold and the damp steps are hard to maneuver, made even harder by the fact that there's blood on my hands and the guards above me are chucking chunks of wood at my head.

As I move upwards, rung by rung, one piece of wood clips me in the forehead and hot blood streams into my right eye. Ignoring it, I reach the platform and climb through the man-sized hole at its base.

A boot kicks me in the center of the back the moment I'm through and my body slams into the tree trunk. I nearly lose my grip on the floorboards as the pressure of the boot against my spine knocks the breath right out of me. I gulp in little sips of air.

Twisting around, my feet slip over the wooden beams, but I manage to brace my side against the edge of the manhole and my feet against the tree just in time to see a second foot driving towards me.

I don't stab, but slice.

Catching his boot against my shoulder, I bring my spade across his Achilles tendon. The rusted edge manages to cut deep and he clings to his goon-friend to try to keep himself from falling over. The friend helpfully pushes him back. He grabs the guy's arms and together, both men fall off the edge of the rail-less platform with fairly little effort on my part.

I cringe when I hear the sound of their bodies hitting the carpeted forest floor below, knowing that it's that softness that will keep them living for who knows how long, and in a level of pain I don't want to think about.

Pulling myself out of the precarious tree hole, I start towards the rope bridge connecting this platform to the next.

Built around the far tree is a small house, barred by a closed door. Guessing that's where Drago's keeping my pack, I move toward it tentatively, one slat at a time.

My hands grip the worn rope rails like a madwoman, but no matter how softly I step, I continue to swing wildly on this stupid death-trap. The sounds from the fight below seem so much louder at this height and I can hear my teeth grinding against one another with how hard I'm clenched.

I tell myself not to look down, so naturally, I look down immediately.

I find Kane in the chaos quite quickly, standing in the center of a pile of bodies like the last piece of some bloody chess game. *Check mate, Drago.* He's doing better than I could have expected. Especially alone and against dozens. Dozens — maybe two dozen — but *not* forty, as I originally calculated.

As I canvas the carnage, I realize that the odds aren't actually what I thought they'd be.

Candy's intervention in the battle must have started a chain reaction, because when Rick stepped in to defend her, he wasn't alone. Looking around now, I can't tell who the enemy is anymore. Kane is fighting humans, Drago is fighting humans, and humans are fighting each other.

A group of four men stand slightly apart from the fray and after a fleeting hesitation, dart off into the night. Another couple stragglers follow soon after.

Then I see Drago's wives, clustered around Rick and Candy. One of them is wielding a big stick like a club and takes a guy down when he comes within a foot of her. Two more men run up to the group and wrap two of Drago's wives in huge hugs. I see one of the women crying and in the next second, the entire pack is running off, taking Rick and Candy with them.

I wonder if I'll ever see them again…

My chest tightens at the thought. I don't know why I should feel abandoned by a group of people I don't even know. Maybe it's because Candy reminds me of Ashlyn in a way and I have the strange urge to want to see this through, and protect her. Maybe it's because Candy reminds me of me in the love she had for her brother. Maybe it's because seeing them hug one another and move as a unit reminds me of what it was like to have friends and family and something almost resembling a community.

What do I have?

Nothi…

A roar from below makes me jump and I glance down to see Kane charging a group of humans. Bodies fly away from his so fast it hardly looks like he's touching them and of all the things I could do in that moment, I have the audacity to laugh. He looks ridiculous, though he's earned it. The battle is won.

I wonder where Drago disappeared to as the number of living humans dwindles from around twenty to four. The creak of the platform's wooden base causes me to swivel my head around just in time to answer the question I just asked myself.

Well, hello.

Drago lifts his head through the man hole and stupidly, I chuck my spade at him, missing him by a good three feet. Propelled by a fear greater than my fear of heights, I sprint across the rest of the rope bridge, make it onto the opposite platform, dive into the tree house and slam the bottom half of the weird two-part door shut behind me.

Light filters in through an overhead skylight but it's still too hard to see anything distinct amidst the endless piles of junk.

I land on something hard and pull a decrepit doll with ratty blonde hair and one eye missing out from under me. Blech. *Grooooossssssss.*

I kick aside more kids' toys, broken bottles, maggot-infested magazines, aging books with dog-eared pages and jaundiced bindings, and occasionally the useful oil lamp or lighter.

Clothes and equipment litter the space too, and are piled on top of the suitcases and packs of all the people that must have been captured before me.

I grab the oil lamp and a box of matches and just as I do, something thunderous shakes the foundation of the tree beneath me. I hear a crack and then a shout that sounds distinctly like my name — no, the name Kane calls me. The tree wobbles, but holds at the last second.

Scrabbling back to the door, I open the bottom half and spy Drago halfway across the bridge, foot caught in between two wooden planks. It won't stall him for long. I glance at the oil lamp I'm carrying and throw it. It shatters on the wooden planks between Drago and me, the rope bridge and the platform. He looks up and our eyes meet, but I've got six matches in my hand and I strike them all simultaneously. I don't wait, but throw them all.

Wait a second. *Is there another exit out of this place?*

A cloud of flame sends me cantering back and for a moment my sleeve catches fire as I drop back into the supply closet. I kick the door closed with my foot while Drago curses me from beyond the flame-embellished doorway.

Smoke floods the building, but so does the fire's light. With that help, it doesn't take me long to find my pack shoved underneath a pile of clothes that look too small to fit anyone I've seen so far at the camp. *They'd fit Ashlyn though…*

I wince as I lift my pack from the rubble. It feels lighter than it did and when I look inside I see that they've emptied it of everything useful, which of course means that the key is still there. Without knowing what the key does, I still manage to feel fleetingly grateful.

I swing the pack onto my shoulders and scramble hand over foot in my search for the sword. I curse when I can't find it, but by then, smoke filters around the frame of the door so thick, I can barely see or breathe through it.

I'm still watching the door, wondering what to do next when it explodes open and a massive body steps into the little building with me. My eyes are watery and for the first second, I hallucinate that it's Kane standing there, like the Prince Charming of my own post-apocalyptic fairy tale. But instead of Prince Charming, I'm left with the dragon.

He's got flames licking up his arms and covering his vest, which falls around his shoulders in pieces, and he looks extremely unhappy to see me.

Bye then!

I scramble up onto my feet and hurl myself towards the far wall, which is marked by just one window. Then I drag my body through the termite-infested frame.

Choking on smoke and soot, I realize that the last thing under me now — apart from a whole heckofalotta empty space — is one precariously thin bough that doesn't look thick enough to take my weight.

Wonderful. Here it goes, anyway...

I crouch down and wriggle along the branch until I start to feel it bend, then I stop. Now what?

My eyes are burning and I'm not sure what kind of damage I'll sustain trying to jump, but I remember the sound of bones breaking and breaths choking on sobs — the other two humans I'd pushed from this height — and I don't want to find out.

Carefully, I unclip my pack and let it fall to the ground. It takes a full two-seconds to hit the wet leaves below and in my head I quickly calculate that I must be up over sixty feet. I shudder and mutter a quiet curse.

"Fuck's right, Sweets." Drago barks out a laugh just behind me.

Sparing a single glance back, I see him standing at the window I just came through, unbothered by the raging fire that has fully claimed the building at his back or the ash thickening the air between us.

I make a mental note — next time I set a tree on fire, maybe make sure there's another way off of it.

"How long do you think you can hold on there, Sweets? I'll give you about two more minutes — five if you're as strong as your Notare thinks you are — but I don't mind. I've got all the time in the world."

Five minutes? That's seriously optimistic. Each breath I take fills me with ash and smoke and leaden weight. I'm in a kiln.

I edge another couple inches out along the bough, but it dips, creaks and splinters and I know that it's met the last of its resistance. Looking towards the ground, I see that the next tree branch belongs to another tree and hovers about ten feet down and twenty feet to my left.

Mmm, since I'm not a spider-monkey or a squirrel, that's not an option.

I'm going to have to let go…and break every bone in my body.

Lovely. Just great.

"Abel, Hold on!" Kane shouts somewhere below me.

Croaking through the smoke, I fire back. "Your pack is down there with the key. Take it!"

"Shut up. I'm going to get you down." Kane's voice is followed by a thunderous crack followed by the entire tree lurching.

Dried branches plummet past me wreathed in flame and though my sweaty hands are slipping, I squeeze the bough as hard as I can between my thighs. The next thunderclap shakes the tree to its foundations. I'm going to fall. I'm definitely going to fall. What in God's name is happening?

Drago apparently has the same concern and roars, "Kane, what are you doing! You can't carry the fucking tree."

Oh seven hells. Is *that* what he's doing?

"Kane, this seems like a bad idea!" The tree cracks again, bark splintering with all the sound of a truly glorious thunder, and I squeal.

My bodyweight pulls me to the right. I'm scrambling to hold on now. Every inch of me is sweating. I hear a roar — Kane's this time. He sounds like he's in pain but I don't have time to think about that as the entire tree takes a sudden daring leap to the right.

Drago shouts. I start to slip, my fingers struggling to catch the slick wood. I lock my ankles together as the tree lurches back up, then begins a slow descent to the left. I hazard a glance down only to see the ground rushing up to meet me at an alarming rate.

Fifty feet in closing, then I'm thirty, then twenty, and then…

Kane curses and whatever impossible grip he had on the tree releases. I'm diving towards the forest floor and I know that I'm going to have to take a literal leap of faith and jump if I don't want to be impaled by two tons of flaming branches. I can't get on top of the branch — that would be impossible at this point — so I wedge my knees up against my chest, bracing them on the underside of the bough, and then I push.

I launch every part of me away from the tree as far as I can. No sooner have I hit the ground than thorny branches come down to claw at me like skeletal fingers. Burning embers sprinkle my face and arms, but luckily the leaves beneath me are wet and soft. I roll over, dousing the fire that threatens to catch and when I'm finished, I lay still for just a second before a spark-like cough catches in my chest.

A cracking sound is followed by a heavy weight slamming against my back. I scream, and for a second, I think it's Drago, but when I start to fight it, it doesn't fight back — not like that changes the outcome of the situation, or anything. A large branch has me pinned to the ground and when I look past it, I see feet stomping towards me. *Sprinting.*

Oh shit.

"You filthy bitch," Drago screeches, arriving at my side before I can so much as flip myself over. At least on my back, I could watch him kill me...Oh joy.

Drago tears easily through the tree branches holding me down. His heavy hands grab the front of my sweatshirt, rips me off of the ground and, while my feet hang suspended, shakes the shit out of me.

I cough in his face — not intentionally *of course* — but he still gets a wad of spittle and blood to the cheek. Apparently, that was the last straw, because he screams his head off and starts beating the life out of me.

The padding provided by my many layers does little to cushion the force of each blow and soon my ribs and cheeks and mouth are all singing songs of agony. My fiery lungs sizzle up and dry out as I desperately try to take in air. White spots flood my vision.

"You stupid little bitch," he shouts. "I had it all and you ruined everything!"

He shakes me again and strangely, my new rule crops up again, this time with a slight amendment — never give up, ~~not while you're breathing~~ even when you're dying.

My hands still work, and I've got just enough coordination in me to lift my right arm and poke Drago in the eye. Drago screams a scream that might have made me laugh had my lips not already been bloodied, and had I not already been sailing through the air.

He throws me. I hit the ground hard a few seconds later and am thankful for the dead bodies that cushion my fall. They squish upon impact, and while the world continues to revolve dizzyingly around me, I smell smoke and I taste blood. I choke up a lungful of what looks like charcoal and pink ink. The sludge burns my mouth, tongue and lips and tastes like metal.

My feet slip and slide over the wet leaves and my heartbeat drones along weakly while the world doubles in front of me, then triples. As such, I see three giant hands reach for me instead of just the one.

He touches my chin almost fondly, then wraps his fist around my throat. "I'm going to enjoy ending you and afterwards, I'll enjoy *you*. Then I'll watch the animals feast on your corpse."

I couldn't have responded even if I'd had something witty to say. Not when he lifts me from the ground by the throat. My eyes roll back into my head and I black out and just when I expect for the suffocating to start, I hear Drago whisper, "Impossible."

His voice is hollow and haunted and in that terror, pierces me with a little shrapnel of hope. I peek my left eye open and in the darkness, catch a bright red shape rising up from the forest floor.

I smile a little as Kane staggers once, then straightens, then bursts into an all out run. His shirt's on fire and so are his pants, but he doesn't seem to notice or care. His eyes are fixed on Drago or me or both with an unrivaled fury.

"Drago," he hisses.

Drago starts to canter back, but he's got nowhere to go that Kane wouldn't find him. He's been marked.

My vision fades out again, but I feel as Drago releases the hold he had on me. I fall into warm arms — I fall into arms that are on *fire*. I squeak out my pain and feel as I'm lowered surprisingly gently to the forest floor.

Kane moves out in front of me and he and Drago begin rotating around one another. I struggle to focus, ignoring the fight that commences, but concentrating rather on the funny thing sticking out of Drago's back… Is that Candy's knife?

Squinting a little harder, I see the knife Candy stuck Drago with sprouting from his spine like a gimp limb. Surprise makes me focus, and even as my sandpaper lungs threaten to burst, I sit up and slowly roll onto my feet.

Drago hits Kane in the face hard enough to split his lower lip and draw blood, but Kane doesn't react except to spit once, then fire into Drago with both fists, so fierce and so fast that Drago stumbles away from him and towards me. I know that this is the closest I'm likely to get to Drago and even though I'm half convinced every single bone in my body is broken, I lurch forward and rip the knife out of his back.

He screams and starts to turn, but I'm already moving forward, lunging forward, *falling* forward. Using two hands, I plunge the knife into his lower abdomen. Drago curses before swiping the back of his hand across my face. I'm thrown onto my back this time and I can feel the heat from the fires not too far off, but instead of concerning myself with them I use the last of my energy to lift my head so I can watch Drago and Kane dance like fire gods in the dark.

Drago swings for Kane's head, but Kane ducks beneath the blow and lands on one knee. With one swift flick of his wrist, he grabs the short handle of Candy's dagger that I just released and finishes the job I started. He drags the knife all the way across Drago's belly.

Drago doesn't scream this time. Instead, he looks down at the rivulets of his own intestines slipping down into the packed earth and spilling over the golden brown leaves, like scarlet ribbons. His lips part and he staggers back, narrow eyes full of surprise as he looks up at Kane. In contrast, Kane's face is frighteningly expressionless. He takes a step towards Drago like a leopard stalking wounded prey, then begins to circle him.

Drago holds up a glistening red hand. "Mercy. We are brothers." He calls him that word again, *Notare*, and Kane snarls.

Kane whispers something in that sibilant language that means nothing to me, and then in English says, "Though you lived like a coward, you can still choose to die honorably. Get on your knees."

Instead, Drago shouts. He turns like he'll run, but before he manages to lift one foot off of the ground, Kane closes the distance between them, snaps Drago's neck and lets him fall.

Coughing racks my lungs again, distracting me for the seconds it takes for Kane to remove Drago's head from his body and toss it far away, into the flames. The head makes a dull sound when it lands wherever it does.

Squish, squish. Crackle, crackle. Pop.

Eew.

I don't bother moving. I probably should, but I don't. I don't exactly remember ever feeling this close to death before and right now I feel the distinct urge to just sit and wait for it. *Never give up, even when death is coming.* I groan. Why'd I have to add that rule again?

"Human, are you alive?" Kane's face appears in my vision and for a moment, I see a ferocity in his expression that reminds me of my rule book and urges me to fight.

Then his face softens. *Ugh. Stop!* Emotions, emotions, emotions! I hate them and will them back.

"You hate what?" Kane says abruptly.

Shit. Did I just say that out loud?

"Yes, you are speaking out loud. Now what is it that you hate and I'll do my best to kill it." He glances around, but he must be pretty satisfied that he already killed everything in the vicinity because he's got a smile on his face.

I groan. Everything *hurts*. It hurts too much to fight the agony. I just lean into it and let it wrap its grizzly bones around me. "I hate *you*."

He frowns. Actually frowns at that. "Why?"

"You look like you just got off a runway."

His forehead crinkles. "Runway? What have I got to do with flying airplanes?"

"Airplanes? No. No, that's not what I mean. I mean the runway where you..." Cough, cough, cough. Stammer, stammer, stammer. "The thing hot guys walk up and down wearing clothes. Modeling clothes. The World Before."

Nothing I've just said makes sense, but to be honest, I'm more familiar with 'runways' as an expression, than I am with them in actual practice. Models, I'm pretty sure, were among the first humans to go.

My incoherency doesn't seem to phase Kane at all, because a slow Cheshire grin spreads across his face. The firelight behind us flashes across his straight teeth and makes his eyes glimmer electric green and honey. Like molten gold.

"You think I'm *attractive*," he says, as if testing the word.

My whole body breaks out in heat so much more terrible than my current spiking levels of pain. Luckily then, I start to cough. Kane, seeing me try unsuccessfully to roll onto my side, rolls me the rest of the way.

I manage onto my left shoulder just in time to hurl my guts out. Pink goo mostly. It smells like smoke and bile.

"You are injured," Kane says, a hint of *something* souring his tone. I don't know what.

I laugh as I fall onto my back and rub my sleeve over my face and mouth. I swallow convulsively, wishing for water. "I'm dying."

"*Dying?*" Then he just says, "No."

All of a sudden, I feel hands on my arms pulling me out of my clothes. "What...what are you doing?"

"I'm checking your injuries."

"Oh God, please don't."

He doesn't listen, but I don't like his hands on my body like this, *undressing* me. It reminds me too much of the grocery store. Aisles and aisles of bloodstained tile. Screaming. Laughing. I remember Candy. I remember what it was once like to have a brother I'd have done anything for.

"Kane, stop," I say, trying to make my voice loud.

He doesn't stop. His fingers are on the hem of my shirt. He's muttering to himself — something about humans and how fragile we are — but he isn't listening.

"Kane! I said stop it!" I flap my hands, slapping his arms. My chest heaves and when he finally looks up at my face, I can't recognize his expression for the concern it carries, all I see is the fact that he's a male and he's bigger and I'm injured and I'm in enemy territory because everywhere is.

I sink my heels into the ground and kick myself away from him. Tension threads through my deflating muscles, and as Kane reaches for me, I kick his raised hand. He grabs my shoe and holds it.

I gasp. I can feel my neck muscles working to swallow and keep my head up in equal measure. His gaze is pinned to mine and there's something weird rolling across his expression. And then it settles. His furrowed brow flattens. And then he pulls.

He wrenches my body over the leaves and plants his fists on either side of my face. I grab his shoulders, but my arms shake as I try to hold him back only to realize that they're shaking and I'm *not* holding him back because he isn't moving forward.

"Kane," I accuse.

"Shh and listen." His black hair drips towards me. There is fire in his eyes and in his expression that makes my blood run cold. "I am not Drago."

I know what he's trying to say, but it makes no difference. "You're still a man."

His front teeth clench behind the brutal slash of his lips. Slowly, he takes both of my wrists in one of his big hands and as he pulls them in front of my body, he slides something hard into my fists.

I lurch, fearing the worst, then glance down and see what it is…

"If I ever attempt to take from you that which you do not freely give, I give you every permission in this world to take my sword and gut me with it."

With that, he lurches off of me and rises to stand. He extends his hand down to me. "Do your injuries prevent you from moving? I have no desire to linger here."

I'm still holding my breath. Still thinking about what he just said and what he's just done. I feel like bursting into tears. But I can't do that. Population doesn't allow for injuries or weak women or sacrifice or anything good.

"Abel," Kane says, and his voice is softer now. Soft enough to cut me open and pull everything on the inside out.

I clear my throat and look away from him, then struggle to sit up. Using the sword he just put in my hand, I manage to stand without his help.

My eyes flutter as I try to keep them open. It's hard. I can feel my right eyelid swelling and absconding with a good chunk of my vision. My left cheek feels like it's been rubbed off with a cheese grater. My spinal column feels like it's got its own damn current.

Heat and energy radiate out from between my shoulder blades, piercing me through to the sternum. My left leg is weirdly wobbly and the cuts on my hands from days before have reopened in places.

It hurts. Everything hurts. But nothing hurts more than the weight of the sword in my fist.

I stare down at it, hard, pushing back those damning, threatening emotions. "What is this? You're letting me borrow your sword?"

"I said have, didn't I?"

"No."

"Well, that's what I meant. It's yours."

"Mine?"

"Yours." He scoffs all of a sudden. "I'd have thought you'd be happier to be reunited with your faithful companion. You're quite good with it, you know. Where did you train?"

It takes me a few seconds to answer him, because my heart is still pounding as the emotion monster rears its ugly, malformed head. *Cut it down!*

"Uhmm..." *Rule number three — don't get personal — remember rule number three!* But right now the emotion monster has its warm, loving hands around my throat and is shaking the shit out of me.

"I..."

"Has anyone ever told you, you make a truly appalling conversationalist?"

I snort...*snort*. And when I look back up at him, my mouth opens and the words come out before I can hack them to pieces and bury their corpses. "Becks's dad. He was a martial arts enthusiast. We all thought he was a freak until the Fall. Then he was our saving grace."

Kane breathes out half a laugh that I can tell is meant to be encouraging, but when my only response is to smile shakily back up at him, he rolls his eyes and runs a hand back through his hair, tousling it in frustration.

"What is the matter with you?"

"Nothing..."

"Your lies are starting to bore me."

"I've got...rules," I blurt.

He considers, tilts his head. "Now this is more interesting. What kind of rules?" As he speaks, he starts off towards the fallen tree and the fire that's ravaging it.

A few paces away from it, he veers to the left, then glances back over his shoulder. "You coming?"

Coming? I don't move towards him, but I don't move away either. "I...You want me to come with you?"

He grins and raises one eyebrow. I never knew an Other could be so expressive. In my mind, they were all cold, bloodthirsty savages.

Just like me.

"You think I covered this distance to come back for you, only to leave you here?"

"I…You…" I waver where I stand. Bloodloss must be affecting my speech *and* my hearing. I shake my head and grunt, "You didn't come back for me. You came back for your key and your sword."

He doesn't respond right away, but turns to face me fully. Behind him, a section of branches fall, sending embers spiraling up to meet the grey while a gust of warm energy careens towards me.

It would be more than possible for me to camp out here tonight and not freeze to death. Plus, I'm fairly confident that I wouldn't be attacked where I slept. I could make it to the morning, clean out my injuries once I found where Drago and his *community* stored their supplies and their water. I could make it without Kane…

"What?" I say abruptly, realizing he's answered.

"I said, that's what I tried telling myself, too. Now come on. I told you before, I won't make the same mistake twice."

"Mistake?"

"The mistake of leaving you."

Silence. Then my very pitiful, "Oh."

Kane sighs. He tugs at a bit of cloth around his neck. The last remnants of his shirt. It's entirely blackened even though his glowing, blood-spattered chest is bare and without a single scratch. His shorts are badly singed too and yet, despite everything, he still saunters towards me with his heavy hands clasped casually behind his back.

He comes within arm's reach of me…then takes another step. My hand tenses around the hilt of his sword and his eyes flick to it. The smile at the edge of his mouth dips, but only for a moment. He stops moving forward.

"Abel," he breathes, and somehow, when he says my name, I feel it's *mine*. Not necessarily the one I was born with, but the one my soul sounds like. "Must I beg?"

I shake my head rapidly. I don't want to hear him beg — he, who just ripped the head off an alien and took down a tree to save my life. I don't know what that would do to me.

"Good, then can we go now?"

"Ashlyn…"

"Yes, your sister." He remembered her name. "I will take you to the Diera."

I take an involuntary step forward, but my right leg shakes. Kane glances down at it and frowns quickly, before lifting his gaze back to my face.

"Really? You'll just…take me to a territory filled with Others? Just like that?"

"Yes."

"Are you going to make me into a soup?"

He laughs, hard and loud. "No. If you were another human, perhaps I'd consider it, but I've found you to be a particularly tough chew to swallow."

My cheeks burn again as I remember those words from before. Did he memorize our *entire* conversation? I scrunch up my nose and firm my grip on my sword.

"I don't trust you."

But the weird thing is that I do. Rule number six says to trust my gut. And my gut is telling me that what he's telling me is true.

"The path to trust is forged in faith." He holds out his hand.

I just stare at it. "I don't know what that means."

"Yes, you do."

I take a deep breath — at least, as deep as I can. I cough a little bit and feel my head get light because of it. Having someone watch my back…would be a good thing. He did it once before, back in the townhouse. I was vulnerable then, and he didn't kill me.

I take a step and this time, brush right past him. "If you make me into a soup, I'm going to be pissed."

He laughs lightly at my back as we make our way around the wreckage of Drago's fallen community.

I'm uncomfortable.

No, I'm *dying* and I'm uncomfortable. It takes a lot of concentration not to bolt. Almost as much concentration as it takes to see where I'm going.

I'm uncomfortable because even though I can only barely see him in the darkness, made darker now that the fires are so far behind us, I can tell that he's *staring* at me. He also seems to know exactly where we're going even though the night is at its most sinister and the woods are close around us.

Finally, I can't handle it and blurt, "What? Do I have broccoli between my teeth or something?"

"You'd more likely have some other man's skin between your teeth, than broccoli. I saw the way you fought those men on that platform."

"You saw that?"

"Yes. I had to make sure you acquired the key."

"The key!" I lurch to a complete stop and spin around, face-planting directly in Kane's chest and lighting up a whole host of new wounds.

I hiss and might have keeled right over, possibly for good, had Kane not taken my shoulders and held me steady. "I have the key. But are you sure you're alright?"

No, no and hell to the no. "Yes. I'm fine."

"I'd offer to carry you, but I can already anticipate that the response will be…"

"No," I say emphatically.

"No," Kane huffs.

"But you got the key?" I ask again.

"Yes. Thank you for retrieving it for me."

"Okay, whew. I thought for a second that, after all that, we left it behind." I turn around and continue clomping forward in the direction that Kane guides me.

After a few more clomps, I finally ask the question that's been eating at my mind ever since I woke up to find his stupid note. The one still in my pocket somewhere crumpled and bloodied and burned.

"Why didn't you take it, back in the house? You knew where it was and I was asleep. You wouldn't have even had to fight me for it." I try to keep my voice light, but the ripe curiosity in my tone is obvious.

His heat rides up against my shoulder. "I already told you. Perhaps I wanted a reason to have to come back," he says in a low voice.

I wish he would have said something else, and in an effort to crush the mounting tension between us, I blurt out another question, "Where are we going?"

"To the Diera."

"No, I mean right now."

"To the Diera."

"Is it close?"

"Closer than you'd think."

"Hmph."

More silence. He doesn't move away from me either, staying persistently a foot or two behind my awkward, lurching steps. Every time I make a misstep, he's close enough to catch me. It seems like he's touching me more and more often. I don't like it. I don't *not* like it, but I definitely don't like it. And his nagging heat. I don't like that right now either. And his glow, illuminating my steps...

Oh God damn him. Is he walking close to me like this to keep me warm and light my path? No. Nononononono.

"You know, you could give me some space. You're basically breathing down my neck."

"Apologies."

He pulls back and the world in front of me is plunged into almost pure darkness. I trip over a branch immediately and plummet forward, only to feel Kane's hands come around my waist.

"I'm not interested in watching you gut yourself on the sword I just gave you, so I'll continue to walk right here, if you don't mind."

I take another step and jump in surprise when Kane lightly places his hand against the back of my neck. Gently, he guides me to the left.

"Ditch," he says quietly while my heartbeat pounds.

He keeps his warm hand on the back of my neck, distracting me, and I struggle to breathe evenly for more reasons than one. His fingers are rough and warm and his thumb strokes upwards into my hair, sending a soothing balm slithering down my spine.

I grumble something unintelligible and shrug free of his grip, but don't try to move out ahead again. Instead, I ask, "So why *does* your heart glow?"

"It's not an interesting story."

"I'd find it interesting."

"Pity, as I have no desire to share it."

"Humph," I pout. "Well, can you at least tell me about all your crazy extra senses?"

"That doesn't sound like a complete question."

I can tell that he's patronizing me and huff, "Can you see in the dark?"

"Yes. It's incredible that you can't. Just walking through the woods like this, you're perpetually one step away from death." He sounds downright angry about it and his voice comes out loud enough to make me flinch. "And still you ask me to move away from you. It's incredible. Truly.

"You're basically blind at night and hardly more observant than that during the day, and you seem to be almost completely deaf. Do you know how many times I've had to repeat myself since meeting you? I think more times than in the cumulation of the rest of my entire existence."

I think this is the most I've ever heard him say at once, and of course, it's to disparage me. I try to round on him, but trip over my own two feet, forcing him to have to catch me or let me fall. I wish he'd do the latter, but he doesn't. He never does.

Not even when I'm caught fifty feet up in a tree that I lit on fire.

"Hey," I accuse, trying to put some distance between us. And I don't mean the physical kind. "If it wasn't for *your* kind, I'd hear twice as well. I lost hearing in my left ear during one of the first attacks, so bite me." And then when I realize what I've said, I stammer, "Wait. Don't *actually* do that…"

He laughs hard, then harder still. I quickly pull away from him and stomp out into the woods. He catches up to me in a nanosecond, but instead of lapsing back into silence, he leans down so close I can feel his mouth brushing my hair.

"Who knows, you might actually enjoy it."

"Is this flirting? Are you flirting with me!" I sound shrill and a little like a lunatic.

Kane doesn't laugh. I expect him to laugh or condescend to me in some way, but instead he just says, "You really can't tell? How many men have you been with?"

I turn from him, every intention of running away from this line of conversation and naturally fall flat on my face. This time, Kane is too slow to catch me. I feel his hand brush the back of my coat, but I twist out from beneath him and land hard on my wrists, the sword flat beneath me. My lungs surge up into my mouth and I vomit again, this time something sludgy.

"Alright, that's it." His arms come around me and I feel my feet leave the ground, along with the rest of me. I'm tilted and tossed until I find myself plastered against his chest, cradled in his arms, head wedged between his shoulder and his neck.

"I can't watch this any longer. It's causing me physical pain and there is nothing the matter with me."

I start to wriggle, but he tightens his grip around me, and prods my butt with the hilt of his sword. "Don't fight it."

"Give me back my sword," I choke. "You said I could run you through with it."

"When I'm trying to violate you yes, but not when I'm trying to save your life."

Violate me. I shudder, not liking the term.

We walk for a little longer in silence, and I hate that I'm sinking into his grip. It hurts in some places where he touches me, and my back definitely stings, but it beats concentrating on walking by a long shot.

I find myself strangely *relaxed*, and soon feel my head tip and lean more casually on his shoulder. It puts our faces close together. Super close.

"Why do you travel alone?" He asks me out of the blue.

"They all got killed," I sigh. My eyelids flutter closed.

"How many were you?"

I yawn, and just like last time, tiredness seems to win out over the rule book. "Just after the Fall we were about one-fifty, then the Others started their attacks and we realized staying in one place wasn't safe. We found an underground garage that we managed to convert into a makeshift city for a few months. But then internal fighting broke us into factions…"

"Internal fighting?" He sounds surprised.

Honestly, it had surprised me too. "Yeah. We were low on food and supplies and some of us wanted to go above ground to try and regroup — create a little community where we could grow food and stuff. The Others hadn't attacked in years, so we thought there was hope. The other group was too scared and wanted to stay."

"You were in the first group?" He confirms, curiosity coloring his tone in a way that makes me fidget in his grip. Why is this interesting to him?

"Yeah."

He takes a few large steps, and I see why a moment later. Bodies. But so far out? I wonder what killed them.

"Did you leave the garage eventually?"

"Yeah." He hoists me up higher on his chest and gives my waist a light squeeze when I wince.

"Apologies," he whispers. Then, "Do you regret it?"

I shake my head, curling and uncurling my fingers because I can still feel the ghost of his lingering touch. "No. The night after we left, we heard that the compound was attacked by gangs. Everybody was slaughtered. Then again, so were we. At least we lasted longer than the other guys." I chuckle morbidly.

"And your family?"

A stinging touches the center of my chest that has nothing to do with the bruises I got tonight.

I don't answer right away and instead allow myself to be impressed when the trees part before us and the wet leaves beneath Kane's feet give ground to harder pavement. We're back at the freeway.

When we reach the road Kane walks right up to a big black car that hadn't been there before. It's the kind that the president drives. Well, the kind that the president *used* to drive, back when Population had some sort of leadership.

It's still in good condition, which is weird. Weirder still, he reaches into his pocket and pulls out a small black box which he uses to open the passenger's side door. It's a *key*.

Gawking, I ask myself two impossible questions:

Does it *run*?

Is this *his*?

"Your family," he says, coaxing me into the front seat. I unfurl my legs, place my feet on the floor of the car, and gawk at him standing there in the open doorway.

"This is a car," I say dumbly.

He glances around at it and makes an incredulous face. "Goodness, I hadn't noticed." A grin settles over his expression.

I peg him with a glare. "This is a *car*."

"Yes, and I believe I was asking you about your family."

"How do you have a car?" I say, ignoring him.

He rolls his eyes, slams the door shut in my face and makes his way around to the driver's seat. "Enough about the car. You have asked me plenty of questions tonight. I want to know about your family."

The road blockade that had sheltered the older woman is gone. Distantly, I wonder what happened to her as he starts the car, takes the wheel and pulls into the center of the street. Within moments, the dark world passes by on either side of us, trees fading to give way to farmland. With my fingers pressed to the glass, I wish it had been daytime. This moving world fascinates me.

"You mean Ashlyn?" I ask, knowing he doesn't.

"Your other family."

I glance over at him. I want to tell him to shove it — that I won't talk about it — but he's looking at me expectantly with eyes that are wide with guileless curiosity. It's too hard to deny. I inhale, cough into my fist, then inhale again.

"My family, Becks's family, and a few stragglers were the last left of our initial host community. We found a complex of townhouses just outside of DC that hadn't been raided yet and thought we'd just gotten lucky. Turns out, the entire block was gang territory and when they found us a few weeks in, it was a bloodbath.

"They killed everybody. My dad and Becks's dad stayed behind to give us enough time to run. We waited for them and scouted out the house for weeks after, but they never came out."

"Who escaped with you?"

"Me, Becks and her husband."

"And Becks's husband? He wasn't with you the night that we met."

Met. Somehow that doesn't seem adequate enough to describe the evening where he'd died and I'd lost everything.

"Gangs again," I say. It's not a lie, but it's definitely the abridged version. "A small gang had been…"

It's hard to breathe and harder to speak.

"…they'd been following us for days — probably because they realized we were only one guy and two women. They cornered us in an abandoned grocery store and when Matt went down, I realized that we'd all die if I didn't do something."

"So what did you do?"

"I killed them all."

He pauses. "How many were there?"

"Four."

"How old were you?"

Somehow that question snaps me out of my reverie and I straighten. I look over at him and feel myself grimace, hating that I answered these questions and threw the rule book away.

"It doesn't matter." I was sixteen.

"It does to me."

"It shouldn't," I snap breathlessly. "What's with the twenty questions anyway? You're just an alien and I'm just a human, so let's just cool it on the water-cooler talk, alright?"

His fists tighten around the steering wheel and he doesn't try to talk to me again. At least, not until I lean my head against the window and close my eyes.

Once again, trying to cheat me when all I can see behind closed lids is imagined starlight.

"You know you'll have to answer me sooner or later."

I press my lips together fiercely and don't dare rise to the challenge. I refuse to give him the satisfaction, which is why I'm surprised as all get out when he offers answers to questions I've wondered, but haven't had the courage to ask him yet.

"My family died, too, and much in the same way yours did. To protect me."

I lift my head and glance over at him. "How?"

"Do you really not know?"

"How would I?"

Kane heaves out a breath and rubs his face with his hand. "No wonder."

"No wonder what?"

"You hate me."

"You hate me, too."

"I do no such thing."

I frown, wondering why he's telling me this, wondering why we have to have this conversation here and now while I'm bleeding out all over his upholstery.

"Our galaxy crashed into its neighboring galaxy and our planet, *Sistylea*, was pulled into the orbit of their largest planet. This catapulted us into their sun. Evacuation protocol brought us to your planet through *slext*. I believe your kind call this an Einstein-Rosen bridge or a wormhole.

"Because of Earth's ability to sustain life and the fact that the dominant species of your planet was and is so similar to our biological makeup, your planet had been selected millennia ago, expressly for this purpose.

"But by then our population was too large and our government too lax. There were not enough life rafts to accommodate every citizen on my planet so my parents sacrificed both of theirs so that I could get away."

"One pod per person?"

He hesitates, then nods again. "Yes."

And I hear something in that hesitation that makes me ask a question I otherwise wouldn't have thought of. "Who took the other life raft?"

"What?" he says, though I know he'd heard me the first time, what with supersonic hearing and all.

"You said *both* life rafts. If you took one then who took the other?" When he doesn't answer me, I feel my vocal cords contract, strangling my next question. "Was it your wife?"

If I hadn't asked I'm not sure I'd have ever gotten the real answer, but the shock is enough for him to grunt out, "No, no. Of course not. It was my brother."

I hope he doesn't, but know that he must hear me exhale. "Where is he now?"

"Dead."

I nod, staring out of the window while the dangerous noose of emotions tightens around my neck. "Yeah, mine too."

"What was that?"

"I'm sorry about your family," I say quickly.

A long stretch of silence passes before Kane finally says, "That is not what you said, but I do appreciate your condolences and I offer mine in return."

I scoff, "You do?"

"I do."

I open my mouth, but don't have anything to say to that. Kane must sense my discomfort and takes pity on me. "Sleep, Abel. I'll let you guard your answers for one more night."

I grunt and cross my arms tight over my chest, as if that will somehow prevent him from seeing straight through me. I rest my head on the window and as the car glides so smoothly down the street, one final question occurs to me.

"How did you know where I was tonight?"

Kane laughs. It's a secretive, carnivorous thing. "While you guard your secrets, I will not give you all of mine. Now sleep, Abel," he tells me for the second time, and it's like he pushes a button.

Darkness descends like a cloud, bringing dreams with it.

Chapter Six

Faces fade in and out. Sometimes, I imagine I can hear them speaking. *"…possibly cracked ribs, lacerations all over her face and arms, and this bruising…did you see the bruises on her sternum and in the center of her back? They must be causing her unbelievable pain. What did you two do? Fight a war?"*

"Just a small one…"

A dark brown smear. Black hair haloed in red wallpaper. A woman's face. Eyes, looking at me. I don't recognize them and for a moment, I try to fight.

Then a heavy weight lands on my forehead and green eyes consume me. "Sleep, Abel." Concern. It's everywhere. In his expression, in his throat. "Will she heal?"

"Yes," comes the sigh. "So long as she's done fighting wars."

"I don't think she is."

I close my eyes and I'm alone, dreaming of things I'd have no way of dreaming of because I've never known them.

Fluffy pillows that crinkle under the curvature of my skull. Pure white sheets that don't have one drop of filth on them. A fire in a fireplace surrounded by dark-colored stone. It crackles and hisses and pops and makes me think of that rabbit I found not so long ago, back before I met some guy named Drago and his young wife called Candy.

I'm toasty warm.

Dry, even.

I've been damp my whole life up to this point.

Dreams are the only place I've ever gotten any reprieve from the constant saturation of the grey into my clothes.

Funny then that as my fingers twitch against the sheets, I could be so stunned by their softness.

Or that I could be so dry when I'm awake.

My eyes are open. It's a thought that, once arrived, takes a long time to settle in and stay.

My next thought is the immediate consideration that I'm awake, but dead. It's very possible I died in that car. Maybe I never made it to the car in the first place. The answers Kane was feeding me were pretty outlandish. Things about space ships and galaxies far from this one.

Things that sounded like concern about my human body.

About my family. The one that was alive once.

I *could* be dead. Yes, that's a definite possibility. But if I *were* dead then wouldn't they be here with me? Maybe I'll get a chance to see my brother again. I'd like that. I go to call out to him. *Aiden.* But somehow, that's not the name that comes out.

"Kane?" Aw hell, this is *not* death. Or if it is, it's not the heaven that lady from our first camp was always ranting on and on about. This death *hurts.*

My throat feels like I swallowed nails. My chest feels like I swallowed a grenade. My eyes feel like they got sprayed with hot pepper, then blindfolded.

I hurt.

Tears come to my eyes and I feel like a little wimp, so weepy. I want to see something that makes sense. Something that can ground me.

"Kane?" I call out.

I surprise myself.

And before I have too long to be damned by my own tongue, the door on the far wall swings open silently. Not a creak to be heard.

An older woman that I don't recognize glides into the room and I slide off the bed and jump up into a fighting stance. I grab the sword lying on the bedside table and swing it around and gut her before she can kill me.

Just kidding.

I lay where I am, broken and drained, and croak like the fearsome warrior that I am, "You're not Kane."

The older woman with the white hair trills in a way that might be laughter, but I'm not sure. It sounds far too giddy for that. "No, I don't believe I am."

She gives herself a very dramatic look over before meeting my gaze again. When she does, her eyes crinkle. She takes a step closer and I notice she's got a silver tray stretched between her two hands. She sets it at the foot of the bed, then comes and helps me up to sitting.

Oh. My. Freaking. Baby. Jesus.

My head spins for a long time, which is the only reason I think for a minute that I might be hallucinating. The foods on the tray...the fact that there *is* food is already a feat, but this...this is unlike anything I've ever seen.

There's...fresh vegetables. At least they look fresh. She tries to offer me a fork and a knife, but I haven't used either of those in years and they feel clumsy in my hands when I take them. I toss them aside, and pick up lettuce by the fistful. I never thought anything so bland could taste so wonderful. I eat the salad and then the potatoes that have been mashed into a sort of purée, then the meat and the fresh freaking *bread* and then the peach. I savor the peach.

I realize the woman's been talking the whole time, but I haven't heard a word of it. I look up at her as my eyes slink back shut. She gives me a disparaging look that I've seen Kane make before and my stomach clenches.

"Are you Kane's wife?" I ask, humiliating myself all over again.

The woman gives me a pointed look. "You must truly have hit your head. Master Kane could be my grandchild."

"Master?"

"Yes, dear. We are on Master Kane's estate."

"Estate?" She's using big words that I don't understand.

"Yes, dear. He brought you in two days ago."

Two days? My body gets hot at the thought. Also when I realize I'm not wearing the same clothes I arrived in. I look down and the oversized black tee shirt reminds me of the last one I saw Kane wearing. *Master* Kane. I'm wearing some sort of short black boxer pants, but I'm not wearing any underwear.

At least I'm still dirty. That makes me feel better.

"Master?"

The woman at least has the decency to blush. "It's what we've taken to calling him. We are his servants, in a sense." Human servants to a blood-thirsty alien? Is *that* what he brought me here for? To serve him? Was he lying about everything? Bringing me to the Diera? Finding my sister? All of it?

And then the creeping, selfish thought that should take precedence over Ashlyn, but in this moment, doesn't. Because this thought feels too imminent. Too dark. Too scary.

He brought me here to serve him. But serve him how? What does he want with me?

"Master Kane…" The woman starts, then stops. Her gaze lifts over my shoulder and her blush darkens.

"How are things, Maggie? Is our visitor awake?"

"And rearing," Maggie answers all in the time it takes me to swivel my head around. The movement must be too much, because right away I release a loud belch.

Kane grunts out laughter while Maggie shoves a cup of clear liquid into my hand. "Water, dear," she says kindly, but I don't trust it. I don't trust her.

I toss it onto the ground.

She looks at me completely stupefied, then up at Kane. None of the gentleness has faded from Kane's gaze as he raises his palms up to the woman, then lowers them again. "She's spent most of her life in Population. Her trust must be earned."

He's talking about me like he knows something about me. He doesn't. Whatever happened in the woods didn't really happen if his intention is to enslave me.

"What am I doing here?"

"I told you, I brought you to the Diera."

"Why is she calling you Master?"

Kane's jaw works, but he doesn't answer right away. He takes another step towards the bed and my gaze rakes over his form. He's clean now, and standing in front of me in all his broad-shouldered glory, I can see his naked chest. It gleams with muscle and all, but it's also not got a scratch on it.

I shift back against the pillows and tuck my legs slightly beneath me. They'll get all tangled if I have to jump, but right now, I just want to be away from him. At least until I'm sure that every stupid emotion I had last night wasn't...wrong. Being cut in the flesh is one thing, but I won't let this big brute cut me here...in the chest...beneath the sternum where it hurts most.

"So?" I stammer. "What is this? What's going on?"

He moves towards me gracefully, like a predator stalking its prey in the night. At the same time, his hands are tucked casually in his pockets. He's looking at me with glossy green eyes that are so finely detailed I can make out each strand where the gold and emerald meet. And in those eyes I find safety and sin and curiosity and hunger.

"Say something!" I nearly shout.

Maggie jumps where she's standing and places her hand on her heart, like *I'm* the scary one between the three of us. "Shall I call Sandra to have her sedated again?"

Sedated? Again? I'm not sure which is worse, but I can see Kane's eyes start to round as my expression changes. I start breathing harder while my heart pumps too fast, and then when his full, burgundy lips pull back and he tries a placating smile all I can see in his face is Drago. Does that make me Candy?

Maybe, but only in that moment when she stabbed the shit out of him.

"What did you do to me?"

Kane comes even closer. I edge even further back. He stops moving, but looks down at the bed between us as if it did something to offend him. Bed. The word sticks in my mind like glue.

I grab the tray and even as the rest of the food that was on it sloshes off and into my lap, staining those white sheets — hopefully for good — I hold it as a shield between us.

"Abel," he says.

"Don't call me that. It isn't my name." Only it is. It's *mine*, because it's the one I gave myself when I needed a shield. And I still need one.

"Abel," Kane says again. "You need to calm yourself. Our medic took a look at you and found that your injuries were severe enough that you warranted sedation. She needed to stitch your forehead." Forehead? I feel along my brow and find stitches drilled above my left eyebrow in a neat little row. Stitches? Medics? I feel panic well in my chest and tears well in my eyes.

"Where am I? What is going on?"

"Where you are?" Kane's face scrunches, but he's made no less attractive by it. With his glowing golden chest, he shines like the sun. Every inch of him. And I haven't seen the sun in so long… I'm overwhelmed by it. "I know you're deaf, but you can't be dense enough to have forgotten what I told you? Or did you hit your head?"

He comes around the bed, pushes the woman aside gently and reaches for me, like he'll presses the back of his hand to my forehead. Like he cares. Emotions. It confuses me. It *hurts* me. I don't understand.

"I don't understand. What is all this?" I gesture around at the room and feel my panic rise.

His face falls. "You're serious? We're in my house in the Diera, where you wanted to come." He mumbles that last part.

I'm still hung up on the first half of what he's just said, and feel my tattered throat close. I look around the room. There are paintings on the wall. Paintings of *humans* painted by human hands by humans who died a long time ago. These…these Others killed everyone then built their empires on our backs. But I didn't know…the opulence…that there were slaves…I've never been to one of their territories. How could I have known?

"Your *house*?" My voice is shaky. Terribly so. I've never heard it like this before. "You…this…is how…you live?" I'm panting now, voice heaving. I can't seem to get the words out, no matter how I try to say them.

He reaches for me again, but this time, I use the entire tray to block him. The sound of his fist meeting metal rings, but it makes no difference to his expression.

He yields to me though he doesn't have to, and canters back a step. "Does it offend you?"

"Does it *offend* me? You fucking bastard." I don't know where the energy comes from, all that power, but my whole body lifts off the bed and I throw my torso at him.

My legs tangle into the sheets, but my momentum sends him cantering back *even as he tries to catch me*. He catches my wrists and my knees clack against his abdomen, which is so intensely muscled it looks like he's smuggling paint rollers. He calls my name as he canters to the side and I knock him back into the dresser.

Something shatters against the glossy hardwood and wherever in the room the human has gone, she shouts, "Please! Watch the porcelain!"

Porcelain! "Porcelain! You goddamn ass hole. You *live* here? You live here and you have food and electricity and you promised me that you'd take me to the Diera and now you want me to be your servant and you…lied. You *lied* to me."

I'm not fighting anymore. I don't have it in me. My body has melted completely into his arms. He pulls me against his body and he just holds me there. My breasts are flush to his chest, held there by this magnetism between us. He's not wearing a shirt. My forehead falls against his pec when I lean forward because that's as high as it reaches.

"I…I haven't eaten…" I punch him in the gut, but there's no force behind the blow. My fingers unfurl. My hand drips down to the band of his pants. I feel his whole body stiffen beneath my touch.

Because this is what he wants from me. A slave in his pretty white sheets.

My breath comes hard and hot as it washes over his skin. I try to push myself away, but he holds me tight and I can't get away. I'm not as strong enough as I was last time I had to kill them all. I have to kill him before…

"Abel, you have to calm your breaths."

I'm hyperventilating. My vision goes all fuzzy. Kane grabs my right wrist firmly but gently, and lowers me onto the cool hardwood as my knees give out.

"I haven't even seen that much food in…in…since the Fall and there are people dying on the streets of Population. Tearing one another apart for crusts of bread. *Fighting.* What I wouldn't have given six months ago for a single piece of pork for Ashlyn. And a peach?" I start to cough. I hear Kane say my name gruffly, violently almost, but his voice sounds distant even though he's quite close.

His hands press lightly against my back, but they are hesitant in a way that suggests he's never done anything like this before.

"Maggie," he shouts, "what is wrong with her?"

"She's having an anxiety attack," the older woman says, though I can barely hear the sound of her voice over my heart pounding. An anxiety attack? Who would have thought, among all the dangers of Population, my own body would kill me?

Kane lifts me into a sitting position and holds me in his lap. "Don't touch me! You're a monster." I send my elbow back into his belly and though I know it doesn't hurt him, I feel his whole body tense beneath me.

He growls into my ear and I remember too well the feeling of following his voice in the dark. The emotion monster had been there spewing its malignant threats. It's gone now though. By the sight of those paintings, cleanly eviscerated.

And I'm glad for it.

"You think *me* the monster? After all that your humans have done. They lied to you, Abel. No!" he says when I try to free myself. He holds me to him and the heat at my back feels like I'm chained to a goddamn furnace. "No. You will hear me now."

"No!" I scream.

He holds me even more firmly. "I told you the story of my people. Our destruction. Our sacrifice to arrive to this stone among the cosmos. Did you not hear me? Or did you think that was just petty drivel?" He tightens his grip so that he's got both arms strapped across my chest, my wrists locked in his hands. I can't even kick my feet really, useless as they are flopping around on the hardwood floor. So I've really got no other choice than to listen. Especially when he speaks directly into my good ear, and he speaks slow.

"We arrived depleted, diminished. With nothing but the clothing we arrived in. We were rounded up by each continent's world leaders and we begged them to accept us. We came in peace."

"No…No, I saw the fires. The explosions…"

"Your leaders, being so small of mind, could not fucking fathom that beings from another planet would have made their way to earth's door, so they did what small, simple animals would do. They reacted in terror and violence.

"They rounded us up, attempted to perform experiments on us, but they were still human. Stupid and weak. Even at their attempts to enslave and torture us, they were clumsy.

"Our leaders escaped except for one who was tortured for almost a decade. By that point, we had regained control of the world."

"Of *our* world. Of our world," I cry, though no tears come. There's no such thing.

"No, Abel. *My* world. And I regret nothing I have done in order to survive. I would have expected understanding from you, of all creatures in this wretched wasteland. How many have you killed? How many lives have you stolen for that meager crust of bread?"

I start to thrash now in earnest, which doesn't help issues of air flow. I can't breathe. I can't breathe *at all.* "Kane," I hear a voice blustering. "Kane, release her at once!" What is the servant doing issuing orders to the alien?

Weirder still, what is he doing obeying her?

He drops me at once. My body hits the hardwood and he shifts out from underneath me. Everything is suddenly so cold, all except for the heat rippling up from my stomach to reach my throat.

Finally a huge, racking breath comes to me and I choke through it. As it passes, I can hear a voice speaking to me though it sounds like she's underwater. "Follow my breathing." Delicate fingers touch my face and my concentration is torn. I look into Maggie's eyes.

It's good advice and I try to follow it, but just as I start to marshal my breaths I see Kane shift behind her. He's standing at the door. Why hasn't he left yet?

My gaze slams into his like a fist into concrete. I hate him, I decide then. My head spins and my stomach churns while heat claws its way up my lungs like cracked fingernails, climbing for survival. I feel sick, and more afraid than normal because I've never had an anxiety attack before. The sensation is entirely foreign. Almost as foreign as meeting one of the Others and realizing a set of truths, each more harrowing than the last:

Either he's lying to me or our leaders did — and even though I trust him as far as I can throw him, I'd still bet on the latter. None of the information that came out after the Fall made any sense. Leaders telling people not to panic, and then to arm themselves and begin stockpiling supplies, from one day to the next. There was no information and then too much information. And then everything went dark. When the internet went, sanity went with it. All thoughts of not panicking were moot.

And the second truth is that he's right about me on all accounts. I've killed over bread before. I've killed over much less.

Am I the same as him?

His eyebrows are drawn together and his hollow cheeks betray a color that's way too human. His glowing gold chest pulses and he looks more alive now than ever, but his expression is cruel.

He crosses his arms over his chest and at the exact moment that I begin to feel that I just might be able to regain control of my spiking adrenaline levels, he says, "I should have known you were already ruined by Population. I should have left you outside with the other rats."

I curse and push Maggie out of the way. She falls onto her butt while I scramble around the bed with every intention of attacking Kane with my bare hands. Not my smartest idea.

Also not my dumbest.

I punch him square in the face, but only because he lets me. Meanwhile, he slides his shoulder under my stomach and flips me over his head. I think he'll throw me to the ground and kill me for good, but in a move too quick to catch, he slams me against the wall by the bedroom door.

Glass shatters, but I don't see what falls. I'm too busy watching the way Kane's expression oscillates so seamlessly between hate and something else infinitely more toxic. His skin burns every place we touch.

"Are you going to calm down?" Burgundy clings to his hollow cheeks and when I don't answer, he levels his arm across my chest. The pain in my lungs reaches an abrupt climax and I cry out. He drops me to the ground and when I struggle to push myself away from the wall, back onto my feet so that I can finish what I've started, Maggie stalls me. Shouting still, as she has been for the past five minutes, she tells Kane to move away from me and forces my head between my knees.

"Breathe," she coaches me when I put up no resistance, "you need to breathe, Abel."

"I'm trying," I grunt, residual anger making it hard for me to speak.

Maggie tries to urge Kane from the room as I recover my breath, but he doesn't listen. Instead, he switches back and forth along the wall hung with all the paintings. Every time he switches in my direction, he shoots me a furious glare.

Realizing he won't leave — he doesn't have to, he's *master* after all, isn't it? — Maggie stands me up and forces me into the bathroom. She draws a bath and steam rises from the water like cinders in the wind. She pours oil beneath the spout that smells of roses and lavender then strips me butt ass naked. I let her.

I slip into the water and it scalds my skin. I've never felt anything like this. Never. In the time before the Fall, I don't remember baths. I took showers, I think, but now I'm not sure what's real and what's a figment of my imagination. Most things, I imagine, are.

My father's voice. My mother's awful singing. Aiden's laugh. Were any of them really the way I repeat them? Or am I just a lonely girl carrying around the ghosts of her family?

Maggie disappears and there's murmuring on the other side of the door. Well, it starts quiet. "I want to see her...no right...she shouldn't..." And then glass shatters against the bathroom door.

"Animal!" I shout at the top of my lungs.

A fist pounds once on the other side of the door, but just the once. "At least that makes two of us!" He roars.

A door slams and then there's silence.

I close my eyes and let the hot water blister my skin, loving every second of it. Maggie comes back in and helps me wash. She soaps my skin, shampoos my hair, adds conditioner and even manages to work a comb through it.

The whole time, she works in silence.

It's me who breaks it. "Is it true?" I say.

She surprises me by shrugging. "Does it really matter? You already seem to have your mind made up about him."

I frown. "You think he's the hero in this?"

"He's a hero to us."

That's all she says and I hate her for making me draw this out of her. Maybe she's right. Maybe none of this matters and neither does she. A little more rest and I'll be ready to go back out into Population to go after Ashlyn.

My fingers tighten on the edges of the tub. Oh god. Going back out into Population *alone* knowing Kane would never come for me? That hurts in places that don't exist, because in Population, you can't have a heart.

"He's a hero and so you let him enslave you?"

She smirks. "You think I am here against my own will?" She shakes her head. "I was a baker in the World Before. A good one, but not particularly successful. I wasn't rich. I often defaulted on my rents. I had a hard time dealing with credit. In the digital world things just got," she sighs, "away from me.

"And then the Fall happened. You've spent a long time in Population. Do you think I would have done well, even ten years younger than I am now?"

She pulls back enough for me to be able to take in her face. Laugh lines surround her eyes. They are the most threatening thing about her. I frown. "No."

"Luckily, I didn't have to. Kane took me and my son in. He let me bake. There were no rents. There was only total freedom. Even though the Fall was awful — for both sides — I can say that for me personally, I live better now than I did before. The children born here know nothing of survival."

"Children?"

"Yes. Do you think I'm the only human here?" She smiles at me softly and removes the curls stuck to my cheek. "We are over four hundred and each of us owes Kane everything."

I lay on the bed after she's gone. I lay there for a while.

She brings me more food eventually and I eat every single thing on the plate before licking the plate clean. I also down two full jugs of water. Poison be damned. If he'd wanted me dead, he'd have done it by now.

But then what does he want with me?

He *should* have left me out with the rats. I don't know why he didn't. I'm no better than them. I'm certainly no Maggie. She's a woman that shines with her own light, even though she doesn't have a glowing chest and is just an old human lady. She's a lady who has laugh lines instead of scars, and a smile perpetually tilting up her lips.

I'm just a half-deaf ghost chasing after corpses. A rat clinging to survival. A rat, but bigger.

What keeps me going? The promise of more baths could. Even now, even knowing that it's an alien that offers it, I would still take it.

What are morals in the face of misery? Where is my line in the sand when there is no sand and the enemy has formed a circle around us? When the enemy is everyone?

I don't sleep. I should be sleeping, but instead, I'm wandering the halls of a house that seems to have no end. Marble. Wood. Paint without a single chip. It's all so perfect, I don't dare touch anything. *I don't belong here. I belong out there with them.*

I don't realize I'm looking for him until I see the door hanging slightly ajar. At the sight of it, my whole body reacts with a visceral shiver. *Kane's in there.* I don't know how I know it, but I know it's him. Maybe because he's right. He *is* me — if I were an alien.

I peek inside and see the back of Kane's head resting on the back of a brown leather couch. He's fully reclined in front of a fire that simmers gently in the black jade hearth at the end of the room. It illuminates the space, which is massive and full of beautiful things — hundreds of leather-bound books, a golden music stand, a marble globe covered in sticky notes, like a conqueror in the planning stages.

I brace as I enter the room and drift lightly across the carpet towards him as if hoping I might make myself invisible if I just keep my mouth shut. He doesn't move until I reach the edge of the couch, and even then he only lifts an eyelid. Just one. He sees me, sighs, then lets his eyes fall shut again.

Watching him like this, I forget why I'm here at all — if I ever knew. My fingertips brush the arm of the couch and I use it to keep me centered and steady as my gaze roams over his body, fascinated all over again. It's the glow that does it. At least, that's what I tell myself. Nothing more than that.

Mesmerized, I follow the rise and fall of his chest with each of his shallow breaths. My eyelids get heavier and heavier. I sway forward, and then catch myself on supple leather.

"Yes?" he says and his tone betrays nothing.

"So the humans like living with you?"

"Wouldn't you? You already smell better than you did."

Embarrassment makes me clench. I feel myself rise towards a ruthless insult, but I'm not that clever. I use my fists, and right now I don't feel like fighting a fight I know I can't win. Scratch number five from the rule book.

"Kind of hard to smell good when there's no water or soap out there."

"So you've come to shame me for mine after having used some of it?"

"No," I pout.

"Then what is it? Why are you here? You've made your opinion of me quite clear."

"You're the one who called me a rat." I point my finger at his nose.

Looking at it, he hesitates before meeting my eyes. "Yes, I did. And I should not have. You are not a rat. Do you accept my apology, Abel?"

Emotions. They come swiftly, the little cockroaches, skittering all over me. I shift my weight between my feet and wipe my palm off on the boxer shorts I'm wearing. "I don't…you don't have to apologize."

"I do. I behaved dishonorably in my attempt to shame you."

"Stop it. I did the same thing."

"Yes," he says slowly. "This is why you should apologize, too."

With my shoulders clenched by my ears and my arms hugging my sides stiffly, I stammer. "Hit me." Apologies I don't get. Punishment, by contrast, is something I can understand.

"What the fuck are you talking about?" he says and it startles me. I can't remember the last time I heard him curse.

"I'm not going to apologize. I had the information I had and you still live like this," I say, sweeping my hand around at all the books and the shelves and the carpets, "while I was living like a rat. You weren't wrong and neither was I.

Nobody needs to apologize. But I did hit you, so you can hit me back."

"Have you considered that I don't want to hit you? That it brings me discomfort to see you in pain?"

Emotions creep, creep, creep. I close my eyes and shake my head quickly. "No. You're an alien." The response sounds weak, even to me.

A whoosh of cool air causes me to canter back. Heat rises up against my chest, sinking through the thin material of the tee shirt I'm in. Can he see how hard my nipples are? God, I hope not. It stings a little bit to think that it actually doesn't matter. He's an *alien*. He's not going to be affected like that by me.

I close my eyes and brace myself — a little surprised he's actually going to hit me — and then even more surprised when the punch I hoped he'd land, falls short.

His cheek touches my cheek. I can feel his jaw work as he whispers, "Your pride is going to get you hurt one day, or killed." His hand wraps around the back of my neck and his thumb smoothes up into my curls. "But not by me," he breathes. "Never by me."

All at once, he moves to the door. "I brought you here because there will be a Heztoichen gala at which I have been named the guest of honor. The man who stole your sister will be in attendance. The gala will be in three days' time, after which you are free to rid yourself of my bestial company."

He disappears through archway while my lips keep uselessly flapping.

When he disappears, he sucks all the air out of the room, taking it with him. And in its absence, I feel a strange hollowness in my stomach that I've never felt before. Maybe it's because I've never really been alone until recently. Or maybe it's because…I sort of like his company. How messed up is that?

"Very," I whisper to myself, collapsing heavily on the couch in the same position I found Kane. I stare up at the ceiling and let the scent of his skin, and his residual heat, sink into my bones.

"What are you doing, Abel?" I say, and it's strange, because the word comes to me like it's the only name I've ever known.

Later that night, the effects of our encounter really seep in. They manifest in ways that I don't expect too, because I can't sleep. I keep waking up, thinking that there's someone in the room with me, hoping that it's him and that he's there to slide into the bed next to me just like he did once before.

But why would he? He was only doing it then to keep me from freezing. Now there's no chance of that in this heated house that looks like it was ripped straight from a fairytale written before the Fall.

Giving up, I roll out of bed, tug on a pair of jeans that are only a little baggy on me, boots that fit a little too snug, a sweatshirt and a coat.

I find my way to the kitchens and try to stuff as much food inside my body without vomiting, then I head outside. The world seems...lighter here. Yeah, the grey still hangs there, but it doesn't seem so dark today and the mist that rolls over the grounds ducks and dips, like a playful dancer even though there isn't much wind.

I carve a path through it, following a paved road leading away from the house. I'm surprised to find people milling about. They look like they've been up for a while.

Three little boys wearing backpacks rush past me talking animatedly amongst one another. One of them pushes the other and I feel my muscles tense, prepared to intervene, but then I see they're laughing. Frozen with one foot off the ground, I don't know what to think. I follow the boys along the trail until I reach a school.

A man with pale hair and bright eyes is shouting at about thirty kids to get in order and get inside, to stop wrestling, for someone named Anthony to stop pulling someone called Jill's hair. The man stops speaking when he sees me, and waves at me as I walk.

Speechless, I wave back. Rule number nine says not to talk in the grey. But what about laughter? Does that count? Like the mist that rolls across the road in front of me, rule number nine fades away.

A little while later, I spot a group of men moving towards me down the path at an alarming rate. Fear steals into my bones, but they don't even notice I'm there. My eyes fall out of my head when I see why. They're chasing an escaped *pig* down the road. The pig is barely a blur of pink on the ground, but I anticipate its trajectory and quickly jump over it. The little animal squeals beneath me and all the men cheer.

"Whoa! You're really good," one of the men says. He's about my age, maybe a little younger — or maybe much, much older considering that Population hasn't hardened him in the way it does most people I've met over the years.

He's got blonde hair and a crooked tooth in his crooked smile and says, "You must be Abel." He takes another step towards me and I edge back. He notices, and his face scrunches up like he doesn't understand my reaction.

The squealing pig removes some of the awkwardness between us. He looks over his shoulder and laughs while the two other men struggle to get the pig into a sack.

"How do you know my name?" I say.

"Everybody knows. You think Kane brings hot women… sorry," he blushes deeply, "I mean lady guests around often?"

I have no way of knowing, but something irks at the thought. "I don't know. Maybe."

He shakes his head. "Well, he doesn't, in case you're wondering. New people only join if they make it up to his estate and knock on the front door. Nobody's done that though in ages."

"So what — the rest of you are just born here?"

"Or were taken in at the beginning, yeah. You're the newest face that's shown up here in years. Rumors have it you can kick some serious ass. You took on a Heztoichen?" He uses that same word Kane does, which bugs the crap out of me. Why is a human out here speaking alien? "How'd it go?"

"What do you mean?"

"I mean how bad was it? How long did you last?"

Offended, I make a face. "I killed it, obviously. If I hadn't I wouldn't be standing here now."

"Woah...that's amazing." His eyes grow large and I realize that the guys gathered behind him have gone quiet. He wipes his palm off on his dirt-stained jacket and sticks out his hand. "I'm Calvin, by the way."

He already knows my name, so I don't know what to say when I shake his hand. What did I used to say, in the World Before? God, I don't remember. Good? Thank you?

"Want a tour?" he says, sparing me from my own doubt. The fact that I can't remember the basics about being civil is a little disappointing.

I nod. "Um, yeah. Sure, that sounds great."

He shows me the school, which I've already seen, then the housing units slightly further west. They're little cottages built in orderly rows, disaggregate by single, double, and family units. Small though they are, each of them is worked with electricity, a stove, and a fireplace. I'm green with envy. Stationary housing units *with* heating and appliances? Sounds like utopia.

He explains that about four hundred people live on Kane's estate and that they each perform an integral function that keeps the city thriving. Their numbers are growing with new babies being born, and when I ask him if he ever thinks Kane will kick them out he just laughs.

"I mean, it's not like Kane consorts with the humans, per se," he gives me a funny look when he says that, but doesn't elaborate, "but he doesn't despise us either, like some of the Others do. He likes his human stuff too much, and it really does take a whole city's worth of people just to keep the most basic services afloat.

"You got your electricity, water, and waste management centers," he says gesturing to two huge steel buildings nestled in the tree line against the eastern horizon, "not to mention your manufacturing workshops. We have to make clothes, sheets, towels — everything that we used to take for granted in the World Before.

"Though we have search parties that used to go out raiding almost twice a month, there's nothing really left worth taking, so now we only go out maybe four times a year. Plus, there's the other humans to deal with." He grits his teeth when he says this, though when he mentioned the Others he didn't react at all.

He continues explaining to me the ins and outs of Kane's estate as we pass a large barn. I hear at least half a dozen different breeds of animals complaining inside of it.

"Plus, Kane likes eating human food," he tells me as I try and stare through the barn slats, hoping to catch a glimpse of a horse. Becks had loved horses. I've never seen one before, but I'd like to.

"Even though he doesn't need to eat human food to survive, he still enjoys it. And we need it to live, obviously, so we have to cultivate the produce, harvest grain, tend the livestock…"

"Kane doesn't eat?"

Calvin shakes his head. "No. He doesn't need to. The Others, they live primarily on human blood…or flesh. Didn't you know that?"

No. I don't know much of anything, other than what it looks like when Kane rips out a man's throat and drains him dry. Like that juice box man. Slurp slurp.

"So what, every now and again he just offs one of you? Population control?" I try and keep my voice light but it just comes out condemning.

And then Calvin shocks me by looking even more horrified and appalled than Maggie had. "No. We tithe. Nobody has to that doesn't want to, but every six months, we go and donate blood. It all gets swirled together and Kane and the other Heztoichen who live in the Diera use that. Nobody gets killed here by Kane. Actually nobody gets killed here pretty much ever."

He smiles at me. I just glare back in disdain. Does he know what I've been through?

Two women pass us carrying shovels and wearing jeans and a long-sleeved tee shirt, only. Like they're not worried about piling on all their clothes just in case they need to make a break for it. Like I was when I got dressed this morning.

When Calvin waves at them, they share a glance and giggle loudly between one another. Like their biggest concern really is whether or not the sexy farmhand is into them. Calvin cocks his head and squints his eyes, at least pretending not to have noticed.

"Calvin, is that the warrior princess?"

Up ahead, a big guy starts to make his way towards us down the path. His skin is blacker than anyone's I've ever seen, which makes his teeth stand out in bright white. He's also only wearing a fitted long-sleeve shirt, which accentuates his easy muscles. I've already determined that I could kill Calvin, easy. But this guy might actually put up a fight.

"Yeah. Yeah, it is." And then out of the corner of his mouth, he whispers, "That's Gabe. Other people just call him Beast. He's the only one I've ever heard of to take on an Other and live." I notice that he doesn't include me in this category. The little shit probably doesn't believe me. Makes me like him less than I already do for having his green face and his unscarred hands and his stupid smile that says that all things, deep down, really are good.

"I'm Gabe," the Gabe Beast says when he's within earshot. He holds out his hand and I shake it firmly.

"Abel," I grumble.

He nods and crosses his arms over the rake he's carrying. He leans on it in a way that spells confidence. "I hear tell you're a pretty impressive fighter. Care to give us a demonstration?"

A group of about six boys and men loom up behind him. Not very clever eavesdroppers, they pretend to be doing work even though their rakes and hoes dangle limply in their hands. Instead, their bright eyes watch me, awaiting my answer in anticipation. But the idea of fighting this guy just for fun doesn't sit well in my gut. I've only ever fought for survival.

"I don't think that's a good idea," I say slowly, "I don't have good technique, and I don't fight clean."

He grins at me to show all his teeth and by now the farm hands have formed a semi-circle around us. "You afraid you'll get hurt?" He goads.

I'm already hurt. What more could this oaf do to me?

I shake my head. "Quite the opposite. I'm afraid *you'll* get hurt."

He laughs. "I think I'll take my chances."

I see that he's insistent and I'm not sure what to say. I've never backed down from a fight before, but I'm also not used to showing restraint. What if I *do* actually hurt him? At my side, Calvin nudges me with his elbow.

"You don't have to fight him, you know."

"Fighting is the only thing I do know," I grumble under my breath. "Fine. How do I know if I've won?" I say to Gabe.

Beast's eyebrows lift up, as if my consent surprises him. After a few seconds, he strips his shirt off over his head. What is he doing?

"Until first man yields. Or woman." He winks.

"How do I yield?"

A few of the spectators share uneasy looks. They should. In Population there's no such thing a yield. There's only alive or dead.

"Tap your hand twice on the ground, or just say that you yield," Calvin says.

"Okay."

I quickly take in our surroundings. We're in a small clearing, the barn is about thirty paces away, there's a small cluster of houses to my left surrounding a large barn that Calvin called the dining hall, and near the tree line there's a well.

The people filing out of the dining hall watch us curiously, but they're far away still — about a few dozen paces off. It's the clear fascination and apprehension oozing from this faraway group and also from the closer spectators that makes me wonder how often fights happen around here, if ever. I cringe and cling to any emotion that's not jealousy. It's difficult. To know a world other than the brutal one I do, would be a blessing.

I glance around at the male and female faces standing astride one another without fear or lust or panic and recognize that Kane has blessed them all. By giving them this sanctuary he's allowed them to keep what's left of their humanity. They're not animals like Drago's pets, like gangs, like scavengers, like rats. Like me.

I wince as I realize that, when I find Ashlyn, Kane probably won't let us stay here. I'm not just broken, I'm ruined. Population has ruined me.

Gabe squares up against me, but there's confusion in his expression as he glances down at my outfit. "You're going to wear *that*?"

"Yeah." I shrug, looking down absently. "What else?"

Gabe snorts, but doesn't respond. Instead he starts stretching.

"Are you sure you're up to this?" Calvin says, voice dipping low in a way that makes me want to hit him.

Gabe beams. "Don't worry, I'll go easy on her."

I roll my eyes. "Just attack already."

I realize quickly that Beast is most comfortable using his size and strength to wrestle his opponents to the ground, so I don't give him that chance. Instead, I hit him early with a few quick slaps to the face and one to the throat. He seems surprised that I actually touch him, but otherwise unconcerned. I don't hit him very hard, and he doesn't seem to realize that I'm not trying to break him down — not yet. I'm trying to find his weaknesses.

He's slow but freakish strong and when he does manage to catch me in the gut, it's enough to knock me onto my back. He lunges towards me while I'm down, but I propel myself backwards across the dusty ground, ignoring the rocks that dig into my spine through all my clothes.

When he's just close enough, I wait for him to reach for my legs before kicking him in the face once, and then again in the gut. He cries out, but he really should be counting his lucky stars that I didn't go for his groin. That's the only concession on offer.

I'm able to use my momentum then to skip back up onto my feet. I duck and dodge around him, hoping to tire him out, but he doesn't tire easily and suddenly I realize that *I'm* the one getting tired. That's when he catches me.

He hits me in the side hard enough to make my ribs sing. Ordinarily, this would be nothing, but I didn't take the pain pills Maggie put on the dresser for me, so this *hurts*. The force of the blow sends me skidding back, but I keep my balance and charge.

He isn't expecting me to come at him in the way I do, and his stance is all wrong to ward the blow. I kick him once in the knee, then again in his other knee. He starts to crumple and as he falls, I clasp my hands together and use the strength of both arms to bring my right elbow up against the side of his face.

He stumbles and I make the mistake of thinking that I'm in a better position than I am. When I hit him again, he swipes my legs.

We fall to the ground in a pile of limbs, but being twice my size and three times as heavy — not to mention well-fed and uninjured — he's able to take the dominant position easily. He uses his whole body to pin mine to the ground and

I quickly recall some of the self-defense moves for girls that a woman in my first settlement taught me. She said that men often aim to get women on their stomachs in the submissive position, but with a few tricks I counter it.

First, I take his pinky when it locks around my throat and I rip it back. The hand goes where the pinky goes and he's forced to release my neck. Next, I smash the crown of my head backwards into his nose and, judging by the way he roars, I take it that I've broken it. Now, he's given me just enough space to flip my body over so that he's straddling my waist.

I hoist my hips up, lock my ankles around the front of his throat and lean my full bodyweight into my legs. He cries out and we rock like a chair until he's on his back and I'm seated above him. I'm breathing heavily, but not hard, and I sit up straight with very little effort. Leaning just a little further forward until I can reach his face, I cup my hands and box his ears. He roars and writhes but doesn't give up or give in, so I box them again.

"Do you yield?" I say.

He tries to unhook my legs from beneath his chin, but he's choking and gasping and his sweaty grip slips. His desperation to beat me makes me frown and I find it much harder to believe his story about the Others when he probably couldn't best a human child from the outside.

"Do you yield?" I shout again.

I snatch up a stick lying in the dirt and imagine how easy it would be to stab that stiff piece of wood straight through his eye socket, blinding him or killing him depending how far I jab. Moving in for the final kill, bloodlust grips me and distantly, I hear a woman gasp and another release a short scream. That innocence breaks through my need for this big man's blood and so does a single word: *ruined... This is supposed to be for practice or something, isn't it?*

I actually can't remember why I'm here, straddling this big man, anymore. This isn't real. This is fake and sick and so am

I and I hate it. I drop the stick I'm holding and release the sad little Beast from the bind I've locked him in.

I amble stiffly to my feet, dust off my hands and see that we've gathered quite a following. At least two dozen spectators have crowded around to watch us fight, and not a single one of them isn't gaping.

Many mouths whisper all at once, "Can you believe that?" "She really didn't..." "There's no way..." "...killed an Other!" "...can't believe Kane is here..."

My ears perk up and I look through the thickets of people and see him first. It's hard not to. People are bunched together quite closely, but they've marked a three foot perimeter around him that nobody dares to breach.

He's standing with his arms crossed over his chest and when our eyes meet, he lifts just one brow. Like he's impressed or something. I feel my skin warm. Maybe Gabe was right after all. I feel too hot underneath my coat and jacket.

"So you can fight." His voice is low, but his pitch carries over the crowd. Everyone watches him in silence and reverence. So do I.

He moves within three feet of me and I'm suddenly apprehensive that he's going to teach me a lesson out here in front of all these people.

I ball my hands into fists and hold them at shoulder level, angling my body to the side so that I present a smaller target. His expression is difficult to make out as he glances between my face and my stiff posture once and then again. At no point, however, does he look away from me to the crowd.

Then he holds out his hand and says, "But can you dance?"

Chapter Seven

We walk back to his house — his freaking castle — in silence and I know that he's still mad at me. I think about saying something…but I don't. Instead, I let the chasm between us get bigger and bigger.

I'm grateful when Maggie comes rushing down the path towards us. "What happened?" She flutters, gasping when she sees the welt on my cheek and the blood on the backs of my knuckles.

"Was she attacked by one of ours?" Maggie's eyes glisten with shock and I'm so distracted by the way she says *ours* that I don't respond right away.

"In a sense." Kane hides a smile with his hands. "And in a truer sense, no. She had a practice round with Gabe."

"Oh lord." Maggie shakes her head and looks at me as if I really am the stupidest girl in the world. "You were already injured. Are you hurt badly now? Should I call for Sandra?"

Kane laughs. "I think Sandra's services are needed, yes, but to attend to Gabe. He lasted six minutes against Abel, and is in a sorry state." He takes me by the arm and guides me around Maggie who stands there, stock still, mouth open. "Send Sandra to check up on him. Abel will be just fine." Inside, Kane leads me to an enormous ballroom. Wide landscape windows line the far wall and tower thirty feet over my head. They overlook a sprawling forest, wreathed in that familiar-yet-not-so-familiar mist.

Two fireplaces stud opposite walls at each end of the room and the heat they radiate through these big bronze furnaces makes it possible for me to take off my coat. I toss it onto the floor, but Kane picks it back up and hangs it on the coat rack I hadn't noticed six feet away from me by the high, arching door.

He rolls his eyes, then sweeps his gaze over my face and blood-spattered sweat shirt. It's big on me and I feel very small in it. I feel even smaller under the weight of his stare. He grunts in a language I can't interpret, then comes and stands before me.

He touches my jaw with his fingertips only, and electricity flies from his hands into my cheeks as he tilts my head to the left and then to the right.

"I want no more fighting until after the gala." His voice is low, and fills me all the way up like a cistern in the rain. "From this moment, you are made of glass. Nothing and no one touches you. No scrapes, no cuts, no bruises. Do you understand?"

I nod like I do, even though I can't think straight with the butterflies in my stomach trying to chew their way out. He releases me and places something in my hands that makes my whole body tense. I'm absolutely sure that if I could have seen my own brown face in that moment, I'd have been sheet white.

"You can't be serious."

He nods so I put them on, and as I do I have to use his arms to help me stand up straight because I'll fall otherwise. My knees and ankles tremble like a newborn colt's and I look up at him helplessly. What sort of cruel and unusual torture is this?

Kane's expression troubles me, but only for the instant before it fades. "Don't look at me like that."

"Like what?"

"With such terror."

"I can't do this," I say with another wobble.

I'm going to break both my ankles, of this I'm absolutely sure. My grip on Kane's bare arms tightens. I wish he was wearing a coat. I wish he was wearing those pants and nothing else. My cheeks warm and I try to pull away from him, but in these shoes, I can't.

Kane huffs like a horse. "You can take down a full grown man three times your size without batting an eyelash but you can't make it three feet in ladies' high heels?"

I grimace and try another tottering step without breaking my ankle. The shoes I'm in have a three-inch platform and a nine-inch heel, putting my heel-to-toe differential at six inches.

I shake my head. "No."

"You didn't look frightened at all in the woods."

"In the woods, I was in Population. I was in *my* element." With the rats. "I've never had to wear high heels before. These are a nightmare. Seriously, why do I have to do this?"

"The gala," he explains. He peels my hands off of his skin and goes to the gold gramophone into the center of the space. He presses a button, then lifts a slender black needle and lets it fall onto the record beneath it.

A chillingly beautiful song begins to play. I haven't heard music in ages.

The song wraps around me like a caress as a woman's voice wafts into the space in low notes, as sultry and seductive as smoke. And I am pleasantly seduced. The back of my neck breaks out in heat when I realize that Kane is watching me again with one ear cocked to the ceiling. His eyes glisten as they stare and I see about a million questions hiding in that gluttonous green, but when I lift my gaze to meet his, he shakes his head and looks away quickly. I wonder, not for the first time, what he's thinking.

He clears his throat. "You'll need to play the part of an extremely high class escort that none of the other Heztoichen would be able to afford."

"You mean aliens?"

His lips flatten. "You are aliens to us."

"We were here first."

"I'm sure your indigenous communities said the same to their invaders."

I balk. "That doesn't make it right."

"No. It makes it history. History does not change."

I open my mouth to retort, but he speaks louder than I can. "As I was saying, you'll need to be my date to this affair and any date of mine will wear shoes like these to elevate her puny height, so that she can more believably be seen as equal to me."

"I'm not your equal. We're not even on the same team. Can't you just bring me as your blood bag?"

He winces when I say that and doesn't answer except to return to my side and lift my arms away from my body. He takes my left hand in his right and places my right hand on his left shoulder. Then he starts to waltz. Surprised, I don't even know where to begin, what to do, how to follow…

Clutching Kane's hand and shoulder fiercely, I try to follow his steps and, when that inevitably fails, I work on staying upright. Both are struggles.

"I am the guest of honor and as I have never brought a human escort to one of these functions, you will attract attention. They will expect you to be exceptional. Beautiful, intelligent, delicious of course," he whispers that last part in a way that makes me shiver. We do a turn and suddenly I'm aware of his heat pressing against me and that stupid, nagging desire I have to be closer to him. *Close* close.

Then I trip and fall and not even the clever move he pulls is enough to keep me standing. I crash in a heap onto the floor. He stands over me, massages his eyelids and says, "They also will expect you to have attended these types of functions before and to be graceful and irresistibly charming. We will have to pretend you're both."

"Yeah well you're not much of a charmer yourself," I lie as he helps me back onto my feet.

"Unlikely."

I smile a little as we settle into the same posture and start again. I stumble three times within the first cadence, almost as if I'm trying to prove his point rather than disprove it.

Before he can make some condescending quip, I say, "So why are you the guest of honor?"

His cheeks flood with unexpected color. The emotion takes me a few seconds to process, but slowly I understand that he's *embarrassed*. He clears his throat, but doesn't respond.

"You're somebody important, aren't you?"

Again he remains silent, eyes carefully avoiding mine though the color in his cheeks holds.

Stubbornly I press, "Like some kind of rock star?"

My voice is teasing and reluctantly Kane grumbles, "No."

"A rich guy?"

"Clearly," he smirks, "though that isn't why I'm being honored."

I try again. "Are you some kind of government official?"

"Sort of." He takes my hands in his and begins the waltz again. I use my game of twenty questions to ignore the friction between our palms. He might be important, and he might be an alien, but his palms are still callused. Rough and dry, they're the hands of someone who works hard.

"Are you…like a king or something?"

"No," he says voice so quiet only rats could hear it.

"No?"

"No, I'm not *like* a king. I am a king."

This time when I fall, he just leaves me down on the ground. He mutters something condescending about this being a stupid plan, but I'm still hung up on what he's just said. "A *king?*"

His cheeks cling to that heat and I see his chest pulse vibrant orange, just once, through his tee shirt. "That is the closest word you have for it in English. We use the term *Notare*. There are ministers that work beneath me as well as other Notare dispersed across the continents, but at any given time we are only seven."

He licks his lips and looks away as I try to gracefully glide back up to my feet. I end up tripping over my own shoes instead and crashing face first into his chest. He sighs, and after he rights me, steps away from me.

"You asked me once about my heart and its glow. The term Notare means one who bears the light. We are considered strongest of our kind. I was born with this light, named Notare, and when we were cast to Earth my light remained.

"I govern, but my power is not absolute. I can be challenged. And when I am unfit to continue for whatever reason, my light will fade. Another will be born then and will take my place."

I'm gobsmacked. *Gobsmacked.* Here, I've been picking fights with a king among the aliens. What is the matter with me? He watches me struggle to articulate, but when I come up short his mouth twitches and flattens and he runs a hand back through is hair.

"Never mind. This will take forever. I don't have time to train you." He turns from me and stalks towards the wide, double doors. Over his shoulder, he says, "I don't want to see you with those shoes off for the next forty-eight hours. I'll send Calvin to coach you on the other five dances."

"There are *five?*"

The door swings shut to the sound of his subtle laughter.

Calvin meets me in the ballroom some minutes later, and we begin a different dance, one where we don't touch at all except for our palms. We spin dizzying circles around one another and finally, I manage to nail it without falling down. By then the gramophone has already played the record once through and Calvin has to reset it.

"How do you know these weird dance moves?" I ask him when we sit down for a lunch break.

He smiles at me and bobs his head in time to the music. "I actually get invited sometimes to these things by Tasha. She's one of the Heztoichen and once in a while, takes me along instead of Kane."

My spine sizzles as I picture Kane in all his glowing, glorious decadence, dancing at one of these balls with another girl. What is *wrong* with me? Kane is a total ick monster. I mean, a good looking ick monster, but still the enemy. *Who's trying to help me.*

"You know, I never got a chance to tell you how amazing that was today," he says as I chew on the thick cartilage of a roast beef sandwich.

"What?" I speak through a full mouth while the fat of the cow melts on my tongue and horseradish and mustard dribble down my chin. I remember the unfamiliar vocabulary Kane used today — graceful, he said. I'm about as graceful as a cow.

"Fighting Beast. I've never seen anybody take him on so easily. You smashed him." He laughs and shakes his head. "I guess we'll have to rethink that nickname."

I wipe my face with the back of my hand and dare a smile. "Thanks."

"No gratitude necessary. I just hope that you'll stay, even after you're finished with us and whatnot. We could learn a lot from you. From someone who's spent so much time on the outside."

I know what he's trying to say, but I also don't know how to ask him what he thinks my chances are of Kane taking me back, and letting Ashlyn in. I mean, what can a little girl offer him? I choke down a knot of roast beef and emotion and change the subject.

"So what are these galas like?"

"Well, they're pretty intense. A bunch of Heztoichen elite all with their perfect human escorts. Sometimes Kane goes with Tasha, but other times he just takes one of the humans offered to him." He rolls his eyes and leans back onto his hands. "And there are *always* humans offered to him."

My back and shoulders burn. Must be the pain from my injuries. Yeah, that's it. "Yeah?"

"As far as the Heztoichen go, I think he's a pretty big deal."

I grit my teeth again and remind myself that this doesn't matter. This is a transactional relationship. One where he helps me find my sister, and I…accept his help without a lick of gratitude.

I push the guilt in my stomach aside. I try to, anyway, but it's like moving a boulder. "Anything else I should know about the galas?"

Calvin considers, then says, "Don't talk unless you're spoken to first. Oh, and try and look like you're enjoying it."

"Enjoying what?"

"Everything."

I laugh humorlessly and dust off my hands as I chew on the last bit of my sandwich. Then I stand up again even though the arches of my feet are throbbing and I'm pretty sure my feet are covered in raw blisters. I hold out my right hand and bow.

"May I to this dance, sir Calvinus?"

He laughs as he sets the gramophone back to the original recording. Then we begin. Again. And again. And again and again and again until my heels bleed and the guilt boulder sinks like a stone all the way through my little rat heart.

An eternity later, I leave the ballroom. I keep my heels on — not because Kane told me to, of course, but because I need the practice. Of course.

I say goodbye to Calvin in the massive marble entryway and he gives me a quick hug before heading back to his house. The hug is *weird*. Someone closing their arms around your shoulders without the intention of trying to put you in a sleeper hold? What's the point?

I awkwardly return the hug before making my way down the halls towards the room I've been squatting in. As I walk, my mind wanders...and so do my feet...until I hear words whispered from the next doorway.

This is Kane's room.

A sudden nervous energy steals into my bones. A sudden fervor too. *I'm sorry.* That's what he wants me to say. Maybe if I say it, he'll let Ashlyn stay here. I don't even need to stay here with her. Maggie will look after her and give her a better life than I ever could out in Population, of that I'm sure. He doesn't deserve a sorry — or if he does, I'm still not going to give it up that easily — but Ashlyn does. *If she's still breathing.*

I wince, but practice the line over and over and over in my head until it ceases to sound like English. *I'm sorry imsorry imsorryimsorryimsorry.* I take strong strides down the hall. Well, I try to, but it's hard to look confident when you're stumbling over perfectly flat carpet every third step.

My ankles are swollen, but I use the pain to fuel my adrenaline because I know I'll need it if I'm to accomplish the arduous task that I'm there to accomplish. No battle has ever seemed so daunting as this.

I burst through the door and start talking before I even process the scene. My eyes are closed as I blurt out, "Imsorry." It sounds sort of like I said I'm slobbery, so I feel like I should maybe try that again. "S-sorry." That time had a hiccup. "Sooorry." Why am I adding emphasis on the O? That's not right.

I inhale deeply, about to give it one last go, but when my eyes open the scene sharpens and the words punch out of me hard and hot and slow. "I'm sorry." I sound like I'm underwater. Drowning.

Maybe because that's what it feels like. Why? I'm not sure.

Kane is standing in the center of his bedroom wearing nothing but a pair of blue boxers. There's a woman in front of him and she's got her long, skinny arms wrapped around his bare torso.

The muscles in his back shift, and though he's turned away from me I can still see his surprised expression reflected in the face of a full-length mirror a few feet in front of him. His eyebrows are raised, lips slightly parted.

The woman with her bare hands on Kane glances at me from over his shoulder. She's nearly as tall as he is and like him, is fiercely beautiful. She has pale, ivory skin and brilliant red hair. She wears makeup that highlights her high cheekbones and accentuates the startling green of her eyes, which peer at me from between heavy, black lashes. The dress she wears wraps around her like a second skin. Graceful, beautiful, elegant.

She is all the things Kane asked me to be, but he knew better. This woman is those things and she's my polar opposite.

Emotion monster rears it's stupid, squishy head and tries to break free. It wants to claw at something with its little rat hands and bite that woman with its little rat teeth. I want to punch Kane in the stomach. Yeah, that would feel good. But first, I need to flee.

I wonder what my face must look like as I stand there stupidly, absorbed in the way Kane's shoulders shift easily beneath his olive skin when he turns to look at me. He starts to say my name, but I'm feeling a rush of emotions too strong to stomach, so I back out of the door, an apology rattling past my teeth.

"Sorry, I didn't mean to…" I don't finish.

I slam the door and book it down the hallway.

It doesn't take me long to realize that it's actually a lot harder to run in heels than to walk and I fall eight times before reaching my room. I also get lost somewhere between the second floor and the third and when I finally sprint through the door to the room Kane let me sleep in, Kane is already there — still in his boxers — and so is the woman.

"How the hell did you guys get here before me?" I pant. I bend over and place my hands on my knees, then reach down and massage my ankles.

The woman looks to Kane with dark eyebrows arched high over her forehead. Her crimson mouth whispers foreign words that I don't understand and Kane grins as he responds.

He watches me as he speaks with bright, clear eyes and I get the crazy idea that he's happy, which I hate only because it makes being angry super duper hard.

"What are you doing here?" My face burns. I can't remember ever having been half so embarrassed. "Get out of my room."

He and the red head exchange a confused look before Kane slips his hand around her upper arm. The emotion monster stomps on my chest, demanding feeling from me. It hurts and I can't fight it — not when it's made its nest inside of me.

"I believe this is *my* room, Abel," is all that Kane says.

I kick the leg of the dresser next to me and pain shoots up my leg. While I curse, the woman says something else, but Kane holds up his hand. He looks surprised and also… hopeful.

"Give me my shoes back and I'll go."

"Where will you go?" Kane takes a step towards me full of menace.

Panic! I turn towards the door, every intention of plunging blindly through it and running at the top speed that I can muster in these shoes. Ankles be damned.

But Kane's suddenly there, hand on the seam of the door, holding it closed while I pull with all my might. I glance around wildly for something I can bash him over the head with, but the gold candlestick is too far and the vase to my left is too heavy, judging by its looks.

I keep my hand on the knob, daring him to defy me, which he does. "Look at me," he whispers.

"No."

I do everything possible not to look at him, which is hard given that his current wardrobe includes boxers and nothing else. His heat hits me like a slap in the face while his chest radiates a calm, even glow. He even smells beautiful. Like cinnamon and blossoming moonflowers.

I turn my head to get rid of the sight of him even in my peripheries, but Kane slips his finger beneath my chin and with the easy pressure of his thumb and forefinger on my jaw, demands my attention.

My gaze snaps to his and I suck in my next breath. The muscles in my legs stiffen and my face lights up in heat and my little rat brain goes completely blank.

Is he...no...the alien...is...going...to...

Is he going to freaking kiss me?

Do I want him to kiss me? Hell no! Well, maybe it wouldn't hurt. I could do it for Ashlyn. Maybe, it would feel good. Maybe isn't good enough. Well, he's not going to let me out of the room until I do. Maybe I've got no choice in the matter. Maybe it's okay. Okay? Fuck it.

Kane brushes his lips over my lips very lightly, just enough to make my stomach clench. I...I haven't ever kissed a boy before. I don't know what to do with my hands. I'm not sure what to do with my feet. Should I be moving away? — sprinting with all I've got! — or should I be leaning into him?

My body makes the choice for me and I lean forward onto the balls of my feet as his tongue snakes past the barrier of my lips to press against mine gently. He's so, so gentle. It makes the emotion monster reel and cower. My knees lock to keep me standing. My arms dangle limp at my sides.

His lips are *soft*. They really don't have a right to be soft like this. But they're soft and at the same time, commanding. I feel a little afraid. I feel *very* afraid. His smell. The pressure. His fingers gently touching my face.

He pulls back before it's over.

Because it wasn't over. *Nothing* is the same, now. *Nothing* is finished between us.

I wobble and realize one of my hands is still stupidly welded to the doorknob. I grip the brass fiercely as Kane stands up to his full height and looks down at me while I bathe in his golden glow.

"Abel." Kane's voice is thicker when he speaks and I have the audacity to wonder, for just an instant, if he could possibly be *affected* by me.

"I wanted to introduce you to Tasha. She is one of my oldest friends and came to help us with our clothing for the gala tomorrow evening. She was taking my measurements when you interrupted us." Oh. Shiiiiiiit. That's what she was doing…

His eyes crinkle at the corners as he searches my gaze, reading my thoughts because I do absolutely nothing to hide them. "She will be tailoring your dress for the gala tomorrow evening." He takes his thumb and brushes it firmly across my left cheek.

"Uh huh." That's what I say? Uh huh? What is the matter with me?

Kane smirks. "Cat got your tongue?" he whispers.

I lick my lips. His chest seems to shine brighter as his gaze drops to my mouth. His hand stills. He's going to kiss me again and it'll probably shatter me into a thousand little pieces.

So I quickly say the first thing I can think of. "I ate a cat once."

"That is disgusting." The woman's voice clangs between Kane and I. He gives me a disparaging look, which is good, since grossed out is way better than heated.

"I don't have all day, Kane, and this is very last minute, so will you please let me fit your toy into her little outfit now?"

"Tasha," Kane grumbles under his breath.

"It's fine," I say quickly. "It's the truth of it."

I turn from him to face the alien lady who's giving me a weird look. "Hmph," she says, then she shakes her head. "Come."

I see Kane's hand flinch towards me out of the corner of my eye and quickly evade his grip. He's like glue or wet cement. Something that I won't be able to crawl out of if I get caught in it.

"I'll send Maggie up with dinner. Tasha, please see me when you're finished."

"I will," she says.

"Abel."

I don't dare turn around to face him. Like a petulant child, I shake my head.

"Look at me."

His voice gives me the chills. He isn't asking. I'm worried that if I don't look now, he might come closer to me and the emotion monster will swallow me whole in the end.

I turn and meet his gaze out of the corner of mine. His green eyes are fire. I'm charred from the inside. "I accept your apology."

I think about telling him that the kiss wasn't the apology and that I only apologized so he'd take Ashlyn in and that really, I don't mean it. I think about all those things...but I don't say any of them. "Okay."

Kane frowns, then rolls his eyes. "Impossible woman. This is not over between us."

"This?"

"Yes."

"I…" I lick my lips, knowing exactly what he means. "I don't know what you mean."

"Oh for the love of Sistylea, he means he intends to sleep with you."

"Tasha," Kane hisses, while I stutter wildly. "I…er…no, I don't…I'm not a sleeping…I mean, I don't sleep. I don't sleep ever."

And that's how I end my speech. I don't sleep ever. Clever idiot.

Tasha is just staring at me like I'm a moron while I hold tight to my opposite arms and squeeze my knees together. "You're sure this is the human female you were telling me so much about? Because it would seem that you grossly misrepresented her intelligence."

He was talking about me with her?

"Tasha, that's enough. Or do I need to send you to the human settlement to provide them with another series of sewing workshops?"

It's Tasha's turn to pout. "No. Once was enough."

"That's what I thought."

"I'll play nice with your special guest."

"I'd expect nothing less. Abel, we'll speak later." He doesn't wait for me to answer, but steps outside and closes the door softly behind him.

I exhale the breath I'd been safeguarding and plop down on the little bed at the foot of the bed. As if one wasn't enough for these people.

I don't realize Tasha's watching me until I look up and meet her expression with a surprised one of my own. She's watching me in a way that's invasive. Like I'm a bug she's trying to decide whether or not to squash.

"You are a tiny thing, aren't you?"

She keeps one long finger resting on her chin. Her eyes are narrowed.

"But you've got a nice figure. Wide hips, a decent set of shoulders. You're too thin, but I suppose that can't be helped at this stage." She strides towards me and the gown she wears flutters out behind her in varying shades of lavender.

"Stand up," she says when I don't automatically. She looks down the length of my body and rests her gaze on my feet unhappily. "With all that height and you're still a shrimpy thing. We'll have to find shoes more suitable for the gala, otherwise the dress I've imagined will never work."

"More suitable?" I say as she drags me by the arm to face the full-length mirror at the end of the room.

She moves the heavy leather ottoman in front of the mirror with one hand, then pulls me onto it. Even then, and with heels on, I'm still only barely taller than she is. She seems to recognize this as well and scoffs, "Absolutely. We can't have Kane waltzing with a mouse now can we? The shoes will have to be at least four inches higher."

"No."

"No?"

"No."

"What makes you think you have a say?"

"If you try to put me in shoes taller than these, I'll stab you in the eye with my stiletto."

"Colorful, but I don't think you will."

"You're right. I'll go barefoot."

She freezes with her mouth open, but she can't think of anything to say. Not so bad for a rat, huh? Her lips twitch and she goes back to measuring my wingspan and waist.

"No wonder he likes you." She shakes her head softly and a hint of a smile twists up the corners of her thin lips.

In the mirror's gaze, I see a shimmery pink spread between my cheeks, running across the bridge of my nose. I look younger than I did a second ago. More like Calvin, and less like Drago.

"I'm a human. He doesn't like me."

"You think Kane buys *my* dresses for every annoying, pint-sized human that waltzes through his front door?"

"I'm perfectly normal sized. You're the alien who's freakish tall."

This makes her smile outright. She rolls her eyes, then makes me strip down to my bra and underwear. "Good heavens," she gasps when she sees the bruises that cover most of me.

She says another word in her language, then, "I had hopes for a two-part dress with an open midriff, but I now see that this will be impossible." She pokes at a particularly nasty bruise on my stomach and I wince.

Sucking air in through my teeth, I say, "Do you mind?"

She finishes taking my measurements in silence. "I'll be back tomorrow to fit you for your gown. I've also given instructions to Lady on how I'd like your hair and makeup.

"And please, for the love of all that is good in this world, get rid of all that pesky body hair. You are not an animal. Oh, and no more fighting — for Kane's sake. I'm not sure he'll like his new treasure black and blue and bruised in the center."

She leaves before I get a chance to retaliate and just as she does, Maggie comes in with a plate of hot food that makes me forget my irritation. Did Kane plan this? He's good, I'll give him credit.

He's good at other things too.

I glance at the bedroom door, shit scared that all of a sudden it'll open and I'll see him walking through it. *This isn't over between us.* What is *it?* I don't want to find out, because if it feels anything like his kiss did, it has *power.*

Not carefully at all, I move the dresser kicking and screaming in front of the door, making sure to line up a few porcelain vases on top of it. I also close and lock the windows, draw the curtains and make sure to put some more porcelain and glass bobbles underneath those, too.

I slide into bed and as I sleep I dream of wolves hunting me in the forest. They're larger than average wolves too, with teeth like a saber-tooth's and vulture's talons.

I'm running as hard as I can, lungs jerking and arms pumping furiously, but no matter how hard or fast I sprint they're always there right behind me. Persistent, but without gaining on me either.

I know that if they do catch me I'll die, so I don't stop even though I can feel every muscle in my body screaming in rebellion. And then, as dreams go, my feet suddenly become so much heavier and when I look down I see that I'm wearing ten inch heels made of thorns.

I fight against them and try to kick them off without breaking stride, but the harder I pull, the more they shred my feet bloody.

A ditch appears up ahead and I jump to clear it, but the farther I jump, the wider the chasm becomes until I'm falling through sheets of ice and glass into pure darkness. Cold assaults me. I release a scream and call for help.

"Kane!" I say his name again and again, without meaning to.

Or maybe I do.

Heat breaks through the frost at my back and coils itself around me like a snake, and as the dream slowly fades I wake to the knowledge that he's in my bed, beneath the covers with me. I open my eyes but the world is black.

"Kane?" My voice trembles.

"Yes," comes his easy response, as if this is totally normal and my heart isn't about to leap into my stomach.

I'm too afraid to move, too afraid to get up, too afraid to turn him away. "Wh…what are you doing in here?"

"You called for me, didn't you?"

"No," I say.

He pauses. "Would you like me to leave?"

"How did you get in here?"

"The window. The door would have been a noisy option."

"But I didn't hear anything smash."

"This isn't the first time I've broken into your room in the night, Abel. The first time, I learned my lesson."

The stupid townhouse. "Ah." So...what now? I'm definitely too scared to ask him.

I feel him moving up onto his elbow behind me and can see his face in the glow of his chest. His eyes look like two sparks. I can't look away. Goosebumps break out over my every inch.

"You're cold." He rubs my right arm gently and after a moment, slides out of bed.

In the next second I hear the gas fireplace ignite and see the light of the low fire further illuminate his face and his bare chest. In only boxers, I gulp when he comes towards me, evident implication in his eyes as he comes at me over the sheets.

He looks hungry and in the quietness of the night, I finally admit it: I'm hungry too. Just a little bit. Just enough not to fight and not to scream bloody murder.

I lay on my back with my legs limp and my hands up by my face, fully exposed. I'm only wearing his boxers and tee shirt and right now that doesn't feel like enough.

His body hovers over mine for a moment and his green and gold eyes watch my face, seeking out something in my expression that I wonder if he's found.

His eyebrows pull together and he tilts his head, that one little superman curl flopping down in the center of his forehead.

"You're afraid."

I think about lying, then nod.

Kane's face softens as he sinks more of his weight onto me and collapses onto his elbows. He brushes my hair out of my face and plants the tenderest kiss in the center of my forehead.

"I've seen you slay monsters and lay waste to armies. You fought me when you had everything to lose. You burned a tree down in order to beat Drago when you were in it. None of those times were you ever afraid.

"But you're afraid of me now, here, when you know I won't hurt you?"

He's talking, but the warm imprint of his lips against my forehead speaks so much louder. It's deafening and unbearable. I feel like squirming, but I know that his weight on me like this will make me feel claustrophobic and that it will make everything so much worse because it'll be like back then, and this is nothing like back then.

This is good.

"I didn't mean to light the tree on fire," I whisper. "I mean, I meant to, but I didn't mean to be in it. I just…was stupid."

"Abel," he says, voice a little sterner. "I can't believe I'm having to say this, but tell me to leave if you want me to leave."

I shift on the sheets, but it doesn't feel claustrophobic, like I thought. Why doesn't it feel claustrophobic? "Wasn't the barricade a clear enough sign?" I say with a laugh that sounds as shaky as dead leaves in a dry wind.

His chest rumbles against me. He bows his head. "I need to hear you say it."

We're nose-to-nose now, our lips separated by a breath. I can taste him and he tastes good. Really good. I want to kiss him, but I don't want to embarrass myself.

"I've never done that before," I whisper, as soft as death.

Kane sucks in a little breath that only serves to humiliate me even more. His fingers comb through my hair very gently. It makes me unsure. I don't know what it feels like to feel good, so this is all unknown and overwhelming and scary and I feel guilty because Becks is gone and so is Ashlyn and here I am in an actual bed with food in my belly and the promise of good hovering over me and petting me like I'm adored.

Like I'm beloved.

"Would you like me to kiss you again, Abel?"

I don't answer because the emotion monster is sitting on my face, squeezing my eyeballs and making everything shake.

I shake my head, but as he starts to shift off of me, I reach up and lock my fingers together around the back of his neck.

"I don't want to embarrass myself."

I'm honest with him in this lonely darkness that seems so full of consequences that I can't discern their danger level except to say that *I am in danger* if the emotion monster decides to linger. And that seems to be its intent.

Kane exhales his next breath onto my lips. They taste like rain. Like how rain used to taste before the grey took and ruined that too. "There is no risk of that, Abel."

"Okay." My word is a garbled half-laugh.

Kane strokes his thumb down my cheek, over my jaw, and massages my neck. He tilts my face up to his and leans in towards me, then kisses me for the second time.

His lips are so, so gentle as they nip and pull at my upper, then my lower lip. He concentrates there, running his tongue across it, heating me up from the inside. He pushes my hands down into the soft mattress and tangles his fingers with mine.

"Relax," he says between little nibbles and dammit, if I don't try, but it's impossible.

The fire in my mouth has moved down to my stomach, and then further south still. My thighs are clenching together in little pulses, and I can feel my body fighting as a sharp pressure in the juncture between my legs builds.

Meanwhile, his mouth continues gently coaxing mine into some form of submission and submission isn't something I do well. I realize that if I'm going to survive this, I might need to do what I do best: fight to the end.

I open my mouth and his body shifts above mine, like he's surprised, when I start to kiss him back.

I don't totally know what I'm doing, but I emulate his movements — biting, sucking, puckering and releasing with my lips, then the dangerous dance he plays with his tongue.

I trace the line of his lips with my tongue before pushing past his teeth and plundering his mouth. He groans above me, moaning in a way that makes me flinch because it isn't a sound a man has ever made around me.

My pulse picks up as he pulls back just enough to growl my name against my lips. Whatever restraint he'd been showing before seems to be unraveling faster now as his hand slips behind my neck. He angles my face even further back so that I'm at his total mercy. His other hand drifts down my body, slides behind my back and scoops up my pelvis.

He lifts and I gasp at the sensation of his hard erection at the warm space between my legs. He's moving faster now, frantically almost. It's gotten to the point that I'm very aware that when it comes to Kane and his ability to please, I've only just scratched the surface.

My left foot starts shaking involuntarily as he crushes his mouth to mine and feasts. He holds me down, holds my hair back, touches every part of me.

I fight to keep up, but I'm quickly overwhelmed, overpowered, over...overeverythinged. I feel like I'm falling, but there's nowhere to go. I feel like I'm drowning, both in an intense pleasure unlike anything I've ever felt before, and in memories that cut the pleasure down and make it hard to stay in this moment.

He starts to lift my shirt and I flinch at the sensation of his heavy hand against my bare stomach. I free my trapped fingers from his grip and I rake my nails down his back. Because I like it? Because I don't? I don't know.

I just want him to kiss me.

I just want him to stay away from me.

"Abel, are you alright?" He's panting — shaking even, or maybe that's just me. Am I shaking? Am I alright? My lips feel swollen and my thighs are tingling and there's a cramping in my gut where I want his body to be.

I nod feverishly and stroke the side of his face with my fingertips, trying to be gentle like the way he was gentle with me.

His eyes unfocus and he starts to lean back down to kiss me, but he rears up and back and shakes his head, like something's got a hold of him and he's trying to break free.

"You aren't fine. You're frozen and shaking like a leaf."

I pull on his neck, trying to bring him back, but he resists and that's bad because if he resists much more, the spell will be broken and this will end and he won't want to do it again and worse, he might even want to *talk* about it.

I lift up and bite down on his earlobe. I didn't even know that would do anything, but it seems to have the desired effect, because his elbow buckles and he's all over me again.

"Abel," he growls as I work my way down his neck, kissing and biting and tasting the salt on his skin. He tastes so reassuring and I know I could taste him for hours, until he does the one thing I hoped he would…and also, would never do.

He slides one knee between my legs…and then the other…and when he sinks lower onto me, he spreads me open underneath him.

I resist. I resist *hard* but it makes no difference. My stomach jumps up into my throat and even though there's still heat there, it's not the right kind. It feels like needles. It feels like pins.

My hands that were on his body press against his shoulders violently now, but I'm shaking too bad to have any real effect. I close my eyes and my head rips to the side. I feel panicked as he slides between my thighs, but he doesn't enter.

"Abel, look at me," he says, and the fire is gone from his tone. Instead, he sounds all full of worry and when I look up at him all I see is that concern radiating down from his gaze, which looks tortured by something small, something angry, something beautiful.

I find that I can't speak, so I don't even try. It's like my throat has sealed itself up for good. Pleading the Fifth on my own behalf. I feel all the early warning signs of an anxiety attack ready to overwhelm me, but I can see the solid pulsing of his chest and I cling to that serenity in an attempt to keep my own heartbeat from running away like that frightened rabbit I caught in the woods.

Caught and devoured.

A memory revisits me, and it isn't a good one. I block it from conscious thought and focus instead on the shape of his eyes and their color, the feel of his hard shoulders beneath my fingertips.

He lowers himself down onto his elbows so that his face is very close to mine and our bare bellies touch beneath my scrunched up shirt. I'm breathing hard, but he moves slowly and in a way that is careful and deliberate.

He brushes the stray curls back behind my ears, licks his lips and says very softly, "Tell me what happened to you."

"Nothing." My voice is a strangled yelp. Not a lick of confidence in sight. Confidence? What's that look like anyway when you don't have a sword in your hand or the will to fight?

He says nothing, but I see his jaw harden in a way that spells murder. And then his eyes close. He looks like he's steeped in some kind of argument with himself. Or like he's fighting a battle with an unknown opponent — an opponent that only *I* know, and that I have no desire to bring back to life.

"You were assaulted."

I shake my head quickly. "No. No, I wasn't."

I try to squirm out from under him, but he doesn't let me. "Shh." He kisses my forehead, anger gone from both his tone and touch. He presses his warm lips to each of my eyelids, to my chin, and to my nose.

"Sex can be aggressive."

He kisses my neck so tenderly I'm lost to the emotion monster now. The pain behind my eyes manifests into real tears that I've denied for years.

He kisses the little droplets that slip down my cheeks and says, "But there are other ways."

His voice is soft, lips even softer as they trace delicate patterns over my face, down my neck, between my breasts through my tee shirt. He pushes my shirt up to my ribs so he can kiss his way down my bruises. They don't hurt when he kisses them. They should hurt, but they don't.

I exhale and it feels like the ghost of the person I once was floats up and out of me, excised like a demon.

I'm reborn as Abel in his arms.

I gasp as he moves lower, over my belly button to my hips. His tongue is pure fire as he licks a line between my slightly-too-prominent hip bones. His tongue leaves fire wherever it touches. Wet fire that makes my toes curl.

I'm *relaxed* when he starts to tug my boxers down. So relaxed it's hard to compute what he's doing.

"Kane," I say, brain short-circuiting.

And then he does something wonderful with his mouth. He presses the whole thing over my core and breathes hot air through the thin barrier of my boxer shorts. I come alive.

My back arches. I think I hear three joints in my right shoulder pop. My mouth opens. I cry out in a language I didn't even know I spoke.

A quiet laugh, one that's fully mocking, slips from Kane's throat. I'm not even sure I was meant to hear it, but that laugh is what does it.

It's so him.

It's so *normal.*

This isn't a grocery store aisle where I'm separated from my brother and he's killed while I'm defiled. This is *Kane.* The monster who came for me in the townhouse, and again in the tree house. He didn't hurt me. He *never* hurt me. He took a bullet for me, killed a gang for me, carried a tree for me, and then took me home and took me to bed.

I spread my legs wider and he releases a low growl. It sounds appreciative. He nuzzles his nose into the soft flesh of my upper inner thigh. I didn't realize skin could be so sensitive. My right knee kicks when he bites down softly.

"You're going to need to put your legs together if you want me to take these off."

"I…" My mouth is dry. My cheeks are wet.

He answers the question I didn't ask him yet. "This won't hurt."

"It won't?" I'm speaking in a tone I've never heard before. I sound a decade younger than I am. I feel so unsure.

"No. And if you want me to stop at any point, all you have to do is say it, pull my hair, get my attention in any way you want. Do you want me to stop?"

I don't hesitate, but slide my legs closed and let him inch my boxers down just a little bit at a time until my lower half is fully exposed to him.

For a moment nothing happens and in my chest, I feel little bursts of panic. "Kane?"

"Sorry. I just…you are incandescent."

I hack out a laugh. It helps ease the ache that he's freeing from my soul. "My vagina?"

"Yes," he says, laughing with me in that light, honest way he does. "That too. But I meant your vulnerability. Seeing you open for me like this. I would never exploit this."

Emotions, emotions, emotions! The monster chomps through my flesh and licks my bones clean. I'm done. I'm so done.

I mean to tell him that he better not. That we're on dangerous ground. That I've never felt anything like this and I'm not really…capable of processing it. That I have the emotional fortitude of a clam. That this doesn't end well for me, no matter how it ends…

I mean to tell him all these things, but the little, fragile weirdo that lives in my chest that Kane's somehow drawn out, says, "You…you'll take care of me?"

I glance down and see him lying in between my legs, my knees draped over his shoulders, his mouth inches from that very sensitive bit of me.

It's too much. I look away, throwing my head back into the pillows and blankets.

Because even in the precarious position I'm in, nothing could have had the ability to throw me like his gaze. I have to black it out and block it out. But I can't ignore the way he shivers. *Shivers.* What does that mean? Do I want to know?

No. I definitely don't want to know.

His lips brush my lower lips and I tingle all over as he says, "I won't let you down, Abel."

I won't let you down, Abel.

I'm lost to the sentiment until his mouth closes over my core and his tongue presses against my clit and it's hot like an ember that turns the rest of me to ash.

I crash as he uses that expert mouth of his on a part of me I never expected to receive such…attention.

My whole body breaks out in heat and sweat. My hands fist the sheets. My back arches and my hips buck. He has to hold me still enough to kiss me there, but he still lets me move the way I want. He lifts my hips so that they're higher than my head and I feel all the blood rush every whichaway.

I don't know what to expect…didn't know…but it wasn't this.

"Kane," I cry out in a panic.

He slows and I feel my fever break just enough for me to be able to blink my eyes open. "Are you alright?"

I nod quickly. I'm more than alright, I'm just…climbing and I'm afraid of what I'll find when I reach the top. "Is this…right?"

Kane laughs against my clit again, then blows air on the insides of my thighs. They're damp. Everything is damp, and it's not from his mouth. It's from *me*. I'm wet somehow. Did I pee?

"Yes, so long as you feel safe, everything is right."

"I feel safe," I somehow manage to stutter. I even manage to lift my head again even though my chest is rising and falling like a wave. "But I feel like I'm going to explode."

Kane's expression changes. He clenches his back teeth and closes his eyes again. He fights another battle and it's only when he comes out victorious that he opens them. I gasp at how charged they are...but I don't retreat. Not this time.

"The point is for you to explode. For me to make you."

"And it won't hurt?" Explosions, in my experience, hurt.

"Trust me, Abel."

I don't answer. I just hang there on the cusp of this ledge, unable to pull myself up, unwilling to let myself plummet to my own death.

Then he says softly, "The path to trust if forged in faith. Believe in me, Abel. I won't let you down. Not in this. Not ever."

I don't know if it's his words or if it's the soft little kisses he's peppering up and down the insides of my thighs, but I fall back on a whisper, "Alright."

It's not exactly a *yes*, but it's not a *no* either. And that's likely the best he'll get from me right now while I'm on this path with no ending.

"Abel," he whispers, and that's the last warning I get before he descends on me.

Ruthless.

That's not a word I would have used to describe Kane — except on the battlefield — but it's the word that comes to me now along with one other...

Ruthless and reverent.

He devours me, tongue snaking inside me, fingers... He touches me down there and spreads me even wider before slipping one finger inside my body and pumping that digit in and out.

And while he works me over, I keep climbing. I resist as much as I can, but it's like the story my dad told me once about the guy carrying the boulder up the hill. He keeps sliding back, like I keep sliding back.

There's no pushing that boulder. The emotion monster's already escaped out from under it and it wants its revenge. It's coming for my body. Maybe my soul too. Maybe the thing that pumps blood through my chest.

Kane's tongue or whatever hot wet thing is on my clit starts to suck and a second finger joins the first inside my body and I've never *felt* so much.

I want to ask Kane if this is it — have I crested the summit? But the answer is clear as the explosion ricochets through me and tears my whole body apart.

I explode, just as explosions do, but he's right. It doesn't hurt. Not even close.

My legs kick and my hips twitch and the tee shirt I'm wearing feels suddenly so heavy and scratchy on my breasts. I reach up and grab my tits and my *god* they're so freaking sensitive. I touch my own throat. I've never felt like this. I don't want it to end.

"Kane," I say and this voice is definitely not one I've heard before. Hell, for a second I think there might be another woman in the room. I sound sultry and successfully seduced as the pleasure wreaking havoc through me starts to abate and eventually, I come down the mountain.

No, I'm *carried* down the mountain in Kane's arms, against his chest.

I know people call it coming, but to me it's more than that. *I arrive.* I feel present now, possibly for the first time, and grounded to the earth. To that mountain.

When I open my eyes, I see the ceiling. It's dark, but it's not the scary kind of darkness. I didn't know there was another kind. Darkness usually means grey and damp and danger.

And while things are definitely slick below my waist — there's a damn puddle of water under my butt by now — I'm not afraid.

Kane drags a finger up from my *back* hole through my wet slit, up over my clit and into the small mane of dark fur that encroaches on it. I shudder involuntarily, shocked that he can work my body like this and there's nothing I can do to stop him — worse, that I would willingly let him do it to me again.

I try to sit up, but Kane's hovering over me, brushing back my hair. He drops onto his side next to me and I rotate onto mine so I can touch him. I should be touching him, right? I had my explosion, but nothing so far has happened to him. Can I make him explode too? I don't know. I feel sluggish and confused.

I reach for the bulging mass at the front of his boxer shorts while the sweat between my shoulder blades turns to ice. I'm so lost right now. He's smiling slightly, but stops my hand as it brushes the mound between his hips.

Momentary shame washes over me. "You don't want…" I can't even finish, and flush on a cause of it. Here I am, a short, skinny human with an anger problem and solid right hook, but completely stupid when it comes to sex.

He just gives me another warm smile, and manages to look smolderingly satisfied even though he hasn't even… gotten any himself.

"Of course I do," he says. He touches my earlobe in a way that makes the nerves at the base of my spine tingle. Then he brushes my hair behind my ear and lays down beneath the blankets. He gestures for me to do the same.

I feel awkward crushing myself to his side, so I don't even though I want to. Instead I just lay there stiff. He laughs that mocking laugh, but considering the fact that he's the reason the insides of my thighs are still wet and pulsing, I let him get away with it. Just this once.

Kane turns to face me and I do the same to him. Everything seems so conspiratorial in the flickering orange light of the fire and the golden glow of his chest. It keeps pulsing evenly. Thump…thump…thump…

I reach out and touch the place above his heart tentatively. After a few seconds, I start to pull back, but he lays his hand over mine and draws me close.

"Did I let you down?"

I feel so hot at the question — and not just in my cheeks, but down there, too. *I want more.*

I shake my head. "Why did you…" I clear my throat and struggle to find words appropriate enough to describe how I feel, but there aren't any. I've never felt so hopelessly lost, grateful, full and simultaneously inadequate.

When he sighs, he sinks further into the pillows beneath him and I sink into the crater his body creates. He opens his arms to me and I don't know why he does it — why he thinks I deserve it. Or maybe he does it with all his humans.

"Because," he starts and I'm surprised when he doesn't say anything else. He's a being with a true command of words and emotions and everything he freaking touches. He should be able to offer me an explanation for this.

"Kane?"

"Did you enjoy it?" he says and he sounds momentarily annoyed.

I don't understand, but I don't want to ruin this. I nod.

"Then the rest does not matter."

I nod again. He touches my cheek.

"Thank you," I whisper.

"My pleasure."

He touches my hair, and then slides his hand down the length of my body until he reaches the dip in my waist. It feels silly, still having his tee shirt on.

"Will you tell me what happened to you?" he says.

I cast my gaze to the side and right now, after the gift he just threw in my lap, I see no point in withholding the truth.

Fuck the rules.

I shrug. "There's not much to tell. Me, Becks and her husband went to a grocery store. We were four at the time. I lied before. My brother…he was with us. We got overtaken by a gang. We all made a stand so Becks could run — she was pregnant with Ashlyn at the time.

"They killed my brother and Matt. They wanted to use me to trade with another gang, but first one of the guys wanted a test drive.

"The rest of the story you already know." I exhale, close my eyes, find some sort of release. "I don't know what came over me, but all those men died. I think that was the first time I unleashed the monster that lives in me."

Kane grumbles low and in a way that's hardly intelligible, "Please tell me that it was recent. That you were not a child."

"I was sixteen."

Kane closes his eyes again as he reenters that battle. I wish I could see what goes on there…the adversaries he imagines. Veins bulging in his forehead and his corded neck are the only signs of life for a full minute.

Then he exhales, "Thank you for telling me. I am sorry, Abel. Deeply so."

"You didn't do anything."

His jaw ticks. His hand on my cheek flinches and he draws it back into his chest. "I let you down."

I balk. "You didn't even know me then."

"It doesn't matter." His voice is ice cold and not open to discussion, so I don't try. I'm too warm to try anyway. Sleepy, too.

My eyes start to shut until Kane says, "What was your brother's name?"

"Aiden."

The moment I say his name out loud, a small weight lifts from my chest. Somehow, through it all, I always blamed myself for their deaths.

"That's madness," Kane says and again, I've spoken out loud.

I offer Kane a small smile that seems totally inappropriate for the topic at hand, but it feels right. Good.

"I know," I exhale. "Saying it out loud sounds crazy, but I've never said it out loud before."

"You carried too much."

Kane's lips part and I long to taste them again. See what I taste like on them. The thought stirs me and I glance back to his boxers, wishing…but I'm too shy right now. At least for the first time, I need him to guide me.

"Everyone in Population carries too much." The weight of ghosts.

Kane's jaw clenches again and that vein pop, pop, pops. He wraps his arm around my head then, and drags my whole body into the cavern of his chest. He holds me like this. Just holds me against his heart.

"Goddammit, I wish I'd found you sooner," he growls into my hair before he kisses the top of my head. "And Aiden, and Becks and Ashlyn and Matt."

The emotion monster that owns me now goes and plays the bongos on my head. "Aiden," I whisper, closing my eyes as tears come. "I wish you'd found us too, or that we found you. Then Ashlyn wouldn't be…"

"If she is alive, I swear to you we will recover her. I will not fail you twice."

"Fail me?" I look up into his face while he looks down into mine. "You never failed me once."

"That's not what it feels like."

I part my lips, but I don't have an answer. Who am I to tell him what his emotion monster looks like? So instead, I just bow my head and lean back into the embrace of his arms, coming closer to him than I've ever been to another living person.

I dare myself to ask him if this is just a once off, and if he's got another girl, or two or ten, or if this is all part of the tithe and he's got a whole retinue of lines he uses to make soft, broken girls feel good about themselves…

I'm lucky that he speaks first.

"Aiden," Kane repeats. Silence simmers between us for another breath. Then Kane says, "I had a brother as well. His name was Mikael."

"What happened to him?"

Kane closes his eyes and inhales deeply once and then again. "He's dead."

Kane exhales as he reaches for me, and his hands and arms have softened just enough for me to believe he has a better control of his rage than I ever could. He turns me over, and I press my back to his chest and let him pull me close, close, closer.

I like the feeling of his warm arms around me, and though I know it goes against the rule book, I still feel an unfamiliar sense of safety when he breathes into my hair, "You know that nothing like that will ever happen to you again."

"You can't know the future."

"I know what is within the realm of my control, and keeping you safe is one of those things. I will keep you safe." His voice is thick with rage and I recognize the tone again that says that this is not up for discussion.

I yawn and feel about a ton lighter than I did as I selfishly shift the weight of my own traumas off of my shoulders and onto his. Or maybe not onto him, but I at least spread them out in the open. *Aiden.* He was a good man. A good kid. And he died as any of us Population rats should hope to — fighting for the people we love.

Love. It's a strange word I haven't considered for a long time. A word that, in Population, is among the forbidden.

"Kane?" I say as sleep comes for me.

"Yes?"

"I'll keep you safe, too."

He laughs lightly and the last thing I feel are his arms strapped across my chest and waist and his warm breath on my earlobe.

"I know," he whispers. "I know."

Chapter Eight

K ane isn't there when I wake up and I have an unfortunate case of déjà vu. It's so bad, I actually expect to find a note on the bedside table and am only a touch relieved when I don't. I'm even more relived when he comes back.

With food.

He eats breakfast with me. He seems to find the foods I like and don't like fascinating in a way that makes me feel self-conscious because I'm pretty sure he listens to me chew and makes mental notes in that giant head of his about the weird things that humans do. Or that I do.

He also has me blushing every other second because despite how hard I try, I can't forget the feeling of his lips between my legs. I want to feel them again. I want to return the favor, and then explore the rest of him.

As such, I'm nearly grateful when Calvin comes to me mid-morning and asks if I'd like one last dance lesson. I accept as a way to escape even if it means tottering awkwardly around in the torture contraptions Tasha picks out for me.

Dance practice ends just after lunch when a younger woman named Lady and another woman named Lanis shepherd me back to my room. They soak me in fiery hot water, scrub, buff and paint my nails and toes. They wax every last inch of hair off of my body while I protest in rebellion, lather me up in lotion and fit me into particularly skimpy lingerie that has *Tasha* written all over it.

Seated in front of the vanity in only a satin robe, I fidget uncomfortably while the two women — clearly twins — work tirelessly at my hair and makeup. Lady cuts my hair into a bob that tapers in the front to frame my face, then Lanis blow dries it. They scrunch up the curls until they're perfectly springy, before finally twisting and tying my hair up into the most incredible contraption.

When they finish, it looks like I'm wearing a crown, though the crown itself is a fluid braid. Curls flutter out to touch my hairline and a few drape down the length of my neck. I nearly choke to death in a cloud of hairspray before Lanis finally stuffs about a thousand pins in my hair to keep everything stable.

Wow. What a ridiculous ceremony. I'm going to look totally ridiculous fighting anybody in this…though I guess, I'm not really meant to. I harrumph at that.

The makeup portion of the evening takes another billion hours and has to be applied and then reapplied half a dozen times in order to fit Tasha's specifications just right.

Lady uses silver and black makeup around my eyes and silver blush high on my cheeks. The foundation they use matches my skin tone perfectly and successfully conceals all my war wounds. Or nearly.

Just as they conclude by applying dark, blood red lipstick to my mouth, Maggie walks into my — Kane's — bedroom with Tasha's dress. My jaw drops.

Working together, the three ladies manage to wriggle me into the thing, though the twins have to hold me upright and support most of my weight when Maggie fits my feet into nine-inch platform sandals.

I realize that Tasha *tried* to compromise. Even though they're higher than the last set of shoes were, they aren't stilettos and I can walk in these a bit easier.

"Hey, Abel, I just wanted to see you off and say good…" Calvin steps into the room just as I'm standing up in front of the mirror giving myself a critical look.

I turn when Calvin stops talking and see that his face has turned bright red. "That bad, huh?" I start to sweat. Shit! I can't be sweating. I'll smell like shit before we even get there.

Calvin gulps. "You look incredible."

"Ugh. Great."

I frown at the dress in the mirror. The bodice is tight, black velvet and, with the help of the slutty lingerie, pushes my boobs up to my chin. The sluttiness is curbed slightly by the sleeves, which are long and tight — likely to hide more bruising — and by a veil-like-cape thingie that stretches up from the floor up to my shoulder blades.

"No really, you look amazing," Calvin tries, but I wave him off.

"Yeah, yeah, yeah."

He turns to leave, but his gaze is pinned on me and he trips over one of the chairs Lanis had been using and goes sprawling.

"Get out of here!" I'm laughing now. "Before you hurt yourself."

Still bright red, Calvin shoots me a goofy smile and high-tails it out of the room. The door closes behind him, but is opened again a second later and Kane appears in his place.

Kane moves into the room and freezes.

"Master Kane, you look resplendent this evening," Lady says, holding out her skirts to curtsey. He might not be a *total* ass hole but seeing a human bow to him still sort of makes me wanna gag.

Mockingly, I bow, too. "Oh Master Kane, how exquisite you look on this fine hour."

It might have been funnier if I hadn't slipped off the ottoman. Maggie and Lanis catch my either arm and help me to the ground while blood rushes to my head.

I think Kane might have gone spontaneously deaf because he doesn't respond to my jeers or to the other ladies' actual compliments. Instead he barks so loud it makes me flinch, "Ladies, leave us."

The women slip out into the hallway amidst laughter that doesn't make me feel good at all. Kane and I are alone and they were right — he does look hot — and there's a bed... and right now the only thing on my mind is the fact that he and I didn't finish what we started...

"Erm...You clean up well," I say, though isn't that the understatement of the century.

Kane's black tuxedo is perfectly tailored to fit his broad form, and silver details match my dress. The shirt beneath his tuxedo is made out of a strange matte material, thin enough to see the glowing pulse of his chest through.

I understand that Tasha must have specifically engineered this shirt to react in this way, and again I can't help but be impressed by the woman.

I lift my gaze from his glowing pecs up to his black hair, which has evidently been cut, washed and styled, as it rolls in onyx waves away from his face and also brings out the darkness of his eyebrows. His bowtie looks to be made from the same shimmery black material that my cape is, because it glitters ever so subtly when the light catches it. Still, he says nothing.

"Kane, you're freaking me out. Say something."

Kane's gaze drops to the floor. He shakes his head. "Forgive me, I..."

"What — cat got your tongue?"

"Precisely." He sighs out of the corner of his mouth and runs his hand back through his hair. "And I've never even eaten cat."

That superman curl flops down into the center of his forehead and I fight the urge to brush it away from his face. "I came here to give you this."

He moves towards me and holds a black velvet box between us. He opens it when I don't. Nestled there against cobalt-colored fabric are a pair of silver earrings.

"Thoughts?" he says when I don't say anything at all.

I don't know what to say. "They're gonna mess up my ears in a fight."

Kane rolls his eyes. "Luckily your ears aren't pierced, and these clip on."

"Oh, well in that case, they're beautiful."

Kane laughs and helps me put them on since I have no idea how. As he does, he says, "They were my mother's."

"Shit! You can't tell me stuff like that. What if I lose them?"

"Shh, Abel." He pinches my chin, leans in like he'll kiss me, then at the last second kisses my cheek. "It's just a thing."

"But it's a special thing, and I'm not all that responsible. They're precious to you."

He looks into my left eye, and then into my right. He doesn't look again at the earrings. His attention shifts down then to my breasts and I almost jump straight out of my dress when he cups my right tit and squeezes. That wetness I felt yesterday surges out onto my panties and I immediately shift my weight between my hips.

I gasp. Kane hisses. He wrenches his hand back and clenches his front teeth together. "Tonight is going to be more difficult than I imagined."

"Why?"

"I want you and I don't want to share you."

"Share me?" My palms get hot and clammy. "I don't want you to share me."

"Your goal for tonight is to attract Memnoch's attention. It won't be difficult. He and I share a sordid history and he will want to steal you from me when he sees my interest. It is not something I will be able to hide," he snarls.

"But I find myself loathe to allow him to look at you, let alone *touch* you." He spits out the word, starts to pace away from me, then paces back and stops.

"And then the next phase of the plan..." His eyes flare white hot and I waver back. Strange, that I never thought to ask him about the plan. Then again, I don't really ever plan anything. I'm more of a fly-by-the-seat-of-your-pants kinda gal. That he's been making plans this whole time to help me, is something I find even more touching than the earrings I'm wearing. At least, just as touching.

"What's the next phase?"

"You will need to make him like you enough that he offers you an invitation to his home. Once he does, you'll need to go there, *alone* and find your sister."

He rubs his face roughly and does that pacing thing again that's definitely freaking me out.

"That sounds easy."

"Easy for you. I don't know how I'm supposed to be able to bear letting you into his home unprotected."

"I...you..." He's on dangerous ground. It sounds way, way too much like he *cares* in that awful way that Population only punishes you for.

I clear my throat and grab hold of the wheel before he derails us completely. "Thank you, Kane, for planning and organizing all this. I don't know how I'll ever repay you."

His eyes flash. He still looks like murder. Only now, he looks like he's ready for two different kinds of battle. The kind he fights with me at his side, and the other kind he fights with me between his bed sheets.

I suck in a hard breath, ready now for either.

"Thank me when you have your sister." He shakes his head and ruffles his hair. I step up to him and he stills when I reach up and run my fingers through it, combing it back.

Standing so close to him, I feel…calm. It's a nice feeling. Kane's looking at me like he's trying to memorize my face, but right now, it feels like there's nothing bad in the world. Like nothing can hurt me. Or either of us.

"Let me see your throat."

My hands still on the lapel of his suit jacket. "Uhm, what?"

Kane pulls a scalpel from his inside jacket pocket and I hate that my immediate reaction isn't to defend myself. I'm *curious*. Already, I have too much confidence in him. Just because he licked my…

"You are my *human* escort. It is presumed that human escorts also serve an invaluable function as…"

"The meal."

He looks at me sternly, but in his eyes I see a quiet hesitation. "I need to mark you."

"Golly. Sounds like a fun time."

"It can be." Kane smirks. "Depending on where you're marked."

I don't have any idea what he's talking about, but that doesn't seem to matter to my body because the molten lava in my gut erupts in little splashes. The seat of my dress is going to be soaked through before we even get to the gala if he keeps this up.

I hold out my wrists. "Cut away."

He shakes his head and reaches for my throat. "I will make the incision along your jugular."

"Why there? Why not on my arm or someplace else less visible?"

Kane cocks his eyebrow. This time it's his turn to look skeptical. "You're concerned about scars *now*?"

I smile and sigh, "Just wondering…" I turn my head to the side and wait for the sting.

"I could cut your wrist or the inside of your upper thigh, but each cut carries a different meaning." He places the steel against the side of my neck and I clench my perfectly manicured nails into my palms.

"Oh?"

He nods. "To only have your inner thigh cut implies that you are a whore. That the Heztoichen who feed from you take blood and body in equal measure." I shudder, remembering Candy and the bloody spots on her dress. Drago was such a bastard. He deserved his beheading.

"If I cut your wrist, it's to suggest that you are nothing but a blood bag to be served at restaurants like a bottle of wine. But those that have cuts marking their necks..." He draws a line down the side of my neck with his finger that makes me shiver.

"They are the ones who the Heztoichen have selected. There is a certain prestige in having your throat cut. It suggests that you are intimate with and respected by the one who cut you. Very few humans can boast of these marks."

"Candy had all the marks. What does that mean?"

"Who?"

"Candy," I repeat. "One of Drago's wives?"

Kane shakes his head slowly, jaw angrily set. "Drago is not one of us." He brings the scalpel down just as I open my mouth to argue, but the sting of it quiets me. A slight pain pricks me but what's weird is that Kane hisses louder than I do, like he's been cut himself.

Quickly, he presses a handkerchief to the wound and tells me to hold it in place, then he moves as far away from me as the confines of the room allow. He reaches the door and when he takes the doorknob in his fist like he's hungry for a quick escape, I think that he might just take it. But he stops, and when he turns to the scalpel in his left hand, like it's speaking to him in more than just words, I realize that he's actually hungry for something else.

Kane holds the steel at eye-level and watches it with crazy eyes. It looks like he's having one of those internal battles again — one that he's about to lose.

And then in a sudden, sharp movement, Kane passes the blade, which is dotted in only a faint shimmer of my blood, across his tongue. He licks it clean.

I'm too surprised and weirdly turned on to react at all, especially when he staggers back and drops the blade so that it lands point down. He doesn't bend to retrieve it.

Instead, he clenches his fists so fiercely that his knuckles turn white and the muscles in his arms and neck ripple violently. His eyes close and he breathes in and out slowly through his mouth, like he's concentrating very hard on something.

"Kane?" I whisper in a hushed voice.

Silence.

"Kane?" When I take a tentative step towards him, his eyes fly open.

"Are you alright?" He asks, voice dripping with a genuine concern that makes me feel like he just planned and executed my murder in his head and is surprised to still see me standing.

I nod, mute.

He exhales, grins ravenously, and exhales again. "Has the bleeding stopped?"

"I...I think so." I step back to the mirror and lift the cloth away from my throat. The skin is red and slightly inflamed but I don't see fresh blood. I wipe away what's dried and use a dab of water to clear away the rest. What's left behind is a bright red strip, about three inches long, against the side of my neck. I frown at it.

"So much for looking perfect."

"Trust me. You do. Unquestioningly." From the doorway, he lifts his hand and beckons me forward. "Shall we?"

I walk to his side and when I take his arm, I see that I come up to his chin, rather than his chest. Guess I've got

Tasha to thank. I exhale insecurity and inhale strength as we move from the bedroom. About two dozen residents have crowded in the main entryway to see us off. They gasp and ooh and awe, much to my chagrin.

Kane encourages me by telling me that there will be much more like this, and much worse. Adrenaline flows through me in rushes, and this time when I climb into the back of his car in my stupid shoes, I don't stumble.

A human man I don't know drives while Kane and I sit in the converted back seat of a black Hummer, which is made to be like a limo. Kane faces me and I face forward. As we drive, Kane reminds me that the Heztoichen have exceptional hearing and that I shouldn't talk to him until he tells me it's okay, likely on the drive home. Otherwise, I should write down anything urgent I have to say on paper.

He keeps a pad and pen tucked in his breast pocket and after about thirty minutes of driving, Kane doesn't say anything anymore. Instead, he just stares at me while I squirm under the weight of his gaze. I can't really look out of the car, because of the tinted windows, so I close my eyes for a while. When I open them, he's still staring. It's mad spooky.

The gala is hosted in a house like Kane's, though it's somehow even larger. A human in an all-black uniform opens our door and the attendant offers me his hand. I take it and when he helps me out of the car, I trip for the first time that evening and practically throw myself all over him to keep myself upright.

The guy garbles out an apology and kind of screams? Either way he struggles to put me on my feet and when he steps back and looks at me, he stills. Spooky as hell.

He doesn't even seem to see Kane until Kane speaks to him directly. "I have it from here," Kane snarls, snatching my fingers from the attendant's.

"What was that about?" I say.

Kane snarls, but doesn't bother to answer.

The mansion doors are two wide archways that join together like McDonald's golden M, only these are stone and engraved with grotesques. I fight not to make a face as we pass beneath their dark stares into a world of light.

The foyer is massive with vaulted ceilings and a crystal chandelier dripping towards a sea of alien guests. There must be dozens — possibly hundreds — of aliens here. My spooky meter has just hit the ceiling and I stumble again as I take it all in.

Kane looks down at me with slanted eyes and smiles and I realize I should be smiling too. I try the fake mask he's got on, but I've never done this before, so I can't imagine how awful it looks.

Kane, beside me, chuckles a little under his breath.

I should be terrified. I should be shitting my pants. I'm surrounded by the enemy. Completely surrounded. But…I feel nothing but safe. Curious, and safe. I don't have to wonder why, or what changed.

Countless faces peer at Kane from between the folds and I notice that chatter gets quieter where we walk.

"Notare," a voice cries and suddenly eight or nine Others are moving towards us, human escorts tucked against their sides or trailing ever so slightly behind them.

Kane tilts his head towards the woman, who responds with a full bow. Her male companion is a good looking human dude, and shockingly only a few inches shorter than she is. He bows as well, and stands only after she does. His eyes touch mine but they don't linger.

"How positively enchanting to meet you again, Notare," the woman says, taking his hand in her two. "I am Rivonia. We had the pleasure of meeting several times last year at the Convening of Counselors. I am your fifth Sheriff of the eastern province."

"Of course Rivonia, I haven't forgotten. We rely on your humans for your grain harvest. How is the crop yield this season?"

They talk about food for the next thirty hours while I waste away inside, trying to stay interested. Then the next thirty hours they talk about some Notare called Tanen and problems he's having in his territory. Or maybe he's creating the problems? I don't know. They keep mentioning that he's holed up in a place called Stalia, and I forget where I am for a minute.

"Where's Stalia?" I say and the conversation comes to a brutal halt. All eyes turn to me. The human behind Rivonia looks like he's just seen a ghost.

Kane doesn't react at all, even as Rivonia looks to him for help. He just stares at her, as if with every expectation that she should answer my question.

"Stalia is what was once known as the city of Istanbul, I believe," she chokes. Then she turns back to Kane and keeps talking to him in a flourish as if, the faster she talks, the more distance she'll put between her and this moment.

The irony is, I don't know where Istanbul is either. For all that, and I learned nothing.

After way too long, Kane excuses us and Rivonia shoots me a withering scowl as Kane turns from her first to leave. Like it's my fault she lost points with the boss. Ugh. Whatever. Maybe now we'll get a break to eat or drink something or speak with a normal alien…Nope!

We don't make it more than four feet before another group of aliens see Kane's face and kiss his ass. I'm confused as to the etiquette and when a man who introduces himself as the Council Minister and the host of this gala bows so low his nose almost touches his knees, I go to curtsey. Before I move so much as a millimeter, Kane's hand hardens around my upper arm, keeping me unflinchingly vertical. I don't try that again.

The Council Minister introduces us to two, dark-haired Others who look so similar I assume they're sisters if not twins. They both compliment Kane on his choice of human. He thanks them coolly, but gives no further explanation.

This seems to strain the already burgeoning amount of attention I get, for though no one dares speak directly to me or stare at me while in Kane's presence, I can feel eyes canvassing my body from afar at all times and with increasing intensity.

I hate it.

I'm a rat, remember? We aren't used to the attention, and if we get it, it's usually because someone wants to stomp us out.

Then again, I might also be surprised if I saw a rat walking around in a frilly dress.

People are packed into the parlor around us, so I'm not able to get a true sense of the number of guests until we're shepherded into the dining room. The table is shaped like a giant T, and what's fascinating is that it's not two tables pressed together at the tangent, but a single table carved from one massive slab of stone.

Given Kane's prestige, he sits at the top of the T in the very center so that he looks straight down the length of the long table while shorter wings spread off to his either side. I take the place to his left and the Council Minister and his human sit to Kane's right.

The Council Minister's human is a pale blonde with thin arms and a narrow face. She wears a strapless blue dress that fits her like a glove and illuminates the red scar that rips down her neck.

There are probably two hundred and some-odd guests in attendance — a hundred plus Others and the rest, their humans. Human servants pour into the massive chamber and number at least that amount — enough for every guest.

They all wear black and stand against the walls, trying their hardest not to look too important as they pour champagne into our cups. Kane is served first followed by the Council Minister and the rest of the aliens at our table.

The Others seated at the long table are served second, and then the humans are served, me first among them as Kane's cute little pet.

The Council Minister says a few words and leaves the floor open to Kane, who only raises his glass. Immediately, the Council Minister and everyone else follows suit. We all lift our glasses and say something that sounds an awful lot like *hssterssgss*, but I just mouth along and smile and say absolutely nothing.

I'm not used to alcohol and don't plan on drinking too much, but all of the other humans finished their first glasses in one gulp and are staring directly at me, like they're waiting for something.

One of the waiters is standing at my shoulder urging a bottle of champagne towards me so, cursing to myself, I drain my glass and let him refill my cup. I gulp that down too and repeat the whole thing a third time. My head is spinning, but my stomach is full of warm bubbly flies.

The Council Minister pitches his voice loud so that it carries over the light chatter. "I believe now that our guests have enjoyed their fill, we may also take a moment to enjoy ours."

He sweeps a long, gaunt hand across his balding head. A few strands of hair dance upright before falling down to the sides. I thought all of the Others were in peak physical condition, but the Council Minister certainly proves me wrong. He looks sickly, and smiles to reveal a mouthful of yellow teeth.

When he claps twice, each human lifts their right hand over the table. All I can do is mimic at this point, and keep that same stupid smile strung between my cheeks.

I wait for something to happen and hear a servant at my ear whisper, "Pardon me, miss."

He rolls back my sleeve three inches, slides a martini glass underneath my wrist and reaches for something I hadn't immediately noticed hiding there in stainless steel glory amongst the other silver utensils: a scalpel.

My face fills with heat and I try not to betray my emotions because if I do, I'll be the only one. Every other human at the table seems perfectly at ease even when the waiters slice a horizontal line across our arms in fire and blood. No one reacts, so I don't either. And I feel like *I'm* the crazy person...

I fight not to look at Kane. I want to box his ears and make a promise to myself that I will later. Couldn't he have warned me or something?

The Others at the table continue to make light conversation with one another while us humans are bled out. Alright, not *out*. But enough for my lightheadedness to get even lighter and headier.

I'm grateful when the waiter folds a white towel around my wrist and rolls my sleeve back down to cover it. Without saying anything more, he gives my shoulder a light squeeze and sets the glass in front of Kane. He bows then, and moves away from the table.

Kane doesn't reach for his glass as quickly as he should. Even I can see that. Instead he stares at it and I'm reminded of the staring competition that he had with the scalpel earlier.

Meanwhile, the other members of our short table lift their glasses halfway to their mouths, pausing only when they see the guest of honor taking his time with his own cup. At least I hope that's what it looks like to them because to me, it looks like hesitation.

There's a pause, light murmuring picks up, and all eyes lock on Kane. After what feels like forever, Kane glances down the length of the table, picks up his martini glass and holds it out at eye level. I think of the scalpel. He's losing again...

Everyone falls silent and despite the size of the room, his evenly pitched voice resonates. "To Sistylea. May she live forever here on Earth."

"To Sistylea," comes the resounding cry right before Kane takes the smallest sip of my blood.

The sound that slips from his throat is *not* part of the program. I know it and if I know it, they know. And I hear it. And if I can hear it, they can definitely hear it.

It's a sound of pure pleasure.

Heat chars my cheeks and that wetness between my legs makes my pussy *hurt*. It needs something. It needs more of what it got last night. It needs Kane right now. There are no consequences. There are no rules. He can have as much of my blood as he wants.

I look directly at him and my lips part. I can feel my gaze unfocus because of the booze and the blood that he took, and also just because of *him*. He's so hot. Has he always been so hot?

Dammit. Why am I thinking like this?

And why isn't he moving?

He's frozen and his jaw is grinding and he looks like he's in pain. Instead of shrugging off his reaction, Kane rounds on me and lowers his voice and everything is so unexpected I flinch where I sit.

"*Disgusting*," he hisses and though his voice is pitched low, I know that everyone in the room can still hear it, "What have you been eating?"

The waiter rushes forward while my jaw works uselessly. The waiter says, "Apologies, my Lord. We will have her removed from the table at once..." He grabs my hand and starts to usher me away from Kane, but Kane stops him with an indifferent wave.

"No," he says gruffly, "let her stay. She is a pretty thing to look at even if she does taste...sour today." He frowns and I notice that as he speaks, he doesn't look at me. At the same time, his hollow cheeks betray not one ounce of color. I don't know what to think. "Just have a new glass sent over."

The waiter rushes off and eventually chatter resumes with some level of normalcy. Well, normal for them. None of this is normal.

The distance between me and Kane feels like miles even though he's still just as close. He takes great effort not to speak to me and after a few seconds, turns from me entirely to engage the Council Minister in conversation.

The woman to my left is tall and blonde and talking animatedly with her human — why on Earth would she want to talk to the Notare's pariah? — so I sit there alone, remembering Calvin's wise words. I pretend like I'm enjoying absolutely everything even though I've just been humiliated... at least, I think? And now there's a different, pretty human standing over Kane's right shoulder with her ample bust thrust in his face like she really does want him to just take a bite out of her.

Starting with her left tit.

The waiter cuts her arm and gives Kane a new glass. The woman tosses her glossy blonde hair as she leaves and throws Kane a coy smile that he either doesn't see or pretends not to.

Instead, he sips at his cup of blood casually, making no sounds of disgust this time around and for a fleeting second, I have the gall to wonder what is wrong with *me* even though I'm one of the few non-blood suckers sitting at the table.

Silently, I watch as the courses come and go. Everything is decadent. I don't know what most things are, but I know how they taste. Like meat, like butter, like bread, like some fruits that used to exist and that, out in Population, people would fight to the death for. Some cheese even, and other vegetables. Nuts. I don't know what this brown thing is, but I choke two cups of that down, too.

My stomach complains uncomfortably on the other side of my dress. It's unforgiving. Still, I'm determined to make it through the thing I hear someone call *cake* but I'm stalled when I feel eyes on my face, watching me at a distance.

I look up. I don't know how I didn't notice him sitting there first thing, or why I didn't look harder to begin with. Maybe it's because I'm afraid of actually finding him, trying to get his attention and then failing. Letting Ashlyn down. Letting Kane down. Ruining everything.

But with his one great green eye watching me like that from the farthest end of the long table, he doesn't look like he hates me. In fact, it looks very much like he wants me and in that wanting, I find anger. My insides rage and roil and a riptide of homicidal thoughts crush the plan that Kane concocted.

My leg muscles clench, itching to push me up onto my feet and across the table. I glance to the right, find a cutting knife and reach for it. But just as I do, Kane takes my wrist in his hand and sets it back down on the marble.

He doesn't look at me. He doesn't speak to me. But he reads my thoughts.

Because as he takes my wrist so casually in his and places it away from the knife, I realize that it would appear to anyone else that I'm not reaching for the knife at all. It probably looks like I'm reaching for him, and he's rejecting me. Again. Only I know that he's actually saved my life. How far would I have made it out of the door, even if I did somehow manage to kill Memnoch?

The murder in my heart calms and I take two deep breaths before scanning the table's guests for him a second time. He's still watching me with curiosity and when I flick my eyes to meet his one, he smiles.

There's no sign of recognition in his gaze and for this, I am grateful. My heart hammers uncomfortably as I realize just how much is on the line and just how ill-equipped I really am. I'm not an actress, but if I don't pretend to be completely enrapt by him I'm doomed and so is Ashlyn.

In thinking of Ashlyn, I try and hone some of her dramatic skills as I let my eyes dance up to Memnoch's then look away again. As I take small, dainty bites out of my cake,

I hope that my blush looks modest and lecherous, rather than fueled by a deep-seated desire to rip off his face.

Memnoch's smile spreads as he drains his glass of blood and calls for another. I see that he doesn't have a human beside him, but drinks from the same woman that Kane did. He drinks without taking his eyes off my face and I remember a funny moment when Becks found a bottle of only half-stale whipped cream nearly eight years ago.

She'd squirted a line on her finger and licked it, and I'd always remembered that moment because she and Matt had made Ashlyn right after. If Matt had thought that was sexy, maybe Memnoch would too. The trouble is, I'm clumsy as shit. Sexy isn't even a word I know how to use.

I make a show of accidentally dropping my spoon into my ice cream, which splatters onto the side of my hand and almost all of my fingers. Oops. Well, here goes nothing.

I start to lick it off, trying to go slow in a way I think could be hot? I don't know. I glance across the table at Memnoch and I see that he's biting his bottom lip and his eye is fixed to my face fiercely. Is this working? Is this sexy?

Oh god, I don't feel sexy. Not one bit. Then again, I never have, so even if I were, I wouldn't be able to recognize it.

I take the clenching of his fist around his fork as a good sign and continue to hold his gaze as I lick my fingers clean, then drain my glass of wine.

He finishes his blood cup and orders another one. While he drinks that, his free hand slips under the table and I'd bet my bottom doller that he's…adjusting himself. Ugh.

Kane starts to literally *rumble* at my side as I lick the ice cream off of my spoon too, for good measure. Maybe he thinks I'm doing something wrong? I have to guess he does, because he isn't talking to me and I don't exactly speak rumble.

Or any other language beside English, and I barely speak that.

I lose sight of Memnoch after dinner when we head to the ballroom. The thing is huge. I forgot that buildings were even made to be this big. It's like a damn colosseum in here, with soaring marble columns and checkered marble floors and chandeliers dripping from the ceiling like stalactites.

My hand is on Kane's arm as we move through the room and people stare at me questioningly as I pass. Kane doesn't react to them, but instead pulls me through a curtain of bodies and suddenly the ballroom opens up before us.

And we're the only two people on the goddamn dance floor.

Sweet baby Jesus, this can't be happening.

Rule number five begs me to run and I have to quickly incinerate it in order to keep my feet planted and my head held high when Kane lifts his left hand and turns to face me. When he places his right behind his back, I recognize this as Calvin's favorite dance — the one I'm worst at.

Music fades in, clearer than any I've heard before, and I'm startled to see a full orchestra seated two stories up on a gravity-defying balcony. Despite the gentle tenor of the music, in this moment, it sounds like the intro to a horror flick. A slasher. My brother used to love those and though I don't remember much about TV, I remember a movie about a girl falling down a well that scared the crap out of me when I was little.

I don't run, which is good, but I also don't really breathe. How can I with hundreds of sets of eyes on my face? The strange thing is that I'm not so afraid of them. I'm most afraid of the green and gold eyes before me. What if I mess up? What if I embarrass him?

Steeling myself, I straighten up, press my right palm to his and when he takes a step forward, I waltz. I waltz like it's the last thing I'll do, like I'm waltzing for my goddamn survival.

Kane's eyes are on mine and his expression shifts from surprise to mocking. I wanna punch him and I think he knows it.

My calves burn as we continue the dance, moving in awkward steps that I struggle to remember while trying to keep the booze and the food down in my stomach, instead of up in my throat.

The dance reaches its peak and when we take the next spin quickly, my right ankle trembles. I clutch his hands just a hair tighter but he moves so gracefully that I panic and in my panic, my footing slips. It's going to happen. There's no two ways around it. I feel like screaming bloody murder. I feel like crawling into a hole where there's no sunlight.

I start to fall, but Kane's hands slip from their original hold and just as my feet slide out from under me, he lifts me into the air. We complete the spin, which was meant to be grounded, but when I land I step right back into the dance and Kane looks away from me glibly, as if this entire turn had been scripted. My slip up goes unnoticed and I have the strange desire to add another tally to the column of times Kane saved my skin.

"Brava." Rivonia's voice shocks me enough that I definitely stumble again. But Kane's already stopped dancing and when I look past him, I see that the ballroom floor is full of couples spinning stupid circles around one another.

Remind me that, the next time I'm caught spinning around another person, it'll be in a death ring or not at all.

"You look ravishing, Notare, as does your companion. Truly, tonight's iconic couple." Her eyes flash to me warmly, though her grin is biting.

She glances back to Kane. "Perhaps I could impose on your date and trouble you for a dance?"

"Certainly," Kane says with a slight bow. He takes a step away from me, and as he does, the Council Minister appears out of nowhere.

The man rubs his dry, crackling lips and bows to Kane deeply before he says, "It would be such a shame to leave someone as lovely as Abel without a partner." I'm so shocked he knows my name that when he looks at me, I forget to smile.

I see Kane grimace, but only fleetingly. When he looks back to the Minister, he's all debonair cordiality that makes me feel like I've never met this man before in my life. "Certainly, Crispin."

He nods and the bald dude quickly swoops in and places his hands around my waist, leaving his own pretty blonde date standing alone. But she's smiling. Enjoying everything, I'm certain.

By the time the song changes, I've long since lost Kane in the crowd. I only see him again three songs later, and by this time I've managed to shake the Minister who talks to me of nothing but how incredible hunting is this season. Hunting what?

I laugh in a loud, shrill way, though it sounds fake — even to me — and the Minister finds a fresher, more obliging face the fourth song around.

When I next spot Kane a few songs after that, he's dancing with Tasha and I'm pleased to see that she's making him smile, and it looks a little more genuine at this point. For just a second, I wish I were Heztoichen — I mean, an *alien* — like them so I could hear their conversation and know what to say to make him smile like that the next time we're alone.

A hand taps my shoulder and I turn to see a fairly large, imposing-looking Other in front of me, but when he introduces himself as Sylas, his voice is quiet and kind. So I accept his invitation to dance without trying to fight him even once.

The songs slow and the movements become slightly more sensual. Dance number two. I'm annoyed that Kane isn't with me, and more annoyed still at the thought that he's entered this dance with another partner. Though why should I be? I've got no claim over him?

I know that...but I still search...

My gaze canvas couples, mixed human and Other alike, but I don't see Kane anywhere. Sylas spins me and for an instant I catch sight of Tasha standing against the wall beneath the floating orchestra. Kane's at her side, watching me with an expression that betrays no emotion. When his eye catches mine, he shifts uncomfortably and looks away, but I manage to grab hold of his attention just long enough to mouth *Help!* over Sylas's shoulder.

Kane's face, which had been strictly composed, breaks. He lifts one corner of his mouth and takes a sip from his glass, then leans more casually against the wall behind him.

Jackass, I mouth again, hoping that he understands my frustration. I also hope he knows that I *will* make him pay for this later.

Tasha turns when she sees Kane staring. She's stunning in a gown the color of moss with soft white flowers dotting her hair. A heavy crimson braid falls over her left shoulder and in whatever shoes she's got on, she's Kane's height, or a little taller.

Her eyes flash to Kane, she lifts a single eyebrow and then nods her head. I don't know what that means, but I feel my face get hot and then get hotter still when both of Sylas's hands move to my hips. Remembering how awkward this had been with Calvin, I force my focus away from Kane and make polite small talk to distract Sylas. To distract us both.

Sylas's face is nearly as red as I think mine might be, but when he looks over my right shoulder all that color drains from his face in one go.

Thinking perhaps that Kane's finally come to my rescue, I'm shocked when I turn to see Memnoch standing there. *Kill him.* Not yet. Not until I know where Ashlyn is.

And the second I find her, I'm going to rip his remaining eye out.

"Apologies," he says and I shiver, because his voice is exactly the same as I remember it. "Sylas, is it?"

Sylas nods, but doesn't speak.

"Might I cut in?"

Sylas seems hesitant. He licks his pink lips and his wide, cobalt eyes flash to me. "This is the *Notare's* escort." I don't understand what that means or why he says it, but it evidently is enough to stall Memnoch.

Memnoch grimaces and takes half a step back. Where he should be. But then I remember that I'm supposed to be like...seducing him or something and I can't do that and get an invite to his place if he's standing across the room staring at me.

Quickly, I say, "I'm certain that the Notare won't mind."

To my surprise Sylas nods once, bows and pulls away from me, leaving room for Memnoch to coil his heavy arms around my waist and pull my stomach flush against his own.

My whole body lights up as it occurs to me that this is the second closest I've ever been to a man before and it's the male who killed my best friend and stole her kid away from me. I don't want to know what he's done with her.

I just want her back.

And I want him under my stupid stiletto heel, begging me for mercy.

"It would have seemed such a shame to miss my opportunity to dance with the most beautiful woman in the room," he says. His breath reeks of scotch and blood.

I smile like I'm flattered even though all I can think about is yanking off his testicles like a paper towel off the roll. "And your name?" I grit, trying to keep my tone light and the anger from blanketing it.

His scarred face stretches into a wicked grin that's more lecherous than the last one was. And that's saying something.

"Memnoch. And you are Abel. The Notare's prized treasure." He drops his voice, and his face is so close that he speaks into my neck — the wounded side. "I find myself painfully envious."

I release a high, breathy giggle and tense my fingers around his shoulders in a way that I hope feels encouraging.

"It is flattering to be noticed. Particularly by someone of your rank and prestige." By a garbage bag. That's his rank to me.

He hacks out a grating laugh into my ear, spittle wetting the side of my face. "Your charm rivals your beauty. But I am only the errand boy of Notare Elise."

I don't know who that is, but I nod encouragingly and pretend that I do. "Errand boy or not, I have passed by your estate and it is certainly something to boast of," I lie, and I evidently lie convincingly because his satisfied smile holds.

"Have you?"

I twitch when I feel his strong right hand slide down my back and cup my butt. I want to bite his fingers off through to the bone. Instead I smile and touch his chest in the way I touched Kane's last night that he liked. It's the only experience I have to draw on. And it works.

Memnoch is a few seconds behind the waltz as the song transitions. He laughs at his mistake and has to restart. "I'm not certain that your Notare would be so easily persuaded to give you up," he whispers, though I'm sure everyone in the vicinity that is listening can hear us.

"He has many humans. I'm sure he won't notice the absence of just one."

Memnoch dips me when the music comes to a crescendo. I can hear him breathing hard against my throat and I worry that he really might eat me then and there and without warning. "Your blood smells like pure ecstasy. A lucky man's poison."

He pulls me back into his chest and his hands around me tense so viciously that I feel my adrenaline lurch into overdrive. Fight! No. Wait, for Ashlyn.

"I am certain that no one believed the charade your Notare pulled at dinner."

"Charade?" I say dumbly.

"I'm certain you know what I mean. He was lost to the sensation of your blood, and what is enough to tempt the

Notare's noble sensibilities, is something that I want. But why would you leave him — the Notare — for me?"

I can see his incredulity and I can feel his hate. He holds my wrists hard enough to bruise them and doesn't even pretend to dance anymore. We've slowed from a waltz to a stumble.

Panicked, my eyes flash over Memnoch's shoulder to Kane, who stands against the far wall unmoving. Tasha's hand is on his upper arm and when I see the muscles flinch in her neck and Kane's left foot jolt half an inch forward I get the idea that she's *restraining* him.

Just before Memnoch turns to follow my line of sight, Tasha spins around Kane, blocking him from view. A fleeting jealousy ticks, even as I recognize her actions as helping me, and I realize she can help me in more ways than one…

"It's Tasha," I gasp, and the anxiety in my tone makes the lie sound that much more believable, "He loves her. I…I am just a play thing."

Memnoch stares down at me furiously, but I manage to find a very real fear in the lie that I've just told and I cling to it. A few seconds pass and as his face softens back into that carnivorous smile I know that he believes me.

"So you'd like to make him jealous?"

"Yes," I say. "And I know that you two don't have a happy history so I thought, if I want to make him jealous it should be with the man that he hates and fears the most."

Memnoch is pleased. He picks me up, spins me around and steps back into the dance. I'm slow to follow. Couples close enough to be paying attention to the exchange that has passed between us, throw us looks that I wish I didn't catch.

They're condemning and I feel guilt steal into my blood even though I know that this is part of Kane's plan. A perfect plan. One that does so much for me and for him, does absolutely nothing. Why is he even doing this? I don't understand, but I feel guilt pinch me quite painfully.

As the song ends, Memnoch brushes his hand over my cheek. He slides that same hand down the length of my throat and tickles my wound with his pointer finger. Oh yeah, that finger I'll bite off first thing.

"Come to my estate Friday evening and we will give the Notare something to be jealous about." He drops his hands and glides back through the great hall, disappearing between folds in the couples.

I turn and it's only as I make my way across the dance floor to Kane's side that I truly begin to feel excited. I did it. I did it! For Christ's sake I managed to pull off one hell of a lie.

I reach Kane just as Tasha makes to leave. She gives me a look that's half-apprehensive, half-apologetic, but doesn't say anything.

Kane's feet are crossed, one over the other, and he's got a glass of something bubbly and red trapped in his left fist. The sight of it distracts me.

"Is that *blood* champagne?" I ask once I'm within earshot. Then I tap on his jacket pocket and wait for him to hand me the pad and paper, which he only does with a reluctant grimace.

As I scribble down a few words, I notice that his jaw is clenched with the intent of cracking all his teeth. I scratch out what I'd written before and start over on a clean sheet.

I did it! I got the invite. His place Friday night. Also, I like your teeth the way they are so you should stop that.

Kane barely glances at the page before ripping the entire pad and pen out of my hand. I jump. He snarls. Then he grabs me by the wrist and drags me out of the ballroom through the parlor down a long hall.

The corridor is lined in mirrors that reflect my own worried expression back to me. Guests become fewer and fewer and servants more ubiquitous until finally we pass a set of stainless steel double doors and enter a kitchen.

"Thanks but I ate enough at dinner." I try a joke. It doesn't work at all.

"Leave us," Kane roars.

The bodies in the kitchen rush out in no discernible order. They're just trying to move fast. Rat pack mentality. I turn to follow them, sure that they must be sensing a danger I don't, but Kane grabs the back of my dress, keeping me here, with him.

"Kane, I…"

He lets me go as the last of the servants scram and when I turn to face him, he slams both of his fists onto the butcher's block countertop. The force of the blow takes off chunks of wood and resonates like thunder.

My heart rate spikes and I stumble back, losing my balance. "What are you…" I start, but he looks at me and his face is full of rage and when he holds a finger to his lips, I quiet.

Kane stares at me for a long, terrifying moment. I can see the orange pulse of his chest even brighter now than I could before. Like his entire torso is on fire. I wonder if it's his anger that makes the sensation appear so beautiful.

When Kane stands up to his full height, he towers over me. I shake my head, my muscles burn, and I take a tentative step towards him. I wobble in my shoes and he seems to notice because he glares at my feet.

A muscle in his cheek twitches. I don't know what it means, but when his hands form fists, I get the idea that he's come to a decision. An important one that has to do with me.

In a flourish, Kane turns to the cabinets at his back. He starts rifling through stacks of pots and pans and food. He tosses aside bins of dried pasta, tins of sugar and sacks of rice, boxes of beans and cans of preserved fruit. A bag of flour explodes on the floor in a white cloud.

"Kane?"

He turns towards me, but I can tell he hasn't heard me at all. And then I see what he's carrying.

"Kane," I say, harder this time.

He's got a freaking butcher knife trapped in one fist and a single stocky tea cup in the other. Is this it? Did I embarrass him so much, he's got no choice but to kill me now? This was his plan, the ass hole!

I open my mouth to shout all these things, but jump back instead when Kane sets the glass down hard enough on the counter that the handle and base crack, but don't break.

Ceramic shards flake onto the butcher's block and concrete floor. I try saying his name again, but he takes off his tux jacket and rolls back his sleeve. He writes something down and, terrified, I take the paper.

Drink it all.

Then he cuts *himself*. Not me.

Understanding dawns on me when the little teacup is halfway full. He doesn't stop there though, but fills it all the way to the brim.

The smell of sulfur and rotten eggs and *wrongness* floods the room. I'm hopelessly confused but can't ask him about it, which only heightens my desire to run. Then again, I'm not sure I even *could* run at this point because Kane's gaze keeps me planted and I know that if I tried, he'd hunt me down.

Kane snatches a dirty dishtowel from beside the sink and places it over his wound. He wipes the knife clean and slams it into the countertop so that it stands up straight. The force of it causes the whole room to shake. Or maybe it's just me. Something's happening.

What the shit is happening!

Kane's hot green gaze finds the paper dangling limply from my hand. He comes to me, snatches it away and replaces it with the tea cup. Then he holds the paper in front of my eyes so that I see nothing else, not even in my peripheries.

Drink it all.

I gulp. He can't be serious. But with fire in his face and fire in his chest and fire in his eyes, I see that he is. Unequivocally.

I lift the glass to my mouth and try not to inhale as I take the first sip. Doesn't help. The taste is harsh enough to make my stomach lurch and the back of my throat burn. I choke.

I can't, I mouth, but all he does is hold the paper so close to my nose, the words all blur.

I try again and manage to gulp down a single swallow. Three more sips in and the taste resurfaces — along with bile — up the back of my throat. I gulp down everything. One sip down, only ten more to go.

As I try to choke down the rest of Kane's tea from hell, I think about my rule book and how many rules I've erased since meeting him.

Rule number six — trust my gut — is gone in the most literal sense as my body screams at me to purge. And so is rule number twelve, which should have probably included not drinking Other blood in addition to not talking to them.

I drain the glass, fall back against the stainless steel table behind me and try to keep Kane's blood down. My stomach twists, then releases. I relax fully, a strange energy in my bones making me weightless. Something unearthly is happening in my system and I feel weirdly full, but also full of life.

Like someone breathing air into a worn out paper bag, making it new. Cicadas shedding their shells. A snake slipping out of its old skin.

My cheek and injured jaw tingle and a similar sensation grips my ankles, wrists and throat. I cup my neck and scratch at the cut there, but the wound is gone like it never was.

Confused, I gulp down the lingering taste of his blood, coughing slightly as Kane takes the tea cup from my hand and rinses it out in the sink.

He pours cleaning detergent down the faucet, then he drops the glass on the ground, smashing it. He kicks the pieces around, dispersing them, then looks up at me.

His eyes are wide and the anger is gone and not for the first time, I'm desperate to know what he's thinking.

I make the motion for a pen and paper with my hands, but he doesn't move. At least, not in the direction I thought he would. Instead, Kane rushes me and I canter back until my ass hits the edge of a table.

I hold up my hand — to do what with, I'll never know. Kane snatches my wrist and then grabs me by the waist and tosses me onto the table in one desperate motion.

He slides on top of me, onto the table, and I'm pinned under his weight. "Kane," I say his name in the shrinking space between us, but he severs whatever I was about to say when he kisses me ferociously, lips set out to conquer to mine.

Every place our bodies touch is consumed by fire. I suddenly can't remember the taste of his blood or wanting a notepad or Memnoch the Cyclops or the gala. All I know is that I want *him*.

He's my enemy for life, and he's the only male I've *ever* wanted.

"Please," I beg, and I've never begged an Other for anything before in my life.

I grab for the buttons on his shirt, but I can't get them undone. Kane reaches past my hand up to his throat, rips his bow tie and then pops his shirt open. Buttons go flying, scattering off of metal surfaces and appliances.

My hands are everywhere, touching everything. I feel crazy right now, but I can't seem to control myself in this. I feel *connected* to him. And I want to be connected to him in the most literal sense.

"Kane, please." I reach for his belt and palm the bulge beneath it. The heat of his erection beckons to me like promises of warmth in the snow.

He groans into my neck as I stroke him and I shiver when his tongue slides over the place where he cut me earlier. *Where did the wound go? How could it just be gone like that?* It must have something to do with his blood…

"I need you in me," he moans, pulling me from my thoughts.

That doesn't sound right. How could I be inside of him? And I feel it…the hard edges of his teeth. They aren't sharpened or anything, but they still sink through my flesh when he bites.

I scream as pain stabs me in the neck, then moves down my side in little ripples. "Kane," I squeal, but not because it hurts — oh no. But because, on the heels of that pain there's pleasure unlike any that I've ever experienced…that I don't even have words for.

"Fuck. I'm so sorry, I don't know what came over…" He starts to pull away from me, but I claw at his back in an effort to keep him close.

"Don't stop," I moan.

Holy shit. I can feel the blood on the side of my neck, but it feels…oh my god…it *feels*. My mouth, my tongue. I can taste heaven. "More."

Kane's pupils dilate and he grabs the front of my dress with one huge hand and tears it straight down the middle. My back jolts up off of the table with a fleeting flash of pain as stitches break, then unravel.

He says something in an alien language as his fingers trace the line of my lingerie, over the swell of my breast to reach my heart. He taps the beat of my pulse and when his gaze greets mine, this time there are words in there that I'm not ready for.

He opens his mouth. I brace, panicked, but Kane is a merciful alien. "I'm going to take you now," he says huskily.

Panic comes again, but the sweeping rush is followed immediately by a desire too thick to swim through. It pulls me under. I nod and reach for the side of his face, but he shakes his head.

"Need to hear you say it."

"Say what?"

He slides his hand meaningfully up my inner thigh and cups my core. "Tell me you want this just as much as I do."

How can I tell him that I've never wanted anything like this before? How can I tell him that he's completely unmade me and rebuilt me into a woman I don't recognize, but that I'm proud of? How can I tell him that I appreciate him so, so much and that in only the span of a few weeks, he's come to mean just as much to me as family does?

And he's the enemy.

How can I tell him that I'd fight Population for him? I'd even wear high heels for him.

He pauses and I worry he's mistaking my silence for hesitation. "I don't ever want to make you do anything you don't want to do," he says gently.

I know that. I know. But does he know?

"Kane, I…can't say that I want this as much as you do…" His face falls and his hand starts to retreat, but I clasp my thighs around his wrist. "I'm absolutely sure that I want it more. Much more. I want you to drink my blood. I want you to be in me." I reach down and cover his hand between my legs with my own palm. "I want you to show me all the things Population never taught me."

His eyes light like kindling and his smile grows wicked and wild. He kisses me hard, and just as he pulls back he growls, "I won't let you down."

Everything comes together suddenly. All I can do is grab his neck and hold on.

His hands are everywhere and his tongue is in my mouth and his lips are on my neck and his fingers are palming my breast and flicking my clit.

I've never felt like this before. Like I could just come apart and that would be just fine.

We had a plan at the beginning of this night, didn't we? Something about a Cyclops, but as Kane rips the rest of my dress off of me, scoops me up off the table and plants my ass down on the butcher's block table top, I can't remember past this moment.

Past my need.

I'm fumbling with his belt gracelessly while Kane tears through Tasha's armor. I gasp as I glance down at my own naked body and for a moment, I don't even recognize me.

I don't have a bruise, scratch or abrasion on me.

Kane takes that opening to his advantage and invades my mouth, moving in and out slowly as he penetrates me with his tongue — like he's trying to give me an idea of what's about to come. *A warning…*

And I'm ready… I suck on his tongue and rake my nails down his chest. I pinch his nipple and he grabs me by the hair, tilting my head back while he yanks my hips forward.

His mouth dives for the side of my neck where droplets of blood still run hot and pool in the well above my clavicle. He reopens me with his teeth and again, it hurts for the first instance before a new wave of euphoria slams me down into the floor, then lifts me back up through the ceiling.

I'm making all kinds of sounds now and there's no hope to censor them. Not when Kane's got his pants down and is shoving his boxers down with them.

He pulls me off of the counter and lowers me to the tiles. On his knees between my legs I get my first glimpse of his naked body.

Shit. It's glorious.

His cock is long and thick but it looks…manageable. Not something that will rip me in two. It's slightly curved in a way I didn't know cocks were and the bloated mushroom head is weeping from a single slit. I want to lick it, but Kane's moving too fast. I don't get that chance.

Dropping forward, Kane touches my face…the side of my neck. His fingers come back bloody and when he licks them clean, I feel spiders explode out of my dormant sex drive as he clears away all the cobwebs.

I'm reanimated. Alive.

I reach between us and wrap my hand around his erection. My fingers explore its incredible length, swirling around the head. I like touching him. I like watching his face. Eyebrows bunching and flattening. Pupils dilating even more until there's almost no iris.

I whimper when I manage to brush the head of his cock over my lower lips. It's so close, yet too far to make the connection I'm looking for.

"Kane, please. I'm ready," I tell him.

Kane curses in that alien language, grips the side of my face with one hand, locks his gaze with mine. Below my waist, I can feel his hips sinking low as his cock lines up with my entrance.

Then he tilts my head to the side, lowers his mouth to the curve of my throat. He drinks from me, and slides forward into me at the exact same time.

Heaven.

There's no pain at all. Not even a little. I thought there would be. I've only done this once before and that was almost a decade ago, but right now heaven is all I can feel.

It hits my tongue, sinking into my tastebuds, and it claims my tits, every place that his chest is crushed against me. My legs are shaking already and we've barely even begun. He's pumping in and out of me in smooth strokes, grinding down hard against me.

As he moves, the slapping sound of his body meeting mine completely grounds me to the moment. I can't believe this is happening. I can't believe it hasn't happened before. If I'd known I could feel like this, then I'd have thrown him down to the ground and mounted him long ago…

"Heaven," I cry out, when I mean to say something else.

Kane laughs his condescending little laugh in my ear and pulls back from my throat just enough to look at me. He's got my blood on his lips and the sight of it turns me on in ways it definitely shouldn't. *What's wrong with me?*

And for once, I find that the answer is *absolutely nothing at all.*

He slams forward and I cry out. His pubic hair is rubbing directly on my clit with each wave and oh my god…the way it's rubbing…it's way too much. I'm about to arrive…I'm about to come.

The explosion that I felt in his bed erupts within me, only this time, he's inside there with it. My walls cling to his cock and I dig my nails into his ass to hold him against me. I need him there…exactly right there.

I scream some rendition of his name and Kane bellows out a roar. I'm clenching around him in waves and pulses, the walls of my core squeezing, squeezing, squeezing. He's tight as a bow string and there's heat between us, and wetness…so much of it. I can't see anything. I'm caught in the vortex of some kind of storm.

"Abel," he chokes, "I did not know it could be like this…"

There's a sudden rush as he empties himself inside of me. I open my eyes and I see his hooded gaze on my face. His lips are slack and parted. I lift up and catch his mouth with mine and he moans and slides one arm around my shoulders and wrenches me to him as my right leg starts to shiver and my belly starts to ache.

"It's…again," I mewl, voice stolen from me as a second, unprecedented explosion rides over my first.

It happens so suddenly and with such overwhelming force that tears erupt from my eyes. I grab hold of Kane's shoulders as Kane shudders above me.

"Again?" He pants, sounding strained. "It can't be…" And then he groans.

I scream.

We both moan simultaneously.

We're caught together in this cycle for so long, time erases itself. I see sunrises in reverse, wounds unmade, colliding galaxies charting a new course.

There's only Kane.

He comes every time I do, and I come each time he does. We're caught like this in some sort of cycle that might kill me, but that I know I don't want to break free from.

I come again and when I open my eyes, Kane's face is scrunched up tight in concentration. "You're trying to get us off the tracks?" I gasp, laughing a little hysterically.

The tenor of Kane's laughter matches mine and is just as crazed. "We will lose ourselves to this."

I release all of the weight in my bones and flop backwards onto the floor, panting. "What do you mean? I'm already lost."

I'm sopping wet below the waist and the rest of me is sticky with semen or sweat or both. I've also got flour all over me. I can feel it between my fingers as they trace imaginary lines over Kane's back and shoulders. I cling to him and, after many moments, he exhales and drops forward onto his elbows. He licks my neck clean, sending bolts of euphoria through my tongue and lips, but doesn't reopen it.

Never thought I'd be so disappointed.

"I did not think it would be like this," he says and when he lifts his head and looks down at me, I notice that his eyes are glossier than usual. I don't like that. Don't like it one bit. The emotion monster is clapping its hands. It knows it's won everything.

Everything.

"Like what?"

His cock is still inside me, fully erect, and my inner walls flutter shyly in his presence. He groans and kisses me instead of answering.

We kiss on the floor in the flour for a while. Long enough for him to lose the battle he'd been fighting and start thrusting in and out of me for two more cycles. Two more shared arrivals. Two more trips to heaven's shores.

I collapse, completely gone. I've been in battles to the death before that didn't drain me like this.

Kane doesn't seem to be doing much better. He's shaking with the effort it takes to keep his entire weight off of me, but when I suggest he roll to the side, he says, "No. I'm not leaving your warmth yet. I want to be in you."

I shiver at the manic look in his eyes. "We have time."

He snarls and takes the side of my face in one hand. He's angry again. He looks like a madman, rugged and wild. "Not enough."

Love. The word floats through my mind and sticks. Like the emotion monster is sitting there fishing for words and *Love* is the only catch.

It makes no sense. Am I even sure about this? I've never loved a man before in my life. Maybe I'm just confused. Maybe everyone feels this way right after…right after what? What *was* that? I overheard Becks and Matt sometimes — it was almost impossible not to in the cramped quarters we so often found ourselves in — but I never heard them do anything like this.

Infinity sex. Compounding and confusing. Consuming. Overwhelming. Love on repeat. Love on steroids.

"Kane, I…"

He looks down at me and is wearing an expression that's so full of hope, it needs to be rewarded. Because for as much as he wants me to have faith in him, I want him to believe in me. I want him to believe that I'm capable of more than just surviving and living and bleeding.

That I'm capable of loving.

"Abel," he whispers. He kisses my lower lip tenderly and the gloss on his eyes finds its way to mine.

His arms tighten even more around me and I've never felt so safe in all my life. "I…"

The kitchen door flies open with a bang and when I look over Kane's shoulder, I see Rivonia standing there agape.

"Notare, I am so sorry…"

"Out!" Kane roars over his shoulder, loud enough to make her flinch.

She backs away with both hands raised, like she's trying to ward off a dangerous animal. "Apologies, sincerely, I did not realize you were still…" The door swings closed between her words and Kane looks down at my face.

"What were you saying?"

His cock twitches in me and I suck in a shaky breath. "I…" Do it. Tell him what you're thinking. Be honest. "I've got flour all over me." *Coward.*

I laugh and Kane grins at me. His fist appears and before I can fight him off, he starts sprinkling flour over my forehead and hair. "You mean, this flour?"

"Kane!" I smack his hands, but he holds me steady, and when I grab a fistful of flour myself and smush it against his sweat-slicked spine, his gaze heats all over again.

"Kane…"

He closes his eyes, shakes his head. "No. I want you home where I can have your screams all to myself."

He stands all at once and brings me with him, somehow without removing himself from my core. The friction makes my eyes roll back. I wrap my legs around him and can feel him pulsing in me just a little bit.

He collapses against the island and pumps into me a few times, like he can't even help it. "I can't…" He gasps and that's fine. I can't either.

I'm sore from the inside out and I've got rice stuck to my butt, but I'll be damned if I'm the one to put a stop to this.

So we screw each other senseless until the backdoor to the kitchen opens and someone I think might be our driver appears and then Kane takes me to the car where he lies me down on the floor between the seats.

Cramped, the only position for us to be in is me on top and Kane loves it. I've never done it before, but it feels even fuller than when I was on bottom and Kane doesn't last long, which means I don't last long.

I think the car is parked for a while and the driver has long since made himself scarce by the time Kane carries me out. I can't walk. I can't think about walking.

The house is empty when we reenter, thank heavens, so Kane takes me on the stairs — Kane takes me on *every* stair — until we finally make it back to his bedroom.

We don't make it to the bed, but I tackle Kane onto the floor and it's on the floor that Kane does something weird. *Weirder.*

He reopens my throat again, but this time, he opens *his* throat too. I drink from him because I'm too lost not to, and even though I don't like the taste, I feel made stronger by it and when he pulls blood from my own throat, I feel the cycle between us intensifying. Almost like...we can feel each other.

But that's crazy...right?

Blood from his neck drips onto my body and Kane smears it over my breasts. I smear my blood from his mouth down his chin and down his neck.

We're still connected in the way it counts, but now Kane's kneeling back on his heels, with both hands around my hips so he can pound me down onto him.

He pauses just long enough to pant, "I don't know who I have to thank — the universe or your planet's many gods — but I'm beginning to believe you were made for me. And I'm the fool who waited so long."

As usual, I can't handle the things he says to me, so I latch onto the least important bit. "It hasn't...been long at all," I say between thrusts.

And as usual, he refuses to be unseated. "It's been longer than I can bear, knowing I had you and then left. I should have stayed to worship you then."

He kisses me ferociously, sparing me the grief of having to say something poetic, and the cycle continues, and as it continues the emotion monster sighs contentedly before it winks out of existence. Because the emotion monster is me now, and the rule book is gone, because no matter which broken rule kills me now, it'll all have been worth it to have basked even just this once in Kane's golden glow.

To have felt well and truly loved.

I toss my head back, and surrender.

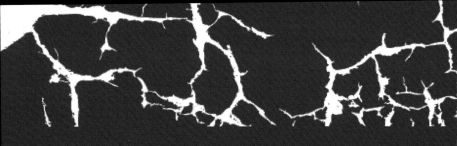

Chapter Nine

The bath water is warm, steam rising from its surface in cute little tendrils. Kane and I sit in his massive Jacuzzi tub facing one another. He has one of my feet in his hands and is massaging it and sometimes kissing my toes, even if it's just to watch me squirm away.

"It tickles."

"It's supposed to tickle."

"Tickling hurts," I complain.

He laughs against my calf, kissing his way down to my knee. He's been in a kissing mood since he brought me back. A kissing, biting, sucking, touching, licking, fucking mood, to be more specific.

Which is good, since it's matched my mood completely.

"Tickling does not hurt. In its very nature, it tickles."

"I say it hurts."

"I say, you are a very confusing female. You arrived on my estate covered in a motley of injuries and never complained, but this?" He holds up my foot. "This makes you quake?"

I giggle — *giggle* — in a way I'm damn sure I've never done as he chews on the arch of my foot and works his way down my ankle. At my calf, his chewing turns to licking and I feel my lower lips pulse open and clench together.

I slip my hand below the water's surface and for a second, I feel like touching myself until I register the ache. "Don't start unless you intend for me to pull you out of this bath again and ravish you for the next two days." He's breathing harder, chest rising and falling in time with his increased pulse. "I can't resist you, Abel."

I gasp a little and he pulls me closer and I can't help but kiss him and line my body up with his erection. "I can't resist you either."

I sink onto him and we both bellow out mirrored groans as I start to move, gyrating in a way that comes naturally to me. Kane spends himself in my body and I clench around his, and we get caught in the cycle until we're both spit out by it in the end. A little worse for the wear.

The water's chilly now, and Kane fills the tub back up and tries to grab hold of my foot again, but I kick him off. "That's how we got into trouble before."

"Trouble. I'd say it ended quite well, wouldn't you?"

I blush. "Yes."

Kane smiles and laughs lightly to himself, but at least he doesn't make any more advances...Darn it.

Instead, he leans his head back against a towel he's rolled up on the edge of the bath. He closes his eyes, leaving me to inspect the totally healed wound along the side of his neck. Mine's healed too, I notice again as I reach for it.

"How come all my bruises are gone?" I say.

Kane's smile twitches. "You're a gifted human. Why shouldn't you heal quickly?"

I narrow my eyes and poke him in the stomach with my toe. "That's not an answer."

"Yes, I know."

Warm water laps around us and when I realize he isn't going to give me any more than that, I try a second question. "Why did I drink your blood?" Why did I *like* it?

He pauses before he answers. "Because I asked you to."

"Come on."

He laughs lightly and I feel him take my foot again and gently rub the outside of my ankle. The movement is one thing above all others: possessive. It makes me heat. I didn't know it could feel like this. That's what he said to me on the flour-covered floor. I didn't know either.

"I know. And I will have to tell you eventually, but please don't ask me to give away all of my secrets in the span of one night."

"*All* of your secrets?" I say incredulously. "You keep so many from me."

"I don't. You know more about my life than any other human has."

"That doesn't say much. No human knows anything about you."

And then he has to go and spoil my irritation when he says, "You know what I look like when I'm vulnerable. No other human knows that."

My heart floats, just like so many bubbles on the surface of the water. The lights are dim in here and it feels like we're the only two people left in Population.

And that's alright.

"I won't let you down," I whisper.

Kane sucks in a breath. "You shouldn't say such things to me right now."

"Why not?"

"Because they make me want to make love to you, but we both need rest, and right now my restraint is as thin as a razor."

My chest jolts. He opens his eyes. Electricity fires like a live wire between us. I'm ready to get scorched.

Quickly trying to redirect, I blurt out, "So why didn't you tell me we'd have the first dance *solo*?"

Kane eases back against the basin and fails to disguise his taunting grin. "I didn't want to frighten you."

"How generous." I roll my eyes and look at the window to my right, where I can just barely discern the driveway and beyond that, the road, and past that, the treeline, in the lightening grey sky. It must be near morning.

I look up when Kane shifts against the bath with a small squeak. It makes me smile. Or would have, had Kane not been looking at me with a suddenly serious expression.

"You didn't…" He pauses to clear his throat. "You don't *really* think that I prefer Tasha to you, do you?"

I feel my face flush as I remember that he heard every word that passed between Memnoch and me. "Well, no. Yes and no," I amend, tracing the outline of a larger bubble with my middle finger. It pops silently.

"I just…"

"What?" Kane's looking at me in a way that makes me blush.

I struggle for words in the English language — the only language I know. "It's not just Tasha, but I sometimes…have been thinking…about the others…" Oh lordamercy am I really saying this to him right now? Naked in his bathtub?

His forehead wrinkles. "The Heztoichen? What about them?"

"No, I mean, the other *women*."

"This is one of the most frustrating conversations I can recall having," he pouts. "I am no nearer to understanding what you're talking about. The other women at the gala? Tasha? You believe I prefer…"

And then it hits him. His hand on my ankle stills. I don't know what I expected from telling him this, but outright anger wasn't it.

His hooded gaze sears and I feel a distant fear wriggle back in. I stiffen and edge back, but he grabs my foot and reels me in.

With his hands on my hips and my tits at his eye-level, he rasps, "Do you mean to tell me that you think there are other females who share my bed?"

I don't dare answer.

"Answer me."

But I'm too scared to. I shake my head no.

Kane leans in and sucks one of my nipples into his mouth and then the other. He bites very softly and a spasm rips down my left side. "Kane…"

"No," he says gruffly, pushing me back to my side of the tub. "That was a punishment, not a reward."

The only punishing thing about it was that he didn't continue. Though maybe that was the point.

He rubs his face, pushing water back through his hair and says, "There are no other females — Heztoichen or otherwise — for me, Abel. Just as, for you, there are no other men."

His words are thick enough with implication — and threat — that even someone as dense as me has no trouble understanding him. "I just thought, maybe you do this all the time."

"This? Abel. Listen to me clearly. Whatever you think *this* is, you are mistaken. This is not a passing pleasure. This is a bond. A mating. This is for life."

For life? I don't understand and shake my head. "So… there aren't other women?"

Kane groans, "I have slept with other women before you — both here and on Sistylea. I have been alive for three hundred years. How could I not have?

"But this…" His hands move through the water, gesturing at the space between us. "I have never had this before with anyone. And I do not intend to let you go."

My heart jerks. I feel dumb. Numb, while pleasure radiates through my once broken bones. Three hundred years? And in that time, he's never done *this* with anyone?

I don't know what to say, so again, I say the wrong thing, "So, I can stay here with you…even after we get Ashlyn back?"

"Abel," Kane snarls, voice jumping up an octave. He grabs both my ankles and yanks me back onto his lap. He wraps both arms around me and stares deep into my eyes.

"This house is not mine without you in it. It's yours now too. I am a selfish, jealous male. I will not give you up. Not when I'm so deeply in love with you."

My heart does this thing where it just kind of…stops. I think I black out. Or maybe I don't, but whatever happens, my fingers arc on his face and my lips are on his lips, my tongue meeting his with gentleness. I wilt. Something I've never done.

"I…" He stares into my face and I can still read anger there. He told me he loves me and he has no expectation of me saying it back. None. It makes it all that much more special.

"I love you too."

Now it's his turn to freeze. His eyes widen. A grin transforms his face. He pulls me close and buries his face between my breasts and I close my arms around his head and bend to kiss his crown and for a long time we just hold each other. We just surrender in each other's arms.

"I did not think I would win you so easily. Part of me thought I never would. But I was willing to try for as long as it took."

I don't know what to say to that, so I just touch him softly, hoping to soften the tension in his arms. He's still stiff though. Not at all the reaction I would have expected from a confession like the one I gave him. Honestly, I'm a bit peeved we aren't having sex again.

Then he groans and he sounds like he's in real pain.

"What's wrong?" I say.

"Your words just remind me of what I stand to lose."

"Lose?"

"With this plan. And it was *my* idea." He shakes his head against my sternum, then looks up at me and pushes the wet curls off of my face and neck.

"Perhaps I deluded myself into thinking you would fail, or maybe that the risks would not be as great as I realize they are now, but if he takes you into his home there is a chance you won't come back out."

Kane's voice is loud and dogged in its intensity. It sounds even more like love than his admission did.

"You're worried about me?"

He barks out a hollow laugh. "I'm in love with you, Abel. Do you have any idea what I've sacrificed..." His words cut short. He shakes his head again.

"You performed far too wonderfully at the gala." He reaches down and strokes the sole of my left foot. "Even in the shoes."

I smile shakily, so thrown by this conversation, and stutter, "Thank you. You did too."

"I did not." He laughs in a way that is cynical and humorless, and leans back, but pulls me with him, too.

He runs his hands up and down my body, but doesn't look at my face as he says, "Even someone as dense as Memnoch was able to see straight through me. And the way he *handled* you was deplorable. I should have ripped off both of his hands at the wrists." Kane clenches both fists and speaks through his teeth.

"But...this was just part of the plan, right? He had to like me. I had to be pretty and graceful and charming and pretend to be into him. Right?"

"You were quite convincing."

His tone is incriminating and my jaw drops. "You can't be serious. Are you really mad at me?"

"No," he grunts quickly — too quickly. "Of course not."

"You weren't...I mean, were you...Were you jealous?"

"Of *course* I'm jealous," he snaps as if he's been waiting for me to ask him this question all day.

He breathes hard and I can see the way his chest beats with brilliant light but I don't say anything. "But now I'm about to send you into his home, alone and unarmed. I'll be completely powerless and worse, I'll have to be far away to avoid his notice. He could rape and kill you in the time it takes me to reach his estate."

He's getting visibly upset now and I shush him, trying to offer him comfort in the only way I know how. By being blunt. "You know that I can take care of myself. Memnoch won't lay a hand on me."

He slides his arms around my waist, turns me around and pulls me into his lap where he holds me so tightly that not a hair could have fit between us.

"I know," he says, planting a wet kiss on my shoulder. "I know…I just wish you didn't have to. I swore to keep you safe and I'm not one to lightly break an oath."

"I made it a long time without you in my life. I think I can make it three more days."

"Another fact I loathe." He mutters, but there's a less hostile edge on his tone now. I take his hands and kiss all his knuckles.

I sigh.

Everything just feels good. He doesn't say more and we lay there, touching one another in ways I've never been touched before. The motions are all lazy caresses that make bubbles rush to my belly and bring a smile to my cheeks. I'm smiling still as dreariness comes for me.

Barriers down, I whisper something sweet, "I'm really grateful for these moments."

"As am I," he breathes into my hair. "I truly do love you, Abel."

"I love you too, Kane."

He squeezes me tight — and then tighter — so tight that I laugh.

When I settle again in his arms, I lean my head back on his shoulder. He whispers in my ear, "It seems strange that I should call you Abel, still. Do you not wish for me to call you by your true name?"

I close my eyes, a smile on my face, and shake my head. "No."

"Why not? You still don't trust me?"

"I trust you," I tell him. At least, I think I do. "But my old name is unlucky. It's the name I had when my world was destroyed, when my parents were killed, when my brother died trying to stop me from being raped, when my best friend was slaughtered because I wasn't quick enough, and when the last of my family was stolen."

I can feel him nodding behind me, his body stilling for just a moment. I stroke his arms, trying to pull him from the darkness of my history. Here in the light, there's no place for it.

"Abel's a good name. A lucky name."

"Oh is it?" he says with a little laugh.

I turn around and kiss the underside of his jaw. Then pull his chin down so I can devour his mouth. When I pull back, I'm breathless.

"Yes. It's the name I got when I met a Notare named Kane, fell in love, and he helped me get my little sister back."

Chapter Ten

The next three days pass in periods of alternating insanity and monotony. Kane leaves for a whole day to tend to official kingly business in some place called Laera — also known as Vancouver, according to Calvin.

There's a ton to do around the property so I busy myself the first day working with the seamstresses at spinning yarn. I'm god awful at it, so they send me the next day to work with Calvin and some of the other men to skin animals. I'm much, much better at that.

When Kane returns the third day, he's unhappy and foul-tempered. Well, anytime outside of his bedroom, or mine. I didn't think it was possible, but the cycles between us are only intensifying. Or maybe it's desperation that does it.

Kane's worried. I can feel it. And by the time Tasha comes to fit me for my dress for Friday night, he's shut down. Despite Tasha's deflection of most questions I ask her as she measures and mocks me, I get the impression that she's started to like me and that she really does want me to survive this.

Thursday evening, I stand in front of the mirror in my bedroom while Tasha makes a few final alterations. The dress she's designed is a slinky little thing that you can see my bra and panties through — though Tasha assures me that this is an integral part of the outfit. Of course.

The front and back flaps dangle down just low enough to cover my crotch and some of my butt cheeks, though the sides ride up nearly to hip level. Kane comes by to check on us and has about seven simultaneous heart attacks when he sees the dress.

He and Tasha argue for the better part of an hour before leaving the final call on whether or not I wear it up to me. Kane doesn't talk to me for the rest of the day after I side with Tasha.

I mean, I'm not happy about it either, but if I'm supposed to play the part of an escort then I have to do it convincingly, right? Plus, I like the shoes. In each stiletto is a knife.

Friday afternoon, Tasha helps me into my dress and Lady and Lanis do my makeup. Nervous that Kane will refuse to see me off, I'm happy to find him in the main hall.

"What are you doing?"

His hair is disheveled and his hands are working rapidly at something. He doesn't respond immediately and when he does, he doesn't answer but holds up a fur coat.

"For you."

"Cool," I say warily, slipping my arms into the sleeves. "Your mom's earrings by the way..."

"Are not relevant now." He grunts, "But yes, they were returned to us by the cleaning staff. They'll be waiting for you in our room when you get back."

"Don't you mean my room?"

"No. You're sleeping with me every night until old age kills you."

"Okay. That's an uhh...lovely sentiment. I kind of thought I'd have my own space though."

"Out of the question."

"Didn't you say it's my house, too?"

"Didn't I tell you that I am a selfish, possessive male? Or have you forgotten that you belong to me, Abel?"

"Well, you belong to me, too."

"Yes, which is why it makes no sense that I'm not going with you." He bends down. We're nearly nose-to-nose, or lip-to-lip. He licks his and it nearly derails me. I think that was the intent.

"Don't do this," he whispers. "I changed my mind. I'm not strong enough to allow it."

"You have to. It's a good plan. He won't suspect anything. Do you have the syringes?"

He hesitates, then nods. "In the lining of the coat."

"See? I'll be fine."

"I can find another way. I'll just burn his fucking estate down."

"With Ashlyn in it? I don't think so."

"Then I'll invade…"

"Tasha already told me why you can't. You could lose your title for that and then what would happen to me with you in jail? Hm?"

Kane's face twists up. He grumbles something I can't hear under his breath.

I place my hand on his chest. "You already are in trouble with the Lahve anyway for going into Population on your own to get that key."

The key. I haven't thought about it in so long. I'm about to ask him about it, when he barks, "I went back for *you*, and the Lahve does not rule me. His rules…"

"Are meant to keep you safe."

He shoves his hands back through his hair, exasperated. He kicks the air. "This is the last time I leave you alone with Tasha."

He reaches into his pocket and hands me a six inch needle filled with murky liquid. "This one is a backup. Less powerful, but should be enough to keep him down in an emergency. Use these on Memnoch at the first available opportunity."

"I don't plan on drawing this out," I say, slipping the syringe into my coat pocket. Filled with a bull tranquilizer, Sandra, the resident doctor, was sure these would be enough to take him down without killing him.

I hope she's right.

"If he touches you inappropriately even once, I'm going to rip his head off and feast on his organs. The consequences are irrelevant."

He buttons up every single button on my coat — even the top one that practically strangles me. I don't stop him though.

"Hey Abel, I'm ready when you are," Calvin says — my driver for the night.

Kane tenses. I mean, I thought he was tense before, but he tenses even *more*. He's a pile of gunpowder waiting for a light as he runs his hands up and down my arms over and over.

"Abel," he growls.

"I know. Tell me when I'm back with Ashlyn."

I untangle myself from his grip and head out after Calvin into the darkness towards the big black SUV.

I amble into the back seat and roll down the window. Kane isn't looking at me though, but at Calvin as he says, "Drive straight there. Drive straight back."

"Yessir."

"You don't come back without her." This time, I hear the unspoken threat.

"I...of course," Calvin stutters and I wonder if he's reconsidering having volunteered at about this moment.

Calvin pauses before nodding in agreement. Even from the backseat, I swear I can hear him gulp.

Then Kane hands Calvin what looks like a phone from the 1990s. It's big and blocky and yellow with a short black antennae and only one button on its flat face. He also hands Calvin a gun.

"You use this if and only if there's trouble on the road." I can't tell if he's talking about the gun or the walkie-talkie or both.

"Or if there are complications at Memnoch's," Calvin adds, as if repeating a script.

"There won't be," I interject.

Kane pretends he hasn't heard me and says, "I will use my receiver to phone you in four hours if you have not returned with Abel by then. Four hours."

Calvin looks at his watch. "Midnight then, sir."

Kane nods once, then exhales and looks at me. "Four hours," he repeats.

"Four hours," I agree.

Kane licks his lips and pulls a scalpel from his sleeve. "The wound won't heal up in time for him to notice anything strange."

"What's strange?" I ask as he cuts me.

His eyes meet mine and he rubs his nose on the inside of his arm. He licks my blood off of his fingers and shudders at the same time a foreign euphoria rolls through me.

"I'll see you at twelve, Kane. Not a minute later." I hope. Pray.

Kane closes his eyes and nods once, then straightens up and backs away.

"I won't give up," I tell him. Not for anything.

Kane shakes his head and as the car begins to roll, says, "That's what I'm afraid of."

The road is paved, but lonely. Or maybe the loneliness is all mine. I got so used to Kane's presence over these past days that it feels strange now to be without him.

How messed up is that?

Scavenger rat and the alien king living happily ever after…

If only Population ever allowed for things like happily ever afters…

This is the part where the nerves set in. Will she be there? What if she isn't? What if she's dead? What if Memnoch gets suspicious? I also recognize that I haven't had to fight anyone to the death recently and I hope my skills haven't gotten rusty in the interim. What if I fight like Beast now? I wonder if Population missed me while I was away…

To distract myself, I make light conversation with Calvin, but when he starts responding in "oh yes, ma'ams" and "certainly, madams", my frayed nerves peak. We must be getting close. And then I see it through the front windshield.

A small compound stands fully lit at the top of a low hill. There aren't any trees near it. There are only stumps, like the crooked gravestones of the ones who died to make space for his massive driveway.

We approach the gate at the bottom of the hill and Calvin rolls down his window. "Hello, I am speaking on behalf of Miss Abel, here to see Lord Memnoch," Calvin says into the tiny speaker box that juts towards our car like a mouth.

I hear static for a second, and then a voice that is unmistakably Memnoch's. "Who is this?"

"This is Miss Abel's driver."

There's a long pause before the gate swings open and we crunch over gravel up, up, up to the house. Calvin swings the car around so that I'm as close to the front door as possible and I wonder for a second if it's because he sees how much damage I can inflict upon myself in these stupid high shoes on a *flat* surface. Gravel is basically a death trap.

This whole thing is basically a death trap.

Swallowing down my mounting reservation, I open the door at the same time that the front door to the house opens. Memnoch leans against the threshold, arms crossed over his chest. He's wearing suit pants and a shirt, unbuttoned. The sleeves are rolled back to the elbows. He smiles at me and even with only one eye, he might have been dashing in some other life. One where he hadn't stolen my little sister.

"Apologies, Miss," Calvin says, scrambling to help me out of the car. Calvin's eyes are bright and when I look into them I realize that I've made the first blunder. I should have waited for him to open the door.

I overcorrect and wave him away. "Next time, be quicker." Facing away from Memnoch, Calvin shoots me a tight-lipped glare. I'll pay for that later.

For now, I move forward, standing tall as I try to hone some of Kane's confidence and when I approach Memnoch, it's thankfully without wobbling.

"Good evening," he says coolly.

"Good evening." I hold onto the collar of my coat, feeling the syringe beneath the furry yolk. I wonder if I'll have time to grab it and stab him now, or if it's too soon. If I'm being too hasty. And then the moment is gone and I transform the twitch of my fingers towards the seam of the fabric into something much less dangerous.

"I'll take your coat, if you like," he says in a deep, rumbling voice that does nothing to mask his hunger.

"Then there will be nothing left for desert," I muse and I sound sexy only because Tasha told me what to say and how to say it. She was ruthless in her critique.

Memnoch beams. "I can see why the Notare keeps you close." Then he shuts the door between Calvin and me and seals me into this crypt alive. "Is that his car?"

"Not anymore. It was gifted to me," I say, spewing more lies.

"By the Notare?"

"Don't sound so impressed. You don't know what you'll be prepared to give me when I'm through with you."

As I turn around my voice gives out when I register how close he is. He's not more than an arm's length away. He edges closer still and I have to fight not to move back as he reaches behind my head, then pulls the clip from my hair.

My curls spill down around my face and I realize that he's going to kiss me and that I haven't prepared myself at all for this. His mouth moves towards mine, but I turn my head in the final instant.

"Don't get greedy." I force out a laugh as his mouth tastes my jaw and the edge of my bottom lip. Tingles sweep through me, but they're the kind that accompany nausea, rather than the euphoric tingles I get from Kane.

I think of Kane and feel a strange sensation ripple across each inch of my skin that Memnoch touches. I don't understand it, but pull away anyways. It feels oddly enough, like guilt.

Memnoch grunts, but seems to enjoy the charade. He rolls his one eye and says, "Patience has never been one of my strongest attributes."

"You know the humans say that patience is a virtue."

"I didn't think you were here to do anything virtuous. I can smell your blood from here and it, at least, is certainly sinful."

I turn to face him. My heartbeat is light and quick and I imagine that I can feel Ashlyn in that house with me. It'll all be over soon.

"I'd love a tour before we begin," I say, unbuttoning the top clasp that Kane worked so hard to close. I fan open my coat to reveal my collar bones. And more importantly, the cut Kane branded me with.

Memnoch nods, but he doesn't see my eyes anymore and instead allows himself to be taunted by the smell of my wound. I twist my neck so that he gets a better look at it and when I glance back to meet his gaze, he bows to me. I don't bow back.

"It would be my pleasure," he says, voice rough around the edges. "And perhaps as we move towards the bedroom we can remove a few more of those buttons."

I nod, acquiescing with a smile that only just masks my revulsion as I make room for him to lead. As he drifts past me, he leans in towards my neck and breathes in deeply and then deeper still. Inhaling me.

"Where shall we start?" He gestures around at all of his many things. The paintings on the walls are of boxes and shapes. The furniture is all sleek and modern. Nothing like Kane's.

"Upstairs or downstairs?"

"Whichever," I answer, though really I want to see the basement. "Though we should save the bedroom for last."

He grins at me devilishly. "Then we begin with the basement."

I think I've gotten lucky until I actually see his basement. It's a game room, fully equipped with a Pac-Man machine, video game console, miniature arcade, and billiards table. He tries to coerce me into a game, but I've never even seen pool played before. I've never used any form of entertainment.

The tour of the rest of the house is tedious, Memnoch explaining to me different artifacts and which important person I'd never heard of gave them to him. It must be tedious to him too, because when he shows me a secret passage blended into the wallpaper on the ground floor, it leads us straight to his bedroom.

Now or never then.

Let's do this.

I step into the space and glance around, noticing immediately that his bedroom is nothing like Kane's. Everything is black and red, like it's meant to terrify. Like it's meant for pain.

Memnoch stares past me and glances at his red satin sheets with implication. "The bedroom," he says, speaking when I don't.

"Hm." I clutch the collar of my coat and will my fingers not to shake and give me away. It's hard. I *am* nervous. I'm nervous, weirdly, because I'm no longer on the streets of Population. Population, I know.

I know the grey, I know the dark alleyways, I know how to outlive the scavengers and steer clear of the Others and fight the gangs. I know how to survive, because I stick to the rule book. But the rule book is gone, replaced by just one — never give up, even in the face of death, or something. And now I'm entirely out of my element, under-clothed and overfed in an alien's house by choice rather than by force, willingly edging myself back onto his bed.

"Incredible," he says when I have the coat fully fanned open. His eyes sweep up and down the length of my body again and again.

I smile while a cool burst of air caresses my middle. Tasha's stupid dress is satin and leaves a lot to be desired in terms of warmth and practicality. My bare legs rub against one another in a way I hope is distracting as I free the needle. Successful, I quickly toss the coat behind me onto the bed, the syringe beneath it. Then I lay back down against the soft mattress, holding myself in a position that keeps the syringe fixed beneath my left shoulder blade.

I marshal my breaths and say calmly, "Are you just going to stand there?"

He doesn't hesitate, but covers me with his body right away. He's a heavy bastard, but I was prepared for that. I was prepared for all of this and I'm not afraid when his hands paw at me now. He goes immediately for my panties — so much for foreplay — but Tasha used metal threads in order to stitch this dress together. He can't get anywhere.

"How do you get this thing off?" He growls, anger rising.

"Let me show you." I push on his shoulder and he hesitates, then lets me roll him onto his back. I straddle his waist and reach up to massage my breasts.

"Yes," he hisses, settling back. "You're beautiful," he says, grabbing my ass and squeezing it, "I want you now."

"I want you too." Your life. For a moment, I hesitate — maybe I should go for the knife in my shoes instead of the syringe on the bed. Maybe I should just end him. There's no reason for him to be among the living.

That wasn't the plan though. I shake my head and say through clenched teeth, "I've been waiting for this moment for too long."

He moans as his fingers dig into my ass cheeks hard enough it hurts. "I want in you now, Abel. Take this off."

He grips my hips and gyrates against them so forcefully that I can feel his erection against my crotch like a thick length of rope.

Smiling genuinely now, I drop forward onto my hands, planting one on either side of his face. I look down at him and lean in like I'm going to kiss him. At the same time, my right hand frees the top from the syringe and points it at his neck.

He doesn't even notice, he's so focused on my mouth as I say, "This is for Kane."

I insert the needle into his neck and push the plunger. To his credit, his confusion doesn't last and he manages to react in time to knock me off of him and onto the floor.

My butt gets rug burn as I scooch over it towards the wall and watch Memnoch rise from the bed like a demon. Shit shit shit! Was that not enough? Momentary panic that the dose was too little grips me, until Memnoch takes a drunken step to the left.

"You bi…" he starts to say, before staggering down to his knees and collapsing onto the carpet at my feet, face first.

Well, that was close.

I quietly snatch my coat off the bed, debate sticking him with the other syringe…debate stabbing him…debate sticking him with the other syringe then stabbing him, but I don't. Better if we're in and out. That was the plan. Because I don't want to know what the aliens would do to me if I got charged with murder.

I don't know exactly how much time I have, but Sandra said to be out of the house in forty-five minutes at the latest.

I start canvassing right away, slipping from one room to the next, throwing books out of bookshelves, feeling up the walls in the hopes of finding more of those secret stairwells.

Nothing.

There must be forty rooms in his house all connected by about half a dozen visible halls and staircases on top of the countless hidden ones. I've only found three secret passages so far, in addition to the one that he showed me, and none of them lead to anywhere interesting. I rip through the bathroom, hurtling objects around with so much force that I break both the glass shower door and the mirror.

Nothing.

I thunder into the last room at the end of the hall on the first floor. It's a study. Bookshelves wrap around the room and a window covers the entire width of the wall to my left. There's a computer sitting open at a massive oak desk just in front of me. I go to it and press down angrily on the keys, hoping that I might see something on his desktop that reads: THIS IS WHERE I'M KEEPING YOUR SISTER.

When the monitor unfreezes I'm nearly stunned — not by the folders and documents that are on his desktop, which number at about three dozen — but by his screensaver. The picture on the display is of a young, pre-pubescent girl. She looks human and is standing in the center of Memnoch's bedroom — the same bedroom I'd been in fifteen minutes previous — wearing a stretched smile and nothing else.

I wait for a second and try to force my mind to cooperate with me, because I'm drawing a total blank. My stomach drops even though this girl isn't Ashlyn, because I suddenly remember what Memnoch said when he took her. *I like little girls.*

The slideshow shifts to the next image, which is of another girl, only this time Memnoch is in the photograph too. She's seated on his lap and has blood dripping down her right arm. Her pale face is red and splotchy. She looks like she's been crying. Breathing hard, I look away quickly down at the floor.

I check my breath, as my insides war and rebel. I realize two things in that moment: there can't be a God, because what manner of Creator would subject her children to this? And then I realize that there is definitely a God because as my gaze drops to the floor in horror, it's drawn to a small brass grate.

And there are sounds coming out of it. Human sounds.

A sniffle, barely hushed, is followed closely by a voice. It's a child's voice and it whispers, "Shh…"

My heart pounds. I fall onto my knees and tear the grate from the wall, but when I look into the hole, I don't hear anything and I see only darkness. "Hello?" I say into the space, which is much larger than just another air duct.

No one answers. But I do hear motion. The light from the room behind me shines only far enough to illuminate a soft gleam, about six feet away, and nothing else.

"Hello," I say again, "If someone is there, then answer me. My name is Abel. I'm here to help."

A soft whisper answers my call. It's a voice — one that I recognize — and my heart thunders to a short, sweet stop. Because despite everything, before that very second, I never truly expected to hear her voice again at all. Ashlyn calls me by my name from the World Before, but I answer with the one from the World After. The one that led me back to her.

"Ashlyn, holy fucking shit! Are you there? It's me. Becks sent me for you."

"Becks?" she says and I hear tears on her tongue even though I cannot see her. "Mom?"

Strange sounds come from the direction of her voice and even though I know she's in there I'm weirdly terrified to crawl into that space after her. I can't see how far it goes. I can't even see the floor. Where is the bastard keeping her? What *is* this place?

My blood runs cold and goosebumps break out across my arms and legs. "No. It's just me. Are you in there alone?"

"No. No there are…"

And then there's rattling and a separate voice whimpers, "Ashlyn, shut up."

Another says, "Please, stop talking…"

"Ashlyn you're going to get us killed."

"Who knows who that is…"

"…what kind of trap he's planning."

"You're going to die…"

"Don't…please…"

The voices speak in overlapping waves, like water against the shore and there are so many of them. "Shut up, all of you," I say loudly, meaner than I needed to. "I'm here to help you get out. Now, Ashlyn, is there a light down there?"

"Yes," she whispers, and I can hear the surge of panic in her voice that sounds so much older than it last did when I spoke to her. Like she's gone miraculously from eleven to forty.

"Yes, it's in the middle of the room. You…you have to come inside first."

I gulp down a knot of nerves, bottle the last of my reservation and shimmy into the cubicle of darkness, feet first. There's a wall at my back and I use that to leverage my weight against as my toes stretch to reach the floor. Dropping the last few feet to the ground, I stumble in my heels and reach out to catch myself on the nearest object. My hand hits something hard and cold and I hear a gasp and a short scream, followed by sobbing.

"Shhh," I say, though I've already been drowned out by a chorus of voices that evidently agree with me. "Ashlyn, you have to guide me," I say into the darkness, trying to keep my voice even.

I can't see a damn thing and I think of how much easier this entire ordeal would be if I were Kane. Then again, I doubt he'd have had the same degree of success trying to seduce Memnoch.

Ashlyn speaks to me, but from a distance. "Take about ten steps from the wall towards my voice." Her pitch trembles in a way that is uncharacteristic. I don't think I can remember what fear sounds like in the throat of an eleven-year-old. Now that's all I hear.

I hold my hands out in front of me and feel my way through the darkness, totally blind. Twice, my fingers fumble against more cold, hard edges and once more my ankles wobble, but I don't fall and no one else in the room speaks. They don't even whimper. For a moment, I imagine that there's no one in there with me at all.

"Ashlyn?" I say, more for my sake than for hers. I have to break up the silence.

"There's a string that hangs down, you should run into it." Just as she speaks, I do. This makes me nervous. Cringing, I wonder how long she's had to study this room.

I grab ahold of the string and give it a gentle pull. The cord bounces back towards the ceiling and a light comes on about four feet over my head. It illuminates the stark and startling world around me. My jaw drops and my heart breaks.

Dozens of metal cages are stacked two-high in meticulous rows, and each contains a different little girl. My eyes over rake the scene again and again and I don't cry. I can't. That wouldn't help them. Tears in Population never help anyone.

Ashlyn's little voice calls me by the name I used to own and drags me from my own thoughts.

"Ashlyn," I answer, voice steel now, hard.

She's in the last row of cages against the farthest wall, clinging to a metal, chain-link door. Her little pink nose sticks out at me like a dog's. I step closer.

"Ashlyn," I whisper again, but my throat catches. I think about Kane and the kids running to school, laughing. And then I think about the kids that die out in Population, too used by gangs to even trade anymore. And then I look at Ashlyn here, naked in a cage, cuts covering both of her arms to the elbows.

I thought I was out of Population, and safe in the Diera, but no. Nowhere is safe.

Only that's not true...

Kane. Kane is safe. I need to get her out of here and to him, if it's the last thing I do.

"I'm going to get you out of here," I tell her. My voice is even, but I still choke.

She sticks her fingers out through the cage to touch mine and I struggle to touch her back. She's so dirty. So filthy. I feel like I failed her a thousand times in this moment.

"It's locked." I tear at the heavy metal bolt keeping her from salvation.

She points over my shoulder. "There's a key to our cages, over there. He keeps the key to the door with him though."

I turn and spot a silver key hanging beside a large brown door and run to it before Ashlyn can say another word. I streak past two rows of girls, and rip the key from the wall.

As I do, I'm shocked to see that the girl in the cage closest to the door is actually near enough to reach the key beside it. My face twists up as I wonder why she didn't take the key and liberate herself... And then I look at her. I look at her closely. She cowers away from my gaze and quivers when I hold the key towards her.

"No," she says. Her grey eyes lock with mine and for just a second, I see me. Her skin is the same creamy brown mine is and her hair is a mess of ratty, rampant curls.

It's strange, looking into a mirror like this and seeing what could have happened to me. The thinking that, for all that I've been through, I was one of the lucky ones. She doesn't have a list of rules telling her to keep fighting. She doesn't even have one.

"Never give up," I growl as heat streaks up the backs of my arms. "And I will never give up on you."

I won't let you down.

I won't let any of them down.

I can't afford to.

I wrench open the door to her cell and drag her out of it by force as her skinny arms thrash feebly against me. I pull her with me along the ground and return to Ashlyn's cell, unlocking that one next. Ashlyn climbs out and hugs me as tight as her thin arms can manage. For only a second — because that's all we have — I forget all thoughts of murder and vengeance and simply hug her back. I feel relief at the same time that I feel regret. It's impossible not to blame myself. I couldn't save Becks. And I couldn't save Ashlyn's childhood. Only her life. Because that's all that's left.

I take the remaining syringe and stick it between my breasts, then I throw my coat around Ashlyn's shoulders, handing her the key. "Ashlyn, we've got to work together. You have to help me with all these locks, okay?"

I glance up at the open window and in two-seconds, form the outline of a terrible plan, but I don't have much time for ingenuity. "When you get the girls out of the cages, send them to me. I'll help them through this window. There's a car waiting outside." I glance down at my watch. We've got twenty minutes.

Ashlyn nods once, and I can tell that even though her glossy eyes are bloodshot and ringed by deep indigo bags, she's still alert enough to understand how to help me. She's off.

While Ashlyn works to liberate the girls in the far cages first, I remove the spike from the bottom of my left shoe and whittle it around the window frame high in the far wall.

Eventually, I manage to snap it free without breaking any glass. By this point there are already six little girls crowded around me, the first of which is wearing my coat. I glance up at Ashlyn, who's naked again and working fiercely to unlock the cells. I see that she's already enlisted some of the older girls to help coax the younger, more fragile ones from their cages. I can't even believe it.

This was the girl who ate first, who got all of the best things that we scavenged, who was sheltered from anything and everything cruel. Now she's entirely naked and gives up the only semblance of protection she has to help a stranger.

I remember what Becks said to me and what Kane repeated the first time we spoke. *Selflessness will only get you killed in this world.* Unfortunately, that selflessness has rubbed off on somebody else.

And I'm so proud of her.

I drop to one knee and look at the girls around me. I focus on the one in my coat and say, "My name is Abel. I'm a human just like you, but I have friends that are also Others."

Several of the girls start to cry at the mention of the word, but I shush them and continue quickly, "There is a human outside in a black car. His name is Calvin. He's going to take you to my friend's house. My friend is one of the Others, but he's kind and he will take care of you.

"There are lots of humans living with him now. He will give you food and water and a warm bed to sleep in. I promise. But you all *need* to find the front gate. That is where Calvin is. Can you do that?"

The little girl before me blinks, without understanding. I don't know that she can even hear me. It's a taller girl just behind her that says, "Yeah. Yes, ma'am, I mean," she stutters, "We'll find Calvin. At the gate. He'll take us to the Oth... Oth...Other and...and he'll help us."

"That's a good girl," I say, taking my hand to her cheek. "What's your name?"

"Ju...Judith?"

"Judith. That's excellent. Now what is your name?" I say to the lost girl.

She shakes her head. Then after a few moments, whispers, "Rebecca."

I just stare at her. *Becks?*

Population plays dangerous games with my heart and for a moment, I'm distracted by longing. "Rebecca," I breathe.

I tuck her hair behind her ear and button her fully into my coat, just like Kane had done for me. "Can you follow Judith?"

Rebecca's head swivels around on her neck. Vacantly, she nods and I know that I'm unlikely to get a more definite response than that.

"Good," I say, even though it isn't. She's malnourished and likely on her last legs. If I can just get her to Maggie and Sandra... But she has to actually get there. "Now Judith, you first. I need you to stand on the other side of the window and help get the other girls out."

I push Judith through the window though she barely fits, and I know she can't be much older than ten. Together, we manage to get the girls out one-by-one and when I turn around, I see that Ashlyn has helped the rest of the girls form a rudimentary line.

I lift thirteen girls up and over my head and through that tiny window until just three are left. A roar is followed immediately by a crash. Ashlyn trembles and the weepy redhead next in line screams while the girl in line behind her collapses.

I grab the two girls from the floor and toss them roughly through the window, scratching elbows and bumping heads. The crashing overhead gets louder and I quickly run to turn out the lights. I check my watch.

Shit. It's been forty-seven minutes.

"Come on, you're the last one," I whisper to Ashlyn.

Ashlyn's gaunt face tilts up to me before turning towards the window. She shakes her head. I grab her by the arm and physically drag her forward but when I lift her, she braces her feet against the wall in resistance.

"You won't fit." She's clever for a kid.

"It doesn't matter. You've got to get out and help the other girls." I know that she probably wouldn't go for any reason any less altruistic.

I see her resolution waver and her eyes glance up to the window with hope. "What about you?" Her voice is as pale as she is, and as light as a shadow.

"I'll be fine," I respond, though I only half mean it, but by then I've already scooped Ashlyn up beneath the arms and lifted her over my head. She kicks her feet weakly in protest but I push her through the opening and into Judith's outstretched hands.

"Well done, Judith," I tell her when Ashlyn's outside. "You saved them."

Judith stares down at me with horror. She's still clutching Ashlyn's hands.

"I need you two to be strong for the other girls. I need you to make sure that you all find Calvin, and if you can't find him you have to get past the gate, onto the road. There, you run west. Do you remember what direction west is?"

Judith shakes her head. "I don't know…"

"I know. I can lead them."

"Of course you can, baby girl." I nod up at her. My voice is thick as I say, "You run west about ten miles until you find an Other named Kane. If anyone stops you, you tell them that you belong to Notare Kane. Repeat that after me, okay?"

"Notare Kane," the two girls whisper, as something above us sounds off like an explosion.

"Notare Kane will help you. He is one of the Others, but he's my friend." I can see the hesitation in her quiet eyes as I blatantly tell her to defy every rule I've ever taught her all at once. "Do you trust me?"

Ashlyn nods without hesitation. So does Judith.

"Good. Now go."

"I love you," she whispers.

"I love you too," I tell her. "And when you find Kane, tell him I love him and not to do anything stupid."

Ashlyn's eyes widen, but a second later Judith is pulling her arm and both of their pale faces disappear like the grey hunting down the stars.

I can hear Memnoch thundering across the floor above me, screaming something about being cheated and lied to and ripping something off of someone's neck. Probably mine.

Well, big boy, the feeling is mutual.

I had a plan earlier about making this whole operation an in-and-out, super stealth kinda thing. Fuck that. Right now I'm feeling pretty stabby stabby.

I take my remaining syringe in hand with every intention of knocking Memnoch out, then torturing the hell out of him.

I recognize the futility of my plan if he were to catch me down here amidst all the cages, and I quickly wriggle back up into the study. Not five seconds pass before I hear the sound of his voice ripping through the walls and I realize with alarm that he's headed straight towards me.

There's a window seat behind the desk between two bookcases. I run to it and rip the curtains closed so that I'm concealed — so long as he can't hear me breathing.

"She lied to me…tricks…he is behind this. All of this… he knows!" It takes me a second to realize that Memnoch isn't talking to himself like an insane person. He must have another one of those walkie talkies. I wonder fleetingly who's on the other end of the line…

"He sent a spy to come for me and the fucking human bitch tricked me and drugged me and stole valuable materials…Probably that have to do with his brother…why else would she come here? He had to have sent her…*Notare Kane*," he sneers, and then his voice softens and becomes more imploring.

"Of course I told her nothing of you, Notare." Notare. Notare? My memory tickles, old folders dusted off and opened. I remember the gala — more than just what happened in the kitchens — and I realize that what he's just said isn't quite true. He *did* tell me something about a Notare. Only her name, though.

Elise.

Is that who he's speaking to? "She knows nothing of your involvement. Only that I have the key, probably…had the key. No. No, Kane took it." I took it. Don't I get any credit for anything? "I nearly killed him for it but I cannot kill a Notare…Notare," he says, stuttering now, clearly lost.

"Why? It's illegal…the Lahve — our Chancellor — would have my fucking head on a spike. You know he's been looking for someone to make an example of and he's always hated me…Of course I serve you and only you. You are my Notare and my Queen."

He says more in the HeztoiGn language before breaking completely. "The human klees!" I don't know what that means, but judging by the intonation, I can hazard a guess that it's not a nice word he's using to describe me.

"She was in my den rooting around on my computer… Why else would she be? It is obvious that Kane sent her to do his bidding, because he knows…she must know…she must know that his brother isn't dead and that we have him!"

It's pretty cliché that I gasp at the drop, but I do. Oops.

The room goes dead still. All, except for my heartbeat which pounds out a wicked tattoo. I try to stay calm as my pulse accelerates and my stomach pitches and my muscles all tense, preparing themselves for one final smack down that could end with me in a bodybag. It will, if I can't kill Memnoch, because I'm not going into one of those cages. He won't take me alive.

At the the unmistakable plod of giant footstep against the carpet, I raise the syringe. Memnoch rips the curtains back.

I'm up on my heels but his wild, bloodshot eye sees me and knows where I'm going even before I do. He'd have killed me immediately — long before I ever managed to get the tranquilizer in his bloodstream — if it hadn't been for one little, miraculous thing: Calvin. There's a crash out in the driveway below us and it shakes like thunder and spits like lightning.

Flames crackle and my panic at what the shit is going on down there is only displaced by the knowledge that Memnoch is wondering the same thing. He's distracted, which means I can't afford to be.

Smashing the syringe into his chest, I push the plunger quickly. Unfortunately, I'm not quite quick enough.

Halfway through the vial, Memnoch reels away from me. He latches onto my wrist and rips my hand back with enough force that something cracks. I scream and while pain radiates up my arm, Memnoch removes the needle from his chest and stabs me in the neck with whatever's left in the capsule.

Shit.

I watch him struggle against the effects of the tranquilizer just long enough to smash through his desk chair. It shatters to pieces upon impact.

Meanwhile, I slump down into the window seat and lay my head against the soft pillows. I close my eyes and fold my hands gently in my lap, as if I were always meant to die there.

Chapter Eleven

I wish that I'd stayed passed out for longer.

That's the first thought that comes to me when I wake up to a miserable pain. The drugs batter back the ferocity of my agony just enough for me to be able to access my senses. Opening my eyes, I can just make out the ripple of water rising and falling about a dozen paces directly in front of me. Otherwise, I see nothing.

It's dark. Darker than dark. Dark like the inside of an eyelid.

The only light in the room is the keychain hanging off Memnoch's belt, reflected in soft pale shades against the rock surrounding me. And it *is* surrounding me. Each time my body lurches forward, the rocky ground slashes the backs of my calves. My legs are wet and the ground beneath them is cold, rugged and craggy.

It takes me a second to understand that I'm being dragged and that there's a gash in my throat. I can feel my own hot blood leaking across my chest. My head lolls on my neck like it's attached in paper and string rather than bone and muscle. I try to pick it up, but it doesn't cooperate with me. Stupid head.

The whole world spins as the drugs in my bloodstream make it almost impossible to tell up from down or left from right, but I do realize that I've still got Tasha's heels on my feet. Oh Hallelujah.

Though I can't see him, I know that it's Memnoch that's got me by a single wrist. My entire left side screams as it supports my dead weight and fire ripples through my shoulder blade.

That pain explodes louder still when my lower spine connects with the hard shelf of what feels like a particularly jagged rock. I try to stay quiet, but can't. I grunt.

Memnoch ignores me and continues muttering to himself. "Can't believe that I'm here and that I'm doing this...I could have just killed her — should have just killed her — if only... fucking Notare!"

When we hit another larger, sharper rock about a second later, I bite my bottom lip so hard I can taste the metallic twang of my own blood. Memnoch shakes me violently and the pain in my back stretches down to meet my legs.

A section of the hard rock falls free when he drags my limp body over it. I grab it. I'm not even sure why I grab it. It must be the rule book. Because when I swing it around and smash Memnoch's shoe with it, I knew that there would be consequences.

He kicks me. I choke on the taste of blood and he kicks me again and again and again. Darkness is a welcome reprieve. The pain is so bad, I don't even feel it when I wake up again. I don't feel anything.

I hear the distinct shuffling of something big break from the silence. I turn to look ahead, but as I do Memnoch drops my arm and picks up my ankle. He drags me a few feet further and the hard rock beneath me becomes smooth, even though it's covered in something brittle that crunches under my weight, like twigs that snap and pop in a dry forest.

Not sticks, bones.

Memnoch snaps something heavy, hard and cold around my left ankle. I can hear the distinctive sound of a chain being dragged and the next thing I know there's a second manacle locked around my left wrist.

Memnoch rolls my body over the smooth floor, pressing me up against something hard and chillingly cold. I'm completely wet, though I don't know how. Freezing. My teeth begin to chatter.

I force myself to focus hard, and in the darkness I make out the dim outline of something strong and vertical. Beams. Metal beams. They press against my arm and I can tell that they've been built into the foundation of the stone around us. Each post is nearly three inches in diameter, with only about enough space from one to the next to fit a wrist through, maybe a thin ankle.

"Hey," Memnoch shouts, banging on the bars with an open palm, "feeding time."

A hollow ring fills the tunnel, echoing back to me as I try unsuccessfully to sit up. My heart starts to pound and I rattle the shackles, but they don't budge.

"Memnoch," I shout, but my voice catches on vocal cords that no longer seem to function. Coughing, I say instead, "Fucker." What is it that they say about antagonizing your jailers again? Oh yeah... Don't.

Memnoch stands and pushes my head back with enough force that I hear it crack against the ground. But I don't feel the pain. I suddenly don't feel anything anymore. That can't be good.

"You are a human who thinks they are equal to one of us, but you will see soon enough just how wrong you are. If it were up to me, I'd have ended your life while you were sleeping. But having tasted your blood, my master feels that it's better to let someone else do the job."

I think about answering, but can't. And apparently, that's the end of his monologue. He leaves and I stare after him, but am only able to see the outline of his receding form for a moment. Then darkness takes everything.

Sound carries in a strange way in this tunnel, and just as his footfalls fade out altogether, I'm startled by a second echo — this one quite close. I look to my left, towards the bars and stare at them so intensely that after a few seconds I stop seeing bars and beams, but instead see yellow and purple blocks of color. There's no light down here. I'm not actually seeing *anything*.

I close my eyes and shake my head at the sound of a large animal shifting just beyond the beams, willing myself to see it. I don't. And I can't get away from it either as the chain charges over the ground, dragging me with it.

My fingers claw at the things beneath me, hoping for purchase. Instead, my palms pad through bones and things that are *softer*. Clothes, maybe? Some of them are hard and crusty and all of it reeks of death. Soon I'll be nothing more than a skull and the dress Tasha made for me that's indestructible.

A hard hand latches around my left ankle, dragging it through the beams. Chipped nails claw against my skin a second before a set of hard square teeth snap through my flesh and this feels *nothing* like when Kane does it. This is pure pain.

I scream and the echo of my own agony comes back to me a dozen times more. My thoughts dim but I'm not dead yet because the mouth around my leg retreats as whatever has me spits me back out.

I smile at that deliriously and think, maybe I really *am* a tough chew to swallow.

"Fuck." The voice is definitely male and scares the piss out of me. *There's a living, sentient being back there?* What the what?

He coughs and then spits, "I haven't fed in months and the bastard brings me my brother's wife."

He coughs again and the sound, like his words, echoes down the tunnel so many times that I know I've heard him right. Even though he's dead wrong.

From my position sprawled out over the floor with my chewed up leg shoved crudely between the cold beams, I choke out a single word. "Wh…what?"

"You're my brother's wife."

Whoever's in that cell smashes a fist against one of the walls. There's a snapping sound and I wonder if it's the wall cracking, or the bones of his own hand. Then I feel warmth on the other side of those beams and I hear the sound of a body sliding against the wall and sinking to the ground.

"I'm fucking starving," he breathes. "Of course he'd bring you here to torture me. But I can be strong enough not to kill you, even if you do smell so good. Your taste…"

He growls, "Your taste is even better." I don't know if he's assuring me or himself, so I don't respond. It's not like I could have fought him off — or even moved — if I wanted. I still have Tasha's other knife in my shoe, but I don't have the strength to lift myself up right now, let alone saw off my own hand and foot, kill the guy on the other side of the bars and somehow limp away from all of this.

"But I won't kill you. I can resist killing my brother's wife, right?" Is he asking *me*?

I moan, laughing at the irony of it.

"Fuck," I hear the sound of something hard hitting something harder, "you don't even make a convincing case in your own defense…"

"Mikael," I say, remembering. "You're Mikael."

Silence. "You know who I am?"

"You escaped with him from Sistylea. You took the other life raft." I croak. There's blood in my mouth, on my lips, coating my teeth. It's all I can taste. It's all I can smell. I think I'm dying one minute, but in the next I think of Kane and focus on the slightly sulfuric smell of my own blood, mixed with his. I find it easier to breathe.

Mikael, grunts, "I guess you are Kane's wife then. He doesn't talk about his family to people he doesn't trust. So how did that happen? Kane married? And to a *human*?" Mikael says the word cruelly and I know that they really are brothers when I feel my smashed face frown. Even in death, I'm still being belittled.

I groan, "What are you talking about? Kane and I… married?"

"You drank his blood didn't you?" He rumbles and the sound he makes is either frustration or a deep hunger. I didn't really plan on being eaten alive, so I'm really hoping it's the former.

I nod. "Yeah."

"And he drank yours?"

"Uh huh."

"There you go. There's a whole ceremony attached, but that's the essence of it. You drank his blood, he drank yours, badda bing badda boom, as the humans say. Hell. Humans… Kane's always had a soft spot for your kind, even if you are inferior."

"At least humans would have treated you better than your alien host. You're *dead* as far as the rest of the world is concerned," I growl, pain making me irritable.

My wounds make me want to wound.

"Kane thinks I'm dead?" It's the first true emotion I hear in him and it's a sadness, one that I can understand. It's how Ashlyn must have felt each day I did not come for her.

I wince, feeling guilty. It doesn't last as a wave of nausea rolls over me. I keep talking to distract myself from it. "Yeah."

"Shit." He speaks like he's one hundred percent human. For a moment, I forget. Then he says, "Does he know about the experiments?"

"If he does, he hasn't talked to me…about them." Pain shoots through my left leg, and I struggle to speak through it. "What are they for?"

"Notare Elise has been collecting my blood. I heard Memnoch talking about some of the other royal families to Elise on his communicator, once. I think she's doing it to those families, too. I don't know how many others they're keeping, or where. I've never seen any of them."

"What are they doing with the blood?"

"I wish I knew."

"How long have you been here?"

He pauses and I can hear him whispering something quietly to himself, like he's counting out loud. "Thirty-eight months."

"Thirty-eight months? That's…" It takes me a while to do the math. A long while. "That's three years." Stuck down here for three years all alone? I shudder. I'd have long since gone mad.

"Don't fucking pity me. I don't need it from a human, even if you are Kane's wife."

Wife. There's that word again. "What do you mean, wife?"

"I already answered that." He mutters something else. Likely more insults.

"No, I mean…" And this is embarrassing. "What does it mean to be a wife…for an alien, I mean?"

"It's the ultimate bond. The ultimate sacrifice." Mikael hacks out a laugh. "It's insane that he bonded with you."

"Why is that so crazy?"

"Because you're technically a queen now. You're *Sistana*. You co-own all of Kane's estate. You co-own the entire fucking Diera. You're bonded to Kane through your emotions. He'll be able to find you and feel you no matter where you go, and you can do the same.

"He gave up everything when you convinced him to bond with you. Don't know what you did to get there, but I'm assuming it was on your back…"

I swat the bars with my left wrist, the shackle there ringing loudly and interrupting his slanderous, scandalous insults. "You are a bastard and you don't know anything about your brother or about me."

The temperature in my chest is rising. I feel lightheaded. I should be trying to conserve my energy, not fighting the idiot in the cell next to me.

Instead, I spit, "Kane forced me to drink his blood before we even had sex and before I knew anything about any of this. He didn't tell me. He just told me to drink his blood and then he drank mine and I never knew why, so if you think that I'm out here trying to steal stuff from your brother, then you're an ass hole.

"And an idiot."

Silence falls like a barrier between us. Mikael doesn't breach it and neither do I. Instead, all I can think about is what Mikael's just told me about Kane. About me. About our bond.

It explains a lot about the orgasms and their intensity. I felt each one of Kane's just as he felt each one of mine. It also explains why it didn't hurt to have my throat opened by him. It tasted good to him, so I felt that shared euphoria.

And it also explains how Kane was able to find me all the way back there in that townhouse.

I remember the way he'd looked up at me, broken in the center of the road, with that cocky smile. He'd taken a scratch of blood from me then. Could that have already have linked us? I can see no other explanation, and I hope that our bond is even strong now.

Because as much as I'm prepared to die here for Ashlyn and the rest of those girls, I really would prefer dying beside someone else. Someone who isn't a jerk and who might actually like me.

"You're nothing like your brother," I exhale.

He kicks the bars near my head and I jolt. "And you're a bitch. Memnoch should have killed you. Too bad you're Sistana now and he couldn't."

"Too bad you're Kane's little brother and he couldn't kill you either." I shift, trying to get comfortable when there's no such thing. "How did you even end up here, Mikael?"

"It's Mikael," he grunts. "Can't sit here listening to you while you butcher my name like that."

"Mikael," I try again.

"Meek-eye-elle."

"Michael."

"Mee-kai-el."

"Meekle."

"Fuck it. You're worthless."

"I'm worth just as much as you, apparently, if they threw me down here next to you, *Mikey.*"

He hits the bars again.

"That's not my name."

"It'll do," I exhale. "You never answered me."

"And I don't have to."

Silence spreads its wings and I start to take flight into the realm of dreams when Mikey's voice attacks me in the dark. "Humans," he says.

"What?" My voice is weaker than it was. I cough to try to clear my throat.

"Humans were the ones to bring me to Notare Elise."

"I'm sorry for that," I say, because I am. Nobody deserves to die in this place. "How?"

He hesitates, then drops his pitch to a grumble, "Memnoch and another Heztoichen raided my house with like fifty humans. They made it look like an ordinary human gang, robbing and looting. Like maybe they didn't know that I was still in the house and somehow managed to kill me. I don't know...

"Kane was out of town on official Council business so when he got back I assume all he found was rubble. They torched the place. Burned the whole thing to the ground."

"Sad story," I simper a little crueler than I meant to. "But how exactly did you not hear a bunch of noisy humans robbing you blind? Couldn't you have just run?"

He mumbles something, but I can't make it out.

"I'm half-deaf and a human, and also sort of dying, so if you could please speak louder." My own pitch rises to the point that it echoes off of the walls around us. I can hear it for seconds after my words die away.

He blurts out, "I was enjoying myself."

"Enjoying yourself."

"Ever heard of it?"

To that I can't help but laugh. "I just pulled fifteen little girls out of cages in Memnoch's basement and you're about to ask me if I've ever enjoyed myself to the point that I didn't try to fight against an army coming to enslave me?"

"Population is hell. You can't freaking enjoy yourself out here and expect to live to tell the tale."

I did enjoy myself. Back at Kane's estate. And now I'm here. Worth it? Yes. Inevitable? Definitely.

"Cages?"

"Yes."

"What was he doing with them?"

"They were little girls and I found them bloody and naked. What do you think?"

He hits the bars again and this time when he growls, he sounds like he's in pain. "That's fucking disgusting. He was molesting kids?"

A little spark ticks in my heart. This is the first time Kane's brother has said anything to make me like him, or think more of him than a bitter, tortured slob.

"Yeah," I whisper, eyes closing again as my blood cools. "And yes, it is. So no, I haven't really spent the last eleven years enjoying myself."

Mikey grumbles low in the back of his throat. He barks, "I was drunk. There was a woman. She was human. She was a gift from Memnoch and between the woman and the booze…"

I can't help it, I laugh a little bit. Mikey reaches down and wraps a fist angrily around my shin. Agony chars me through to the bone, but I'm still laughing.

"Sorry…" I cough. "But for someone who hates humans, that's pretty human of you. Kane took on fifty humans by himself sober, but getting lost in the bottle? I saw way too many go down that road."

"Of course he did," Mikey says, shoe or foot or whatever clanging against the bars again and making one hell of a racket. "He's a better fighter, anyway. I'm sure he'd have been out of this prison by now. Would have come up with some great plan and Memnoch wouldn't have seen it coming. He's always been the better brother. The one who carries the light, the fucking Notare."

Jealousy like that doesn't need poking. Because he isn't just jealous of his brother, is he? He's envious. The kind of envy that bleeds.

"You love him?" He asks abruptly.

Don't know how to answer with what I've just heard. I opt for the truth. "Yeah."

"He love you?"

"Yes."

"Are you dying?"

"Probably."

"Don't give up."

I grin. "I never do."

"If you die, then the bond breaks and Kane won't be able to find me and get me out of here. I want fucking out!"

He kicks the bars again with every word and as I cringe away from his ire, Mikey shouts, "Kane, if you can fucking hear me, she's dying and unless you want to lose your wife, you better get your ass here now."

It's quiet after the echo fades and I fade in and out for some time. There's lapping water somewhere not far from here. I wonder if there's a pool in this tunnel, and if that's why I'm wet? Goosebumps cover my entire right side, though my left is a little warmer in the shadow of Mikey's heat. I guess all aliens run warm.

"You still alive?"

"Yeah," I answer. "I actually feel a little better."

It's true. I actually feel good enough to sit up and might have tried were it not for the shackles. "That's Kane again," Mikey sneers. "That's what his blood will do to you."

So the scavengers were right!

"Alien blood is healing to humans?"

"It's healing to all things. You're not gonna die down here, not unless they drain you completely."

More questions answered, though this was one I already suspected. There was no other explanation to the vanishing cut on my neck or my healed rib cage, or how, the first time I found Kane he was a corpse resurrected.

"Can you hear that, human?"

"My name is Abel, Mikey."

"Whatever. Just listen."

I tilt my good ear up to the ceiling, then shake my head,. "Got nothing."

"Footsteps," he says quietly. "Two sets. One close, one farther away."

Cool air replaces the warmth that had been at my side a moment ago and I get the impression that he's standing up and pacing now because I hear the sound of short, impatient footsteps. After a few seconds, he stops entirely.

"Kane?" He asks the darkness.

I'm entirely shocked when the darkness responds. "Mikael?"

My heart leaps once for dramatic effect before settling back into its normal, frenetic murmur. "Kane...fuck!"

I start to discern the sound of footsteps. They're running, splashing through shallow pools. I stare down the tunnel where I can just make out a distant point of light. It grows brighter and brighter and soon, it warms the space around me, even from so far away. Or maybe it's just the relief that warms me.

Seconds is all it takes for Kane to emerge from the darkness. He tears it in two with the gleam of his chest that illuminates the small, disgusting, dungeon around us. His pecs are bare and just visible through a rip in his shirt that worries me.

He's covered in sulfurous blood, his raven hair matted to the right side of his face, concealing what looks like a deep wound.

But it doesn't dim the brightening of his eyes as he sees his brother alive before him. "Brother." His golden eyes are round and his mouth is slack, though his jaw and shoulders are both squared and hungry for battle.

"You were supposed to be dead. For years, you were supposed to be dead." He reaches through the bars and takes his brother's forearm, then bows his head over Mikey's hand. The light from his chest catches his face then and illuminates his smile.

"I suppose I was, in a sense, until your wife found me." Mikey's voice breaks as he speaks.

"Where is she? Is she in there with you?"

"Uhm. Look down, man."

Kane's face tilts down and his eyes bug out of his head as he takes me in, sprawled out spread eagle over a pile of corpses. Honestly, I'm not shocked at all that he didn't notice me at first. I blend right in.

I smile up at him while he stares down at me murderously and wave at him with my shackled hand. "Hey, hubby."

Kane sucks in a breath and I swear that his cheeks shine with just a little pink. "Abel," he whispers, brother immediately forgotten. "Fuck."

He drops to his knees at my side and reaches for me slowly, like I'm made of glass. He doesn't seem to even know how to help me. Which blood is mine, which blood is

Memnoch's, which blood is Ashlyn's and those other girls'? I couldn't tell him.

"Memnoch did this to you? I'm going to fucking slay him."

"I guess she wasn't kidding," Mikey grumbles, "You do love her. Even though I specifically remember you telling me one time at Stess's place that you weren't ever going to get bonded — let me see if I've got the exact phrasing right... It was something about bonding being too much trouble and too much risk for someone of your importance."

"That's enough, Mikael." Kane's face turns up to Mikey and I understand in his tone and expression that Mikey is *definitely* the younger brother. "Abel taught me that some risks are worth taking. I hope only that one day you are capable of taking a risk for someone other than yourself."

Mikey's expression hardens, but Kane doesn't give him an opening to talk back. He looks at me instead and says, "Can you move at all?"

"I don't feel that bad, really. Just the chains and stuff." He tries to help me up, but I cough up some blood, which doesn't exactly help my case.

Kane rips away the rest of his shirt and holds his forearm out to me. He opens it with his own teeth and presses it to my mouth without warning.

"Kane, wait. Are you sure you want to do this? It'll make you weaker."

Kane growls, but doesn't respond to his brother. At least not immediately. Instead he combs his fingers back through my hair and as his perfect eyes hold me still and I suck in blood from his arm, I hallucinate those pearlescent beaches of heaven, where we once bathed.

"Of course," Kane says, eyes soft and mocking as they meet mine. "I would do anything for this woman and I expect the same from my kin. She is your Sistana now, too." And then to me he whispers, "After she agrees, of course."

"I didn't exactly sit down and sign a contract," I say, pulling in another sip of his blood and this time, I actually understand why I'm doing it.

The effect is almost immediate. I drink and feel sustenance fuel my muscles and fill the broken bits of my skin and bone, mending them anew. And not just new, but better and stronger than they ever were before.

"No, it was a verbal contract."

"When?" I scoff around his wrist.

"In the bathtub."

"Oh, you mean when you told me that I owned half your house, you were moving me into your bedroom, and I didn't really have a choice in it?"

"See? You remember the conversation quite clearly." I laugh and let Kane take back his arm.

"Are you sure?" he says when I wave him off.

"Yes, I really do feel better. Just the chains. And did Ashlyn and the others…"

Kane nods once, bends down and kisses my mouth ferociously. I love the taste of him. I can't and won't ever get enough.

"Yes, Ashlyn made it, along with all of the rest. Calvin led them home. The car didn't survive the crash through Memnoch's gate, so they had to walk until I was able to retrieve them. Calvin had to carry three of the girls. They fainted. Your little Ashlyn helped carry another that was nearly as large as she is."

He touches my cheek, my nose, my lips. I sigh and clutch his hands fiercely as pain and panic swim in my stomach, and then dissolve. Relief guts me and the emotion is so unrecognizable I have to fight back tears.

Kane kisses my forehead and as he pulls back, says, "Sandra is tending to the girls now. It seems that they will all live."

I nod and wipe my cheeks. "Good," I sniffle, "Good…"

Kane smiles and wipes away a tear I didn't catch. Then he looks away from me. "Though I *struggled* not to kill Calvin when he returned home without you."

He bows his head, but I lift his chin in the same way he's done to me so many times before. I kiss him, this time quite gently. The heat of his blood drips down my chin and onto my chest. I can see it on his mouth when he pulls back and trails his fingers down the length of my legs. The touch is affectionate, but fueled with purpose. When he reaches my feet, he snaps both heels at the base so that I might actually be able to walk.

"Don't forget the knife," I say, and he slips it into his back pocket.

"Tasha is a ruthless female." He shakes his head, then turns his attention back to the bars holding me and his brother back from our freedom.

"I don't know how you plan on getting us out of here unless you've magically got a key in those fancy pants of yours."

Kane reaches into his pocket and I feel like I got smacked in the face when he withdraws the key we spent so much energy fighting over — against Drago, against Memnoch, against ourselves.

It all comes down to this.

"I thought that it would unlock your tomb. That is what Memnoch led me to believe when he would taunt me with it. I recovered it from him, but it was stolen from me later by a wily human scavenger I was later forced to hunt."

His gaze slides to mine as he approaches the keyhole carved directly into the rock. He slides the key inside, then twists once around, then twice. The reaction is instantaneous.

The entire hall rattles dangerously and the posts begin to shift, freeing Mikey – freeing us both. Kane and Mikey hug, but only briefly.

It's Mikey who pulls back first and says, "We've got to go. I hear footsteps. Is Memnoch who you ran into earlier?" He gestures to the blood staining Kane's chest.

Kane doesn't answer Mikey right away. Instead he watches me with a grimace as I gather the chain to my chest, which is heavy and still links my left arm to my left wrist. I'm wobbly at first on my new shoes with my new muscles with my annoying chain and my head buzzing pleasantly while trying to convince me that now's the time for a good nap.

Kane slides his hand beneath my elbow to hold me steady, and says, "Memnoch is inside the tunnels, yes. But I managed to lose him quite a while back."

"Great." Mikey's already off, nearly sprinting down the tunnel away from us.

Kane shouts after him. "But Memnoch is not the problem, Mikael."

"Fuck. Don't tell me that there's more bad news," he hisses.

It irks me that he still hasn't thanked Kane for unlocking his tomb and almost dying to retrieve that key in the first place. I frown at him, but he's ignoring me, as I imagine he'll keep trying to do for the rest of his life. He's already made his opinion on humans clear.

"He called Elise. She's on her way, and she'll be here soon if she's not here already…"

Kane stops short and, as if choreographed, both he and Mikey tilt their ears towards the ceiling. I don't hear anything at all, but they exchange a meaningful glance that I'm able to interpret only because it's a look that Becks and I shared many times and is usually proceeded by panic. Kane doesn't have to tell me to start moving. We all run as one.

I'm surprised by how easily Kane's willing to leave the key he almost died for, behind. But he does. In a split decision that I'm not confident about, I waste the few seconds it takes to turn around and go back for it.

When Kane sees what I have, he smiles. "Allow me to upgrade you." Without prelude, he pulls a familiar sword from his belt. In the darkness, I hadn't noticed it before and I take it gladly. I shove the key into my bra, take the sword and run as fast as I can. It isn't fast enough and the chain is heavy and only getting heavier.

"She's too fucking loud," Mikey says, too far ahead of us for me to be able to see him well. Or at all.

Kane looks down at me and furrows his brows so that they come together above the bridge of his nose. Without warning, he snatches me up around the waist — chain and all — jumps over an inappropriately placed pool full of water in the ground, and flies down the length of the corridor with me in his arms.

A few seconds later, we're nearing a blacker darkness up ahead that I struggle to make sense of. Michael's standing in the center of the slightly more cavernous space, but Kane sets me down just before we reach it.

"Mikael," he rasps through clenched teeth. "Come back here." His voice is fueled by a sense of urgency.

Mikey turns and I see a flash of his white teeth in the darkness. I can also hear the smile in his voice when he speaks. "Why? I know the way out."

He gestures around wildly, and as my eyes adjust to the dimness, I begin to make out the charcoal outline of five or six entrances leading out of this small room. Mikey points towards one of them — the second from the right.

"All we do is take this tunnel, then the next right, then the third left after that and follow the stairs out onto the mountainside. We'll be home before fucking lunch."

He lets out a whoop of exhilaration and I feel his infectious excitement seep into my skin. I move forward towards him an inch. But only just that inch. Kane grabs me by the shoulder the second my foot leaves the ground and shoves me down onto the hard rock behind him. He crouches onto his haunches beside me.

"Mikael," he says again, and this is the voice that a king uses on an insubordinate soldier. One who's about to get himself killed. Maybe everyone.

"Get the fuck out of there!" Kane shouts.

But it's too late. Chaos claims everything the moment that Memnoch enters through the passageway on the far left and takes Mikey by surprise. He's all hands, feet and fists until I see the glimmer of at least two knives. Memnoch swipes for Mikey's chest and before I have time to hand Kane the sword, he's already entered the fray.

Kane's light makes the entire scene hard to interpret. It's made even harder by the fact that they move so fast — too fast for me to keep up with. Finally, I just have to judge who's winning by their grunts of pain. One Mikey. Another Mikey. One Kane. Then the rest from there on out belong exclusively to Memnoch. They have him.

I see Kane stab Memnoch with the blade from my heel. He cries out in pain and Kane uses Memnoch's lapse to steal away one of his daggers. Kane tosses a blade to Mikey and together, the two brothers cut Memnoch from throat to naval and I'm so confident in the outcome of this battle that I choose that moment to stand up.

It's a bad moment.

A slithery, slippery voice simmers into the space, coming from the exit Mikey had just been prepared to take. "Seems to me that the fight is a bit unequal, don't you think Notare?"

It's a woman's voice and her pitch, though high and breathy, sounds malicious. *Only* malicious.

Fury flickers through Kane's expression as he looks up towards the owner of the voice, giving Memnoch precious seconds to slither out from underneath the brothers and amble up onto his feet.

A soft pulsing light draws my attention away from Kane towards the female moving towards him in the darkness. When she steps in range of Kane's glow I see that her hair is so blonde it's nearly white. Like her skin, it seems to glow silver. The combination is unsettling, made more unsettling by the onyx of her eyes. They are utterly opaque and stand out from the ivory of her face like doll's eyes.

Her chest is entirely visible in her low-cut white top and from beneath her nearly translucent skin, she emits a soft white light. It's nothing like Kane's, which is a strong and dazzling orange. It's so bright it illuminates the entire chamber and then some. This woman's light is weaker than that of a single candle.

The others must notice the same thing I do because Mikey shouts, "Holy shit, your light is dying."

Notare Elise's doll eyes pin Mikey with menace. She shrugs out of her white leather coat so that now she's only in a skimpy ivory top and a pair of white leather pants.

Weirdest outfit ever. And I've seen some of Tasha's more daring combinations…

The only thing Tasha would approve of here, I'm sure, are her heels. They're stilettos, and judging by the way she's squaring off against Kane, I feel like she has every intention of fighting in them.

I scoff. Did this woman really come here for a fight? Because I'd bet my bottom dollar that it'll be over quickly. They're huge. She's petite, for an Other. And Memnoch is stupid. Even *I* could take him.

But then why does Mikey look so afraid? And why isn't Kane moving?

"Elise," Kane finally says, angling his body towards her and away from Memnoch, like he's some side note, easily forgotten.

"You have held my brother captive for the better part of four years. You will be imprisoned for the remainder of your light years and slaughtered the moment that light dies, which I gather will take place any day now. You've got minutes left to live, once I've told the Council. Once the Chancellor hears of this."

She smiles and it's truly a blood-curdling thing. I feel my shoulders curl inwards defensively and it takes all the guts I have to stand tall and feign strength while I look up at this cavern full of giants.

"And what makes you think that the Lahve will ever hear of this?" She slinks down low like a kitten stalking a mouse and I realize that she's assumed a fighting stance.

"Come on, baby Notare," she whispers in a way that's deliciously intimate and makes my blood boil. "Let's see what your three centuries are against my thousand."

Kane sets his shoulders and begins to counter her step for step. "So be it."

Kane doesn't stand a chance.

Notare Elise's final words repeat themselves in my mind on a looping chord as I watch her charge for him. Up until now, Kane was the fastest being I'd ever seen. But Elise…she moves so fast light would be jealous.

Within half a dozen moves, she has Kane pinned against the left wall. Three large gashes decorate his face and the talons that are her fingernails work to carve a crater into his chest as if she's actually trying to rip out his heart.

I call for him and he releases a roar at the same time that Mikey tackles Elise from behind. Without releasing Kane, she spins and clips Mikey's chin with her left heel. She kicks Mikey again, this time hard enough that he flies back against the wall adjacent to me and the entire frame of the room shakes like a sandcastle.

Memnoch surges into the darkness and kicks Mikey when he's down. Kicks him over and over again. I catch a glimpse of Mikey's face for a second, and I can only imagine the wrath and anguish of being kicked by the very same monster who held you prisoner for all those years.

With that thought in mind, I surge forward, because even though I might not be able to kill the psycho sorceress, I can definitely take down this hulking piece of garbage.

I lunge for him, forgetting about my chains for a moment. I trip and nearly skewer Mikey instead. He rolls out of the way at just the right second and I slash the blade up, this time with better balance.

I catch Memnoch's stomach cleanly and, without waiting for him to turn around, I stab him in the upper thigh, twisting the blade so that it nicks his femoral artery. Blood spray slashes across the walls and showers my thighs.

Memnoch roars in pain and turns to face me, staggering on his left leg. Mikey's got a look in his eyes that suggests he's going for the attack, but all I can hear in my head is the sound of Kane slipping away into agony at the hands of the other Notare.

"Get Kane," I shout to Mikey.

His eyes unfocus and he looks up, hesitating, but only for a second. We both glance towards Kane who's managed to free himself of Elise's hold against the wall. But he's limping badly and though he's still holding Tasha's stiletto blade, Elise stands before him with her hands on her hips and without a scratch. The only blood on her white outfit is Kane's.

"Go, Mikey!" I scream, voice wretched as I imagine the unimaginable: Kane dying.

I mean, I always knew I could die just trying to save Ashlyn. I was okay with that. But him...Oh god. Is this how he felt watching me leave the house earlier today? Lord help me, he is a better person than I am for letting me go at all.

Or at least, a better alien.

He's got to survive.

I back into the cave behind me just as Mikey reacts towards Elise. Soon they loom out of my sight and I can only hear the fight happening between them. In fact, I can barely see anything at all without the light of Kane's chest. I know that I'm treading dangerous ground, but with the weight of the key in my pocket, I begin to form the outline of what's sure to be a stupid plan.

Memnoch follows me into the mouth of the tunnel and I catch the gleam if his one eye. It hates me. But it loves Elise more and when I hear a female scream coming from the cavern with all the doors, he pivots towards it. I don't hesitate.

I slash his back and then his chest when he lurches forward to face me. He roars and I hop backwards over a small puddle of water, keeping the chain looped over my neck and around my back so that it's out of my way and far from his reach.

He lunges for me, swatting at me like a bear, but I'm good with a blade and he underestimates my skill. Even in the dark, the sheer size of him makes him hard to miss.

This time when I strike, I cut his ear clean off. He's grabbing the side of his head and roaring bloody murder. In his fury, he charges forward tactlessly and all I have to do is plaster my body to the wall and keep the edge of my blade slanted between us. He falls and as he does, rips open his left arm on my sword.

Now that my body stands between him and the only exit, I slash at him again, taking him apart piece by piece as I back him closer to Mikey's cell. He's too big for that narrow space and with the sharp sword between us, he can't touch me.

He manages to punch me once in the thigh, but that's only because I let him. I need the angle so that I can stab straight down into his throat. I nearly decapitate him, but he canters back just quickly enough to avoid losing his head.

In the fading light I hear him splash into that water pool up, falling in it up to the waist. Over his head now, I can just make out shimmery gleam of the prison bars reflected against the mica in the walls. Just the tips protrude from the ceiling. The gate is wide open, awaiting another victim. They're so close to me that I can nearly feel their smooth, ice exterior against my hands. I long for them, yearn to throw Memnoch in a cage just like he's kept so many other victims.

I want him to starve to death and I want it to take a long, long time. His blood will keep him alive, won't it? Because I hope it does. I hope he sits down here and rots for the rest of eternity.

Memnoch thrashes through water, calling me all the foul names I've ever heard used to describe a human and about a million more in a language I don't speak. But it's not Memnoch's voice that draws me. Instead, I'm stalled by a voice at my back.

"No!" The sound of fighting distracts me for a second too long. I turn, seeing nothing, but I still hear Kane roar, "Abel, duck!" Duck? And then it hits me — literally — just to the right of my spine. A rock the size of a bullet with all the force of one to boot. It throws me off of my feet and into the pool, right into Memnoch's outstretched arms.

Memnoch grabs the chain at my back and drags me under the water. Thoughts run through my head too fast for me to catch as I lose the upper hand so easily. Not fair! That's my first thought, followed immediately by, where is my sword, followed by, what else do I have on me? Not a damn thing. Just the rule book and the will to keep going.

The chain weighs me down to the bottom of the shallow pool and Memnoch's foot finds my chest there and presses. I can feel the last little bits of my air rushing out of me. I scratch and claw at his legs, but what's the use? He's too big and he won't stop until I'm dead.

He won't stop until I'm dead.

I thrash and thrash and thrash some more and all at once, I force myself to become still. After a few seconds, Memnoch the moron lifts me out of the water by the throat, shouting to the world about how he's killed me. How I'm dead. I can still hear fighting at a distance but it grows louder and I can hear not one, but two separate cries of agony. They're both Mikey's. And louder than that is Kane.

He shouts and curses and says things in that funny language that I don't understand, but everything that leaves his lips is wrapped in pain. His pain hurts me in ways I don't expect and I feel a sudden heat blossom in the space above my heart. It's tangible, this hurt, and fully consuming. I don't understand the sensation and I don't have time to think about it. Instead, I shove it aside along with my irritation. I mean for real, did Kane think I'd go down that easily to this idiot?

As Memnoch gloats to no one in particular, I open my eyes. I know where his face is even though it's dark because I can just make out the even darker smear of his black eye patch. This gives me a pretty solid sense of where his one remaining eye sits on his face, so I lift my unshackled wrist and I don't hesitate. I stab through his eyelid with my well-manicured nails, and rip his one remaining eye out of his skull.

The slick orb catches, but I pull harder. The tendons or whatever flesh anchoring the slippery ball in place rips and just like that, Memnoch can see in the dark just as well as I can.

Memnoch screams. Memnoch screams a scream that defies all screams. He releases me. He clutches his face and slams his body against both walls, panicked in his blind desperation. The hall shakes and shivers. I hear stones fall from the ceiling behind me but I don't pay them any attention.

Instead, I grab my sword from the bottom of the pool, lift myself out of the water and stab Memnoch in the throat. Blood hits my arm this time, spray slashing across what little's left of my dress.

Memnoch drags himself out of the water, down the tunnel, desperate to get away from me. I slash at him and he stumbles and struggles to regain his footing. He falls, landing like a cockroach on its back. I think he's in the cell now and quickly, I scramble for the key.

Thank heaven its still where I put it as Memnoch writhes and grips his face and struggles to roll onto his side. He's going to try to stand, but I won't let him.

My slick fingers slip across the stone, but I find the lock, jam the key into it and twist. Then I watch the glimmer of iron bars slide down, lower and lower.

In the darkness, it takes me a moment before I realize that Memnoch's not all the way inside the cell. I've miscalculated and only his *torso* is beyond the bars. I think about stopping what's about to happen but I don't. Instead, I watch in satisfaction and horror and total disgust as that first iron post pierces Memnoch's chest with little resistance.

Memnoch seems to understand what's happening, but he's too late to stop it. His fingers, slick with his own blood, reach for the post hovering over his chest. He braces his arms beneath its weight and for only a moment, he succeeds in holding it. The iron strains and the rumbling of the bars grows louder and louder and louder until sand and small chunks of debris begin raining down on us.

More haunting than the sight of it, which I can't totally make out, is the *sound*. The sound of Memnoch's chest being pulverized, ripping straight through his gut like a knife through cloth. Memnoch shrieks and his scream is enough to cause more debris to fall. The next stake must find ribs because I can hear the crunching of bones. Meanwhile, his feet are out by me, kick, kick, kicking.

His head is thrashing against the stone. I can hear the way it clacks. He's still alive. He's still *very* alive. For a moment, I wonder what would happen if I just left him there to suffer, and in that moment I consider it.

But I don't need any ghosts chasing after me.

So I hack the fucker apart.

I hack off both his legs and his arms. I stab him in the torso again and again and even lean all the way up against the bars, thread my arms through them and into the cell, and clumsily use the sword to saw off his head.

Eventually, I know I've freed his skull from the rest of him when a squishing rolling sound echoes through the cell, then stops. His body goes limp and only then do I allow myself the luxury of slumping back against the wall to catch my breath.

"That oughta do it," I tell his dismembered carcass. "And that's for Ashlyn, you stupid fuck."

My chest burns and I know that even though the battle is won the war is still raging. I turn and start to trudge wearily down the hall, prepared to go down with the rest of them, when I suddenly hear Kane's anguished cry and see a small light flash at the end of the tunnel — it's a fading light, not as bright as Kane's — so I know it must be her.

I lift my sword even though my tired arms are shaking and I point it right at her chest. She doesn't speak and she doesn't come towards me, and I wonder why she's able to stand there for so long without Mikey or Kane attacking her. *Are they dead!* They can't be. No. If Kane were dead I'd know. I'd feel it.

But she keeps standing there, and they don't start attacking her, and I listen to Kane's cries of pain with pleasure because if there's one thing I know it's that pain is only felt by the living.

"Come on, you crazy bitch," I say, half to myself though I know she hears me. I take a step towards her.

I think I see the flash of her teeth in the darkness and I wonder if she's smiling. She lifts her hand, waves at me with all her little fingers, then she forms a fist and crushes it into the tunnel wall.

The world rips apart at the seams.

Dust and debris fall at first like raining ash — stuff that I can still run through — but soon small rocks start to pellet me like little bullets. They get larger with each passing second, those rocks, and when I look up, I see that *Notare* Elise is gone, but I can still hear shouting coming from the other cavern.

"No!" This voice is Mikey's.

I run faster, running for my life. Or for Kane's. I'm breathing hard as I reach the mouth of the alley. Peering into the small, rubble-filled room, I see Notare Elise dragging Kane's body down the hall that Mikey had pointed out as the exit. Kane's bright light is blazing across his bare chest, which is covered in blood from about a hundred different incisions. I can barely make out the features of his face anymore. His left leg is bent in at least four different places and his right arm hangs off of the end of his shoulder at an angle that's entirely unnatural.

He sees me, at least I think he does, and calls out to Mikey. "Mikey, save her," he grunts, though his voice is unrecognizable. He can barely speak. He can't defend himself and he definitely can't move. He's dying. And that's the last thing he says before Elise wraps her skeletal arms around his torso and drags him back into the darkness.

I throw myself after Kane, ignoring Mikey as he reaches for me from his position sprawled out across the floor. I don't look to see what's wrong with him and I don't look to see if I can save him. Instead, I dive for the hallway that has claimed Kane.

I arrive at the mouth of the tunnel just in time to see Elise crack her fist against this tunnel wall, too. She looks at me and in the light of Kane's chest, her eyes glitter with malice and wicked intent, then bricks of stone come down between us.

A small rock clips my arm and a larger stone careens into my shoulder, taking skin with it as it falls. If I'm injured, I don't feel it. All I can feel is the thunder of my panicked heart.

"Kane!" My voice is a horrible shriek.

Kane doesn't respond and when a massive boulder falls down to bar my path, I push against it futilely. The thing must weigh a ton and as I struggle with it, little rocks pile up behind me, threatening to seal me into this stone mausoleum. But I ignore those too and try to use the sword to cut my way forward. It's all useless. Suddenly my arm is stuck and I can't move.

"Kane," I scream his name again and for an instant, I think I hear a reply. And then more rocks fall and I'm sure that if Kane doesn't come back for me, I'm going to die. Because I will die there waiting for him.

A strong set of arms wrap themselves around my waist. "We'll get him back," Mikey's gruff voice rumbles in my ear. "We'll get him back."

He pulls me mercilessly and I struggle against him, but it's no use. Rocks fall away from me and I start to think that we've moved out into a safe clearing in the center of the room when all at once, the ceiling gives out entirely.

A huge boulder hits my right arm, knocking the sword from my fingertips. Smaller rocks slash at my face like razorblades raining and a cloud of thick dust fills the space. I start to choke.

Mikey's got me fixed in a hold that's so hard it hurts as he limps down one of the halls that I'm not familiar with. His body canters to the side, falling into something and taking me with him.

I scream when he drags me down into another one of those goddamn pools. I try to swim, but Mikey's pulling me down and then down lower still. He drags me to the bottom of the pool while my lungs jerk and struggle for air.

He pulls me even *deeper*, and then to the side and I realize we've entered a realm of total darkness — some kind of small cave where there's no air and no light and no sound.

The rock walls are smooth around me and stand in complete contrast to the hard, angular boulders that plummet through the water just inches from my fingertips. I can't breathe. I can't breathe at all. Even though I won't die of being impaled, I'm drowning now.

My lungs are jerking with their last sips of air when Mikey grabs my hips and pulls me onto his lap. My legs straddle Mikey's waist and wrap around his hips and I try to push away from him, but he grabs either side of my face.

He holds me steady, hard hands pressing against my cheeks. Then he pulls me down even farther and he...*what the hell is he doing!*...he kisses me.

Confusion delays my panic long enough to realize that he's not kissing me at all. There's no love lost in the bubbles blipping between us. My lips part beneath his when he tilts my head to the side so that there isn't a breath of space between his mouth and mine. And then he does something that is pure magic: he exhales. He exhales *oxygen* into me.

I don't understand how or why, but I breathe in without thinking. It takes me a few tries, but I manage to breathe in again, and then out, shakily. It's unnatural and uncomfortable — not using my nose to breathe — but after a few seconds I start to get the hang of it. Not because I want to, but because I have to.

In order to get Kane back, I have to live.

So I let Mikey breathe into me while the mountain comes down around us.

Chapter Twelve

My chest burns. Mikey's mouth is on mine and I try not to touch his tongue with my tongue. It's awkward. Made worse by the fact that we're waiting for the deluge Notare Elise caused to stop. Waiting for the mountain to settle. Waiting for what feels like years. For what feels like freaking ever.

Kane is all I can think about. Where is he? Why'd she take him? That isn't even allowed from everything I've heard. What does she think is gonna happen? They have some structures in place. Somebody called the Lahve is supposed to protect Kane and if not him, then I will.

I'm going to get him back.

I won't let him down.

Not now. Not ever.

He's the man — well, the alien — I never knew I wanted. The one I didn't know could exist, so I didn't know to dream about. Now he's all I dream about. All I think about.

And I'm trapped and he's taken.

I start to squirm as rocks slip into our little alcove and claustrophobia makes my anxiety even more potent. Mikey has my face in a vice, his lips locked around mine as he exhales oxygen into me. I can practically hear him shouting at me even though we're underwater, trapped in a darkness that's near absolute.

I fidget but he holds me in place until most of my panic subsides, and it's in the dark calm that I find clarity as I recognize what I'm going to do next, the only thing I'm going to do next:

I'm going to get Kane back.

Whatever the cost.

Whatever the cost.

Eternities later, Mikey exhales a little more deeply into my mouth. Something's different. He's filling my lungs all the way up, and now he's pulling back. Cool water claims the space where his warmth had just been, and in its absence, I'm anchored to nothing. Swimming through a vacuum in the dark.

I windmill my arms and hit rock hard enough to grate the skin off my knuckles. I kick out, hitting Mikey, but when I reach for that heat, Mikey presses his hand flat against my sternum and maneuvers my body entirely behind his so that I'm wedged between his broad back and the smooth stone walls. It's a tight fit.

Air bubbles from my mouth and nose explode against my cheeks as more rocks pour into the alcove. I slice my knees and palms as I fight my way through them. What is Mikey doing?

My straining lungs are set to burst. Pressing my palms forward, I find shoulders. I feel my way down his back and take a hold of his belt loops at just the right moment, because when he surges forward then, I do too.

He drags me through an opening in the rocks, which slash and cut at whatever's left of Tasha's dress. The one I seduced Memnoch in.

Remembering Memnoch's impaled body hacked to pieces in the tunnel adjacent to this one fills me with a satisfaction that I need right now when everything else feels like it's gone to shit.

I break through some kind of surface and cough up a lungful of water. My hands grab for rocks, and though most of them fall away, some of them hold.

The problem is the chain. It's still strapped to my body and is dragging me back. "Mikey," I croak, slipping back under.

An intense pressure around my shackled wrist makes my whole arm feel like it's ripping from the socket, and suddenly I'm hurtling up and out of the water. My torso and chest hit something warm, and while the tips of my toes still tickle the water's surface, I'm out. I'm safe. Mikey's underneath me and we're both alive.

I'll have to take that as a win.

His chest rises and falls under me while and I can hear in the heavy way he breathes that he's hurting.

"Do you see a way out?" I cough, spitting up half a lungful of water.

Mikey makes an annoyed sound and pushes me off of him.

I hit the stone hard and its chill comes as a shock. I jolt. Frustrated, I try to kick Mikey in retaliation, but my bare heel hits stone and I yowl.

"You're an idiot," Mikey grunts.

I can hear Mikey moving around me, breath hard and heavy, footsteps labored and short.

"Abel," Mikey says and his voice is a mangled snarl wrapped around another snarl. I can feel, rather than see, as he moves towards me when his heat draws closer. "Get up." His hand tugs at the heavy chain at my back, but right now I don't want to stand up. And it isn't just because the floor is oh so inviting. It's because I can *see*.

"Wait." There's light. I don't know where it's coming from or how. Everything is so disorienting. But it's there, nestled in between the crack separating two stones.

I reach a hand forward and push on the first boulder I find, but it doesn't give way, so I tug on the smaller rocks beside it.

"Careful you don't bring the mountain down on my ass…" My. Everything is *my, me* and *I* with him.

I roll my eyes, though he can't see my face from that angle. "I'm in here too, you know."

Lying flat on my stomach, I push aside enough smaller rocks until I hit boulders. Their sides are smooth and rounded, but between them is a jagged mess of smaller stones. I paw my way forward, throwing them behind me into the pool. Light spills over my fingers and I've never seen anything so welcome or so beautiful.

Mikey drops down to his knees at my side and reaches forward to help me clear the rubble. His hand is pale but strong, lined in blue-green veins. His hand is the first part of him I've seen. Funny that we almost died together, but I still have no idea what he looks like. I tense a little bit, worried that he'll look too much like his brother. That it'll be a constant reminder that I failed him.

"This leads back to that place with all the tunnels," I say. "But that room collapsed."

"It's our only choice at the moment, and there's light."

I nod at that. Must be a good sign.

"I can't fit," he grunts, warm breath near my cheek as his shoulder presses against my own. "But you can."

I nod. "I'm not going to leave you."

"You're damn right you're not," Mikey says, "but maybe you can move the rock from the other side."

He doesn't sound convinced himself, but I don't argue. Instead, I kick my way forward through the opening. The chain slows me down, ripping at my wrist as I wriggle through the tight space. Two frost-flecked rocks come together against my sternum and my spine and I start to panic. "Mikey, you gotta push me."

He places his hands against the backs of my thighs and shoves me hard enough that the shoulder of my dress tears, taking skin with it. Tasha constructed the thing to be indestructible. The downside of that is that nothing is truly indestructible, including me.

I clench my teeth through the pain, curl my fingers into the stone, chipping all my nails and pull, pull, pull.

"How's it looking?" Mikey shouts, though his voice is muted now. I can't feel his hands on my legs anymore. I must be almost there…

My hand hits air. I grab the rock beside it and heave, finally dragging my body into the cavern that once had all the exits. The last place I saw Kane right before he was dragged down that tunnel by Elise.

"Dusty." I cough, as if for emphasis. "Dust everywhere."

"That isn't fucking useful. What about the exits?"

I rub the back of my wrist across my mouth as I squint around, trying to make sense of the rocky world around me. "You know, I could just leave your ass in this rock prison."

"You wouldn't be the first." Mikey's voice is bitter and I feel a momentary guilt that I'd even joke about that after he spent the last three years locked away in here by Memnoch, being experimented on by Notare Elise.

"The exits have all collapsed. There's enough room for me to kneel, but there isn't much more than that. The ceiling is lower than it was, which probably means it's not stable." Mikey curses but I speak over him. "There's got to be an opening, though. I can see in here."

"Fuck. Find the source."

Unfurling my legs hurts. Everything is stiff and sore and tired, even with Kane's blood in my system healing my superficial wounds so fast water would be jealous.

I shake out a cramp in my right leg and gather the chain to my chest as I start inspecting the rocks, careful not to touch any of them until I'm sure I won't be buried alive, at best, and at worst crushed to death. Or maybe the former is worse.

The tunnel entrance that claimed Kane and Elise is well hidden now, as is Memnoch's mausoleum. He'd be trapped forever, even if there had been the slightest chance in hell he'd have survived what I did to him. To save myself and avenge Ashlyn, I'd impaled and decapitated the bastard.

The more distant corners of the cavern disappear into darkness, except for a small ray of pale grey light that filters into the chamber through a small fissure high above the rocks piled up in front of the exit tunnel where Kane and Elise went.

"I found the opening," I say with a grimace. "But it's too small to get a body through, though. Not even mine." I tilt my head to the side and squint while Mikey says something behind me.

"Wait..."

I approach the rocks, pushing on a couple larger boulders to test their stability. They don't budge. Slowly easing myself onto the larger of them, I duck beneath a protruding sheet of stone and climb towards the place where the light filters in. And as I get closer, I notice something that brings a smile to my face.

Tree roots.

I grab at the roots growing by the fissure and pull. Rocks and dirt shower me. I'm greeted by a rush of cool air.

"There's a way out!" I press harder, a tiny stone avalanche sliding back to cover my stomach and bury my feet until the darkness breaks fully and I'm left looking up into a sight I never thought I'd be so happy to see.

The grey.

I laugh up at the grey ruined sky and edge up, up, up, sliding and slipping over the scree in order to be able to stick my head all the way out and up.

The cold air freezes the moisture to my skin and I shiver, teeth clacking together already. Looking down, I see the mountain from the outside for the first time. The surface is solid stone. It curves down to meet a ledge about twenty feet across and four feet wide, on the other side of which is absolutely nothing.

"Shit, Mikey. We're high up." I pull back into the cavern, which feels suddenly so much smaller than it had before. Smaller, but also safer.

I return to the crevice that I crawled through and can hear Mikey shuffling around on the other side of it. I ask him what he's doing. "Trying to get the fuck out of here."

"Hold on a second. Let me help." I drop to my knees only to feel hot pain slice into my shins as I kneel.

"Shit," I curse, jerking back. I reach down to swipe at the stones that are in my way, but as my fingers move, they come back bloody. There's something shiny and *sharp* down there.

Grinning, I dig and keep digging until the familiar hilt of Kane's sword comes into view. It takes a little maneuvering, but I manage to free it. I close my eyes and wrap my fingers around the well-worn hilt and for a moment, it feels like Kane is here, telling me to keep going, to keep pushing, to never give up.

Tucking the sword under my arm, I slide down to the opening. My body blocks out the light, so I can't see anything.

"Any luck on your side?" I say quietly, like I'm afraid that the mountain will hear us and try to keep us inside if it knows how close we are to freedom.

He grunts and I can hear rocks shuffling and sliding against one another uncertainly. A few smaller stones fall, but the big ones remain in place.

"Nothing's moving over here," Mikey grumbles. "I'm going to have to come through the same way you did."

"You won't fit." I pause, then consider, "And if you could fit, then why haven't you?"

He doesn't answer. Then there's a crack followed by pained grunt bordering on a scream. I call out to him, but he still doesn't answer me. There's shuffling. Time moves slower now. Then finally, after my third plea for information, I see his hand clawing through the small space I'd just barely fit through myself. I squeak.

"Pull me through," he rasps, and I don't hesitate.

Carefully bracing my feet against the rocks on either side of the space, I lock my fingers around his right wrist and wrench him straight towards me. It's slow going. My biceps and shoulder blades burn and rocks shift precariously beneath the pressure of my feet, but eventually his head comes through, and then his torso, and then the rest of him.

It's like the mountain is giving birth to a fully grown alien. Eeew. Or just taking an alien-sized shit.

I collapse back and when he falls directly on top of me, I'm crushed by his weight. Thick, wiry hair brushes against my chest and arm — a beard, maybe? He drops forward and his forehead lands square on my right tit but there's nothing at all sexual about this. His hot breath fans over my ribs and he just stays like this, without moving.

"Mikey, are you okay?" I reach down and touch the back of his head, trying to be comforting, but his hair is *gross*. It's one solid sheet of filth and the *smell*. Oh god, the smell… There are no words to describe it.

I laugh a little, hoping to break the tension. "I'm taking it hot showers weren't readily available to you down here, huh?"

"Shut the fuck up. I just broke my own arm and shoulder to get through that fucking hole. I haven't seen hot water in three fucking years. And you're here trying to crack jokes? You're a bitch." He snaps and I know he's in pain and that he's lashing out and that it's for this reason alone that his words are meant to hurt.

But they still do.

Bracing my arm against his throat, I heft his torso off of mine. "Get off me, Mikey."

As he chokes, I catch my first glimpse of his face. Well, what little of it that there is. Mostly he's covered in a course beard that I think might have started out blonde at some point. Now it's just a dense, matted mass flaked with black dirt and brown blood. So is his hair, which tickles my chin as it hangs down towards me in thick, uneven clumps. He smells like shit and sulfur, and he must catch the look of unsympathetic disgust that crosses my face, because he grins.

"My good looks aren't cutting it for you?" His voice is a sarcastic jab.

I raise my tone to match it. "To say the least." I give him one hard push, fingers slipping through blood. He winces, then falls onto his side off of me.

Mikey drags his flaccid legs through the opening while I struggle up into a crouch. My lungs catch when I look down at him. "Holy fuck." I point. "Mikey, your arm." It looks to be broken in half a dozen places and hangs from the stump of his shoulder like an empty sac. "Christ, Mikey…"

"I told you I couldn't fit. Not whole anyways." He coughs blood onto my legs. "I'll heal soon enough, though." He freezes with one ear cocked.

"Oh fuck, what is it?" The mountain groans and I don't wait for Mikey's response.

I shove my shoulder underneath his one remaining arm and haul him to his feet. "Nothing wrong with my legs," he mumbles, but I can still feel him leaning on me.

Keeping a fierce grip on Kane's sword, I scramble onto the boulder and squeeze through the opening in the side of the mountain. Carefully, I drop down onto the ledge nearly ten feet below, pain rattling through my shins and heels when I land hard on the stone.

I glance up at Mikey, who emerges from the opening with fervor, like he's scared something will go wrong now that he's so close to the light. Out under the grey, that low-hanging sheet, Mikey maneuvers awkwardly beside me onto the stone outcrop.

He's barefoot too and though he limps on his left leg and favors his right, mangled arm, he still towers over me. As he ambles stiffly by, chest pressing close to mine, I can't help but compare him to Kane. They couldn't look less like brothers and I'm a little relieved that, looking at him, I won't have a constant reminder of my shame.

His skin is pale where Kane's is olive, hair light where Kane's is dark. His eyes are black where Kane's are hazel and full of light. Despite being cut leaner than his older brother, he has an air of desperation that surrounds him like a stink and makes him look just as lethal.

In Population, I learned to trust things by the look of them and watching Mikey scale down the side of the mountain, moving from this ledge to the narrower one beneath it, I decide that I don't trust him at all.

The only thing that binds us is his brother and I get the feeling that his brother is the only reason I'm alive right now.

"What are you staring at?" he says without looking at me.

I shrug and swing down onto the precipice beside him. "Nothing." I cling to the rock wall to keep from slipping.

He shuffles a few steps forward, leaning heavily against the rock as he tries to keep weight off of his right leg. He peers over the edge before crouching down onto his haunches and scaling his way down to the next rock protrusion.

"Well, fucking quit it. It's weirding me out. I get that I'm ridiculously good-looking but there's no need to make me feel self-conscious about it."

I roll my eyes and follow him, step-for-step.

"It's a quarry," I say, half to myself. "Makes sense why everything is so smooth. Even these protrusions aren't too difficult to scale." I tell myself these things to distract from the height, because the smooth curve of the mountain leads straight down to a hole in the earth full of smooth rocks a hundred plus feet below,

A more gradual slope ahead of us leads to forested terrain off to the right, and that seems to be what Mikey's headed for.

He pauses to rest, or perhaps simply take in the sight of the sky. His eyes crinkle at the corners as he slumps against the mountainside. He tilts his face up to the grey and surprising tears streak through the black filth covering most of his face.

I look away, giving him this moment in peace. I might not like him, and he might hate me, but he deserves to process this moment anyway he needs.

I move past him quickly, heading down, down, down until I finally reach the place where there are no more ledges and smooth stone has transitioned to clustered boulders. At the bottom of this incline there's dirt and soil. I feel like sprinting for it, but am aware that moving too quickly would probably kill me. So I don't.

I take it slow and eventually, earth finds its way beneath my feet.

I squish my toes into the moss-covered soil. There's no grass here. Grass is a bit of a tricky thing in Population. It grows like a weed in some spots, but in a lot of areas around here, it's almost like it's too wet for it.

And it's wet here. The air clings to my skin like a blanket and I shiver when goosebumps break out over my skin. I firm my grip on the sword I carry and take a deep breath, then close my eyes.

"Kane," I whisper.

"What?" Mikey's hard voice snaps and I turn to see him jumping down off a boulder to squish into the soil beside me. He takes the same deep, assured breath I did as he lands.

I meet his gaze and am a little thrown by its intensity. I'm even more thrown by how crazy he looks. He's white under there, I'm sure of it, but right now he's all red and black.

The clothing he's got on...Jesus Christ. It's just a pair of pants, if you can call them that, but I have no idea what color they were before. Right now they're just wet black rags clinging to his legs. They don't fit him, and are definitely too short. His stomach is the cleanest thing about him. Dirt outlines his muscled torso, which clenches the longer I stare at it.

Drawing my gaze back up to his face, I say dumbly, "You don't really look like Kane."

Mikey scoffs, gaze darting away from mine. "Did you expect me to?"

"People always said that I looked just like my brother."

"Was he as ugly as you are?"

I roll my eyes and take off towards the sparse tree line decorating the brow. "Charming. Another thing you and your brother don't have in common."

"Stop fucking comparing me to my brother," Mikey shouts after me, voice and hackles rising. "Heztoichen don't have to resemble their kin, and Kane and I were born two hundred years apart. The only thing we share are parents, and now they're both dead, so just forget it."

"Fine," I say, pitch flat, moving on. I look instead to the desolate world surrounding us while the chill from the mountain numbs my toes. I hug my arms and walk faster.

Is there anything I can use to make shoes? The bark on the trees is pine — not malleable enough — and I can't fashion the needles into anything useful.

I clench my teeth together, grateful for Kane's blood in my system, knowing that it's likely the only weapon I've got at the moment against hypothermia.

"Are you fucking listening to me?"

"No. What?"

He stands on high ground looking down at me. Haggard and blood-drenched and glaring at me like he wants nothing more than to rip my heart out through my chest, he's a nightmare with a face.

"I'm nothing like my brother."

"Yeah, I got it. I heard you the first time. I'm sorry for comparing you," I say, not at all sorry.

"No," he says, staggering towards me. "You don't get it. You don't understand anything. You don't know anything. And now I'm stuck with you." His face takes on a murderous glint that I'm unprepared for.

"What is your problem?" I lift the tip of the sword and the sight of it distracts him.

He glances at me sharply, embers glittering in the black jewels of his eyes. "Do I really need to explain it to you?"

When I don't answer he roars, "Everything! Everything is my fucking problem. I've been waiting for a rescue for three years only to get you instead of my brother and you drag Notare Elise and Memnoch along with you.

"And now I'm out here in the middle of nowhere with nothing to eat and I'm tired and I just want to go back to my fucking house, but instead I've got to go on a wild goose chase to save my brother from a psychopath even though he's probably dead already and I'm going to die trying to save him, and for what?"

He throws out his arms. "For you? For an ugly, skinny, stupid human?"

"You were rescued," I say, heat flooding my face and funneling through my arms. "You let yourself get kidnapped by a human woman and an idiot like Memnoch," I scoff. "You don't have anybody to blame but yourself."

"You fucking…"

"And," I shout, voice rising over his, "I'm the only reason you're even here. Without me, Kane would have *never* found you in the first place and you'd still be rotting away in that cell."

Mikey's rage is reaching a peak that I know I should be afraid of, but I'm pissed off, too, and incapable of being the voice of reason. He stomps towards me, dirt squishing under his big, stupid feet with every step.

He screams, "Yeah. I'm out. But for how long? I can't get Kane back. Not on my own. I'm only a hundred years old and the Lahve won't believe anything I tell him and he definitely won't believe you. So now I've got to walk to my death for Kane — probably gonna get imprisoned again — and it's because of you."

"Are you entirely forgetting that I'm here? That I killed Memnoch, your jailer? The guy who kept you prisoner for three years?"

I lift the sword with conviction now, even as the slack on my chain holsters my movements. It's gonna be hard to take him down. I shake my head. Take him down? This is Kane's brother. We're on the same fucking team! What are we doing here, screaming at each other like this?

"You got lucky," Mikey sneers, but I hear how his voice dips. Nervous, maybe. Or maybe even more pissed. "Memnoch wasn't even that old. He was barely older than me…"

"So that must be why *you* couldn't kill him." I laugh in a horrible way I've never heard before as this creature brings out the monster in me. "No. Why don't you just go home, find a nice drink, and let me save Kane. You're fucking useless anyway. The useless, shitty brother."

Underneath the filth streaked across his cheeks, there's red. A very dangerous red. A red that reminds me that he's actually an alien — not a human at all — but that even an alien is capable of being hurt.

"I…I shouldn't have said that…" I start, but Mikey doesn't hear me.

He roars, "I told you not to compare me to my fucking brother!"

Mikey lurches towards me in a move that's frighteningly fast. I jerk my blade up, nicking his left pec, but he jerks back before I can do any serious damage. Not that I'm trying to. I'm not trying to…I think…or maybe I am.

He shouts again, this time in Other-speak, before he seethes, "Give me the sword."

"It's mine!" I glance towards the trees behind me, wondering if I can make it that far before he rips my head off my neck. "Kane gave it to me." And it's the last piece of him I've got left.

"He had no right to give it to you."

Mikey slaps his chest twice — thwack, thwack — and I canter back, reminded suddenly of a movie poster for some title called *King Kong*. Aiden had it in his bedroom when we were little. Though he'd always been little. He'd died little.

"That is my father's sword. Kane's gone now, so that sword is *mine*."

Mikey moves brutally and without grace. Still, he's fast and manages to punch me in the shoulder *hard*. He isn't holding back.

I switch the hold I have on the sword when he comes at me from the right so that I hold it with both hands. I cut down into his exposed thigh while my feet sink further into the muddy ground underneath me.

"Mikey, quit fucking around. We're on the same side!"

"We aren't! We aren't on the same side. You're a fucking human."

The irony is that, he's absolutely right. We *shouldn't* be on the same side, and two months ago, I would have agreed with him wholeheartedly. Now look at me? Who am I?

I'm a queen among the aliens.

Hah.

How wild is that?

I'm panting, exhaustion making it harder to fight. I hit him again, this time with the flat side of my sword and hard enough to knock him back. His left knee collapses inwards, as if it's made of cardboard rather than bone.

He shouts words in alien that are unintelligible to me, but I don't stop to interpret them. I turn and run. I race for the trees, and as I duck past the first copse, the whole world darkens.

Thunder chases me while branches try to pull me back. I don't make it very far before a soft tugging sensation lights across my left foot and wrist. My feet leave the ground as Mikey grabs the chain I still wear and throws me by it.

A blitzkrieg of heat ripples across my spine as I hit the soft, squishy forest floor. I'm down for a second before the back of Mikey's hand hits my cheek — not hard, but hard enough to shock me — then he rips the sword right out of my hands. A light push and I collapse back into the dead leaves and mud beneath me.

Placing a tree at my back, I struggle up into a seat. I swab the inside of my mouth with two fingers and taste the metallic tang of my blood mixed with Kane's.

"Asshole," I shout after him while hot tears sting the back of my eyelids. I'm not hurt, but I'm angry, frustrated, and cold, made colder by the blood, residual quarry water, and cool, soft soil stuck to my skin.

I'm pissed. I'm pissed because he took the sword away, even though he had no right to take it. I'm pissed because when I was fighting him, I showed a restraint that he didn't. He's Kane's *brother*. He should be like kin. But instead he's this...this horrible jealous thing who hates everything. Including him.

"We're on the same team," I croak.

His back to me, Mikey misses his next step but he continues forward, away from me. Eventually, I get up and follow the muddy tracks he leaves behind into the grey.

I find myself constantly flexing the fingers of my sword hand, wishing I had it back. Wishing I could swap one brother for the other. Wishing I could undo time and make Kane a set of new promises.

To accept that some fights aren't fighting and to forgive his brother for this. But I can't. And I won't ever forgive him.

Chapter Thirteen

I t's dark and my stomach is rumbling in a way that's uncharacteristic, my abdomen twisting in my belly like water snakes. Maybe I'm hungry... That must be it.

I've known hunger before though, and this isn't it. It hasn't been *that* long since I left Kane's and I've got his blood in my system giving me the illusion of fullness.

Must be something else.

I stop for a moment and brace my hands on my knees. "Mikey, hold up a sec. I've got a cramp." Breath puffs up in thick white clouds against the blank backdrop before me. "We need to find food and water."

Somewhere in the darkness up ahead, Mikey snorts. "Sounds like a people problem."

Frosted pine needles tickle my bare toes. I want to build a fire, but I don't. In Population, there's always the risk you aren't the biggest or the baddest thing out there. "You don't want to eat?"

"Don't ask me what I want to eat."

I trudge another dozen steps forward until I spot Mikey's charcoal silhouette. He's found a seat and collapsed against the trunk of a massive moss-covered tree. His eyes flash to me and stand out bright white in the shadows.

I frown down at him. "Don't be nasty."

His upper lip twitches and his lids fall shut. I stalk towards him and quickly snatch for the sword propped up against the tree just out of his reach. He's quicker though, and keeps it from me.

"I will take my sword from you eventually," I say, kicking and scattering some damp leaves across his outstretched leg.

He tucks the hilt under his left arm and crosses that arm over his abdomen. "And then I'll just take it right back." Mikey grunts, groans, and shifts until he's nearly prone against the forest floor.

I shiver as I stare. It's cold. But as I step closer to him, that chill wavers. If I weren't so pissed at him, I'd snuggle right up to his side — smell, be damned. But I am, so I don't.

"So this is your plan, then? You want to sleep here?" I look at the trees clustered around us. They're patchy and the bushes are thin here with barely any leaves on them. Everything is just a moss-covered stick. We're totally exposed.

Mikey doesn't answer. Like he doesn't hear me, or is too stupid to care. I wonder if he'll even bother waking me up in the morning, or if he'll sneak off while I'm asleep. Standing over him, debating whether or not sleeping is worth the risk, I decide that I hate this blonde brother before me. I nudge a lonely rock with my foot and again find myself debating... should I bash his skull in?

"You going to do it or not?" Mikey says, voice slow but otherwise alert. He doesn't open his eyes.

I shake my head, though I know he can't see me, and for just a moment I picture his blood on my hands. That blood makes me think of Memnoch and then of Ashlyn and then of those other girls, of Kane the first time I saw him lying broken on Population's unforgiving city streets.

"No."

A flash of white appears in the dark and I move away from it. His eyes. I feel a pinprick of rage. A pinprick of fear.

I lie down in the hollow at the base of a tree far enough away from him that he won't be able to get up and find me immediately should he wake in the middle of the night debating the same thing I just did.

Though my eyes are shut, I don't really sleep, and reality comes for me well before daybreak — greybreak. As I get up, my concerns about Mikey abandoning me transition to concerns about Mikey waking up at all. He looks like he died several days ago.

His too-white skin looks grizzly in the soft light and the blood and black filth crusted too him looks even more pronounced. It streaks down his neck and over his chest. His hair is black on his face, on his head and under his arms. It's not supposed to be black, I'm sure, but I'd have to guess at what color I think it's supposed to be right now.

"We need to move." I kick his leg. No response.

I say his name several times, then call him all the insults I'd been dreaming about. I'm still flat-lining. Rolling my eyes, I turn from his corpse and trudge through the trees. The forest floor surrounding our sleeping spot is uninterrupted, soft soil covered in thick, dry foliage that crinkles under my feet.

Huzzah for the small blessings…

I siphon water from the large oak leaves, collecting dew and rain. It's not enough to slake my thirst, but it's better than nothing and helps calm the knots in my belly. Then I set to work.

Frustration and physical exertion have me sweating nearly five minutes in as I try to break free of my shackles. Because Mikey's right — I can't even free myself. How am I supposed to free Kane?

I try rocks, sticks, and lots of wriggling and eventually manage to smash the heavy iron weights down my wrists and over the broad of my hand. The effort covers my fingers in a crimson glove, but the pain is only fleeting and already I can see the shredded skin there mending itself anew — another gift from Kane. One of so many.

Massaging my arm, I turn to my bare feet. Together, the shackle and chain must weigh thirty pounds, and no matter how I bend and twist and smash, I can't wrench my ankle free.

"That's not going to work."

I jolt at the sound of Mikey's voice, and look over my shoulder to see him standing just a few feet behind me, arms crossed, sword tucked into a beltloop.

I bring the rock I'm holding down against the iron shackle again. Again, it clangs and makes a small scratch in the surface. At this rate, I'll have the thing off by the time I'm eighty.

"Any…other…suggestions?" I grunt between strokes.

Leaves crunching precede Mikey's arrival. He lowers down in front of me and touches my ankle. His fingers are gentle, so I know not to trust them. I flinch. He meets my gaze.

"I'm not going to hurt you," he grumbles.

"Hm."

"Why haven't you tried the sword?" He pulls my leg out straight and I feel my face heat — both because of the question, but also because of what I'm wearing.

Tasha's dress is tied to me by a few resilient threads at this point. There are huge holes over my stomach, and if I twist my hips the wrong way, I'm pretty sure Mikey'll get an eyeful.

Shoving one flapping shoulder up to more fully cover my right tit, I snap, "I would have if I'd known I was allowed to touch it."

Mikey doesn't respond, though I see the tightening of his jaw, letting me know that this docility only lasts in brief bursts. Very brief.

"Plus, I'd more likely saw off my own leg than get this stupid thing off."

Mikey narrows his eyes as he stares at the shackle. Clearly thinking, but I have no idea what odds he's weighing until he says, "Let me try."

Pressing the sharp edge against my metal cuff, Mikey very carefully leans his weight into the blade and begins sawing back and forth.

As he bends over my calf, I watch him closely. Begrudgingly, I notice that he no longer looks so bad. Maybe he really did need those few extra minutes of sleep.

Or maybe he just laid there to piss me off.

Either way, some of his color has returned and his shoulders seem fuller than they last had. Perhaps it's only how close he is to me. Close enough to smell him. He smells like crap. Actual human crap.

"What?" Mikey barks, stalling for a moment. His eyes flash to mine and I grimace.

"Nothing. Just...loving your look. The mud locks, the caveman beard, the smell of boiled eggs and urine, a little bit of shit and vomit mixed in..."

Mikey's lips twitch like he's going to smile, or trying to restrain the impulse. He doesn't, in the end. But he doesn't hit me, either, which I think may be a step in the right direction for us.

"Yeah, we make quite the couple. You look like a zombie prostitute."

Laughter bellows out of me and Mikey's smile breaks. He grins as he keeps working at my cuff, trying just about everything to get the damn thing off — sawing, hammering, slicing, pulling, ripping, gnawing, tearing. The sword puts a crack in it, but even with Mikey throwing his full weight behind the blade, he doesn't get far. He doesn't get far *enough*.

"Mikey, it's not working."

Mikey spits out a host of what I think are curses in his alien speak and falls back onto his ass.

He tosses the sword into the mud while the swollen muscles in his arms flinch in small pulses. He's got about as much control over his anger as I do. Not a great combination.

Trying to be the voice of reason, I say calmly, "It's alright. Thanks for trying. I'm just going to have to deal with the chain until we reach a city where…"

"I can get you out." He kneads his jaw, which is entirely invisible beneath the thick blanket of beard covering his chin, his cheeks, and some of his neck. It makes me wonder what his face actually looks like under there.

"You can? Why are you telling me this now?"

"I can get you out, but you're not going to like how."

"Is it gonna kill me?"

"No."

"Then it's probably worth a shot."

Mikey grunts and grabs my leg below the knee, making me flinch. "What?"

"That hurts," I complain, trying to shrug him off.

"I'm hardly touching you."

"I mean, it tickles."

His face scrunches up. "It hurts or it tickles? Which one?"

"Why can't it be both?"

"If it tickles, it can't hurt. They're like opposites."

I laugh lightly then and shake my head.

"What?" Mikey says, and his expression is softer than it was. Unlike his brother, who has some sort of unearthly aura about him, Mikey looks so crazy human. So human.

"Nothing. I just happen to disagree with you and with your brother." I smile, lost in the memory. "He says the same thing."

Mikey grunts and tickles the back of my knee, sending my whole left leg into spasm. "Ow," I howl, falling onto my back and clutching my left thigh. "That hurts," I say, but I'm laughing and there are hot tears in my eyes.

"Goddamn, you're weird," Mikey says, but I can hear the smile on his tone and I feel hopeful as he straightens my leg out that maybe we can come together somehow, and this won't be so bad traveling together after all.

I'm still mad at him.

I still don't trust him.

But maybe *hate* was a strong word.

Maybe with a new day things will seem more possible, including friendship.

I decide then to try a little harder.

"You ready?" Mikey's hand is warm and firm around my left ankle.

"I don't know what I'm supposed to be ready for."

"Bite down on this."

He hands me a stick. "Oh fuck." Understanding dawns on me and I quickly shove the stick in my mouth, bear down with my hands, and shout around it. "Go quick!"

In one quick motion, he crushes my heel with nothing but his hand. I scream around the stick, pulverizing it to shards in my mouth, which I then struggle to spit up.

Pain radiates through my whole left side and I fight my way through it, like I've been buried and have to claw my way back to the light.

Hacking out thorny spittle, I roll onto my stomach and lay my forehead on my hands. I try to breathe as I feel heat work its way through me. Kane's blood to the rescue. Hallelujah. I could get used to this…

"Abel? Are you…" Mikey coughs, his throat catching. He doesn't say more. I just lie there and as I lie there, Mikey pats me once on the right shoulder.

I laugh, mad with fever and pain. I sound hysterical, even to myself, but when Mikey asks me what's wrong, I say, "I'm just loving your bedside manner."

"I guess I'll have to work on that." He stands and puts space between us. When I open my eyes, the entire world is fogged over, a warm breath against a clear pane. All I can make out against the ashen background of the forest are his arms folded over his broad chest, his one bare calf visible through his shredded pants, his fingers twitching.

I roll onto my back and drape my arm across my eyes, waiting for Kane's blood to do its work. Even as that funny heat makes its way down to my heel, I know that I won't be able to put weight on it for a while.

As Mikey looms over me, I can sense his impatience. His feet are tapping restlessly and his hands are fiddling with the sword.

I suggest that he goes and finds us something to eat. He stomps off and returns half an hour later with a handful of mushrooms. Most of them are poisonous, but I pluck out the few good ones and we chew in silence. He stares into the forest with flat, black eyes. They are utterly vacant. I wonder what he's thinking, but don't ask.

I tilt my last mushroom towards the pale light above my head and smirk, "So what, you don't know how to hunt?"

It's got dark red spots on the cap and when I check the stem, it's full of dozens of microscopic holes. Lovely. I toss the mushroom over my shoulder and dust off my hands.

"Why would I?" Mikey's tone is harsh but he doesn't meet my gaze, and I can see just beneath that hard, condescending veneer, that he carries a very real insecurity with him. Something I never saw in Kane.

"Because it's a sort of useful skill."

"Perhaps for humans."

"Or for anything that likes eating." He's only a few feet from me and I still can't run anywhere, so of course I bait the beast. "I could teach you some tricks sometime."

Mikey's bottom jaw juts out. "Don't flatter yourself."

I roll my eyes. "Fine. We'll just keep eating poisonous mushrooms until one or both of us drops dead. Sounds like a super plan. While we wait for that one to work out, do we have an actual plan?"

"Get Kane back."

I fight the ever-present urge to chuck something at Mikey's head. "How? Do you even know where he is?"

"No." Mikey steeples his fingers and looks at me over the tops of his broad, flat hands. His nails are crusted in onyx, as are the seams of his knuckles and knees, the laugh lines around his eyes. "But you do."

"I don't even know where *we* are."

"We're just outside of the Diera." Back in Population then. Oh goodie. "And you're wrong. You know where Kane is. You're the only one who can find him."

He answers my curiosity with a groan and punches his fists back through his hair, fingers tangling in the matted locks.

"Have you not been listening? You're Kane's wife. The Sistana. His queen. Your blood bond works two ways. He can sense you, just like you can sense him. You know where he is. You're the map. You just have to find the key."

"You're telling me that I can *find* Kane? Like in the world?" I know that's how he found me, I just thought…I guess, I assumed it was an alien thing. Sounds too much like magic to me.

Mikey nods.

I suck in a breath through my teeth as the pressure in my leg explodes in several simultaneous crescendos. I force myself to ignore them so I can concentrate on what he tells me.

"How does it work?"

"How should I know? I've never blood bonded with anyone before." Mikey flushes for reasons I can't interpret.

"Is that a bad thing?"

"No," he barks, pivoting away from me. "It's just a thing. It only means that I don't know how a blood bond works from the inside so I can't guide you. You should be able to figure it out."

"That's helpful," I mumble.

He points a finger at my chest. "You are so lucky that you have Kane's blood flowing through your veins." I can tell that if it were up to him, I'd have already died a thousand times.

Pushing myself into a seated position, I knead the tender skin around my ankle. It's swollen and stinging and pink but I can feel the bones shifting and the meat and muscle filling themselves up, like a salamander regenerating.

"Can you at least give me the theoretical?"

"Try thinking of Kane." He pauses, then slams the point of the sword into ground and crouches beside it. Only a few long strides from me. "Think about him and what reminds you of him. Think about where and when you last saw him. Where you think he might be. How you think he might be feeling.

"I don't know," he blurts out stormily, and the desperation in his eyes seeps into his tone. Still, he's trying to keep it cool. He's failing. But I can appreciate the effort because I'm failing, too.

I frown.

If Kane were here, he'd know what to do.

I nod once, close my eyes and picture Kane in my mind. I picture his face reflected in the strong glow of his chest that was so much brighter than Elise's. Elise…

I feel a tightening in my rib cage, a ripple of effulgent pain, and wrench myself away from the thought of what she might be doing to him. I can't meet Mikey's gaze as the sudden sense of rejection blows through me.

Mikey curses. "Try harder."

I don't have the heart to be mad. Instead, my shoulders slump forward and I say softly, "Why do you think she took him?"

Mikey shakes his head and tries to ruffle his hair again, but it doesn't move at all, just hangs there like a thick sheet. "I can't be sure, but I have a bad feeling about her dying light. Maybe she's…" Mikey's dirt-crusted eyebrows pull together over his straight nose. "It's not possible, though."

"What isn't?"

He straightens and shakes his head. "It doesn't matter. We just need to find him."

I know he's right, but I hate the sudden responsibility I feel, and with no other outlet, I throw both arms up into the air. "Don't you think I know that! But what am I supposed to do? I'm not an alien! I don't know how this works, and even though you *are* an alien, neither do you. Yesterday, you talked about going to get Kane on your own." I wait for a response, but his face just gets redder and redder.

"Did you forget that? Well, what was your plan? You can't fight. You can't find him... What good are you?"

Mikey roars and surges across the short space between us. He grabs me by the sides of my arms, and the moment he touches me, my heart jumps up into my throat...but my chest isn't empty without it...no, there's suddenly a second kicking...

And then comes something harder. Something scarier. A pounding, like the pressure of a heel against the underside of my sternum is followed by a ripping heat. The tug of Mikey's large, damp mitt against the back of my scalp is firm and heavy, but in slow succession, I cease to feel it.

Instead, I remember the weight of Kane's body atop mine in the darkness of his bedroom, I see the light reflected off of his high cheeks. I think of the easy way he lifted me from the floor, and from disaster, on the dance floor in that monstrous ballroom, and I think about all the ways he was monstrously devoted to me.

Air wrenches into my lungs as I touch the place where my chest heart is trying to jam its way out. My eyes shut when a horrible burn torches my sternum but that darkness is interrupted by a pinpoint of light, far away. It glows like an ember, stagnant at first, and then it's rushing. Or maybe I'm rushing. We're both rushing towards one another like two trains on the same track, headed for collision. I hold up my arms to ward away the blow but it doesn't do any good.

Something sharp jams against my forehead. I can hear the crack and feel the blood drip over my cheek and nose. I can taste it on my lips. *It tastes like sulfur.*

Everything goes dark. I can't move. I can't breathe. Everything shatters around me and then a dark chasm opens up like a mouth under my feet. I fall through a world... through a city...one with streets, and buildings...I fall through the roof of a building and land in a room full of metal tables and grey tiles and I'm not alone here. Inside, there's a person with a voice and they're whispering...

"Abel? Abel!" Mikey's hands are on my shoulders shaking me and when I open my eyes and look up into his face, he exhales, and manages to sound almost relieved. "Jesus fuck. What was that? Are you sick or something?"

"No, I..." I blink a lot. Many times. The foreign feeling in my body is still there, but it's fading away. "I think I did the thing."

His eyes round. He grabs my shoulders and shakes them again with purposes. "Shit! What did you see?"

"Stop that." I bat his hands off me and struggle up into a seat.

"So? What happened? Where'd you go? Where is he?"

"I...I can't be sure."

Mikey looks down at his hand. He's holding the sword, but he looks like he wishes he were running me through with it. In a piss-poor attempt to calm himself, he speaks through clenched teeth. "Try."

I shake my head and knead my chest, wondering about the heat I felt and still feel. The backs of my legs burn, and so does my stomach. Foreign pains of unknown provenance. Implication with no meaning.

"Seattle?"

"Seattle? You're sure."

I hesitate, then nod. "I saw the...the needle thing."

"Yeah, it's still there."

I pause, surprised, "You know it?"

"Fuck. Yeah, I do. That's not even two hundred miles from here."

"Two hundred miles?" Mikey looks west, as if hoping to catch a glimpse of that infamous skyline from here and I scoff, "That'll take us weeks."

He rips his sword from the ground and continues to pace. "Not if we drive."

"Drive?" I use the tree behind me to stand, wishing I didn't need it. I want to appear more aggressive because Mikey isn't listening to me. He's already hundreds of miles from where we are.

"Mikey, you don't know anything about Population. Driving is a sure-fire way to get yourself killed. We're a long way off from anything recognizable. Could be scavengers out here, other gangs, or worse."

"Worse than me? I can take on any humans that come for me."

Frustrated, I stomp my injured foot, only to squeal in pain. "Ouch. Dammit. Mikey! You're not hearing me. There's worse out here than you. Trust me." Much worse.

He clicks his tongue against the back of his teeth and shakes his head. "We'll get a car and get to Kane as soon as possible."

"Mikey…"

"You're not in charge here!" He points his sword at my chest and snarls, "I say we drive, so we drive."

I take a step forward onto my injured foot, which screams beneath me. I hope my face doesn't betray the agony that ripples through the sole of my foot and burrows into my bones. I want to appear strong. Not sure it's possible since I look like a zombie prostitute, and feel like one.

"Today alone I've stopped you from eating poisonous fungi and found your brother *with my mind*. You need me a lot more than I need you. I say we walk, so get your fucking head out of your ass and start fucking walking."

Mikey struts towards me, ever the peacock while I just stand there. I'm not sure what I expect him to do, but I don't expect him to lift his fist and slug me right in the center of the forehead.

Right where I felt imagined blood earlier. *Kane's blood.* What is she doing to him? I think to myself and, as my feet slip out from under me, a second thought follows this one.

His brother and I make the worst team in history. We're never gonna make it.

I'm out before I hit the forest floor.

I don't know how much time passes before I hear mumbled words. Groaning, my head rolls on my neck as my face is tilted to look up.

"You bastard…" I stare up at Mikey's unwashed beard.

I want to punch him, hurt him, bite him, hit him, but what I manage instead is simply another grunt. Pain hasn't set in yet, though I know it will. And soon. How effing delightful.

"I shouldn't have hit you," he spits, and it takes me until then to understand that he's carrying me, my legs and arms bumbling along at regular intervals in time with his steady pace.

"Eff," I moan. Licking my lips, I try again. This time I manage a mostly coherent, "Fuck you."

He snorts and remains silent while my eyes trace the spindly lines of the boughs above Mikey's head. Their faint emerald outlines hang suspended against a ceaseless charcoal sea. Endless monotony. Against the pain that makes me cringe, warmth surfaces in my right cheek and left ankle where Kane's blood is doing its work. I kick my legs and when they react for me, I force my hands to twitch.

Softly, I stutter, "Put…put me down."

"It's fine." Mikey repositions his arms so that he holds me flush against him. "I don't mind holding you."

I make a face and, when his returning expression flickers scarlet, I frown.

"Besides," he shrugs, looking ahead. "What do you weigh? Like six pounds?" He smirks, and I can tell that he's trying to be funny. A strange reaction from him. I wonder what changed while I slept.

"Where are we going?" Syrupy spittle coats my tongue and I cough. I'm dehydrated.

Mikey hoists me higher so that my head hits his shoulder, which is at least better than lolling about as it had been. "Seattle. Like you said."

I lay there for a while in silence while the rest of my senses come back to me. Sight first, then taste, then touch, then sound. There is no wind whistling through the treetops, no birds, no bugs. There is only the sound of Mikey's footsteps crunching over dead foliage, and his heart beating. Thump, thump, thump.

Clearing my throat and trying to dislodge the oppressive weight of Mikey's arms wrapped around, I say, "Why'd she pick Seattle?"

"It's in Population, for a start. Outside of the seven regions, so outside of any turf owned or monitored by the other Notare. It's harder to track activity in Population."

"Still seems awfully close to Kane's territory. Wouldn't he have found out about it?"

"I guess not." Mikey shakes his head and shrugs. "Maybe his informants have gone sour. Maybe they're corrupt. Maybe Elise is just too careful. She's crazy smart and manipulative and ancient." He clenches his front teeth together and I get the feeling that he's lost in thoughts. Unpleasant ones.

"Hmph." I kick my injured foot a little and watch the way it bobs. "What about the Council or the Chancellor or whatever sort of police force you have? Can't they do something?"

Mikey looks down at me, eyebrows knitting together over his strong nose. "How do you know about the Chancellor? Have you met him?"

"No." I didn't even know it was a he. "But I heard a few people talk about him." Kane, I think. But also Memnoch. "Who is he?"

Mikey scoffs and doesn't look at me as he answers. Instead, he veers sharply to the left and narrowly avoids crashing into a thicket of shrubbery. Not quite as graceful as his brother. Tree branches scratch the bottoms of my bare feet and I shudder.

"He's called Lahve and he's not *really* Heztoichen. He's over three thousand years old and he's actually from a tribe that considered themselves above Heztoichen, and above our politics. Because of that, they've always taken this weird, impartial role as watchdog, judge and, if needed, executioner.

"Their job, above everything, is to keep the Notare safe. And if there are ever issues between two or more Notare that the Council can't resolve, he decides."

"The Council being…"

"Comprised of the seven Notare. They outrank everyone."

"And the fact that one of them kidnapped another is not a big deal?"

Mikey grimaces. "Do you see a phone out here anywhere? Who would I call to tell that Kane has been kidnapped? And even if I did call, there's no way that the Lahve…"

He bites back what he would have said next. But it doesn't matter. I already know.

"He wouldn't believe you?"

Mikey laughs and it's a bitter, awful sound. "I'm dead, remember? The Lahve won't hear words from a corpse." He exhales, warm breath touching my forehead.

"What about me? Aren't I Sistana, or whatever?"

"There's no way to prove it without Kane."

"What do you mean?"

"Unless the Lahve tasted your blood on his tongue, how would he know you're Sistana? And it's illegal to taste your blood. Hell, *I* could be thrown in jail for taking from you."

"You didn't know, though."

"Of course," Mikey grumbles, but I'm not sure he's convinced. His fingers tighten around my shoulders until they hurt a little bit.

"Kane would never let you go back to jail," I say.

Mikey hesitates, then nods. "I know. But still, the fact that your blood is in my system is a risk to him."

"How so?"

"Because if you got my blood in you, I could bond to you, too."

I cringe. "Then you would be able to feel Kane, too?"

"No, but I'd be able to feel *you*. It's the worst kind of violation for a Heztoichen to do to another. Worse than cheating, if it's willing. Worse than rape, if it isn't. Double bonding doesn't happen, unless it's in covens."

"Covens?"

"Polyamory. Where everybody shares blood." He shakes his head at that. "Can't imagine, though. It'd be overwhelming. Or so I'm told."

Mikey sighs again. "So no. Getting Kane back is all up to me." He pauses, even in his stride, and glances down at my face. "To us."

A shiver rakes its way through me and Mikey watches me with confusion as I flinch. "I think my foot is better now," I say quietly. "Put me down."

"Just a few minutes. There's a road up ahead." Mikey gestures with his chin and I look right, unable to see anything. "I forgot. You've got those lousy human eyes."

I roll my eyes. "First you punch me in the face, now you're trying to crack jokes? Seriously, put me down."

He lets me drop but doesn't let me go. I squeal as I fall a foot, landing back in his arms. He laughs, but still, gently sets my feet on the ground. I swat his shoulder and stomp away from him, my foot mostly healed by now.

"You've got jokes."

"Do I ever." He chuckles and follows me towards the road which, sure enough, appears in front of me some ten-odd minutes later.

At my insistence, Mikey stays off of it and we stay in the trees, following the road's graveling shoulder as we move past street sign after gratified street sign towards the next city.

"It's a ghost town," I say, as we reach the first building we've seen in miles.

It's a trailer park that looks as if it was abandoned overnight. Portable grills and spits turned on their sides are overgrown with weeds and tall grasses. The doors of the first RV are propped open, screens half-hung from the rusted metal lintels.

In the center of a grouping of three RVs stands a huge television with a fifty two-inch screen, perfectly placed on a high black table. The fact that it's got very little decay is a little freaky.

"Come on," Mikey says when I pause, skirting bits of broken glass hiding in shin-high grass.

He reaches back, palm outstretched. I hesitate, finding the thought of holding hands with him weird. *Don't overthink this.* I begrudgingly take it.

Some miles later, we crouch in the shadow of an abandoned house — an actual house this time, built with some kind of foundation. Blue paint peels off under my fingernails at my light touch and when I press a little further, the damp siding crumbles around my fist. Maggots rain down around my feet and Mikey makes gagging noises in the back of his throat.

"Let's get the fuck out of here."

"I'm following you."

We've evidently reached what was once the more affluent part of town, though now this suburban hellscape is characterized by overgrown lawns, stripped cars, and rotting white picket fences.

Mikey tries to stop me from moving forward from around the back of the house into the next lawn, which is way more exposed and abuts the main road. I shake my head.

"Nobody's been here for years. I think we're okay."

He considers, then nods and leads the way into the yard, past the driveway and into the yard of the next house. I lift my knees towards my chin in order to avoid sticker bushes as I follow him, and I still trip over kids' stuff as I walk — a deflated soccer ball, blonde Barbie dolls with earthworms in their eye sockets, a pink plastic princess castle that's still perfectly in tact, some kind of oversized orange squirt gun.

I pick it up and aim it at Mikey, who snarls then snickers when the trigger locks up. I stick out my tongue, toss the plastic weapon into the grass and move towards the rusting bicycles at Mikey's feet.

"You think these work?" Mikey says, fingers picking apart his beard.

I scratch my neck. "Except for having bald, flat tires and being big enough to fit a four-year-old, sure."

Mikey swipes the pink bike from the ground and takes it out to center of the street. He mounts it like some storybook knight might mount a steed, checks his balance, then places his feet on the pedals.

He scrunches his neck down into his shoulders, brings his torso to meet the handlebars, then kicks out onto the road.

I laugh, and it's the only sound in the world other than the rusting chains of Mikey's bike, squeak, squeak, squeaking. His elbows jut out wildly to either side and are framed by tassels that glitter silver and pink.

"You coming or not?" Mikey shouts over his shoulder, struggling to revolve his knees around the tiny pedals. This isn't going to work. But I'm too entertained to tell him that.

"Right behind you," I say, laughing.

Mikey's *actually* covering some ground and, on a downhill, he's moving faster than I'd thought possible.

"Wait up, Mikey."

I grab the blue bike Mikey left behind, kick up the kickstand and push it out onto the street, finding it a little bit sad that, even though it's a kid's bike, it almost fits me.

I speed past Mikey who somehow manages to keep those thick thighs churning, and soon the houses start crowding closer together and I start to feel nervous of the unknown.

It's been a while since I've been in Population, the land of razorblades and fire, of aliens and madmen, of loneliness and deprivation. My glorious, gluttonous home.

It was different on Kane's turf, in Memnoch's place, because facing up against him alone I knew where the danger was and because I could see it and touch it and anticipate it, I knew I could kill it. But out in Population, the enemy is never certain.

We ride through a small city center, short wooden buildings rushing by on either side, all abandoned. Mikey shouts when we reach the next intersection and I skid off my bike, taking skin off my knees as I hit the ground.

I'm on my feet in an instant, fists up in the air, prepared for battle, but when I turn it's to see Mikey standing, bike thrown to the side, both hands stretched above his head. He says something in his own language and bows at the waist, giving respect to the large, brown building on the corner.

"Mikey, we need to keep going. We've got ground to cover," I bark, struggling to mask my irritation as I coddle the fresh scratches on my knees and palms, not to mention the litany of healing cuts on my feet.

"Since I'm not a rabbit, I'm going to need more than six mushrooms to eat." Mikey doesn't look at me as he kicks open the crumbling front door and steps into the restaurant.

I curse under my breath, but reluctantly drop my bike and follow him. As I step into the space, I pass a sign on the wall. Faded brown and grey — like everything else — it reads: WE NEVER CLOSE, in blocky, Wild Western letters.

I smirk at the irony while my gut begins to gurgle unable to decide if the nausea is physical or mental.

Glancing around, I don't think I would have wanted to eat at this place even *before* the world ended. To say it's dingy would be an understatement. The air lays against me in a thin, wet veneer and the carpet squishes under my feet every third step. Shuffle, shuffle, squish. Shuffle, shuffle, squish.

Faux wooden tabletops stand above blood-colored carpet and the torn plastic seat-cushions lining the benches around them spew black and yellow foam. A menu sits open on one of the tables. Only one. It gives me the chills as my fingers drag through the dust lying thick on top of it, and I wonder what the last person was doing when they placed this menu here. Where are they now? How long did they make it? What killed them?

The words HORSESHOE CAFE are written in the same tacky lettering that hung crookedly off of the sign outside. The same words that Mikey is muttering under his breath.

"Horseshoe cafe, come on…" he says.

Behind the bar against the far wall, Mikey's flung open all of the cabinets. He's throwing everything he finds onto the floor. Plates and glasses smash, utensils clatter, boxes of straws tinkle as they spill and the remnants of disintegrating paper napkins flutter lazily to the tiled floor, landing in silence.

"Can't find what you're looking for?"

He only grunts as I come closer and lean against the bar.

"What are you looking for? Tell me and maybe I can help." I drum my fingers across the tacky, peeling surface. Still nothing.

"There's not going to be any food in there. Why don't you try the kitchen?"

When Mikey remains silent and fixated on the cabinets, I roll my eyes and move on. Following my own advice, I head through the swinging silver doors that lead into the kitchen. A faint smell gives me pause.

I know that smell.

I know it well.

There aren't any weapons nearby, but I'm not afraid of the dead. I hold my nose as I wade through the room, but even then, I can still taste death on my tongue. Ignoring it for now, I flip open cupboards and drawers and look under the sinks.

The kitchens have been cleaned out. Pots and pans and empty wrappers litter the floor. I kick metal bins aside and pick my way through the broken glass until I come around a huge metal island built into the center of the room and see him against the back wall.

Slumped against the white paint, the scent is overpowering. I cover my mouth and nose and blink back the sight. Half his head is missing and there's a gun lying nearby. The rats have been at him, and there's not much left of his torso or legs. Lucky for me, because it makes it possible to reach the stainless steel freezer door to his left and open it without disturbing him.

I fling it open and half a dozen rats charge me, but when I kick at them, they know not to fight a bigger opponent and scurry past me. We're all just rats out here.

I cringe as I try to move forward into the darkness, but the smell of death is even *worse* in here. Worse enough to make me choke.

I stagger back, falling into the island, and I get lucky that it's got a sink in the middle because I retch. I don't have anything to give up, so nothing comes, but the sound must be enough to draw Mikey's attention.

I hear the kitchen door open and then Mikey's voice say, "Yikes." He walks into the room and when I finally stop dry heaving, I look up in time to see Mikey press his bare foot to the dead guy's shoulder and push the corpse aside. Chunks of brain stay matted to the wall, and I start dry heaving all over again.

"No wonder our friend here took himself out. You took the gun, right?"

I nod, not wishing to concede to it. "Yeah." I don't mention that I had to break three of the dead guy's frozen fingers to do it.

"Any bullets?"

"Two in the carriage, I think, but maybe there's more inside," I say, pointing to the open freezer door behind him. "I couldn't though. Wouldn't be mad at you if you can't either."

I've got my hand on my nose and mouth still and my eyes are watering, but Mikey plunges forward. "Hell…"

"What is it?"

"Looks like missus here died trying to give birth to a baby. Oh…but hey! Check this out." There's clanging and then Mikey curses again. "Aw Jesus. Baby's leaking."

An even *worse* smell comes from the freezer and as my stomach hurls up into my throat, I grab the gun and stagger out of the kitchen.

Holding the heels of both palms to my eyes, I slide into the booth closest to the open front door. I only lower my hands when Mikey slams a cardboard box down onto the table in front of me.

"Check it out," he says, a grin on his face and a sparkle in his eye that makes him look like another being.

My stomach sinks even further. "You found booze." My thoughts flit back to what he told me about how he was captured by Memnoch. He was drunk. That's how they got him.

"A hell of a lot of it." He pulls out bottle after bottle of clear and amber liquids. Some are half empty but most are full and all of them make me uneasy.

"We hit the jackpot," he says, holding up a bottle of a clear liquor. Vodka. I look up at him, wondering what the hell he wants from me. What kind of reaction could he possibly hope for?

"Don't worry, I think there'll be enough for the two of us." He unscrews the top and upends half the damn bottle into his mouth before handing it over.

I take the vodka to my nose and wince as I sniff it. It smells like nail polish remover and battery acid and tastes like something you'd sterilize wounds with.

In fact, that's the only thing I've *ever* used alcohol for.

Mikey beams. "Good. More for me."

I frown as he takes the seat across from me and continues to drink in easy pulls, like it's water. I wonder what expression my face betrays, because he rolls his eyes.

"Don't worry, I found a present for you too."

He kicks something under the table and the hard, dry edge of a cardboard box scratches my shins.

The box is full of food.

"Hallelujah," I mutter.

"Gotta thank your human god for the small things," he says, and I know he isn't talking about the same thing I am.

Ignoring him, I crouch under the table and start sifting through the goods. Canned fruits and veggies, dried meats, about every kind of bean known to man, pasta and even spices...

"Mikey, you did..." I start to say before catching myself.

He pauses, bottle halfway to his lips. "What?"

I shake my head, pick out a few items at random and head back towards the kitchen. I open the swinging silver doors with my ass and as I look back at him, nod once.

"You did good."

As I polish off my second plate of spaghetti topped off with some dicey tomato paste mixed with water and a bunch of spices, Mikey finishes his first bottle. It's only then that he turns to the food. He rubs his hands together and twirls spaghetti around the tines on his fork. He takes a bite.

"It beats hunger," he says with a shudder, "but not by much. I guess Kane didn't marry you for your cooking abilities."

"Who needs food when you're drinking your calories? You going to polish off another bottle for dessert?"

"Damn right, I am." His voice is slurred, but only slightly. Meanwhile, that quantity of alcohol would have easily killed me.

I snort and clear my plate, even as my stomach rebels, but I don't let that intimidate me as warmth from my bowl wafts up to my nose, carrying the scent of tomato with it. Well, *sort-of*-tomato.

"You eat like a maltron," Mikey says, one eyebrow raised.

"What's that?"

He lowers the bottle of Jack Daniels he's holding and drops his head so that we're at eye level. "You don't know what a maltron is?" His elbows spread across the table, filling its width.

I shake my head.

He laughs. "Big ugly animal. Fifteen feet tall, black tusks the length of my arm. No? You don't have those here?"

I shake my head again and he looks down at the bowl of pasta in front of him. A tendril of steam dances up from its surface to touch his cheek.

"What?" I say. It looks like he wants to say something.

"Nevermind." He draws lines in his tomato sauce with his fork. "Just thinking about maltrons."

"Thinking about home?"

"Fuck off."

"Geeze," I say, wiping my lips with the back of my arm. Can't get any filthier. "Better stop while I'm ahead. Who knows, my next attempt to get to know you could end with me getting punched."

I toss my bowl onto the table and it clatters against my fork. I can't be around Mikey anymore. Standing, I check out the rest of the food I sorted out meticulously on the next table. Three jars of canned beef sit closest to me and, curious, I pick one up.

"I wouldn't do that if I were you." Mikey pushes his empty plate to the edge of the table. It falls but doesn't shatter when it lands.

I shrug and dig a finger into the mysterious brown substance. "It's protein," I say, glancing at the ingredients list on the back. Barely protein. I slide my finger across my tongue and immediately start to cough.

"Aw fuck," I lean over and spit up onto the threadbare carpet.

Mikey laughs. "I told you."

"Yeah, yeah, yeah…" I can still taste the crap on my tongue, and in this second, I prefer the alcohol. I swipe Mikey's bottle and take a sip before handing it back.

"There's other stuff there too," he says, eyeing me appreciatively as I hand the bottle back. "Check under the food."

Digging beneath the cans, I find a pile of neatly folded men and women's clothing. Baby clothes too. I wince when I find a pair of pale pink shoes, never worn, and quickly place them — and thoughts of the bodies in the kitchen — aside.

I pull out a white long-sleeve tee shirt, a pair of army green cargo pants that look like they might fit me, and two sets of sneakers that are both only a half-size too big. I even find clean-looking panties and a few miscellaneous bras.

I feel a little guilty in the instant where I'm grateful for the stuff because I wouldn't have gotten any of it if they were still alive.

Stepping back into the kitchen, I find a knife, cut myself out of Tasha's dress and don the spare clothing. When I come back into the restaurant, I see that Mikey's done the same. He's wearing a plain blue tee shirt that's too small and khaki pants that are way too big. He's busy cinching an electrical cable around his waist. I laugh.

"Yeah, yeah. If you humans weren't such gluttons this wouldn't be such a disaster."

I roll my eyes, unable to argue with that. "There aren't any bags. How are we gonna carry this?" I look down at the stuff, frowning at the thought that we might have to leave it behind.

Mikey nods once towards the bar. "There are a few. At least one backpack and a few purses."

I scoff. "I'm not carrying a purse."

"Why not? You'd look cute with one." He winks at me and sticks out his tongue.

I stick out mine, trying to keep this light, but inside I'm concerned. "So booze makes you pleasant to be around, does it?"

"Makes you pleasant to be around too."

I roll my eyes — as I've been doing every other second today — and retreat to the bar. "Let's just go." I grab the bags I find, and we do.

Chapter Fourteen

The next few days are warmer, and for that I'm grateful. Even in the tattered coat I found, the influence of Kane's blood in my system isn't as robust as it once was. The winds cut into me sideways and my best guess is that it's winter or maybe even fall, but I haven't owned or seen a calendar in nearly a decade. Time is a vacuum in the grey.

As we walk, Mikey tries to coach me on how I might be able to better access Kane, but each time I reach out with my thoughts, I feel pain. After the first few times he asks, I finally tell him that I can't feel anything anymore. The nothingness is better than the truth and though I know he doesn't believe me, he nods and doesn't question the lies I know he knows I've told him.

"Augh," Mikey says, collapsing down in an office chair in front of a fake wooden desk.

Making a similar sound, I slide down to the floor against the wall opposite him. "How far do you think we've come?"

"What city are we in again?" He tilts his head towards the windows, and I wonder if he sees anything outside of them but blackness.

I snatch a piece of paper off of the floor. There are piles of it everywhere. "Everett," I read, eyes skimming the stationary. "The place is called Honeywell."

"Where's the kitchens?"

"What?"

Mikey yawns. "Honey or wells. Can't draw water or keep bees in here."

I can't tell if he's joking or not and smirk. "They don't make food." I shake my head and stretch out my legs, feeling my knees creak at the hinges. "Probably a tech company. No cubicles. That's why I picked it."

Just big empty spaces filled with toys and slides and all the things software geeks dream about late at night — at least before it was looted. Now it's just an empty room full of broken gadgets and fading paper.

"Why is that good?" Mikey says, glancing around the edges of the desk behind him, as if expecting monsters to jump out at any second. "Kind of feels like open season."

"No cubicles in these offices. No places for scavengers to hide."

"Scavengers aren't what concern me."

"What does concern you?"

Mikey glances up at me only once. His face is mean, but also cautious. "Humans may be stupid…but sometimes they have numbers."

I remember the story Mikey told me in the cave, about how he'd been captured by Memnoch's band of human mercenaries. He'd been too drunk to hear them and distracted by some woman. Three bottles in, I wonder how drunk he is now.

"We're on high ground," I say. Windows are clear. There are six exits on this floor alone. "We'd see them coming and we'd have a lot of options to get out of here."

As I turn to my pack and begin rifling through it, he whispers, "I hope you're right."

We dine that night on apricots and chickpeas before finding the office showers. Water still runs through the pipes and though it's rust-colored and freezing, it's also welcome. I take the risk and when I come back, Mikey's got a fire going right there on the office floor, nestled in a bed of dismembered file cabinets.

He heads to the shower while I draw the blinds and yank on clean clothes. I even wash the old ones in the bathroom sink.

I try not to think of the mother as I hang the cotton by the fire to dry. It squishes between my fingers, reminding me painfully of the sound of a dead baby sliding across the tiled floor...

"Oh shit, Mikey, you scared me." I jump when fingers tap me hard on the shoulder.

Orange light from the fire illuminates his skin and his hair and I start with a laugh. "What?" He grumbles, shifting from foot-to-foot.

"No, you just...I've had no idea what you looked like this whole time. It's nice to see you. I wasn't even sure you were blonde."

Mikey smirks and as I rake my gaze over him he seems to become even more uncomfortable. "Yeah yeah, laugh it up," he says, tugging up his pants. They're the same ones as before and hang so low around his hips, I can see the trail of blonde curls leading down from his belly button to meet his pubic hair.

"Got another towel?" he says, louder than he needs to. I'm standing right here. His gaze darts away from mine like he's nervous or something.

"Yeah. Give me just a second." Hanging my wet shirt over the edge of a chair, I toss him a towel from my pack and take a seat in front of the fire.

I watch him as he tugs on a shirt as takes the place across the fire pit from me. His blonde hair is blonde now. It's clear he didn't bother trying to comb it, even with just his fingers, but the lack of black gunk all over him is a start.

"Trying to make me self-conscious?" He mumbles.

I smile. "Just happy to see you looking more human — or alien. Whatever you are."

He snorts and continues rummaging through his pack until he reaches another bottle of booze. I didn't get the final count from Horseshoe Café, but he must have taken upwards of a dozen. His pack is overfull and clinks every time he touches it.

"What are you staring at?"

"Nothing. Just wondering if you were up for sharing that."

Startled, Mikey looks from the bottle of bourbon trapped in his fist to my face and back again. "Seriously?"

"I mean, I'm not going to fight you for it or anything. I just thought it might help me sleep," I lie. I don't really want to drink. I want to make peace.

Mikey smiles at me very slightly and edges around the perimeter of the aluminum filing cabinet pit — the only thing preventing the embers from burning straight through the floor. He slides the square bottle into my open hand. It's warm from where he held it, and when I take a drag, the liquid itself is fire.

I hiss. "Damn. I feel like I could breathe smoke."

"I thought so too when I first got to this piece-of-shit planet."

Ignoring the jab, I take another swig. "You guys don't have booze on Sistylea?"

Mikey shakes his head and stares at me too intensely as I take another swig, letting the booze burn. Letting it ride. "What?" I prod. "Trying to make me feel self-conscious?"

Mikey picks at his beard, which hangs down past the collar of his tee shirt. "You even pronounce it right." He shakes his head and laughs. It's a sad sound. "Nothing fazes you, does it?"

Warmth settles in my belly though the desolation in his black gaze makes me shiver. Some things do still throw me. The good things. Everything that was Kane. But the bad things stopped fazing me a decade ago.

"I guess not. At least not anymore," I say.

He runs a hand back through his hair. The first time he's actually able. Without the mud and blood matting his locks, it actually looks quite soft. Soft and, like his beard, almost dandelion yellow.

"What about you?"

"What about me?"

"You still surprised by stuff?"

"Every day," he says. "Every day."

I smile, feeling unsettled and hand him back the bottle. "Tell me about your planet."

"Sistylea?"

"No. The other one." I roll my eyes.

Mikey surges towards me and I wince, but the blow I expect to feel never lands. Instead, he wraps his hand around my neck with one arm and grinds his knuckles down onto the top of my head.

"You've got some lip on you," he says, but the humor in his voice catches me off guard and I laugh.

I jab him in the side with my elbow and he curls in around the blow, releasing me. "And you are a madman." I shake out my head, damp curls swatting me in the face and clinging to my cheeks.

Mikey passes me back the bottle with hooded eyes that grow increasingly distant. "Kind of like Earth. A lot of greenery, but our water sources are more dispersed. If you look at it from space, the whole planet looks like an emerald."

He holds his hands in two circles and lifts them to his right eye, like peering through a telescope. "Even though we don't have any oceans, there are rivers, lakes and streams everywhere, and cities are built around the natural habitat."

"Sounds beautiful." My head is turning ever so slightly and when I try to picture Sistylea in my mind, the images that come to me appear fuzzy around the edges.

"It is. I mean, it was." Mikey pauses. "Our house had a river flowing straight through it. Straight down the middle. I used to play in it when I was a kid," he says, talking animatedly now.

"Once, before my mother built the dam, I fell in all the way and got carried straight out of the house. Whoosh." His raised hand falls into his lap and begins picking at the fraying strands of his tee shirt.

"That was the first time Kane saved my ass. Jumped into the river after me, pulled me out. He's been saving my life ever since."

Mikey stares intensely at the bright yellow flames and I would ask him what he's thinking about, but I'm scared to ask. Scared of what will happen if I disrupt this moment.

"Did he tell you that I was supposed to die back on our planet? On Sistylea?"

"No." Chills break out across the back of my neck. I scratch them away and give the booze in my hands needless attention. I take another draught and swirl it around with my tongue.

"There were only enough pods for every family to get two. The Council decreed that each family would supply one male and one female to go into the pods and that not even the Notares' families would get an exception.

"Hell, even the Lahve's thirty-person tribe decided that they would give all of theirs up, choosing only one from their entire race to continue on the new planet. The Lahve was the youngest member in their leadership, so he got picked and he made sure that there was no contest between the Notares and their families on who would get sent. The Notares *had* to go.

"So there was no contest between my dad, Kane and me on who would get a pod. He didn't want to go. Members from the Lahve's tribe came to our house and physically had to strap him in. He fought like hell. He wanted me…" Mikey chokes.

His eyes are still unfocused as he stares directly into the flames. I wonder what he sees. Who.

"He wanted me to take his place, but they were stronger than he was — tens of thousands of years old between them — and they knocked him out and strapped him down and sent him here."

With his knees bent and his arms draped over them, he doesn't look like he'll say more. Then he inhales deeply. "My mom should have taken the last life pod. Our family had no other females. But when it was her time to go, she offered me her place and I took it."

His whole body shudders and a physical pain rolls off of him, slides over the ground, and wraps its fingers around me. I shiver.

"She said she wanted to stay with our father. That she wanted to die with him. It wasn't her choice to make though. There was a reason we were supposed to send a female and a male. We don't birth kids at the rate you humans do. We're going to die off and that rule was mandated for the benefit of the species.

"My mom could have had more kids. I could have had more brothers and sisters. They could have carried on our family's legacy. I could have sacrificed."

His throat catches and he stretches his open palm towards me. It's only after I hand him the bottle that I wonder if he hadn't been reaching for something else.

When the bottle breaks from his lips he gasps, "But I didn't. Because you're right about me. I'm just the shitty brother."

He finishes the bottle and tosses it across the room where it shatters, then he finds another.

I don't know what to say to him. I don't have anything to say. He's right. He was a coward. And anything I could try to say to soften the blow would just be a lie.

"Tell me more about Sistylea," I say, breaking the tension between us. "Something nice."

Mikey cackles. His eyes are glossed. "I don't have many *nice* stories about Sistylea…"

"I didn't ask for many. I just want one."

Mikey sighs and closes his eyes. I don't think he'll answer me at first. Then he speaks all at once. "There's a region where mountains grow upside down. They're small at the bottom, then when they get hundreds of feet tall, they form plateaus that all connect and overlap with each other.

"Huge, ancient castles were built upon them and served as the meeting place for the Council. There's a rainforest where it's rained every day for a millennia. Another cluster of islands exists on Sistylea and never experience darkness. We have two suns."

"Do you have two moons too?"

"Seven. You can usually see as many as four at once."

"Incredible."

Mikey smiles ever so slightly then before looking away. "We don't have deserts or plains — those are new for us — no oceans either. Only streams. We have more stars though. Infinitely more constellations. And our animals are mostly all different — there are some similarities, but different shapes. The types of edible plants we grow are different too."

"Really?" I say, growing more fascinated now as Mikey's face lights up.

His cheeks are red and I wonder if that isn't the booze in his bloodstream or the boy caught in the river's riptide, emerging from its depths.

"What kinds of animals?"

He whistles. "I wouldn't even know where to begin. I can tell you that they're bigger, though. Far bigger. Much smarter too. Would you believe me if I told you that we weren't the animals at the top of the food chain back home?"

I shake my head. "I can't even imagine."

He taps the side of the bottle in a soothing, rhythmic way before, becoming aware of it, he hands the bottle over. I take it and though I know I shouldn't, I tip the base up and my head back.

"There are creatures just about as smart as we are that have their own lands. They look kind of like really ugly horses," he says, and I laugh.

"We stay out of their way and they stay out of ours. They don't eat meat. The other ones are more problematic. The Tolta are hard to describe, but they regenerate even faster than we do and hunt us for our blood."

"Seriously? What do they look like?"

"Kind of like massive bats with bears for bodies. We had a standing peace treaty with the leaders of their kind in place for centuries. Stupid, prideful things, though. They never saw the collapse coming. It wiped them all out."

"That's absolutely insane."

Mikey nods. "We were supposed to have one ship, an ark, with animals on it headed for Earth as well — no Tolta, though."

"What happened to it?"

Mikey shrugs and picks at the carpet. "Probably hit by an asteroid on the way over. Either way, it's gone. Just like everything else." Mikey lapses again into a momentary silence. "Guess we got lucky that human flesh and blood works as well as the creatures we ate back home."

I flash him a smile that seems to surprise him. It surprises me, too. Maybe it's fatigue or maybe it's just the booze, but getting riled up right now seems exhausting.

"Don't forget," I say with a wink. "This is your home now, too."

Mikey smiles and he looks like a child, only larger. He shifts as if to turn towards me, but looks to the fire instead. "I guess that's true."

"Of course it is," I say, setting the bottle down as I struggle to stand.

My goal is to head to the bathroom but the room spins and my stomach bubbles like its angry at Mikey on my behalf. I take a step, but trip over my pack and my hand misses the table when I reach for it.

"Whoa there," Mikey says, suddenly surrounding me. There's so much of him. With my back to him, he steadies me by the arms and lifts me into a standing position. "You alright?"

I let him take most of my weight, but still turn around to face him. I cling to his shirt. "I'm seeing double. Is that normal?" I shake my head, trying to shake off the sensation.

As Mikey chuckles, his breath tickles my face. It smells spicy and saturated with booze. "Have you drunk before?"

I shake my head.

"Christ." He bites his back teeth together. "You gotta pee?"

I nod.

"Let me help you get to the bathroom."

We half-stagger, half-fall to the bathroom and back and when we return, the fire's died down to embers and soot. We're laughing, though, and trading hushed, minced quips as the darkness comes around us like an embrace.

"Come on. Get into your sleeping sack." Mikey fans out his own to my left so that we form an L around the embers with our heads joined.

"Sleeping *bag*," I correct.

Mikey roll his eyes and hits me with the tail end of his sleeping bag once, in the face. I laugh as residual dust rains over me.

"Tell me," he says as we settle down into the dark, quiet warmth, "what is Kane doing right now?"

I inhale deeply and close my eyes, and this time when I think of Kane, I remember the time he came and found me with Mikey in that cave. He looked at me and told me that Ashlyn was alive, that the other girls were safe. He touched my cheek, and I imagine that I can feel his fingers as I felt them then.

Then the fire comes.

Like it crawled right out of those filing cabinets to sit on my face, I gasp at its blistering heat. It hurts. So much pain. My pectorals sear, as if my skin were flayed and a great hand reached inside and yanked out my lungs. I'm melting. The whole of me is melting except for my heart, which continues a faint, irregular thump.

But for how long?

"Abel… Abel?"

I gasp and am wrenched back into reality at the sound of Mikey's voice. His hand is touching the top of my head and I glance up to see him propped on his right side. "What is it? What did you see?"

"Nothing," I breathe, "nothing…"

"He's my brother." Mikey's fist clenches. "Don't lie to me."

I shake my head and try to disassociate myself from my own muddled thoughts. "She's torturing him," I wheeze.

"She's what?"

"I don't know." I clench my hands and pound on my forehead. "I don't know anything. But I can feel something here." I lay my hand over my chest. "And it hurts like hell."

Mikey quiets, and after a long pause, finally says, "We should get an early start tomorrow." He lies down and glances back at me, lines crinkling his forehead as he's forced to look up.

"Thank you."

Shock. I nod and, not knowing what else to say, whisper, "Goodnight, Mikey."

"Goodnight, Abel."

He lies onto his back and I stare into the embers, watching them cling to light before dying, one-by-one.

It's still dark out when we wake, and my head is *still* spinning. I groan as I haul my pack higher onto my back and step into the frigid early morning air.

"Jesus Christ, Mikey, my stomach is in knots and my head is pounding. Is it always like this?"

"What? Drinking?

I nod. Mikey laughs and trudges ahead of me across the parking lot, heading towards the rusted green sign that reads I-5 South.

"I wouldn't know. Human tolerance is different than ours, but for one of your size…" He sweeps his gaze up from my toes to my crown. "Yeah, I imagine the recovery would suck."

"Some warning would have been nice."

"I thought you knew." He shrugs.

"Not all of us are alcoholics," I grumble and there it goes.

All pleasantness is gone between us and it only took five minutes into the trek.

"You're a bitch," he says.

"I know," I tell him.

Hours pass as we weave in and out of trees as we follow the line of the highway. After half a bottle of alcohol, Mikey's in the talking mood again and we make light chatter.

He asks me about Population and I ask him about Sistylea and he asks me about my family and I tell him about my brother and I ask him questions about the animals and plants on Sistylea and am surprised and intrigued by the variance between his planet and Earth.

I even ask him about Kane's former lovers…

"Kane could have had his pick of any woman." He squints in my direction as I rub the back of my hand across my forehead, streaking dirt. "And he picked you."

"Maybe I picked him," I tease as we maneuver carefully beneath a highway underpass.

Mikey starts to laugh until his gaze drops to his feet, and he holds out an arm. "Careful here. Looks like some people had a good time."

"People? Try gangs. This was a big brawl."

Glass shards litter the asphalt, sprinkled across a slick, wet ground. I'd thought it was water from a distance — maybe oil. I was wrong. It's all blood.

But where are the bodies?

An upside-down cross was spray-painted in black on the wall of the underpass. Huge, I'm still staring at it when I slip on blood and glass.

Mikey's there, catching me before I get myself drenched. "Thanks," I whisper, dusting off my hands.

"Any time," he says, but as he starts to move past me, he leans in close and sniffs my hair. "You smell good."

"Okay, weirdo."

Inhaling a second time, his eyes widen and he puts distance between us.

"What is it?" I say.

"Nothing," he barks, but his cheeks are red and his voice cracks. He rubs his palm off on the seam of his khakis and, the minute he's able, moves off of the highway and into the woods.

We break for lunch at a rest stop. These kinds of rest stops have always looked the same — even before the Fall — and this one is no exception.

Whatever fighting that took place on the road didn't make it here and I'm glad to find it empty. A few abandoned trucks sit in the parking lot where an empty QFC bag titters across the asphalt.

I eat a can of pineapple quickly and suck on some dried beans.

"Come on, let's go." I stand up from the stone bench but Mikey doesn't move. He only stares at me.

"What?"

"You're really ready to move? You've been holding your stomach like it's about to burst for the past two days."

I look down, caught in the act, and brace my hands on my hips. "I'm fine."

"The hell you are."

Mikey snatches up a bottle of mostly empty black liquid, the color of tar. I'm no longer surprised by how quickly he finishes it.

"Go take care of yourself." He belches and I can smell the anise on his lips from a dozen paces away.

I groan, "Okay, fine. Just wait a second while I go puke or shit or something."

"Lovely." Mikey snorts. "Are all human women like you?"

"The ones still breathing."

I wade through the crispy brown grass until I reach the toilets. With my hands still on my hips I debate openly with the dented blue door that has a lady in a skirt on it. I don't go inside though. The odor is enough to deter me — not because it smells like human waste but because it smells like wasted humans — so I move around to the back of the short, red brick building instead and yank down my pants.

I blink down at my underwear. I blink a lot.

My pulse starts to thunder at the sight. I'm stunned. I'm horrified.

It's blood.

I touch between my legs, sliding a finger between my lips to be sure. They come back all red. I'm dying. I'm fucking dying!

And then I remember…healthy women used to get *periods* before the Fall. Before every meal was a godsend. Before aliens hunted us like sharks and devoured us like candy. Before before before.

And now I'm out here bleeding like a fucking sieve in a world of sharks.

"Mikey?" I cough into my fist as I remove my pants and pull off my badly stained panties. "Mikey, can you throw me my pack and my canteen?"

My voice is deceptively calm, though my thoughts are screaming. Fucking fuck. This can't be happening. I haven't had a period since...no. I haven't had a period. I punch my fingers — the clean ones — back through my hair and brush the filthy ones off on the grass beneath me.

"So it's true."

"Christ!" I jump and turn to see Mikey standing there *staring* like a creep. The redness in his cheeks brings heat to mine as I turn to face him and shield my crotch with my hands.

"Jesus, Mikey. What are you doing? Don't look." But he doesn't look away. "For fuck's sake, Mikey, hand me my pack."

"Your sweetest blood." He licks his lips and throws my pack to the ground equidistant between us. In order to reach it, I'll have to move closer, though something in the parsed way he speaks makes me want to shuffle in the opposite direction.

Not shuffle. Fucking sprint.

"I thought I smelled it earlier."

"Are you a fucking douche bag? Why didn't you say something?"

"Your sweetest blood. I could smell it on you this morning. Right now you reek of it." He gulps, like a thirsty man standing before a glass of water he can't reach.

My skin boils and I lurch towards my pack, landing hard on my knees while tufts of dry grass tickle the insides of my thighs. My hands are fluttering uselessly as I struggle to unlace the ties.

"Let me help you," Mikey says and I start when he appears directly in front of me.

He drops into a crouch, pushes my hands out of the way, unlaces the leather ties and hands me a pair of fresh pants and a towel.

"Mikey, you're freaking me out." I snatch the items away and use them to cover the space between my legs. The *leaking* space between my legs.

He licks his lips in a way I find totally disconcerting and balks, "You should be fucking freaked out. You're a walking target. Every Heztoichen in a fifty-mile radius will come crawling for what you've got. That's your sweetest blood. It's sacred."

"Stop calling it that. It's so weird." I toss the fresh pants aside for now and bring the towel to the blood between my thighs.

"Mikey!" The single word is a garbled scream as Mikey lashes out and grabs my wrist hard enough to make me drop the towel.

Falling forward onto his knees, he tosses my pack out from between us and yanks my legs out from under me. I yelp as I land on my back and before I know what the shit is happening, Mikey's *mouth* is down there, licking the space where only one other male has ever licked.

And it's his freaking brother.

"Mikey," I gasp, hips bucking as pleasure shoots through my lower back.

He holds my hips down and I should tell him to get the fuck away from me, but my eyes are fluttering and I'm distracted by the climb up, up, up.

Oh my god. What is happening?

"Fuck," Mikey whispers, his cool breath against my core making my head spin. It was already spinning. I can't...this isn't...what is...

"I've never...this is..." And then he says the word that doesn't belong to him. "*Heaven*. This is heaven."

He buries his tongue *inside* of me and I gasp as an unwilling desire scrapes its nails down my body, like fingernails on a chalkboard. And it isn't a desire for Mikey, no. But it *is* a desire for him to keep going.

I gasp, my head kicks back and my body collapses onto the grass. He licks me from the inside out, his lips coming into contact with my clit and I'm too new at this to control my reaction — I come immediately.

Pleasure shivers through me, but it's followed by a ripping sensation somewhere deep.

It starts in the pit of my stomach and then pulls up and out of my throat. My forehead pounds and my stomach tears itself to pieces.

He has to stop.

I have to stop.

My body says to ignore that thrashing pain and keep going, but whatever this is *inside* doesn't feel like heaven at all. It feels like death.

That rotten smell from the kitchens assaults me and as Mikey attacks my wet and bleeding slit with his tongue, I try to *focus* and untangle myself from the web of pleasure making my legs shake and making it so hard to think.

Almost…almost…there!

I lurch up just as a second orgasm sweeps me and the death sensation cuts so, so painfully deep.

I slug him at the same time that a delirious scream strangles me.

My knuckles rake his cheek and toss him to the side. His head hits my inner thigh and I lurch out from under him. He shakes his head and when that doesn't work, he shakes it again. He heaves into the grass under him while I scramble to pull my new pair of pants on and shove the towel into them.

"Oh my god, what *was* that?" I shriek.

Mikey doesn't speak. I don't speak. But I put distance between us.

I grab my pack off the ground and my hands shake as I redo the laces.

"Abel." He coughs. He shakes his head again and when he looks up at me I know that no amount of alcohol could have had such an effect. He looks *wasted*.

"I don't know," he says. "I don't know. I never..." He clenches his eyes shut tight.

I run my hand back through my hair. I'm sweating all over.

His eyebrows scrunch up, pulling together. "You liked it. Tell me you liked it. You wanted it. I felt you...I tasted you come. Tasted almost better than your sweetest blood..."

I don't say anything. I don't have anything to say.

Instead, I turn and walk into the woods without caring that he follows.

Chapter Fifteen

Darkness descends right after we pass the sign that says we're less than twelve miles outside of Seattle. So close now, I just want to plow ahead, but I know that I need to rest if we're going to face off with Elise. *And probably be killed by her.*

It's the first time that it actually occurs to me what lies ahead and the challenge it will bring. It's the first time it occurs to me that I probably won't be alive this time tomorrow. I've seen her in action and I don't stand a chance. I glance up at Mikey, remembering the last time he faced off against her.

She's going to kill us both.

We need to come up with a battle plan, but I can't bring myself to speak. We haven't spoken all day.

I polish off a can of peas and Mikey doesn't look at me over the crackling embers as he picks dried apricots out of a bag. Not even as he says, "You look sick."

He tosses a packet of dried meat at me. It's hand-wrapped in baking paper and twine. Must be something the family hunted. I catch it with one hand.

"You need iron."

I feel my cheeks warm, but I don't thank him.

"Don't mention it," he grunts anyway, looking away from me.

He tosses the empty apricot bag aside and picks out an emptying bottle of amber liquid, marked Hennessy. It's the second lid he's cracked in the span of an hour. He's red in the face and wobbly on his feet and I wonder how he continues to function.

"Eat," he says and I do.

I fidget where I lay against the trunk of a tall tree. It's hard against my back and the ground is icy cold underneath my layered pants despite the low embers that are just enough to keep us from frosting over. Couldn't light anything bigger than this. We're too close to a city for that and have to worry now about avoiding detection.

My eyelids are heavy, but I fight to keep them open. I don't know why. Maybe it's because I'm scared to dream, scared to let my guard down, scared of Mikey sniffing after me in the dark.

He's seated facing away from me, but in the low light I get a good look at his profile. High cheeks, coarse hair covering the same strong jaw Kane has. Neck thick with muscle. He looks stronger than he did when we woke up this morning. Ironic, when I feel like I'm falling apart.

"How is Kane?" he says, eyes on the bottle between his feet.

It glistens when he moves it, silver light shimmering against it like the earrings Kane gave me that one time. They belonged to his mother. A female who would have lived if only the bastard across from me had had the decency to die.

I wince, surprised at the horrible direction of my own thoughts. I don't mean it. At least, I shouldn't...

"I don't know," I sigh.

Mikey shifts his weight around but doesn't manage to look very comfortable sitting there with his arms wrapped around his knees. He rocks back and forth very gently.

"You can tell me. I can take it."

"I said I don't know." My voice is louder now, though I try to marshal it.

Mikey must hear something change in my tone because he stills and doesn't respond right away. "What do you mean?"

"Are you deaf?" My voice is more spiteful than I intended, but I'm on a train to self-hatred with no brakes. I'm taking Mikey with me. "I said I don't fucking know. I can't feel Kane anymore."

"What?"

"How many times do I have to repeat myself? I. don't. feel. Kane. I don't feel anything from him anymore."

"How is...how is that possible?"

"Has it not occurred to you that Kane felt what happened earlier? You said this works like a two-way radio, jackass. Well, he's turned off his end. Rightfully so. His *brother* was eating out his *wife* while he's fighting for his life." I can feel the tears behind my eyelids, but I don't cry. I don't have the energy.

Without warning, the glass bottle in Mikey's hand hurtles some place far away and shatters. He follows it, stalking off until the light no longer reaches him but I can tell that's where he stops because I don't hear anymore footsteps.

When he doesn't return, I try to force myself to calm down and get some sleep. It doesn't work. Not really.

Tossing and turning, I think of Kane and dwell on what he must be thinking and feeling. *Betrayal.*

"I didn't mean for it to happen," says a voice in my sleep. "You should have known better, bleeding all over like that..." So many words, but no apology.

It fades and I wake with words on the tip of my tongue, but as the world sharpens and the face looming above mine comes into focus, the words change.

"You're not Mikey."

The alien looming above me has a narrow face and pale skin that looks shockingly clean when compared to the alien I've been traveling with.

He's well-armed and his gaze is raking over me appraisingly in a way that I don't like at all because it reminds me of the hungry look in Mikey's eyes right before... *Betrayal.*

Behind him, the sky is pale and the light is harsh. I'm cold, too. Colder than I was the night before, though that hardly seems possible. Plus I feel a wet spot on my pants that's either dew or blood and a gaping hole in my chest where Kane's presence should be.

Hope seems distant, especially when I notice four other aliens in the clearing and only one of them is the one I was traveling with.

I look across our pitiful patch of embers and see that Mikey's still sleeping, arms crossed over the bottle he's got trapped to his chest. I growl out his name, but he doesn't so much as wince until one of the Others approaches him and kicks him in the ribs.

Mikey lurches to life, eyes blazing red. Lord. How much *more* did he manage to drink during the night when I slept? He lurches towards the sword on top of his pack, but an alien with a long braid surges in his path and kicks the sword behind him.

They look organized, these aliens and organized aliens are the worst kind. They've all got on heavy black vests with black shirts underneath, black cargo pants and are armed to the teeth.

I squeal as the one standing over me grabs me beneath the armpits and hauls me up to standing. Pangs and pains groan over my body, none worse than the one in my lower back.

Mikey snarls something I don't catch as he lurches towards me like he's going to try to stop the thug. The one with the braid holds him back.

"This is your human?" The one holding me says. He sniffs the air around my head. "She's got Heztoichen blood in her."

"And I can clearly smell her sweetest blood on you," says the one with the braid, sniffing towards Mikey too.

A third interjects, "You claimed her? Married a human?"

Mikey hardens in a way I didn't think he was capable of. He looks like a different man — I mean, a different male — and for the first time, actually looks mean and ready to war against someone or everything.

"Yes," he snarls, surprising me for a second time. I didn't expect him to claim me *ever*. Not even when it meant my life.

Like it does now.

Guess I was wrong.

Maybe this is his way of apologizing.

Does he know it isn't good enough?

"Interesting," the slightly taller one says while the one with the braid spits, "Fucking pathetic."

"I'd consider bonding her too if it meant I'd get to taste that sweet, sweet nirvana…" The taller one sucks his teeth in my direction and takes a casual step towards me.

Mikey lurches towards the alien, which gets him a swift gun to the ribs.

The one with the braid is practically foaming at the lips. He says, "No reason we can't open her up, Trocker."

Mikey bowls over, spittle flying from his lips, while the one above me says, "Have a smoke, Ramil. It'll help mask the smell and stop you from eating her before we get her to the master. He'll want a word."

"But the blood," Ramil grits. "We could just take it and the master wouldn't even have to know…"

His eyes lock on me and I flinch as Ramil lunges, but the contact I expect to feel never lands as Mikey surges into his path. He roars when their shoulders connect and punches Ramil in the stomach and then in the face.

Ramil hits the ground and I shout Mikey's name but he's too slow to avoid the arc of Trocker's weapon. It connects with Mikey's right cheek.

When he doubles over, he spits out blood and two words that surprise me for the third time in as many minutes. "She's *mine*."

The conviction in his tone makes my heart pound while a dark pall falls between the five of us. Someone's going to die.

Probably me.

"Of course," Trocker says, while two of the others grab Mikey by the arms and the hair on his head. "Don't worry about your things. You won't be needing them where we're going."

When they all chuckle over some shared joke, I know with a fair degree of confidence that wherever we're going isn't anywhere I want to be.

Leaving the sword behind hurts, but I try to stay focused on the present as we're led south. I don't know how long we walk. An hour? Less than that? Are we headed towards Seattle or away from it?

Are they planning to kill us?

Will I ever see Ashlyn again? Will I ever get a chance to tell Kane I'm sorry and that I love him? Or will I die with him thinking that I wanted his little brother? I may not know Mikey well, but I know that, with me dead, he'd never admit responsibility in this.

That anger fuels my determination to live as I glare at the back of Mikey's head while we're led through the woods, which eventually open up before us.

I trip over unexpected gravel and gawk up at the castle that juts out of the ground like a mountain in the middle of an enormous field. Its navy towers punch towards the sky in megalithic spindles. Wide windows reflect the grey above and at the end of the long driveway sits an intricately engraved glass door which punctuates the house's pale blue siding. Impossible is the only word I can think of to describe it. Not quite human in architecture or design, they must have built it here for a reason.

But why?

We approach a small concrete post and Trocker punches a series of buttons too quick for me to catch on the panel below the intercom.

"Kaius," Trocker says and suddenly I'm being shoved into his arms. He takes me by the shoulder and leans down to meet my ear.

Standing directly behind me, his lips brush across my earlobe as he whispers, "Behave and you may be able to survive this. Perhaps I'll even keep you as mine…"

Sounds of a scuffle. Then Mikey's gruff voice. "Don't you fucking dare, Trocker. She's mine."

The way he calls him by his first name makes me wonder if they know each other. That could help us…or hurt us. Knowing Mikey, he's not exactly the kind to make fast friends…

Trocker doesn't flinch, but turns me around to face Mikey and lines my back with his body. He reaches between my legs and I try not to let it faze me as he rubs *hard* and then brings his fingers up to his mouth and sucks them *loud*.

"That's not allowed," Mikey snarls. "You can't take the blood of someone who's already bonded."

Trocker laughs and so quietly, I don't know if Mikey can even hear him, he says, "What does it matter when you're already dead?"

He turns towards the house again and steps up to a small intercom built into a massive wrought-iron gate.

"It's Trocker," he says into the black speaker box, "We located the source of the scent. The human girl travels with a companion."

Words float through the intercom in a voice that I can identify only as male. The words themselves are all alien, even if Trocker responds in English, maybe for my benefit.

"Yes, he is Heztoichen."

Light, malicious laughter crackles on the other end of the line and makes me shiver. Then in English, the voice says, "Well, of course. Invite them in for dinner."

Chapter Sixteen

Mikey and I stand next to each other in the doorway of an enormous dining room. I'm weaponless and confused more than I'm afraid for the moment and when I share a glance at Mikey, I can sense that he feels the same.

"Straighten up. Look decent for the Notare," Trocker says, kneeing me in the back.

The force of the blow throws me forward, but he moves quickly enough to catch me before I face-plant.

"There you are," he coos, helping me onto my feet.

I pull away from him quickly, or a I would have if he weren't standing so, so close. He leans in close to me and inhales deeply over and over. He brushes the hair from my eyes and slowly unbuttons my coat. Removing it, he drapes my jacket casually over his arm.

"I believe I'm beginning to grow fond of you, human."

Mikey releases a low growl that gives me flashbacks. Kane's made that sound before. It's not a human sound, either, but something alien. Animal.

Trocker shoots Mikey a slick glare as he takes one step to the left. They're toe-to-toe now. "You don't need to worry for much longer, Mikael," Trocker says with a grin. "And when you're gone, I'll take good care of her."

Ice slides down my shoulders and settles in my fists. I'm not so worried about Trocker getting me alone, but about the implication for Mikey. That's twice now the goons in black have talked about his death like it was already written.

Trocker laughs. "You were never worth very much to begin with, were you, Mikael?" Mikey's jaw clenches. He tenses. Blood rushes into his face. "You don't deserve a female who smells like this. Not even a human one. What did you do to her to convince her to travel with you? Or did you force her?"

"He didn't," I say, anger sitting like a stone in my throat. The skin tightens all over my body. I roll my shoulders back.

I may hate Kane's little brother, but I still don't think he deserves to be spoken to like this. To be made so small when he's already powerless.

"He didn't force me," I say, face heating. "And I liked traveling with him, I just know I shouldn't've. We should have never been...traveling together."

I lick my lips as Trocker glares at me, expression twisted in confusion. He opens his mouth to say something, but another male speaks first.

"Trocker," says the voice at my back.

Trocker straightens, steps back and bows towards the hallway behind us. Mikey and I catch each other's gaze as we turn to face the balding, middle-aged alien hobbling up a flight of stairs towards us. Dressed in clothes that betray his age — even if the wrinkles hadn't done it for him — he looks about seventy in human years, with sallow skin and small, slanted eyes.

His modest, corduroy slacks and oversized, beige button-up clash with the decadence of the world around us — dark wood, flashy carpets, sculptures and paintings hanging on the walls in gold frames.

As he shuffles towards us, the male grins and I immediately feel my body tense and pivot, shifting into a fighting stance. But the male just smiles to show a mouth full of greying teeth and cups my palm in both of his. His delicate skin is cracked like dry leather, and I don't miss the way he shakes.

"Hello," he says, voice kind and warm where I didn't expect it to be. It's confusing, because even though he's the villain out of a nightmare, my gut is telling me to trust him.

"How do you do? I am very pleased to have human guests in my home, particularly of such importance. Sistana Abel, the Notare Kane's queen. You are more vibrant in person than even what the reports suggest."

My voice catches and I glance at Mikey, but with his eyebrows raised and lips hanging open dumbly, he looks just as shocked as I feel. Even Trocker looks surprised by the information, his pale face flushing and his eyes heating as he looks at me again in this new light.

"How do you..." I pause and clear my throat. "How do you know who I am?"

"I am privileged enough to have access to a great deal of information, my dear Sistana."

"And who are you?" I blurt out.

I brush my crusty curls behind my ears and smooth down the front of my white thermal. It's covered in soil and flecks of blood.

"It has been too long since I have been called by my given name," he says with a grin and when he smiles again, even more broadly than before, I can see that his grey teeth are surrounded by bright red gums. "Please, call me Crestor."

"Holy fuck." I glance at Mikey at the same time Crestor does. Mikey's face is ashen as he says, "Crestor, you're still alive?"

When the alien called Crestor does nothing but smile and lace his long, skeletal fingers together, Mikey lurches back and swings his fists at Trocker, nailing him hard in the throat.

Two other guards that had been loitering nearby surge forward while Trocker finds his feet. Ramil surges for Mikey, who kicks him in the stomach.

353 ◗

He lurches towards the dining room and over his shoulder shouts, "Abel, run!"

I don't stop to ask questions, but take off, sprinting past Crestor, who makes no move to stop me. I make it to the end of the hall and hang a hard left, but Trocker is on my ass like a fire on a fuse.

He tackles me against the wall, using his whole body to flatten mine to the silk wallpaper. He's breathing hard in my ear and I get the impression that he isn't tired. He's hungry.

He moans, "Notare Kane's Sistana...a human?" He sounds half-outraged, half-incredulous. "A human with blood that smells so sweet."

He combs his fingers back through my hair, almost lovingly, and the pressure of his hand is just as hard as the wall in front of me. With an ounce more pressure, he could crush my skull.

I kick my elbow into his ribs. He grunts and, wrenching my hands behind my back, drags me down the hall and pitches me into the dining room. I crash into the side of the round table, gasping for air.

Mikey's still fighting in the hallway, and I know already that it's a doomed affair, so I glance down the length of the long table at porcelain place settings, the crystal glasses, the sterling silverware. Dear heavens, this table looks like it's been set for thirty people! Thirty ghosts...Just so long as I'm not among them.

The serrated steak knives are sharp and I grab one when Trocker grabs the back of my arm. Swiveling faster than he expects me to, I manage to catch Trocker across the shoulder, drawing black blood. He staggers back, shocked more than hurt, but I use that opening. I toss the knife up, taking it in a backwards grip and slash down again, this time aiming right for Trocker's heart.

He falls to the ground on his knees and I grab him by the hair and wrench his head back, back, back until he can't breathe. Time for the kill.

Trocker looks up at me, shocked, and as I stare down at him. Does he knew I'm going to cut off his head and take it to Kane as a trophy? Maybe we can mount it to the wall over our bed.

Then Crestor says glibly, "Your Grace." Wait — is he talking to me? I look up and see that Mikey's on his knees with a knife to his throat in a mirror image of Trocker. A parody of it.

"For the sake of your friend's — or should I say your brother-in-law's — health, I suggest you release my guard. I am, after all, quite fond of him, as I suspect you are of your king's brother." He passes his gaunt hand across his receding hairline slowly. It quivers, like his lips, though he looks neither excited nor afraid. Something is wrong. I've never seen one of the alien look so old or frail or get the shakes.

Cursing, I throw the steak knife onto the table, shattering a crystal champagne flute. As Trocker stands up to his full height, I gather my fists in front of me and wait for retribution.

"Trocker," Crestor says, and Trocker freezes, one foot off the ground. He glances over his shoulder once and snarls before turning away from me.

"There." Crestor clasps his hands together. "Now that's all settled, let's take a seat. Dinner shall be served promptly."

I'm guided to a place at the far end of the seemingly limitless expanse of slick black wood. Crestor takes the seat to my right at the head of the table while Mikey's shoved into the seat across from me.

"You give the human the place of honor at your table?" He sneers and I hate him just a little more for it after coming to his rescue earlier.

I glare at him across the table, but he doesn't look at me.

"Better the human than the criminal." Crestor's face flashes and for a moment he's not the same alien he was. He's masked violence. "And from this moment forth, you will address my guest by Sistana or Your Grace. I do not tolerate willful tongues at my table."

Mikey's lips tighten to a thin white line and he rips his shoulder from beneath one of the guard's hands. Crestor's eyes haven't left Mikey and I feel my stomach pitch when he calls Trocker over.

I grip the smooth edge of the wooden table so tightly my fingers turn white around the nails. Low words are exchanged between the two before Trocker stalks out of the room.

He returns moments later with seven human escorts in tow, even though there are only three of us. Then he stands at the wall behind me so that I can no longer see him. But I can feel him. He's everywhere. Staring holes through the back of my neck. Searching low, lower, lower...

The humans pour dense red wine into our crystal cups. Nearly black, it looks less like wine and more like tar, and when Mikey reaches for the cup without hesitation, I balk.

"Mikey," I hiss. Mikey meets my gaze and his hand hesitates over the crystal. I shake my head once, stiffly. "Don't..."

"If I have to be here, I might as well." He lifts the cup to his mouth and drains half in a gulp.

Rage. Disbelief. I don't know which one is stronger. Maybe they both are.

Crestor laughs a little and shakes his head at me indulgently. "My dearest Sistana, do not trouble yourself."

He tucks his white linen napkin carefully into the collar of his shirt and reaches for his own glass. It's a darker red than Mikey's and mine and it *stinks*. Definitely not wine. But it's too dark to be blood. I don't know *what* it is, just that I'm not going anywhere near anything he serves me.

"Thus is the way with all sentient beings. Heztoichen or human, we all have our weakness." His eyes glitter. I don't know what he means.

Just that it's bad.

"Crestor," I say, trying a smile. I swallow hard and clear my throat and unfold my napkin, tucking it into my shirt in the way he just did.

"Thank you very much for inviting us in. It's been a long journey on the road."

Crestor claps his hands in his lap and grins to reveal almost all of his teeth. I was wrong before. They're not grey. They're black and spotted.

"Sistana, I must confess, it is a rare pleasure for me to dine with such beguiling company."

He angles his chair towards me and takes a deep draught from his glass, and it's as if he's entirely forgotten about my haggard appearance, my drunk brother-in-law and the fact that I was about to cut the head off one of his guards.

"Can I offer you another beverage? I see that wine is not to your taste."

He snaps his fingers once and a human attendant comes to my side and whisks it away. There's no eye contact and no recognition at all between us. I can't get his attention. He's like a ghost. *This house is full of them.*

"Water would be fine."

Crestor nods once, though there's something mischievous about him. Trust? Had I felt that once? I don't know what I feel now.

"A bottle for the Sistana. Be sure that it is uncorked."

"Thank you, Crestor."

"Notare Crestor," Trocker blurts out at my back. "Apologies for the intrusion, Notare."

Crestor nods towards Trocker behind me, then lifts a hand to quiet him. "The Sistana has no need to refer to me by my former title. Her rank supersedes mine. Crestor is just fine, Sistana."

Surprise forces me to ask, "You're a former Notare?"

"I am, but as you can see my Tare has long since faded." He gestures to his chest, which I can't see anyway underneath his coat, but I believe him if he says he doesn't shine.

"I was Notare before Kane. He replaced me after my light died. I always viewed him as a son."

"Alright," I say, feeling hopeful. "If you're like a father to him, then maybe you can help us…"

Mikey bangs on the table hard enough to topple another champagne flute and send it crashing to the floor. "Don't you ask him for anything. *Anything.*"

Crestor's dry lips purse and he raises his voice. "If you do not learn to control your tongue, Mikael, then I will see fit to remove it."

He looks up and smiles, shifting in and out of expressions seamlessly, like shedding skins. The snake.

"Ah, look. Here you are now. A bottle of water for the Sistana, and more wine for her lowly servant."

His eyes slide sideways to find Mikey and I get a very bad feeling in the pit of my stomach.

The human servant ghost-robots bring out a corked bottle of water. They make a great show of uncorking it in front of me. They bring food out too. Soup. It's green and smells salty and delicious. My fingers twitch towards my utensils, but at great pains, I manage to restrain myself.

"Your Grace?"

I glance at Crestor. His hands are folded politely in his lap and his eyes are gentle, never prying. He's a big, giant question mark.

"Yes?"

"You are free to request other food if this is not to your liking. However, if I may be so bold as to suggest that your fears are unfounded, I would do so. The food has not been tampered with. As a gesture of good faith, would you like me to have Trocker as well as one of the human servants test your food for you?" He reaches out and touches his alligator skin hands to mine.

I force myself to stay put and speak evenly and say, "Yes, I would like that. Thank you."

Trocker looms over me with a spoon and takes a sip of my soup. One of the human waiters — a tall, gangly boy with bad skin — does the same. When neither drops down dead, I weigh my odds and take a bite myself.

Mikey asks for another glass of wine and as he drinks it, he watches me eat. Only after he finishes his third glass, does he eat too. Like a savage, he gobbles down everything.

"So, you know Kane well?" I say.

"Why, of course." Crestor nods as he picks at his own dish. It's different from ours. I don't know why. No soup, he just went straight for mains, and his plate is full of a black slab of meat that looks absolutely revolting.

"He sends me regular reports from the Diera, as a courtesy. It is very difficult to take on the responsibilities of being Notare as a child. I think I helped ease his transition."

I nod, though can't quite picture Kane as a child, and let the servants clear my plate. A second course of fragrant meat and potatoes soon follows.

Mikey barks my name the moment I lift my fork. His eyes are bloodshot and his cheeks are flushed. The hand he uses to hold his wine is clenched around the crystal so fiercely that a fine crack shimmers up the side of the glass to meet his palm. Deep red wine seeps through it and stains the knuckles of his hand. He shakes his head once more and says my name.

Crestor laughs and sets down his own fork and knife when I do. He rocks back in his chair. "Oh, Mikael, it seems that you fear the rumors about me."

"Rumors?" Mikey says and I don't miss the way he slurs. He's only a couple glasses in though, and I've seen him drink two bottles and still articulate clearly. Something's wrong. Fuck. *Fuuuuuuck.*

Mikey's cheeks flush as he rounds on Crestor. He jabs his pointer finger at him, and it would appear more threatening if he weren't using his other hand to anchor himself to the table.

"*Rumors* imply that they're conjecture. That they might be wrong. You've been tried and convicted of your crimes. The only reason you're still breathing is because you were Notare and Kane has a soft spot for you.

"If it weren't for Kane, the Council would have had your head three hundred years ago — the second your light died and you became irrelevant. A blemish in the history books.

"Parents don't tell their kids about you when they sing songs of hero Notares like my brother. They tell their kids about you to terrify them. You're the monster little Heztoichen children have nightmares about."

Crestor's lips have tensed to the point that I can no longer see them. He snaps with his left hand and with his right, dabs at the bloody spots at the corners of his mouth with white linen. I've got my own napkin crushed in my fist.

"Human," Crestor says to the one that approaches him, "Please fetch Mikael another bottle of wine. Nothing from the bottom shelf. We don't serve good wine to criminals."

"Well, isn't that the sheep calling the pot black?" Mikey laughs, butchering the expression in a way that might have made me laugh had I not been so riveted to the scene and it's impending outcome. Like those machines, the big ones with the blades at the top. You hold the rope and when you let it go…slice goes the neck and thud goes the head when it rolls away from the body.

Whose head will roll? If I had to guess, it'd be Mikey.

And soon.

Crestor raises the glass in his hand. "Silence, Mikael, or I will have you removed from the table before dessert. Ramil," Crestor calls and the one with the braid steps forward. He's got the knife in his hand he was using before to keep Mikey contained. He tosses it up now and with no ceremony at all, he catches it by the sheath and swipes the hilt across the side of Mikey's head.

I flinch, grateful only when I hear Mikey grumbling out curses and trying to staunch the flow of blood running from above his left ear.

"Apologies, Sistana, both for the scene your kin has caused here, and that you had to travel in such undignified company for so long. After all that you have endured, Your Grace, I certainly hope that you find what it is you seek."

"You know that Kane is missing?"

He smiles. "Kane is not the only one from whom I receive reports."

"Then you know where he's been taken." I drop my fork and it clatters loudly as it lands.

"As do you, I'm sure." He glances down at my chest. "Blood bonded to the Notare as you are, it must be a terrible burden to feel his suffering."

"You know…you know what she's doing to him?" Rage. Disbelief. This time, I know which one screams louder.

"I am well aware that Notare Elise has taken him. What she intends to do with him is a mystery."

"Guess," I bellow.

He watches me critically, sizing me up as he calculates something I can't see. I don't dare breathe. I just seethe, pouring my anger out through my gaze. And I don't blink.

He cuts his meat up into small slices, severing the connection between us. He smiles as he chews and as he swallows, says, "Perhaps I have some idea."

He slips the serrated edge of his knife through his meat. It looks tough, and black liquid seeps across his plate, dyeing the potatoes there grey.

He says, "If I were Notare Elise, with ambition equal to her own, it would seem to me that the best way to secure my power would be to eliminate my competition."

"But what does it matter? Her light is dying."

Crestor smiles at me secretly. "And how could you possibly know that?"

I balk. "Because I saw her when she took Kane away. She has him and I want him back."

Crestor nods considerably, like we're discussing our favorite hobbies, and not matters of life and death — *mostly* death. "Unfortunately for you, she needs him if she is to succeed in her experiment. So far the blood of the royal families has not produced the results she had hoped for."

He pulls meat off the tines of his fork with his teeth. He chews, swallows, chews, swallows in a way I find absolutely disgusting.

I look away while my stomach gurgles and the pain in my lower back intensifies. "What results were those?"

"I should have thought it obvious. Using the royal families' blood, she attempts to create her own light."

"You can't fake Tare. It's not possible. Smarter Heztoichen have tried before her," Mikey shouts, though his speech is so badly slurred at this point I can hardly make sense of it.

Looking up at him for the first time in minutes, I see that his eyes are droopy slits. His head lolls on his neck and his hands are relaxed around his utensils.

My pounding heart breaks.

We're not going to make it.

No — we're not *both* going to make it.

And when I find Kane, what would he say?

"On the contrary, Mikael," Crestor says, ignoring Mikey in his sorry state. "Notare Elise's greatest secret is that her light has been dying for nearly two hundred years. Her scientists have discovered a means by which the Notare can keep her light alive by synthesizing royal blood and injecting it into her veins. It is not true Tare by any means, but the shadow of life is enough to keep her above suspicion."

"How do you know all this and why don't you seem to care? Kane was like a son to you and you know that she's using him." I reach across the table and grab Crestor's frail hand. "Help us get him back."

Crestor's eyes dodge mine for the first time all day. His knife clatters against the edge of his plate noisily so he sets it down and, slipping his other palm free of mine, wipes off his hands on his black-stained napkin.

"Apologies, Sistana, this is not a comfortable subject for me." He meets my gaze and I shiver. There's a bleakness in those lying, dying depths. And it's so lonely. "Notare Kane and his family not the first of Elise's subjects. She has been practicing her art of blood transfusion for a long time. Centuries. Six or seven of them, by my count, and long before her light ever began to dim.

"My sister was one of her first victims and unlike Mikael, my sister Lara did not survive the trials Notare Elise put her through."

"So…what?" I blurt. "What happened? Why couldn't you take her down then?"

"If I could have, I certainly would have. But I could prove none of it. I never even found her remains."

Crestor inhales once, sharply, and when his eyes flutter to meet mine the touch of sadness I thought I'd seen in them is gone as if it had never been.

He says softly, "Notare Elise is quite adept at covering her tracks, as you will soon discover. If she has your blood bonded mate, I am sorry for you, for you will not be able to recover him."

Rage. Just rage.

I throw my fork across the table, shattering a dozen glasses simultaneously. "You just gave up, then? Why don't you fight back?"

"Can't leave…" comes the groan from across the table.

"What?"

"Silence, Mikael."

Mikey slumps forward, bracing his arms on the table, one elbow landing directly in the center of his plate. "He can't leave!"

Crestor watches Mikey icily, then throws his napkin onto his plate. "I believe we will have to skip desert. Apologies, Sistana, but alcohol seems to have severed the connection between Mikael's brain and his mouth."

"What does he mean you can't leave? I didn't think that Notare were even allowed in Population."

"I am a former Notare, remember."

Ramil and Kaius grab Mikey's arms and wrestle him from his chair. "That's not the reason," Mikael moans, throwing his elbows back and forth in a failing attempt to get free. His legs drag lamely beneath him.

Crestor drinks more from his glass while I fight the urge to go after Mikey. I wouldn't get far. I have to be smart. Smarter than Mikey, at least, and definitely smarter than Crestor.

"I have been placed under house arrest by the Council. When the decision was made, Kane spoke for me and allowed me to keep this residence along with whatever equipment and support staff I might need. I lead a very comfortable life on a cause of your husband, my queen."

The slight bow to his head suggests an end to the conversation, but I can't not ask, "What's your crime?"

"That is not civilized dinner conversation, my…"

"Cannibal," Mikey slurs from the doorway. He's got a grip on the wall that the guards don't immediately break. When they do, it's too late, because I can still hear Mikey when he says, "Crestor the cannibal…"

Crestor hisses, drawing his head back into his shoulders and clutching the arms of his chair, making him look like some kind of giant, carnivorous bird. The two guards on Mikey's arms drag his limp body out of the dining room while my gaze returns to Crestor's plate.

I don't realize I'm standing until I hear the chair behind me hit the floor with a thwack.

"Where are you taking him?" I say, breathing harder now. In the back of my mind, I already know the answer. What I meant to ask was *how much time do I have?*

Crestor rises from the table and servants flutter around us both. They pick up my chair, replace his napkin, rearrange the plates, glasses and cutlery. "My Lady, you have no need to fear. I would not dare harm my Notare's Sistana. Your food and drink are fine, untampered with and untouched and no humans were harmed in the making of this meal.

"The meat is a particularly succulent piece of Heztoichen. A young woman by the name of Marlina, I believe. She had a daughter who I ate last month. An exquisite rarity, procured by Elise and delivered to my estate.

"She sends me these little gifts from time to time as a torment to remind me of all that she took from me. I am not a perfect male." He shakes his head and when he grins he looks totally insane. "I find it hard not to indulge. There is so little to inspire me these days."

"Not interested in eating people with names." I gulp, putting my chair between us. "Not even aliens."

Crestor just smiles and nods. "I understand, of course, and if you'd like, I'd be happy to prepare you with some cheese and fruits so that you may be on your way. It will be a difficult journey, I imagine, if you still intend to enter the Saltlands."

"I do. You know I do."

"I know."

"But you also know I'm not going without Mikey."

"Ah, but Sistana, you must."

I glance at the doorway, but Mikey's already gone. I can hear the thud of boots on the stairs. Likely the ones belonged to the dead guy from the kitchens. Those damned kitchens.

Why did we have to stop there? Why did Mikey have to find his bottles? Would we have been able to avoid this if he were sober? Would he have heard Trocker and the others approach? Would he have been able to keep himself from tonguing me down there when I didn't give him permission to?

I don't know.

And I'll never know.

"Crestor, please. It's Kane we're talking about here. Your son, remember?"

"Kane may be my son, but Mikey is no relation of mine," he sneers. "The child is barbaric and rude bordering on cruel. I could smell your blood on him and unless you truly are undeserving of Kane's attentions, then I will assume that he forced you. That crime alone is punishable by death."

Crestor gives me a knowing look then. I can either admit that Mikey attacked me and get him killed, or I can admit that I liked it and likely get me killed. I don't know what the punishment would be for that.

Crestor nods again. "No, I do not believe you would be so easily swayed by the affections of this male when you have the adoration of one far, far superior."

Crestor starts to move past me, but I intercept him and grab his arm. "I love Kane," I implore. "And Kane loves his brother. I can't abandon him."

"My darling," Crestor sighs and his dry fingers sweep my hairline. "You do not have a choice."

He snaps and Trocker reappears, grabs me and starts to force me out of the dining room. I grab chairs and linens and anything I can to try to keep myself there, in Crestor's earshot. I've only got seconds left to reason with him.

But he's resumed his seat I shout all kinds of things, but he just saws into his meat and just before Trocker carries me out of the room and down the stairs, Crestor says one last thing.

"Sistana Abel, when Kane spoke for me, it was his intention that I continue living as *punishment* for my crimes. In the wake of my sister's death, I engaged in these *proclivities* that I'd long denied myself for the sake of my family and its reputation." He gestures at his plate and meets my gaze with a smile.

"But I have no family. No reason not to indulge. And while the Council was merciful and wanted me executed, your Notare Kane wanted me exiled so that I could live the remainder of my years in loneliness and bitterness and torment.

"He is a cruel male, your mate. Cruel, but just."

I suck in a breath, feeling my whole body shudder on the exhale while I thrash against Trocker's arms. "So you're going to kill Mikey to get back at him?"

"I was always going to kill Mikey simply for the taste."

"You can't do this. I *command* you," I say, in one last attempt to get through to him. "I'm the Sistana now. *Your* Sistana. I outrank you, you said so yourself."

He smiles just a little with one edge of his mouth and when he looks at me, he manages to look impressed. "Very good, Sistana. Very good. And you are correct. An order from you is not one I dare disobey. So, when you retrieve Notare Kane, I will gladly welcome my punishment."

He cocks his head and Trocker forces me down the staircase and towards the front door. He throws it open, and a cool wind batters back the warmth of the world behind me. He grabs me by the nape of the neck, fingers digging into my pressure points as he drags me outside.

It's still light out, though I can tell that the day is dwindling somewhere above the grey. He shouts an order to another black-clad alien walking the perimeter and the gate swings open before us.

He pushes me so hard that I fall onto my hands and knees. My jacket lands on the ground beside me. Angry, I curl my fingers into the gravel. It's wet, and that's the first I notice of the rain. Somewhere up above the grey, I can hear a mighty growl. It's been years since I've heard thunder.

Trocker looks tormented as he shuts the gate between us. I charge at it, not expecting to be able to make it inside, so it's no surprise when I don't. Through the bars, Trocker punches the heel of his hand against my sternum.

A splinter of pain lights there and fades as I gasp for breath and drop back down onto the gravel. By the time I've got my breath back in order, Trocker's already crossed the driveway and is standing at the front door.

I watch him watch me in the orange glow of the open doorway. His eyes meet mine and they are darkened by the shadows of his eyebrows.

From this distance, he looks like a skeleton. Black suction cup eyes, hollow cheeks, pale skin yearning for sunlight.

He sucks his teeth, and mouths a string of words between us that I can't make out before shutting Mikey in, and me out.

Chapter Seventeen

S ticking to the trees, I circle the house three times, marking the entrances, exits and low-lying windows as I move. The thin mist dampens the sounds of the world around me — sounds that are already difficult to make out with one eardrum blown.

A few times I think I catch the sound of screams drifting along the breeze, but it might just be my imagination. *God, please let it be my imagination...*

Crestor's house is built like a fortress. The fence surrounding it is twice my height and each post is sharpened to a point, sure to shred anything that tries to climb over it. There's no porch, no awning, no terrace, and on the first floor, there are no windows. Aside from the front door, there's no way in.

No way except for the one: a cellar door.

The rain is white and everything else is black — the sky, the castle, the earth, the fence, the basement's camouflaged entrance.

It's one of those cellar doors that's built flat to the ground just a few feet away from the house. Just slightly raised, I can see enough of it if I squint just right and from what I can see from the other side of the fence, even though the wood is dark and looks like it could be old, the lock is silver and shiny and looks new. Recently replaced.

As I crouch under the cover of a prickle bush while two guards scan the woods surrounding me, I debate this for the millionth time.

Mikey is a drunk slob who's slowing me down. I could go for Kane and together, we could come back for Mikey with an armada. Kane could take Crestor apart single-handedly and rescue his brother. *But in how many pieces? How much of Mikey would be left?*

I close my eyes and grit my teeth and clench my fists into the soft soil below me. There are bugs on my fingers. The kinds with the armadillo shells that roll up into a little ball when they get scared. That's what I feel like doing.

I'm not going to make it. The guards are on my trail. They can smell me, even with the rain, of that I'm sure.

Rage. This time it's followed by frustration and that frustration is followed by an idea...

My blood is making them crazy. *Crazy.* So maybe I should let it.

Cautiously, in as few moves as possible, I slip back into the trees. They help block some of the rain, though by this point it hardly matters. My clothes are soaked and muddy and I'm cold again. I dream about the bath that Kane and I shared and wonder...hope...we'll get back to that place.

Yanking my wet pants down to the knees, I pull out the bloody towel and rip it into a dozen strips. Keeping just beyond the cover of the trees, I mark a perimeter around the house, dropping pieces of fabric at arbitrary intervals as I run.

I notice the effect almost immediately and pause long enough to smile and wipe the last of the blood on my hands off onto the nearest tree trunk.

Routes ruined, the guards start pacing now. They're shouting between each other angrily, scanning the woods but without focus. In the rain-dampened distance I hear Trocker screaming orders in alien, followed by the unmistakable sound of Crestor's gates opening.

They're coming. *Perfect.*

I dive underneath a couple thick bushes, my adrenaline spiking and my heart clattering in my ribs. It seems to take forever for one of the Others to appear and there's *two* of them.

A dozen paces away, one shouts at the other, hands him a hunting knife and points to the forest before charging off to the left. The one with the knife turns towards the trees and starts stalking forward slowly...towards me.

He's got a gun on him, but it's lowered at his side. With the rain as thick as it is, dulling his senses, it's like he's walking blind — at least as blind as I am.

Five feet from where I'm hiding, he doesn't hear my pulse or my light breath and with the bushes swallowing me up, to him I'm likely nothing more than a dark smear against a larger darkness.

His right foot crinkles over damp leaves inches from my nose as he moves deeper into the forest. I wait until he passes before springing out of the bush and latching onto his back. He grabs the gun, but I want the knife. I pry it easily from his hand and with way too little resistance, I manage to stab him in the neck.

Remembering what Kane did to Drago, I take the wasteful minutes needed to saw the Other's head off. I can hear the cavalry coming — voices not too far off — and I know I need to move fast.

Throwing his gun across my back, I hack him to pieces where he lies, removing just his arms but keeping his legs. He'd be too heavy to carry otherwise and I've got to make it to the fence.

I haul his body through the mud, which is slick and aids my progress. I slip half a dozen times before reaching the fence's thick black bars. I cling to them with one mud-stained hand. The rain is coming down harder now and when I look to my right, I can see someone running towards me from the forest.

Shit.

I lift the gun, wishing it came with an instruction manual because I've never been any good with firearms — only gangs have guns. By the time the male appears and I recognize him as Kaius, I finally manage to get the safety off.

I pull the trigger and the force of the blow throws me back into the fence. My head hits the metal and the impact knocks the breath clean out of me. Kaius falls, clutching his abs, and I let him writhe in agony. I don't have time to deal with the dying. The living are my concern now.

I slip my shoulder beneath the decapitated corpse and lift it as high as I can. Then I throw. I slip, get a mouthful of iron bar and curse while my mouth fills with blood. My lower lip burns, splitting down the center as I barely keep my teeth.

The once-distant shouting is louder now — right on top of me — though when I look around I don't see anything but mist and rain and grey. I don't know how much time I've actually got, what with my panic making everything feel both faster and slower all at once.

I haul the corpse up out of the mud again and grunt as I throw it up onto the fence. This time it catches and folds at the waist. One of the fence spines pierces him all the way through and black blood rains over me from the new wound in his torso.

Don't care.

I yank hard on his legs. They hang at my hairline and dirt from his boots showers my face. He's anchored there pretty good and, not wishing to waste anymore time, I brace my feet against the fence, grab his legs and climb.

I grapple and claw my way up the length of his body until I reach the spikes at the top. His corpse is a solid buffer between me and being impaled. I wonder just how I'm going to get *back* over the fence as I swing my legs over the other side and drop down onto the gravel. *Eh. I'll deal with it later.*

Mud squishes under my feet and I run towards the cellar. My head hurts, my lungs burn, my mouth tingles and I know that all I've got on my side is time. Rain and time. Rain and time and absolutely no exit strategy.

I come up to the cellar door and point my gun at it. I fire without waiting. The gun has a mind of its own and steers me wildly to the left before taking me off my feet. Tac-tac-tac-tac-tac-tac. Bullet casings rain.

Shouting behind me is loud enough to touch and I turn, finger on the trigger. I shoot the guard sprinting towards me in the head and the one behind him in the stomach. My heart is pounding as I wait to be besieged.

I take in a breath, and then a second, then a third. No one's there. Just the dead and an overactive imagination.

I turn back to the cellar door and fire off another dozen rounds. Eventually, it's not the latch that breaks but the wood surrounding it. I slip my fingers into the woodchips and wrench open the door. I keep my weapon elevated, unsure of what to expect.

"Hello?" I shout into darkness, beyond which nothing stirs. My voice doesn't echo. The rain gobbles it up. "Mikey? Mikey, get your ass up here!"

"Mikey can't hear you, Sistana."

I flinch and swing my gun around. Trocker grins. His gun hangs across his chest, but he doesn't have it raised. I hadn't heard him approach and wonder for a moment why I'm still alive. Then it occurs to me in the way his eyes drift to my pants, that it isn't my life he wants.

"Give me a reason I shouldn't shoot you, Trocker."

Because I can think of one. If I fire, the recoil will send me plummeting into that darkness, and I have no desire to go down there with no clear path back up.

Blood and rain drip from my eyelashes into my eyes, turning the world to rose long enough for Trocker to take a step towards me. I counter by placing my finger to the trigger.

His grin spreads wider. He says, "I can't." And then he dives for me, moving too fast to follow.

I fire and miss, and it's his hands on me that keep me from falling into the cellar hole at my back. He grabs my leg and starts to drag me over the ground, when all at once, a white blur soars out of the cellar and breaks the contact between us.

My eyes widen as I stare after the *thing* sprinting across the gravel. It looks lost. Naked and lost. And it looks…like a person. Like an alien. But it's missing both hands at the wrists.

Bullets fly, taking the escaped alien off of its feet. The sound of approaching guards stirs me to action and I grab for the gun and swing it up, but Trocker blocks with his forearm and the pressure of his arm cutting upward is enough to unbalance me.

I try to stand, but I stagger and lose my grip on the gun and on the soft soil beneath my feet. My heel catches on the opening to the cellar and Trocker is staring at me with horror as I fall forever, then the ground and I collide with unforgiving force.

I can hear movement around me now that I couldn't from up above. Scratching, clawing, shuffling. The world is grey, illuminated only by the pale ring of light hanging like a halo some fifteen feet up. The ground beneath me is black, hard and cold to the touch.

"Mikey?" I whisper.

Then bodies come at me all at once, from every direction. Scrambling over the cool, earthen ground and struggling to regain my breath, I draw the knife from the cargo pocket in my pant leg.

A hand wraps around my ankle the moment I stand and pulls my feet out from under me. I hit the ground hard and when I blink down the length of my legs at the body clinging to my ankles, I don't understand what I'm seeing.

It's an alien, or at least…it used to be. Now, it's got arms and hands but it doesn't have eyes or ears or feet. My heart hammers in my chest and I glance around, realizing for the first time that these aliens are *all* missing parts.

I shove the thing off me, ripping my feet out from under him, only to be approached by a female with arms severed at the shoulders. She steps on my knee and stands on the blind man's back and only then is she able to jump high enough to reach the exit, legs kicking uselessly as her torso hits the dirt above.

More bodies begin scrambling towards the light, shrieking as if they haven't seen any for years.

Maybe they haven't.

Some cower from it and as they move around me like river water around rocks. Heart beating like a goddamn snare drum, I search the throngs for Mikey.

"Mikey! Where the hell are you!" I scream.

A woman with cracked, ashy skin charges towards me from the depths of the darkness. She has only one leg and is using a long, wooden stick as a crutch. She jabs it at me and I spin out of her way only to be pulled to the ground by a heavy arm.

I stab when it doesn't release me and catch only a glimpse of the Other's deformed face. He's got no tongue and is missing his left shoulder. He bares his teeth and I slash at his cheek when he jolts towards me, but he doesn't seem to feel the pain.

He comes at me again as a tower of bodies begin to form, the weaker taking the bottom positions of the pyramid while the others pour out of the darkness and into the world. Into Population.

Blood spray slashes across the opening and I hear Heztoichen words flung between the living. The male attacks me again, this time shouting the same word over and over again. I kick for his face, but a body slips between us, stepping directly on my stomach. It lurches up into my throat at the same time that the guy holding onto my leg bites down.

Roaring up into a seat, I shove the body off of me and stab downward blindly. I hit his shoulder first before aiming a second time for his neck. I stab him again and again, but he doesn't let go of me, and there are bodies now stepping on and over both of us. I'm being trampled to death and this dying guy won't let me go, even as he exhales his last breath with what sounds like relief.

Feet are pressing on my chest and ribs and hands and arms. I keep hold of the knife through sheer will power alone, but I'm not sure how I'm going to be able to get up. Not when I'm the bottom layer.

"Kane," I shout, tears of frustration making it hard to think clearly and rationally about a way out. "Kane..."

A sudden surge of energy blooms in the center of my chest right before a voice shouts very near to me, "Not likely."

It's familiar, though rougher. Still drunk. A heavy boot crushes the skull of the man on my leg and two bloody hands reach through the disembodied limbs to grab the front of my jacket and rip me out of the rubble.

Mikey grabs me to his chest and starts to climb. He steps on backs and arms and legs, some of which break apart beneath him. He steps and pushes and punches and claws and I cling to him with my eyes closed. I can't watch. It's unbearable what Crestor did to these things.

Nobody deserved to die like this. Not even aliens. My mortal enemies.

I'm grateful when Mikey jumps all at once and somehow manages to clear the opening. He lands on the soft soil on his stomach and has to kick his legs free of the hands that have grabbed onto him.

Screams light up from below while more screams light up the grey.

A bullet whizzes past my ear and Mikey curses. Rolling out of Mikey's arms, I look up to see a black-clad guard rushing towards us. The knife I'm still somehow holding nails him in the throat and he hits the ground without ever firing.

Mikey finishes him off by twisting his head off his neck. He swipes the machine gun the guard had been holding, loops the strap over his head and looks back to make sure I'm following. I am, despite the staggering pain in my leg.

My skin is all messed up and mauled, but I can't worry about it now. I don't have a plan or the time to come up with one.

In the time it takes me to wrench my blade free of the headless guard's neck, Crestor's unfinished meals pass like a current between Mikey and me as they shriek their way to freedom. Mikey shouts my name as they inundate us, but they seem to be less concerned now with my free flowing blood than they are with the guards storming towards us.

The guards and the victims clash at the open gates to Crestor's house and I keep my bloodied blade poised at the ready. Mikey fires first. Tac-tac-tac-tac-tac-tac-tac. A whole host of guards hit the ground, and distantly, I wonder what happened to Trocker because he isn't among them.

Resounding gunfire follows us across that muddy arena. I feel the wind rush off of the bullets as I'm narrowly missed. Mikey cries out and collapses against the trunk of a tree just as we follow the bodies out of the gate and make it to the trees.

"You've been hit."

I'm panting now and try to reach for the fresh wound on his shoulder but he shrugs me off and surges to the right. I grab the back of Mikey's pants, noticing for the first time that he has a painful-looking gash across his left pectoral. His right eye is swollen entirely shut and his left is a burning blood red. He's still high and hasn't come down yet.

"Where are you going?" I shout, pulling him to the left. "I canvassed earlier and there's a garage just over here. I think I might be able to hotwire a car and we can try to punch our way out of here and hope to high hell that they don't chase us, guns blazing."

As I say that, I glance over my shoulder. The dozen guards still alive on the gravel driveway are working to finish off most of the dismembered aliens, but those aliens have something the guards don't — numbers.

Numbers and desperation.

They're fighting back.

They outnumber the guards three to one as they fight for their survival. Or their revenge.

I still can't believe the state of them, or that Crestor was able to get away with this. Not just Crestor, either. But Elise, the guards — even the human slaves working the property. How could they have stood by and let this happen? They *knew*. They knew and did nothing.

They deserve to die. All of them.

"I'm going back for my pack," Mikey says, jerking my attention back around.

"What?"

"My pack. I'm going back for it. Kane's sword..."

I nod automatically, until his words actually register. I grab the back of his pants since his shirt's still missing, and jerk him back to me.

"No, Mikey." I shake my head. "I understand it's sentimental, but we need to focus on Kane first. If it's on the way we can stop..."

"Stop fucking telling me what to do. I'm going back for the pack." His one good eye is wild as it looks at me. And then it clicks when he licks his lips.

"How many bottles were left?"

"Four," he answers automatically and in that one word, I learn everything I need to know.

I step away from him, limping on my left and mangled leg. "I went back for you..." I can't believe it. "Why did I go back for you?" I can't think. I don't think I've ever been so angry, and yet…the rage doesn't come in the way I expect it to.

I feel *sad*.

It spreads through me like ink through water. Tears come to my lower lids as I back another step away from him towards the garage, and then another.

"I need them," he grates, voice still a slur.

I shake my head and try to hold onto something. My sanity, above all else. "Your brother needs you, Mikey."

"It's not going to take that long…"

"It's time he doesn't have. And I need you! What about me?"

"What about you?"

"We're surrounded by enemies and I can't run!" I gesture feverishly at my wounded leg. Mikey's gaze passes to it and widens, but not enough. "You're just going to leave me behind? I didn't leave you behind."

Mikey's gaze hardens, sharpening on my face for the second or two it takes him to say, "Maybe you should have."

"You want to be trapped again? You want to end up like them?"

I point to the driveway where the fight is still going on. Far fewer guards stand against the rest of the horde. This is a true battle now to the end, and Crestor, I guarantee, won't live to see morning.

Mikey winces, but takes a step away from me. He looks into the woods and is lost. "I'll get the sword and the packs and catch up."

"You'll get the bottles."

"Those too."

"I hope you drown in them."

"I'll find you." His eyes flick back to look at me but they are unseeing. His body language says it all. He's itchy. Withdrawals from being drunk for the past seventy-two hours.

379 ◗

"I'll find you," he repeats, but he's already angled towards the woods as if he just can't wait to get out of there, and away from me.

"Don't bother." I take a step back and leaves and branches crunch softly beneath my feet.

His eyes flare as some soft semblance of understanding passes through them but like a candle snuffed, it's gone. He opens his mouth as if to say more but I don't wait to hear it. I turn away from him and sprint for the garage.

The chaos has overwhelmed the guards and I don't have any trouble making it inside the squat structure. It's metal and tin and a close gathering of trees blocks it partially from view, but wasn't enough to obscure it from me as I made my rounds earlier.

Inside out of the rain, I grab all the keys from the rack hanging on the near wall and slide into the front seat of a massive red truck. My arms are shaking with a residual rage and I fail three times to stuff the correct key into the ignition.

The truck roars when I start it, choking three times as I back out of the carport and onto the driveway. I haven't driven a car in four years and it isn't an automatic. I thank whatever sick gods lord over Population that my parents taught me to use a stick. My mom always said that it's better to learn how to drive on a manual in case you're ever abducted or need to make a quick escape. I wonder if she hadn't been a sorceress, and predicted this.

The huge vehicle climbs down a narrow dirt road that spits me out onto the highway, that dreaded abyss. On the road, there's no sign of guards or Crestor's victims. Just trees on all sides, and occasionally a pile of metal.

I turn onto the highway and find myself fighting back angry tears again. I want to cry. I want to scream. Instead, I force myself to remember the last time I was driven down a lonely highway road. It hadn't been lonely then, though.

I'd been with Kane and nothing had touched us. I'd slept. He'd told me about his family. He'd taken care of me, dressed me, carried me, put me to bed when I was unconscious. I'd been blanketed by his invincibility.

I clutch the steering wheel, imagining that I'm invincible now...

A leaden weight slams into the side of the truck and I scream and veer wildly onto the shoulder. Mud and rain splatters across the windshield, smeared by the wipers into a paste too thick to see through. Swish swish, swish swish, swish swish.

There's an ominous crunching across the roof followed by a crack. The roof craters. I flinch and there's a pounding above me followed by the distinct sound of laughter.

"Sistana," Trocker roars, "Don't you dare run from me!"

His hand punches in through the roof of the truck like a brick through paper. I slam on the gas. The truck goes airborne over a fallen tree branch blocking the road and my teeth clack together painfully when we slam back down.

I try swerving left and right, but Trocker's winning. He starts to claw his way down through the hole he's created, coming into the truck.

"Don't try to run, my queen," he shouts, spittle flying from his mouth to wet my cheek.

I try to head butt him but he reaches down, falling now, and grabs the steering wheel over my hands. The car spins, but I shove the gas harder while I pull my hands off the wheel and search frantically for my knife in the passenger's seat.

All I feel is urgency as we hydroplane around the next curve and skid along the guard rail. The horrible screech must affect Trocker more than me — hey, who knew being half deaf would be good for something? — because he lets go of the wheel long enough for me to take control.

I slam the wheel right, correcting so that we're back in the center of the road. The abruptness with which the car moves throws him to the side and his arm, which is half-in-half-out of the cab at this point snags on the jagged metal opening.

The sharp roofing tears into his flesh at the elbow, and I scream as half his arm rips free when I jerk the car back to the left. All the way down to the bone.

"You bitch!" Trocker roars, and suddenly he's gone.

He pulls back through the opening and I have to hope that I've managed to shake him…a hope that's crushed when he reappears in front of the windshield. His boots pound down onto the hood of the car and for a moment we lock eyes.

Then he grabs hold of the top of the car, using the opening he created to anchor himself there. He jumps, hangs suspended in the air, then his boots slam forward through the windshield.

Glass cuts through the world and I close my eyes, straighten my elbows and pray that I don't crash. I feel the shards against my face as a large mass of cracked glass shreds the backs of my knuckles. The windshield folds down on itself like a frozen wave, and when I rip my hands back I tear away skin.

As I fight to keep my foot on the pedal and the steering wheel straight, Trocker glides into the passenger's seat like water and the blood on his arms acts as a lubricant between us so my fists deflect off of his arms. I can't get a good punch in, or a good grip on him.

"Fuck you," I shout, slamming the heel of my hand upwards and into his nose, successfully breaking it. The act hardly phases him at all. He lunges towards me and sinks his large, square teeth into the flesh of my right arm.

I scream, hands grappling over the dash as I seek out a weapon. Finding a massive shard of glass, I grab it as hard as I can — until my palms and fingers bleed — and stab it into his back twice, quickly.

He roars away from me and laughs, bloody spittle flying from his lips. "You think I don't like the fight in you?" He sucks his lower lip into his mouth and it's wet with my blood. His eyes roll back into his skull.

"I love it, *Sistana*," he sneers.

He throws his head back and laughs, blonde hair dyed bright pink now with blood from my arm. In the brief lull, I notice the gleam of my knife down by the gas pedal. I try not to react towards it, but he still follows my gaze. He cocks his chin towards my feet and grins. Blood cases each of his teeth. It's mine and Kane's too, and Trocker has no right to it.

"Go ahead," he says. "Take it. You are at a disadvantage, regardless. We can even pull over if you'd like."

I snatch the knife from the ground and clasp it in my right hand, switching to a backwards grip while my other hand holds the steering wheel steady. I don't decelerate. I don't pull over.

"Bring it on, asshole."

We grapple in the front seat of the cab wildly until I gain the upper hand. He's reckless. More and more crazed with each drop of my blood he spills. I've got tears in my clothing and blood streaming from multiple wounds in my arms at this point.

My jacket hangs around my shoulders in tatters, and with each strike, he continues to rip into it, devolving from Other to animal, his most primal functions taking control.

Every time he comes at me, I slash his face, chest, shoulders, arms and hands. His black tee shirt gapes in the center to reveal his strong stomach covered in dozens of shallow grooves.

Bracing his arms against the far side of the cab, he exhales deeply. "You can't keep this up forever." He smiles in spite of the gashes covering his forehead, neck and cheeks, "Didn't anyone ever tell you to keep your eyes on the road?"

He comes at me and I just manage to brace my right arm against his bulging, veined neck, successfully keeping him off. But as my eyes pan out to the road, this becomes a pebble-sized problem, buried beneath the mattress of a much larger problem.

Spikes.

I don't know what they're called, but I've seen them before. They were more common in the beginning when people had cars that other people wanted. Since cars were abandoned, so were these.

Until now.

Across the road, rusted metal spikes unfurl, like a roll of red carpet. I slam my foot onto the brake, but there's no avoiding them. The chain spikes catch the front tires and as the back end of the truck fishtails violently, the momentum is too much. We go flying.

Trocker's teeth slam into my bicep, breaking my arm through to the bone. I don't think he even meant to do it, funnily enough, but we're both thrown up and into the roof of the cab, the jagged opening scraping every bit of my jacket and head it can.

The sheet of folded windshield hits me square in the chest. The airbags explode, punching me in the face, but shred themselves open against shards of glass. A gust of curls float around me and I smell concrete after a cool spring rain.

The truck hits the ground.

Total obliteration.

Chapter Eighteen

I mages hit me, tossed haphazardly against the insides of my eyelids. Paint splashed against a wall. A black hole in reverse.

Blood rushes to my head, making it pound, and for a moment I hear nothing but that thick sloshing sound. I relish that nothingness, because in the next instant agony takes me into its arms.

I cough and pain ripples up my sternum. My eyelids peel apart and gobs of blood dripping onto the roof of the truck from my suspended hands. Suspended? How? I didn't put my seatbelt on…but the glass windshield is wedged across my lap. I'm upside down.

The pounding in my head gets louder and more forceful. Somewhere nearby I hear a scrape, scrape, scraping sound that matches the tattoo of my pulse.

A body drags itself through the collapsed passenger-side window, coming in? Leaving? I can't tell. I'm totally disoriented. Smears of blood decorate white flesh and I think then of the fawn.

It hadn't been my first kill, but it had been the one that haunted me the most. It and I, starving in the forest together. My hand outstretched, it hadn't seen the knife. A swift singing across its throat and blood splashed across my hands. Its eyes had turned up to me in unveiled terror, and then all at once, peace.

It looked at me and was grateful, and in that instant, I envied it.

Scrape, scrape, *scrape*. A face turns up to me and I look back at it without recognition for the first moment. Then I register the hunger in his eyes. My hand fumbles for the glass locked around my hips, but it doesn't obey the commands I give it. The glass I used to stab Trocker cut too deep and now the muscles are mostly severed. Crap.

"Hello there, princess," he gasps.

His body has taken a beating from the crash and his tone betrays both desire and pain. But that isn't the sound that frightens me the most. There's another sound, just beneath his voice, which carries like the rush of a fierce wind or a sea at storm. And that low, dangerous chant carries with it promises of thunder. Of war.

Clapping. Low, malicious laughter. My heart pounds brutally as I start to scramble.

I smell smoke and fire and can hear the tires screaming as they spin even faster now without the concrete beneath them. The gas pedal has jammed. My bloody fingers slip over the windshield, pushing at it.

Trocker, the helpful ass hole that he is, sees my dilemma, grabs the windshield and wrenches it back. I drop into his outstretched hands.

Pain lights in my neck as I land at an awkward angle. Trocker shouts in excitement and then again in anger when I kick him in the face and drag myself out of the shattered driver's side window, glass cutting into my stomach.

Behind me, his fingers slip over my bloodied legs. His nails catch my skin, but I don't care at all about him.

Outside, the air smells like gasoline and smoke. I stand, left knee buckling as I take my first step. There's a gentle buzz floating through my head and my neck hurts like hell, but I don't feel any of my other injuries. Not with my heart pounding like it is. Hard and frighteningly fast.

I feel the strangest surge throughout my whole body as if there's another pulse there, pounding alongside my own. *Kane?* But for the first time since he left me a day ago — or has it been an eternity? — I really hope he isn't there and that he hasn't come back. *Look away, baby. Don't watch from here.*

Because this won't end well for me.

I'm going to die like all things die on the road. Painfully.

Because these guys don't know that I won't give up. I'll die fighting. Or I guess I should say that I'll fight until it kills me.

They won't take me alive.

They have us surrounded, looking like something straight out of a nightmare. In fact, I think I've had this nightmare before. It was the same one I had every day after Matt and Aiden were killed and Becks, Ashlyn and I had to fight the rest of the world alone.

Three women against horrors untold.

The men surrounding me now aren't scavengers, aliens, or even a twisted colony like the Hive. These sixty or so men are pure predators who've taken advantage of disorder and chaos and thrived. The worst of their kind. *My kind.* I hear Trocker fumbling around in the cab of the truck and realize that I need him if either of us are going to survive.

"Trocker," I rasp. "Get out of the fucking truck and I'll give you what you want."

My eyes flit from man-to-man while smoke from the truck wafts lazily on the breeze. The men are dressed in dark leather and wood, black jean and metal. Skulls sit stacked atop most heads — decoration or trophies? — and I can tell by the larger size and high-set cheekbones that some of the skulls belong to the Others, though most are human. I do a second sweep.

Half of the guys hold weapons visibly, though I guess more than that are armed. A few guns, lots of knives, about a dozen machetes, one scythe. My odds are dwindling. *Look away, baby. Don't watch me die.*

One guy at the edge of the ring is holding a torch, but I'm distracted by the man standing just behind him. On top of his shaved head he wears two smooth skulls stacked one on top of the other. Both are huge, both are alien.

He stares harder than his peers and without smiling and, caught in the haze of the torchlight, I catch the gleam of his quiet, troubling eyes that are far too light for his brown skin. His skin is ash brown, lighter than mine — but those eyes.

They're arresting, those eyes. They're the eyes of someone who died a long time ago.

Hollow through and through.

Trocker claims my attention when he rolls, grunting, out of the truck and lands on his back in front of the cab. He staggers drunkenly to his feet and, seeing our new friends, roars, "She's mine." When he speaks, he sounds just as drunk as Mikey did.

He shoves out his arm, hand extended in a claw, while the wounded one hangs limply from the stump of his shoulder. The men don't seem impressed and move forward until they're standing shoulder-to-shoulder.

Trocker snarls around at all of them while I edge to the right, propelled by the sweet scent of gasoline. My injured hand clenches around itself and I will it to work for me just for a few more minutes.

One of the scrawnier men peels apart from the crowd. His torso is bare, but he still wears his many scars proudly. He's got a human head stacked on top of his own and a baseball bat studded in outward-facing nails slung carelessly over his shoulder.

"Every man has the right to a fair fight to decide if he should live, die, or join us. Since we're generous men, we even allow them to choose their opponent. Unfortunately, I don't see any men here."

Light laughter picks up as the man looks over his shoulder towards another. This one is standing just outside of the circle — a spectator to the sport that will ensue. The massacre. And as the smoke clears between us, my breath jerks in my lungs.

Kane?

My heart beats faster. He's Kane, but not.

With black hair and tan skin, he could've been Kane's doppelgänger. He has the same broad shoulders and imposing frame Kane does. The same blood red lips. The same superman curl, even.

The differences lie in the gestures, the aura. This male carries confidence, like Kane does, but it's bleak and damning and desperate and makes me want to curl up on the ground in the fetal position and hide from the world. It makes me want to give up and give in. It makes me want to beg.

He's staring at Trocker with an intensity that makes me feel bad for the alien who was just trying to kill me. *This doesn't end well.* But I get the feeling that it might end worse for Trocker than for me.

I'll take it.

The Kane lookalike nods once and the scrawny guy raises his bat high. "So come on, then, gentlemen," he shouts, stealing impish glances around at his fellow monsters, "What are you waiting for?"

That rumbling chant begins again as every single man standing around us moves forward in sync and I realize that I can't wait any longer for Trocker to do something.

I make a break for the man carrying the torch and I reach him before anyone else reaches me. I use my full bodyweight to knock the guy to the ground where we grapple over the wooden handle.

I kick him in the groin and as he buckles, I snatch up the torch, run back to the truck and toss it into the wetness that smells like gas.

It hits the ground, sizzling in earnest. Bright orange fire licks at the concrete, tearing towards the truck's gas tank. Men start shouting and backing away from me as the fire grows and swells. A flare of sparks shoots up into the sky — I can feel its heat — but as quickly as it appears, cold fills its place.

The man with the alien skulls and empty eyes rushes forward while the others run back, takes off his jacket and throws his jacket and throws it over the encroaching flames, turning them to ash.

In just a tattered vest made of black jean, he looks right at me, and I fall into the void of one man's lonely eyes as several other men drag me off the road and into the woods.

We don't go far, and there's no camp where they drop me. There's just a dirt clearing studded by a single, strong tree that the men are working to ring in stones and big sticks.

The two men at each of my arms drop me in the center of the ring and tie Trocker up to the tree upside down. They coil rope around his feet and it takes eight or nine of them to successfully loop the rope over the largest tree bough and hoist him up, up, up. He kills two of their guys in the process, but they don't seem to care. The ones still alive just loot the corpses of the ones that are dead and use the bodies to form the perimeter of this circle. This arena.

This crucible.

While Trocker thrashes, his blonde and stained hair trailing over the soft, squishy ground, several of the men step forward into the ring. I brace myself to get strung up or attacked, but they don't touch me.

Instead, they pull daggers from their pockets and throw them down into the soft earth a few paces away from where I'm kneeling.

"Is that it? No more takers?" one of them shouts as he throws down his knife. He laughs then, kicking up dirt so that it showers over me.

"Wait for the others," an older man rasps — one of the oldest in the group, though he can't be more than forty. "I'm sure Jack will want a say."

Silence descends while the guys all wait restlessly at the edge of the circle. I don't try to run. At least not yet. I wouldn't make it far. *I'm not going to make it far.* I cringe at the thought and grit my teeth.

Now that I've stopped moving, my adrenaline is coming down and I'm beginning to feel my injuries with clarity. My whole body has been worked over with talons and teeth. Looking down, I see that my period blood has seeped through the crotch of my pants and I grin down at it, shaking my head slowly. The problems of my morning are irrelevant at this stage, aren't they?

"Where's the bucket?" The Kane who isn't Kane at all says, appearing at the circle's edge.

A few men peel apart from the others and drag a large plastic bucket underneath Trocker's head. One of them slits Trocker's throat, the act so fast and so impartial it shocks me in a way I thought nothing could anymore.

Are these things here even human? Or are they less human than the aliens are? They're less human than Kane is, that's for sure.

He's only ten feet away and though I should be used to the smell of their blood, I'm not. It smells like eggs and shit and it's black as it weeps over Trocker's face, like tears cried in reverse.

The droplets wind through his hair before spattering against the bottom of the pot beneath him, sounding like rain. I watch as Trocker chokes on his own blood, dying for a few moments until he's resurrected. Each time he blinks back to life, the same man with that skinny, slender blade reopens his wound, and each time he dies he meets my gaze.

I wince as bile pitches in my stomach and crawls up the back of my throat because he doesn't look like the fawn. There's no peace here. There's only rage and pain.

Another dagger hits the packed earth to my left and I look up at Hollow Eyes. He stands near to me now and is watching me with his head cocked slightly to the right.

Two of the other men who threw their daggers down before come to retrieve their weapons. At this, the Kane lookalike laughs, "So afraid of little Diego, are you?"

He steps into the circle and pulls a blade from his own belt. "Maurice. Come here," he says.

The man who I stole the torch from blubbers something unintelligible and drops to his knees. He pulls a gun out of his back pocket and raises it to his temple. He looks up at the Kane-not-Kane being and fires without hesitating.

I jump, my stomach pitching, my heart pounding. Cold sweat covers every inch of me. What is *wrong* with these people? What is wrong here?

Hollow Eyes watches the dead man drop forward onto his stomach without flinching. Two others near him do the same they did to the others. They steal the weapons off his person, then shove his body out of the arena.

"This girl bested Maurice already in a contest for that torch. It's only thanks to Diego here, that we didn't lose half our numbers."

Kane-not-Kane comes up to Hollow Eyes and places his hand on the back of his neck. He massages him in a way a father might a kid. Or maybe it's *weirder* than that. Maybe it's the way lovers might hold one another. I remember Kane in the woods holding onto the back of my neck like that.

Diego doesn't move though, doesn't lean into the touch. His eyelids don't flutter. He doesn't react at all except for the slight tick in the corner of his jaw. *Wrong*. There's something altogether vile happening here and now and between these monsters.

"You all can take back your daggers now. There will be no contest for this one. I think she's earned her right to a fight. Maybe she'll be a good replacement for Maurice, depending on how she holds up."

Kane-not-Kane moves away from Diego and goes to Trocker. He crouches down next to the bucket and dips his fingers inside. As he stands, he licks them clean and smiles. His eyes flick to me.

"So. Are you ready to fight?"

I nod. "What do I get if I win?"

He laughs and when he does, several of the other men in his group laugh with him. "Your life."

"You've got the advantage. You've got their blood in your system. I should get something else if I win."

He grins at me in a way that shows all his teeth and he suddenly looks nothing like Kane at all. He looks like a vulture. "You have their blood in your system, too. Or did you think I wouldn't notice the way your wounds are healing all on their own?"

He glances down at my hands and arms, the cut on my leg. He's right. The skin in all these places is nearly meshed together. Still red and enflamed and covered with crusted blood, but I have very few open wounds left at this stage. And I should. I shouldn't be walking. Hell, I probably shouldn't be breathing.

But I am. And I'm not going to stop anytime soon.

I don't answer but fake Kane still laughs. He steps forward towards Diego's dagger still embedded in the soil. Though the others came to collect theirs, his was the last one left. He still hasn't moved and when Kane comes towards me, he flinches, like he'll do something.

"Move, Diego. This one is mine. You'll have another chance to fight to get your dick wet soon enough." He kicks Diego's knife free of the dirt.

Diego doesn't retaliate. His expression remains flat as he bends down and wraps his fingers around his dagger's ornately engraved hilt. He stalks to the ring of men, standing stiffly at the inner wall, watching in a way that I find distracting — and I can't afford to be distracted. Not as Fake Kane watches me with his head cocked to one side, bright jade eyes darkening.

The expression is familiar. Appraising. Interested. I see him working things out in his head like a puzzle he can't quite solve. And then all at once he smiles and shrugs out of his coat.

As his faded leather jacket hits the ground with a soft thud, he says, "I can't let you fight one of my men. That'd be unfair, what with their blood in your system and all," he says, tone mocking, "I'll let you fight me, though and if you can beat me." He whistles and it's a sharp, eerie sound. "If you beat me, I'll let you walk out of here in one piece. I'll give you a car and a gun. You can even take your blood bank with you."

That's a good deal. Too good a deal.

But I can take him. I'm sure of it.

"Deal," I tell him and he beams.

"You know, I almost hope you survive this."

Fake Kane moves across the circle, putting a not-yet-dead Trocker at his back while I amble up onto my feet. There's not much hope for a weapon here, but I still take note of the rocks demarcating the outer ring of this battlefield and the few thick sticks lying within it.

The men standing on the other side of those rocks don't say a word, but I can see items being exchanged between hands. It's not hard to guess what they're doing. They're betting. To see if I'll win? Or to see how long I'll last?

"I admire your gusto, little lady," Fake Kane says. He stretches out his arms. "What's your name?"

I don't want to tell him, but something is aroused in me by the sight of his nearly familiar face. "Abel." My fingers curl around my healing palm.

"Nice to meet you, Abel. I'm Jack."

"I always liked that name."

He smiles in a way that fills me with heat and adrenaline. My heart pounds like a fist on the other side of my sternum and for just a second, the flicker of a second beat blazes through me. *Kane, it's only one-on-one,* I'd tell him if I could. *I might just survive this.*

Jack takes a step in my direction and drawls, "Well, aren't you a sweetheart?" His voice holds a distinctly southern lilt, which frightens me. It tells me that this gang has traveled far — that *he* has — and that he's survived everything Population has thrown at him.

"Not really. Now are you going to attack or should I?"

He barks out a laugh and runs his hands back through his oil-slick hair. "Which do you prefer?"

"You first," I say with a pause.

He bats his thick eyelashes at me and nods. "Alright then. But remember what you asked for."

He comes at me like a goddamn hurricane, moving with a violent grace I can't match. No human moves like this, and for a second I wonder if he wasn't lying before. I'd think he was an alien if there wasn't something so human about him. So awful.

He punches without restraint and though the first strike I manage to duck, the second nails me in the cheek and everything under my skin breaks.

I don't give into the pain but whirl around and nail him in the gut with my heel. He flies back and I advance on him, but when I kick at him a second time, he grabs my ankle and hurls me through the air.

I hit the ground hard, along the outskirts of the circle. My head hit a rock and everything fades in and out for a second while my lungs fight for air.

I grab the bloody stone that wounded me and when he comes up behind me and grabs me by the hair, I spin and crush his nose with it, then bound back up — stagger drunkenly onto my feet — and into the center of the circle.

As we approach one another, he laughs and keeps laughing as he reaches up and feels his completely broken nose. Blood pours down his face and it's both red and black at the same time, swirled all together.

"Brilliant, Abel! That's wonderful." He rubs his hands together and turns to face me fully. He bangs on his chest. "Again!" he roars, "Again!"

We fight for hours. For days. Until I'm slowing down and he's still in top shape. I still have the rock in my hand and when I swipe it for his cheek again, he grabs my wrist and breaks it.

I scream as he kicks in my knee and he curses as I punch him with my good hand in the dick. He knees me in the cheek and I fall back.

It's getting harder to move. Harder to fight. Harder not to give up. Rule number one. The only rule. *Not even when you're dying, Abel*, I remind myself.

What about when I'm dead?

No. Not even when I'm dead.

I feel the ground around me for a stick and when he comes and grabs the front of my shirt, I stab. I catch him in the eye, but he shoves my hand out of the way while blood drips down his cheek and grins. He lowers himself onto my body, straddling my waist and as he pins both my hands together with one of his, he pushes my hair back out of my face and speaks to me very gently.

"You did good, girl."

And then he draws his arm back and punches me again and again and again.

Shadows and light. There's no pain at all though. Just the pressure of a heartbeat that doesn't belong to me because mine might have stopped beating a few minutes ago.

I can feel its urgency, and its desire to communicate, but I can't hear the words. All I can see is Kane in the bathtub, my foot trapped in his. I hold onto that image and that memory and I live in it for a while, until the darkness parts and I become aware in ways that I wish I didn't have to be.

Now, I'm aware of me.

"Come on, sweet cheeks." Fingers grab my face and tilt my head up. I feel some small semblance of life return to me as air jerks back into my lungs in one abrupt punch. Jack laughs. "And the angel lives! God really does see you out of the corner of his eye, doesn't he?"

The blood in my mouth is sulfuric, and I know it's the only reason I'm still breathing. Struggling to blink my eyes open, I see dry ground but am unable to reach for it. My wrists are being held in place by ruthless hands, so that my arms are spread wide.

My bare knees are pressed to the soft and icy soil and, against that chill, I recognize that I'm naked and Jack's hands are covering my rib cage and lower back. I shudder, teeth chattering as a panic washes over me, an occultation to block out everything else.

"Don't worry, sweetheart. I don't want what's between your legs." I'd ask him what he does want then, but my tongue is swollen in my slack mouth and I can't feel my lips.

"I want you to watch and see what happens to Others out here when they come into my world." He strokes my hair lovingly. "They think they're so much stronger than I am, but they don't know and you don't know, either. I'm king of Population, sweetie."

He slaps my bare ass, stands and begins shouting orders to his men. My head lolls on my neck and blood pours out of my mouth onto my chest.

"Now I want you two to hold her there and make sure she's got the right kind of view for this."

They lean me back a little so my face tilts up and my eyes tilt open. "The rest of you can start passing the bucket around. A cup for every man except Diego. You know how he never liked drinking with us," he speaks in mock hurt like the whole world is just some big joke to him.

"And you. I want you to keep those pretty blue eyes open, darling. You know, it's those eyes that really do it. You look like you could be Diego's sister, don't you?"

He's absolutely right. And maybe that's why Diego speaks to me on some primal level. He looks like Aiden, resurrected, if Aiden had fallen into the clutches of this madman and lost all the humanity he ever had.

Sadness pulls through me while the pulsing of a heart that isn't mine surges up into my throat with force, willing me to do something that I just don't think I can anymore.

It wants me to live.

"Abel, I know you lost the fight, but I like your spirit, so I'll make you another deal. If you manage to keep your little emotions under control while I kill your alien friend over here, then I'll kill you quick after.

"If you don't then, it'll be slow. Okay?" he says cheerily.

I'd nod if I could, but I can't so I don't.

Smoke chokes my throat and I cough while behind me Jack says, "That counts as a reaction, sweetie. I'll give you this one, but not anymore than that."

I try to hold the jerking of my lungs as suddenly heat bursts against my chest. I open my eyes and see sparks in violent shades of orange, catching the smaller sticks and twigs stacked beneath Trocker's head. Thick, putrid smoke billows as a cloud between us and I have to stop taking in air altogether in order not to cough or choke on the smell.

Trocker was out, but now he's awake again and the hole in his throat sealed itself closed, which is a shame. That would have been a better way for things to end for him.

He starts to thrash, but the fire's already caught his hair and is chewing its way towards his face. I can't watch but the second I look away heat flashes between my shoulder blades. I've never felt anything like it. An incendiary spark, followed by a deep, bone kind of ache.

The sound of the whip striking air is the only indication I have of what just took place. "Don't look away now, honey. You hear?"

I struggle to breathe. My eyes sting. Trocker's eyes are melting in his skull. They're watching me.

I can't do this.

The smell.

The way his melted eyes are puffing up and exploding. The way his skin is charing in sections and falling off in chunks, then mending itself anew only to repeat the process.

It's too much.

My stomach is in my throat and I vomit all over myself while Trocker drips to the ground like candle wax. The lash comes for me again and again and when it doesn't come a third time, I realize that Jack is a special kind of person. He wields hope as a weapon. He's successfully weaponized human emotion. I know in that moment that if he offered me to join his gang or continue on the path I'm on, I'd jump the tracks, throw myself at his feet and beg to enlist.

I can't do this.

And then Trocker's head falls from its perch and bounces across the soft ground, coming to rest at my knees. My throat constricts again. More vomit rushes up into my mouth and I don't swallow it. I physically can't.

I close my eyes and I ready myself for this to end.

The whip comes down and I don't feel it anymore. I just hear the fluttery sound it makes every time it's drawn back.

And as my eyes close, I recognize that I didn't give up on the rule book. I fought as hard as I could. But in a fight, not everybody can win.

Sometimes when you fight, you lose.

Chapter Nineteen

This can't possibly be heaven.

It tastes like burnt rubber and smells like fire. My body is still being held up, but I'm being jerked all around now as the ones holding me step and shuffle from side to side.

People are shouting and they sound a little bit panicked. Crackling fire. Heat. Boots hitting the ground. Thunder.

There's pained gurgles from nearby and I'm falling forward. My chest hits the ground at the same time another body does and when I blink my eyes open I can see one of the gang members lying inches away from my face, his black eyes bright and dead and open.

He's got a cut across his throat and a moment later, there's another thud and another body falls, an arm hitting my back and making everything erupt in me. The pain is so surreal, I pass out.

It doesn't last.

It never lasts.

The heart in my chest isn't mine, but it's exploding with power and the hands on my body aren't mine, but they're hard and lifting me upright.

A jacket comes over my wounds and then arms circle my body. I'm being carried.

Kane?

But when I blink, I'm caught by Diego's hollow eyes looking down at me. He doesn't speak, but I can feel him running. He's carrying me somewhere and I don't know where, but anywhere is fine so long as it's away from Jack.

The thought of him brings tears to my eyes. They wet my cheeks. I've never known suffering like that. Suffering built on the stilts of escape, like there's some way I could have changed my own fate. But I failed Jack. I failed him, so he did what he had to do…the only thing he promised me.

The sounds of screaming become more distant, and when my head swivels on my neck, I see trees.

"What the fuck are you doing!" A voice shouts from somewhere close. "That's Jack's!"

That. No, I'm not a person anymore am I? The things that make a human human, I no longer possess. I'm just waiting, really. Stuck here in limbo, that blood-embellished purgatory, hoping that when I next blink, I'll open my eyes and see Becks.

No. I think, but the thought isn't mine at all. It's coming from somewhere else.

Diego doesn't answer and he doesn't stop. He keeps walking forward, towards the trees, until the man shouts again. Then he stops.

He looks down at my face as he sets me down in the tall grasses. They're scratchy and hot in places I need them to be soft and cool. I cry out, tears coming harder now, and when he pulls away, I reach for him.

I take his hand and hold onto it. It's the only lifeline I've got.

But he untangles his fingers from my fingers and takes a couple steps away from me. I can still see him as he fights. He moves almost as fast as Jack as he he blocks his attacker's first strike with his wrist. With that same arm, stabs into the side of the man's neck. Diego kicks the man in the gut and the corpse flies over the tall grass, disappearing beneath it.

A soft thud pulls my gaze to the right and I look to see a dagger shooting up out of the ground. The hilt is intricately carved sterling silver, poorly polished, studded with three jade beads. I wonder what this means, and wish I could ask, but Diego just turns and walks away from me, shoulders back, face proud, eyes haunted and haunting.

He's going to die.

He's going to die for *me*.

Emotion jerks in my chest, making me wonder if I remind him of a forgotten sister that the world took and, if not, why else he's doing this. He killed his own for me already three times tonight. Maybe more. And now he's giving me his knife. Somehow, my arm manages to move just enough to curl around it.

I bring it to my chest and close my eyes. For a moment, I fade from this world into one of utter darkness. I fade and come back, then fade again. The finale is near, and I would have given myself up to it completely had I not felt a sudden fire burning where my heart was supposed to be and a distant voice whispering my name. *Abel...Abel...*

"Abel!" My eyes flutter open. Dense tufts of smoke billow up into the world. So much smoke. So much fire. I can hear huge trees burning and breaking in the distance. Above me, the tall grasses sway.

"Abel, where are you? I can smell you, but I can't find you. Say something for fuck's sake!"

The thrashing is closer now. I can't draw its attention anymore than I'm doing. I don't actually want to. I don't want to see Mikey now. I just want to sleep...

"Abel."

It's the way he says my name that makes my eyes open just long enough to see him. His face blots out the sky above me. His beard is burned in parts now and I'd smile if I could.

I still have no idea what Kane's brother looks like underneath all that hair, and I've been traveling with him for over a week.

Until he abandoned me.

"Abel." There it is again. Hoarse and cracked, it makes me wonder what he sees. What do I look like now? Like a Mister Potatohead with all the parts in the wrong places? Probably.

His hands are reaching for me, but he doesn't touch me. He doesn't dare.

"Oh God, oh God, oh God. Jesus fucking Christ! Fuck, Abel. Abel, please…please…"

His panic jacks up my heart rate and my lungs contract until I can't get any more air. Oh no. Is this it? Or is this just wishful thinking? The blaze in my chest pulls my focus away from death. How annoying.

"Come on, Abel. I've got to get you out of here," he croaks. There are tears on his face. "You don't…are you… you're going to make it," he says, dropping to his knees.

He pushes the grass out of his way with his arms. He's still missing his shirt, but I can see that he has no new wounds on him, and those he received earlier are mostly healed. He's wearing his backpack and he's got Kane's blade tucked into his belt loops. It's stained in red.

He reaches around my body but I scream bloody freaking murder at the pain. "What…what is it?"

I just writhe. I don't have enough clarity to answer. I cringe away from his hands when he reaches for my body again. He hesitates, then lifts up just a little on one shoulder. He peels Diego's jacket away from me and the sight of his face when he sees…

Two little droplets of water streak in parallel down his either cheek.

"I did this." He breathes heavily, as if he's in a flat-out run.

"I did this." His gaze pins mine.

"I did this."

And then. "Abel, stay with me."

As he tips me into his grip with as much care as he can, I focus on the sight of the trees and the grey above them. I remember the bathtub and stay there.

Mikey's panting is jarring and heavy. His beard drips blood and his cheeks are flushed, probably because of the booze. I hope he enjoyed it.

"Abel, say something." Mikey lurches and I hear splashing just before he tells me that something is going to be cold. "This might hurt."

That makes me laugh, or would have if I could talk.

"Hold on, Abel. And hold your breath." He lowers my whole body rapidly and ice cold water hits my back, then every other inch of me. I gasp, against Mikey's instruction, and suck in a breath of near-frozen water. The shock of it forces my conscious mind to retreat.

I burrow into myself, fighting past the pain to revisit the beating pulse thrumming through me. The bathtub. I sigh as Kane smiles at me, beckoning me into his light and his heat.

Time passes. I'm not sure how much. Hours? Days? I'm cold. Then warm. Then freezing. Is this what death feels like? The motion beneath me suggests I'm in a car, though at another point I wake to find myself in some spacious building with white walls and floors made of cracked tile. It's in this building that Mikey locks me in a room while outside I hear the familiar sounds of fighting, of dying. Mikey roars, and as the door flies open, he fills its width. With blood slashed across his chest, he's got a head in one fist. He tosses it aside as he comes to me and takes my hand while my head rolls to the side. I see a sign in navy, hanging askew. The sign reads: Harborview.

"Abel, no!" He's shouting again, "Don't you fucking dare."

That incessant heartbeat within me is pounding triple time, but it's all that I feel, even as Mikey stuffs needles into my elbows. I pass out. I wake. I feel heat. I feel fever. I feel nothing. Movement. Silence. Calm. Crashing. Warmth. Hands touching my hairline, tracing the patterns my damp curls make. I'm sweating all over.

"I'm sorry," he says, and though I'm not asleep, I pretend that I am. A silence wraps around me and is absolute. I give up and dive in.

I'm swimming somewhere in the darkness, towards an unknown surface. There's a shadow obscuring most of my thoughts, like a thin veil pulled over my consciousness. The harder I fight against it, the more tangled I become in the threads.

A voice calls my name. A voice that my whole body, and not just my mind, remembers. It's accompanied by a growing warmth in my middle that pulses in time with a slow, patient heart. Not my heart to be sure, but another tempo. Its rhythm is fierce and wills me awake, and as I wake, it fades into nothing. Like it hadn't been there at all.

My eyelids are sticky, as if cemented shut. Muted light filters through curtains against the far wall, silhouetting Mikey in darkness.

He kneels before me, head bowed, wearing only beat up, army green cargo pants. He's knuckle down on the hardwood, breathing loud.

"I offer you myhr," he says, presumably to me because there's no one else there.

I'm on my stomach and with a grunt, I register the objects within reach of my right hand. A gun, a baton, a rock, Diego's silver dagger.

The bandages around my right palm make it hard to move, as do the drugs coursing through my system. I don't feel. The whole world seems light years away.

There's a fire in the hearth to my left that keeps me warm, but otherwise I'm naked, covered in flannel up to the waist. The material beneath me is surprisingly soft, though I can't tell what color it is. Actually, I can't see anything out of my right eye at all and when I try to blink, a strange numbness blankets me.

The right side of my face, including my eye, is entirely swollen shut while the left is only mostly swollen. I don't have much depth perception, and when I reach out towards Mikey, I'm surprised to find that he's close enough to touch.

I start to cry. I don't know where it comes from, but it comes.

Mikey moans like he's hurt. He says, "Please, Abel. Choose your weapon. You have to give me myhr. You have to take it. It'll make us both feel better."

I don't know what he means and moan down into the flannel sheets.

"Abel, please."

"You left me," I whisper.

I don't acknowledge that we might *both* be dead now if he hadn't. All I know is that I feel hurt in ways that has nothing to do with my swollen face or my back, which is one exposed wound. I'm not healing like I was. That thought frightens me since blood bonds can only be broken through death and I'm still breathing.

Mikey takes the gun, presses it to my fingers and holds my hand up to his chest. "Shoot."

I do.

My arm shakes as the bullet fires from the tip of the gun, missing Mikey altogether and puncturing the drywall a dozen feet behind him. He doesn't so much as flinch, just repositions my hands around his and moves the gun back to his chest.

"Again," he says, but I've already clicked back the hammer. I hit him in the right shoulder, though I'd been aiming for his heart.

The force of the blow makes my whole body quiver and slices of a tender pain brush across my back. I drop the gun while Mikey straightens, showing no signs of pain. The only action he takes is to scoop a handful of white powder from the bowl to his left and smear it over the wound.

"Thank you," he whispers. "Now please, go back to sleep."

"Where are we?"

Mikey hesitates before answering. "Seattle."

"How far from Kane?" My mouth is gooey with saliva. I can taste fever on my tongue.

"Don't worry about that now…"

"How far?"

Mikey sets the bowl of white powder aside and collapses back onto his ass. Crossing his ankles, he drapes his elbows over his knees.

"Just over a mile," he sighs.

"We need to go. Get to him. We need to…"

I make an effort to slide my palms beneath my shoulders and push the ground away, but I can't flatten my right hand and my left is trapped in a makeshift splint made of wood and gauze, elastic bandages and adhesive tape.

Mikey shifts towards me and draws a set of blankets up over my legs. It's only then that I realize he's doctored all of my wounds and draped towels around my hips.

"You can't move."

"I have to." I lash out with my right hand and, unable to control its trajectory, I knock over the bowl of white powder. Mikey hisses and quickly lifts my hand away from it.

He cleans the mess and speaks in low, gentle tones. "You shouldn't touch that. It's salt." He laughs through his nostrils, though his face is still drawn. "You know why the word for Seattle is the same in English as it is in Heztoichen?"

The question is rhetorical and I don't respond. I just watch Mikey pull a black duffel bag to his side and shuffle through it until he finds the syringe he was looking for.

"It's a word in our language with meaning. It means salt. Ironic, actually, considering that salt is one of the few things that slows our healing abilities. The only thing that creates scars. Figures she'd have set up her torture chambers here in Seattle. The salt land."

I twitch when he changes the dressings on my back as small flares of pain light up across my skin. He presses a needle to my elbow and pushes the plunger, sending a clear liquid running through my veins.

"Don't let me sleep too long. We need to get Kane," I whisper, "I can feel him again."

"I know. You said so last night. When I was about to give you my blood. I should have," he whispers, combing his fingers back through my hair in a way that's loving and welcome.

"But I was selfish and didn't think I'd be able to find Kane without you. I still don't. Please, forgive me."

I close my eyes, feigning a sleep that only comes for me a few minutes later.

Chapter Twenty

I'm standing, though I'm not sure how. The clothes irritate my wounds even though Mikey layered bandages over my skin so thick, my back hunches beneath my coat like a gargoyle's. It smells like mold and lint when I don it and I want to know where Mikey found it, but not enough to want to speak to him. He barely meets my gaze as he tells me that he wants me to rest for another night, and when I look up, he looks down quickly.

"Let's go," I say in a strangled pitch that's hardly recognizable. Even to me.

Mikey opens his mouth but doesn't defy my request. Instead he takes a peek out of the half-boarded-up windows, careful not to flutter the blinds. Just before he pulls a shirt over his head, he crushes more salt into the bullet wound and slaps a bandage over his shoulder. I want to ask him if that's really necessary, but when I next blink, the world is blurred.

He asks me if I'm alright. Blinking, I nod, and when I next open my eyes he's pulling a tattered flannel around his shoulders and the entire world disintegrates around me. My feet slip out from under me and Mikey catches me as I fall.

He curses. "Are you okay?" My face is pressed against his shoulder and I can't lift my neck. He's so warm and I'm so tired. "Abel, please rest."

"Mikey," I moan as the black and blue world returns to living color.

"Yes?"

"Put me down."

Setting me on my feet, he seems as averse to touching me as I am to being touched. We don't speak as we pack up our stuff and move out of the darkness of the apartment and into the grey.

The complex is only two stories. Modern with exposed brick walls and stainless steel appliances, it was probably full of successful young professionals before the Fall.

I take the stairs slowly and carry nothing. Mikey has the sword tucked into his belt and an overfull pack strapped across his back, and when he jumps down to the ground floor landing, glass bottles clink delicately against one another.

He winces and opens his mouth, as if to explain, but I don't comment. I don't care. I don't know why I ever cared in the first place.

The glass in the apartment building door is shattered, so I step through the opening carefully out onto the sidewalk. Strangely, I feel heat, like the sun is shining, and when I look up I have to squint. They grey is thinning, or at least, thinner than it had been.

"What is it? What's wrong?" Mikey's face is severe as he reaches towards me.

I flinch back. "What?"

"You're crying."

"I am?" I touch my cheeks with my bandaged right hand, and on my fingertips, wetness gleams. "Oh. I don't know. Maybe the drugs."

Mikey nods, curling his fingers around his outstretched palm before lowering it. "Are you sure?"

"Yeah. It's nothing." I wipe my face with the makeshift splint on my hand, fabricated from two pieces of wood, cotton and gauze. I take a step forward, stumbling off of the stoop and catch Mikey's sleeve. He tries to encourage me to take a seat, but I say, "Why isn't Kane's blood working anymore?"

Mikey cringes as he speaks. "You lost too much of it."

I nod, glad that that's the answer and that it's not something else. "Keep going."

We walk down a hill, the street marked Pine. I don't expect to survive long enough to reach downtown — we've got no cover, are in the center of a huge city, and the only weapons we have on us are a dagger and a sword.

In low tones, Mikey explains that he had to pass a border guard in order to get into the city. Notare Elise had the whole place blocked off. According to Mikey, the only reason we were able to get in was because a huge motorcade was exiting, leaving behind gaps in security.

Carrying me, he was somehow able to slip in undetected, and shortly thereafter, find the hospital. There, Mikey surprised a small group of Heztoichen guards, killing them and stealing the medical supplies they'd been guarding. With every step Mikey takes, the vials of painkillers and antibiotic rattle in his pack against other, larger glass bottles.

I move so slowly it takes us almost an hour to cover two miles. According to the internal map branded into my mind from before, it's nearly a straight shot. Thank the lord.

We move down Pine, pass a squat, red brick building and signs for an old bookstore called Elliott Bay. Parking meters jut up in vibrant shades of green, and one broken-down sedan has a sticker on the back window that reads, Equality.

A movie theater decorated with crumpled posters looms up on the left. *Carol, Willy Wonka and the Chocolate Factory, Macbeth, The Princess Bride.* I don't recognize any of the titles.

The downtown looms up before us, and the light sky glitters against so much glass. It's beautiful here. The most beautiful city I've ever seen. Water glistens beyond the edge of the metropolis, overtaking it in some places, and from where I stand, I can see a market half-submerged, commerce, shops, a lonely, decrepit Ferris wheel.

The wind smells of salt and sea, and I wish Kane was there to share it with me, instead of his brother. Mikey watches me a lot as we walk and never complains about the pace. He offers me his hand whenever he can, offers to carry me when I stumble. I reject all his attempts.

The guilt he exudes moves with us as we walk, like a third person in our party. It's almost unbearable. A few times I think about speaking, but I don't. I can't think of one good thing to say to him.

A theater comes up on our left, the stumps of shattered light bulbs spelling out the word, *Paramount*. It's just after this that I tell Mikey we're close.

"I can feel Kane. He's only a couple blocks from here, to the left. Inside a white concrete building."

A stitch in my side forces me to stop under the awning of a place called *Pacific P…* Don't know what the rest of the word might have been, as it's too faded now, but when I peer through the murky glass walls, three stories of battered boutiques face inwards as if caught in the eye of a cyclone and frozen there.

"On the eleventh floor."

"You can tell what floor he's on?"

Mikey leans against the glass, watching me with that critical look I've gotten so used to.

I nod, searching through the haze of the drugs for Mikey's face. "Yeah, I can tell what floor he's on. I can feel how big the room is around him. I know that he's alone and that he's hurting but he's hanging on for us."

"For you."

"For us," I correct. "He loves you."

"He did," Mikey concedes after a moment. His gaze passes up and down my oversized attire and he shudders. "But I don't deserve it."

I don't debate him on this.

Mikey mumbles under his breath, and when I ask him to repeat himself, he says, "Can you move?"

We've been loitering here for a while and we're too exposed. The sky has also started to darken.

"I'm fine," I lie. I'm running solely on willpower.

"I can hear bodies nearby," he says, shifting from foot-to-foot. "We should find cover."

I nod and follow Mikey down the road, past a golden plaque that reads Westlake Center. We cross the street beneath the abandoned tramline and enter a Bartell's drugstore.

We move to the far end of the store and I grimace as I slump to the ground against the empty racks. "Leave me," I whisper, clutching my knees so hard my fingertips turn white. The agony is back again and I can't think past it. Everything burns.

"I'm not leaving you anywhere." Mikey presses his palm to my jaw and forces pills down my throat. I suck them down dry since we don't have any water.

"We're almost there. You're not giving up on Kane now."

Mikey reaches for my face and uses his thumb to smear the tears across my bruised cheeks. "Are you with me?"

I shake my head. "Are you going to leave me again?"

He winces and sucks air in through his teeth. "I should never have left you. I'm a rat bastard."

"Yes, you are," I moan pitifully.

Mikey's mouth jerks up into a smile and he ruffles my hair. Even that hurts. "Good. Now that we're on the same page."

Crouching before me on one knee, Mikey starts rummaging through his pack. As he works, he lifts a finger to his lips and gestures for me to look around the edge of the aisle. He points towards the glass wall towards the street outside where two alien guards are wearing all white.

Surprised by the sight of them, I glance back at Mikey and mouth, *How many?*

He holds up four fingers, then points outside towards the guards there.

Four to one aren't great odds — and I'm not including myself in this. I cringe, but Mikey leans in close and whispers low, directly into my ear. "Don't worry. Take this."

From his pack, he produces two more bottles of liquor. I tense until he withdraws two rags and a lighter. He hands them over and it's only then that I break, grinning despite my better instincts.

Mikey shuffles a few inches forward, lifts his hand and grazes my cheek with the tips of his fingers. I would have pulled back if he hadn't lowered his hand first.

He mouths, *I'm sorry,* then he shoves the bottles, the rags and the lighters into the pockets of the man's coat I'm wearing.

The drug store abuts the building where Elise is holding Kane, but there's no direct route to the entrance. We'll still have to exit the drug store and pass the white-clad stormtroopers in order to reach the front door.

On Mikey's mimed orders, I move out from behind the aisle and moan a couple of times. It doesn't take long to draw the guards' attention. They burst into the drugstore and, distracted by the open wounds all over me, Mikey cuts them both down easily.

He pillages their bodies for weapons, passing me a gun whose weight I can barely support. I drag it behind me as Mikey leads the way into the next building. There, my heart lurches and stutters and heat sweeps my limbs. *We're close.*

Signs reading *Medical Dental Center* hang everywhere as we wade through a marble foyer into a stairwell. I'm panting by the time we hit the third floor. My head swims. Though my body is numb thanks to Mikey's drugs, my legs are heavy.

Slumping against one concrete wall, I tell Mikey to go on without me.

"Fuck, Abel. Stop saying that." His jaw clenches and I get the feeling he'd like to shoot me with the gun in his arms.

"Go," he orders, pointing at the staircase. As I move tediously to the next landing, I notice that the dust layered thickly over the concrete has been very recently disturbed. My lungs burn, heat that I can't make sense of blossoming between my breasts — is it Kane's heart or mine that's about to explode?

I'm still mulling over the odds of surviving another flight of stairs when I notice that Mikey is no longer behind me, urging me up the stairs with the butt of his gun.

"Mikey…"

"Shh," he rasps from a few steps below. He cocks his head to the side and his eyes grow wide all at once. "Run." Footsteps echo up the stairwell and I get the impression that it's not one set of feet against the concrete, but dozens.

"Abel, move!"

I throw myself up the stairs and the world rushes by even though I know that I'm moving slow. Way too slow. The drone of feet on concrete blurs and burns until all at once it's disrupted by the sound of bullets firing. I close my hand over my one good ear, hobbled by the magnitude of the sound, and when I turn I see that the guards are already on us.

A horde, they run three abreast, packed into the stairwell like cattle. Mikey fires back and the second row tramples the first when they fall.

They keep coming and Mikey continues firing and, with trembling fingers, I draw the first Molotov cocktail from my inside coat pocket. It takes me three tries to light the rag, only just managing to strike flame when the fourth row of guards kneels over the bodies of the third, and take aim.

I throw the bottle at the same time that three shots hit Mikey in the torso, knocking him backwards. His head hits my feet on the stairs at the same time that the entire stairwell fills with warmth.

Roaring, Mikey throws his body over mine, shielding me as fire chases us up to the tenth floor. He tosses his weapon to the side and half-shoves, half-carries me while bodies plummet over the railing, wreathed in flame.

"Mikey," I shout.

Mikey curses as he looks up at the six guards busting through door marked twelve. They charge us and I try to aim for them, but the gun in my arms is too big and the recoil knocks me back. I miss.

A responding shot punches me in the right shoulder and I gasp as it spins me around. My head cracks as it hits the wall. Mikey swings his body in front of mine as I collapse on the steps. He takes my machine gun away from me and fires again and again and again.

He shouts my name, and it's probably the drugs, but I don't feel pain as he drags me onto my feet by the collar of my coat. He kicks open the metal door with a huge number eleven painted on its front while bullets and fire and screams continue to echo up the stairs.

More are coming.

Soot on his face, blood on his hands, Mikey shoves me hard. "You go and find Kane. I'll stay here and hold them off," he says as I slam into a white wall. My shoulder streaks blood across it. Palm-shaped imprints come off black under my hands.

"What about Elise?" I groan, trying to stay present and focused.

Mikey shakes his head once and pushes the blond hair from his eyes as he turns to face the door. "She's not here. I can't hear her at all and I would be able to hear her."

"How can you be sure?"

He nods at me once, looking more confident than I ever remember him looking before. His eyebrows knit together over his nose and he juts his strong, beard-covered jaw to the left.

"I wouldn't send you into a death trap. This floor is empty. Now go." He kicks open the door to the stairwell and unleashes a round. Screams explode. Bullets explode. Bodies fall. I don't need to hear more.

I can feel Kane burning in my chest like a beacon and I know which way to go. Down the hallway to the right, I take the second left and pass through the broken door. My heart is pounding. It has been all along. So close to him now, I never thought I'd get to this point. I feel like I'm in a video game. Pain making everything so hard to follow.

My hand stills over the cool stainless steel handle of a door. It gives easily beneath my weight and I step into the room, a new terror making me tremble.

It's hope.

"Kane?" My fingers fumble with the light switch on the inner wall. I take a step into the room and the sneakers I'm wearing echo against the tiles beneath me. The room is cold and smells like bleach and blood.

"Kane," I say again, this time with more conviction. Finding a panel of lights, I flip them all and harsh fluorescents flicker in and out of life before beaming bright and strong.

"Kane!"

I rush forward. The room is littered with metal tables and medical equipment so that it looks one-part hospital, one-part science lab, two-parts torture chamber.

Wearing only the same pair of pants I last saw him in, Kane hangs upright in the center of the room. He's strapped to a gurney by metal cuffs at his ankles, neck and wrists. A large metal strap holds him down at the waist while clear tubes puncture his skin in a dozen different places. They don't feed anything into him, but feed out into a single drain on the floor.

His once-olive face is as pale as the walls surrounding us, but he still carries the light. The Tare that Elise so desperately covets continues to pulse in intermittent waves, in time with his precarious heartbeat. I stagger towards him, enraged and afraid.

"Kane?" I stagger into a metal table and trip into a pile of tools, all covered in blood. I shove them aside and they clatter noisily to the floor.

"Kane, wake the fuck up!" I say, falling against his body. I brace myself on his stomach and try to hold myself upright.

I reach for the cuff around his waist, but I know already I'm not getting through this without a key. Not unless he's strong enough to help me.

He stirs. "Mikey?" His voice is a relief and I bow my head, exhaling breath onto his stomach. His skin is unnaturally cool — only as warm as the room around us — but I still hold onto his hips with ferocity and am reassured.

"No, it's me," I sigh, laying my hand over his heart. "It's Abel."

"Abel," he groans, head rolling to the side. "I smelled you, but I hoped it wasn't." His hair drips down around his cheeks. His face is covered in unwashed stubble. "You shouldn't be here."

"You think anything could have kept me away?" His thick black lashes part and he looks at me and whatever color there was drains from his cheeks.

"Abel," he barks. "What happened to you?"

I'm still all swollen and I clutch the gurney he's mounted to in order to keep myself vertical. I shake my head and smile shakily up at him. "You know me." I swallow. "Making new friends."

Kane doesn't smile back. Gloss comes to his eyes that make my knees even jellier than they had been. "Don't do that," I whisper. "We just...we need to get out of here."

He blinks down at me slowly, and beneath the blood, I inhale the scent of his skin. Sweat. Cedar. Spice. He smells like his house or rather, his house smells like him. But whichever came first, I find myself back there, safe now that we're together.

"You always did have a…knack for making friends," he says and pain shifts over his features when he tries to move.

I bark out a laugh and when I look up at him, I'm crying, which is okay, because he's crying to. "Our bond is so weak," he whispers. "Why isn't my blood healing you?"

I shake my head and ignore the question, focusing rather on the problem at hand. All the many, many problems. I can't seem to escape them.

"Kane, I'm not strong enough to free you. You need to free yourself." I shove my sleeve down and hold my unbandaged wrist up to his mouth. "Drink from me."

"You need it." His eyes flutter closed.

I feel a sudden fluttering in my chest where his heartbeat should be pumping strong. The whole time I was dying, he was dying too. He only fought before for me. Now it's my turn.

Gunshots crackle in the hall. "We don't have much time."

I grab Diego's knife from my jacket pocket and bring it down across my wrist without hesitating. "You've got to get us out of here. Please," I beg him when he reels back, closing his eyes at the sight of my blood. "Kane, I need you to save my life."

He opens his mouth, like he'll argue, but I use the opening to shove my wrist in past his teeth. "Drink," I command him, and his eyes slink shut. He moans. And then he drinks.

The response is instantaneous. He pulls in a rush of blood that makes my whole body light in euphoria. I manage to feel horny — *horny* — even though I'm standing all bloody in Elise's house of horrors.

"Abel," he moans and I stagger closer to him, pressing myself to his warmth.

I grab the top of his pants, fingers sliding between his skin and the fabric. "Kane…"

He groans and his chest pulses stronger. Color floods his face and torso and I can feel him pull himself up, holding his own body straighter.

A shiver shudders through me and I feel dizzy with lust and maybe, possibly, also bloodloss and pain medication. I touch his abs until soon, my knees don't really hold up the rest of me. Everything turns a little grey.

"I felt you," I hear him say, though it sounds like it's from a distance.

Metal is suddenly bending and tearing and I hear a pop and a snap that sounds like a gong. My arm is shaking with the effort it takes to hold it up to his mouth, but when it starts to slip, I feel his hands. They hold me at the elbow and wrist as his mouth opens and bites down even more firmly. He drinks.

Stormily, he says, "I felt you receive pleasure and I hated it. What happened, Abel? Abel?"

As his grip on my arm releases, I realize it's the only thing that was holding me up. I hit the bloody tiles beneath me and feel suddenly, wretchedly cold.

"Abel!"

There's a crash before a second voice fires into the space. I know this one too, but it takes me a moment to place it. "Kane? Kane holy fuck, you're alive. Where's Abel?"

"Mikey! Get her."

Scrabbling and scraping as metal is thrown aside. Then Mikey's inhuman roar, "No!"

The sound of his voice reverberating off of the ceiling and walls shocks me to consciousness, like the sharp jolt of a defibrillator. I lurch awake and see Mikey sliding to his knees at my side. He rolls me onto my back and punches his hands through his hair.

"What did you do!" He grabs my wrist and tries to bandage it with the shirt he's wearing.

In the background, I can hear metal bending and breaking. I can hear Kane fighting against his restraints and winning.

"Out of my way."

Kane drops down at Mikey's side and opens his wrist, but the blood that drips onto my face tastes like pennies. Almost entirely human.

Mikey shoves his brother aside and pulls back his own sleeve. "I'm going to have to give her my blood." Mikey lifts his own wrist to his lips, but Kane lashes out so quickly and so brutally, he reminds me of Jack for a moment.

Mikey's face is streaked with red where Kane hit him. His eye is swelling and the bones surrounding it are crumpled. But Mikey doesn't protest.

He just looks at his brother and bares his teeth. "She's dying, Kane. I won't let that happen."

Kane's eyes narrow. He grabs Mikey by the throat. "If you touch my mate again, I will leave you here strapped to that gurney so that Elise can finish what she started."

Mikey grapples with Kane's hands while his face turns from cream to crimson to violet. Kane shoves him back and Mikey spits onto the ground. He looks at me, but doesn't try to offer me his blood a second time.

"If she dies," he coughs into the floor, "it's on *you*."

"Stop talking and get me that centrifuge," Kane snarls, gesturing towards something I can't see with his chin while his hands continue to hold me.

"The what?"

"Those vials!" Kane slams his fist into the floor so hard that loose tiles shatter around my motionless form. "Bring them to me."

Mikey staggers up and returns a moment later with a fistful of empty, clear tubes. "What good are these? They're empty. She's dying, Kane!"

Kane rips the vials from Mikey's fingers with his left hand. His right is trapped around my wrist, stemming the flow of blood. I'm pleasantly lightheaded and prepared to die as Kane tosses aside three of the vials before flipping the lids to the remaining two.

He angles them to my lips, one at a time, and I feel drops of blood hit my tongue. Two from the first vial, three from the second. The blood is tangier than Kane's and significantly more sulfuric.

"Kane, are you fucking kidding me?" Mikey looks poised to kill something, someone, everyone. "She's going to die! A drop of your blood isn't going to save her life…"

"It isn't my blood," Kane says, sweeping his hand over my forehead. I breathe a little more deeply after that and hold Kane's gaze without fading like I thought I might.

Mikey stands at the sound of shouting just outside of the room. "You gave Abel *her* blood?" His voice is a low, quiet threat.

"Better hers than yours, brother."

Mikey rips his sword from his belt and lunges for his brother at the same time that shots crackle in the hall. I jolt, but Kane doesn't react at all. He just looks up at his brother and says something to him in Otherspeak that makes Mikey's shoulders slump. He drops his sword.

"Kane," I croak, drawing both his and his brother's attention back to me.

I cling to his arms and try to pull myself up into a seat. "Can she walk?" Kane asks Mikey. Then, "Barricade the door."

"Barricade the door?" Mikey shouts, but I notice he still starts towards the door and starts barricading it, as instructed. "How are we going to get out of here?"

"Up. Elise has a helicopter on the roof and there's an entrance that leads directly to it from this one. She did not want others to chance by me for any reason."

Smart cookie.

"Fuck me." Mikey races away from the entrance while bodies slam against the other side of the door. Stacked metal tables are the only thing separating us from the reinforcements.

"I found it. Now, come on, Kane, go. I'll get Abel. No, Kane. Don't touch her. Don't…" His voice catches when a scream tickles the back of my throat.

Kane, who just tried to lift me, lowers me back to the floor.

His jaw sets. His eyes read fire and bloodshed. "Where is she injured and how badly?"

"Badly. Let me…" Mikey stoops down to my side, but Kane grabs him by the throat again.

"Why aren't you injured if she is?" He seethes.

Mikey is spared from having to answer by the sound of the barricade caving. Kane shoves him off and scoops me up and I scream through the pain as Kane starts to run.

Mikey fires at the aliens forcing themselves through the opening. The Other collapses, but a second is close on her heels. "Mikey," I manage to say.

He turns to me and I gesture to my jacket pocket with my chin. He grins at me. "That's my girl," he says and I feel Kane's arms tense around me. He doesn't say anything as Mikey frees the molotov cocktails from my pocket.

Kane heads to the back door, bursting through it onto a set of white painted stairs. We reach the top landing just as an explosion goes off below.

The door bangs open and Mikey's thundering up. He meets us on the roof where wind buffets us around and a helicopter sits quietly waiting, that little accidental savior.

"Hallefuckinglujah," Mikey grunts, throwing open the door and helping Kane lower me inside.

They buckle me into a seat in the back and Mikey makes sure to put me on my stomach, drawing searing stares from Kane. They draw the door shut with a thwack and then climb into the cockpit.

"Kane, please tell me you know how to fucking fly one of these things."

"Sort of." I can hear shots refracting against the outside of the helicopter as it lurches awkwardly into the air. But then they fade, and we straighten out and when I open my eyes again, Mikey's flying and Kane's staring at me over the back of his chair.

He says something, but it's too loud to make out.

I smile at him around the blood-taste in my mouth.

He smiles back at me and before I know what's happened, he's unbuckled his seatbelt and is kneeling on the metal ground in front of me. He's kissing me hard and our fingers are locked together and as feelings of safety wash over me, I sleep.

Sometime later, I blink and see Kane asleep on the floor right underneath me.

I gasp, panicked, but Mikey shouts something I can't make out from the front. I look up and he's giving me a thumbs up over his shoulder. When we make eye contact, he points to the right and I look up to see a set of earphones.

I put them on and Mikey does too and when he talks, I can hear him clearly.

"He's okay," he tells me, returning his gaze to the windshield. There are bright lights coming from somewhere that make my eyes hurt. I blink many times against them, but nothing works.

"Abel, you should see this. Can you sit up?"

No. The answer is definitely no. I just laugh into the headphones. Mikey flicks some buttons and undoes his seatbelt. He reaches over Kane's body, but the second he touches me, Kane lurches away and grabs his arm like a zombie with its first taste of human flesh.

"I told you what would happen if you touched her again, didn't I, brother?" I can hear his snarl, even over the wind.

Mikey's face turns bright red and he nods, then pulls back his hands. "I just want her to see this. Show her outside."

Kane struggles up into a seat and then carries me into the cockpit where he sets me on his lap. The pain in my back is surreal and I have a hard time keeping my eyes open, but Mikey was right.

The pain is worth it.

"Sunlight."

I whisper the word with reverence as I look out at the world in front of me.

Clouds line our feet and above them, there's just blue. Pure pale blue and light. It's yellow and bright and turns the grey clouds below us white, making them look like snow.

Kane is very, very gentle with me, but I cling to him hard now as my eyes shut and the emotion monster waves at me from its contented position nestled in the very center of my soul. In each of my bones.

I weep.

I cry like a baby and as I try to staunch the tears, I remind myself that Population doesn't allow for tears.

But we're not in Population anymore.

I try to stay awake for as long as I can, but between Kane's warmth and the jarring pain in my back, it's not possible.

Kane feeds me more pain pills and as their effect loosens my tongue, I smile and say, "We did it. I can't believe we did it."

Kane isn't wearing the headphones, so I don't hear his answer, if there is one. Instead, he pets my hair lovingly while Mikey smirks into the speakers, "*You* did. And you know what else?"

"Hm?"

"We didn't even have to fight any tolta."

"Or maltrons," I whisper.

Mikey laughs then, quite abruptly, and the sound is enough to thaw the ice that sits in my core, covering my flesh which has just begun to prickle. I'm starting to be able to feel again. And I feel terrible.

I cringe into Kane's chest and cower there while the sunlight warms me, inside and out.

I wake with a jolt, disoriented and disappointed that there's no sunlight anymore. My body pitches, but there's a belt across my waist holding me down and next thing I know the helicopter doors are flying open.

I see Sandra first, black hair streaming in the wind the helicopter creates. Maggie and Calvin next, followed by Gabe, several others I can't name, and then finally, Ashlyn. Tears come to my eyes as Sandra shouts orders and Ashlyn, ignoring them, climbs into the back of the helicopter.

Crying, she wraps her slender arms around my head, burying her face in my neck. "I never thought I'd see you again." Her voice cracks as she speaks. "You told me to run and then I did, but you were gone."

She's crying hard now and I rub the tears from her cheeks with my thumb, or at least that's what I imagine I do. I can't move my hands.

"Baby, I'd always come back for you," I say, voice shallow. It hurts to speak.

Her hair smells like lavender soap and is soft against my neck. Someone has recently cut it. Her clothes are clean too. She looks like a kid is supposed to look and I feel nothing but gratitude.

She pulls away from me, rubbing her ruby eyes with the backs of her wrists. "Why are you...what's wrong?" Her cheeks burn a brighter red as she looks me over.

"Sandra," she shrieks, "help me!" She doesn't sound eleven anymore. She speaks with authority. "We need to get a...a thingie," she gasps.

"We need two stretchers immediately. Calvin," Sandra says, completing the sentence for her as she moves to Ashlyn's side.

"On it."

"Only one," comes Kane's low growl. "I'm fine."

"You're not," Maggie argues.

"He's definitely not. He was completely drained..."

Horrified gasps light up the space.

Hands are on me and some of them are Ashlyn's. Others are Kane's.

But soon, I'm being hauled onto a stretcher away from him while Lady, Lanis and Maggie block his path. "Let the good doctor do her work…" I hear Maggie say before I'm rushed around a corner.

Back to my old room. Inside, I recognize the wallpaper.

Sandra shoos away the chaos so that it's just me, her, and Ashlyn. She begins directing Ashlyn in terse orders that I hardly understand. Ashlyn has no trouble, and soon I'm stripped down to my last layer. With the blood and sweat covering most of me, even warm air makes my skin prickle.

Ashlyn takes a pair of stainless steel scissors to my shirt, but Sandra stays her hand. Quietly, she says, "Mikael tells us that Abel has been hurt very badly. Do you want to stay?"

"I want to stay."

Her eyes flare when she peels back my shirt. They roll me onto my stomach and the bandages go next. I'm grateful I don't have to see Ashlyn's reaction, but I can't block out the sound of her sniffling. As Sandra shoves a needle into my arm, she also sends Ashlyn to find Maggie.

Alone now, Sandra squats down so that I can see her face. "I have never met a fighter I admired more." Her lips quirk and her gaze rakes over my back. I wonder how it looks. "You fight until the last breath, and then continue breathing."

She sighs and runs a hand back through her thick, jet-black hair. It's so long it reaches her lower back, even in a pony tail. I remember the first time I met her, I commented on it. She told me that she never cut it because she's Indian and her family was Sikh. Though most of the younger generations have never heard of such a thing as religion, she still adheres to the traditions of her ancestors in honor of their memory.

I blink and hope that can serve as a thanks. Speaking is suddenly impossible as a brilliant warmth consumes me. She fixes IV bags up to a pole and, as Ashlyn and Maggie enter, adds a bag of blood to the drip. *Human* blood. I can tell by the color of it.

Ashlyn's been crying. I can tell by the swelling of her face when she returns, but she doesn't cry now. Methodically, she removes the bandages around my arms and legs.

Maggie there too, and when she arrives at my side, she gently lays her hand on my arm.

"Kane." I cough, but the word's still intelligible enough.

Maggie nods indulgently, laugh lines crinkling around her eyes and lips. "You can stop worrying so much about others, my dear. You just focus on yourself for once. We have him well taken care of. Kane will be just fine."

"Thank...thank you," I say.

Sandra and Maggie exchange a few words rapidly as I begin to fade from this place.

"Sleep now," Maggie whispers, "You're safe."

Chapter Twenty-One

There's light streaming in through the window when I wake. Muted light, but I can tell that it's day. Everything is quiet and I know that I'm home.

Home.

I never thought I'd be able to say that word again.

I sigh. Someone else sighs in response. I open my eyes. Ashlyn is in the bed with me. I can see her knees, but not much else.

"Sorry. Did I wake you up?" she says and I sigh again, whole body tingling.

"I'm not convinced I'm not still dreaming," I croak.

"If this was a dream, it wouldn't be very good."

I exhale laughter into the pillows. They smell like honeysuckle and vanilla and are as soft as ever beneath my bare body. I'm naked again, except that I'm wearing underwear this time that actually fits me and I can feel a fabric pad lining my panties rather than bits of bloodied towels shoved in there all akimbo.

"Don't look pretty, do I?"

Ashlyn doesn't say anything for some time, but I see the bloody gauze pads she throws into the wastepaper basket. "You're hurt real bad."

"What's the prognosis, doc?"

"Good," Ashlyn answers, "Well, it would be better if Kane could give you his blood, but Sandra said he's not ready."

"Of course he isn't." I pause. "How is he?"

Another wad of gauze floats over the edge of the bed. She reaches to the side table then and pulls off a bottle of antibiotic ointment. "Sandra says he still has two more days until he restores his red blood cell count to normal. The puncture wounds in his arms won't fully heal until then either. He might even get some scars."

"Christ," I murmur.

Ashlyn pauses, then adds, "He would heal faster if he took human blood, but he won't."

"He won't?"

"No."

I clench my right fingers around my wounded palm, able to move them more freely than I last could. I can feel the hard ridges of stitching against my hand and imagine that from above, I probably look like a jigsaw puzzle.

"Has Kane seen me yet?"

"No. He's been trying but Maggie said no. She said if he saw you he'd try to give you blood and it wouldn't do any good and he'd only lose more of his own blood in the process."

Ashlyn rubs my back with her little fingers in small, circular motions. They're soothing and I close my eyes, surrendering to the sensation. It's the most comfortable I've felt in days, and again I'm rocked by the fact that Mikey and I emerged from that cave only days ago — a couple weeks, at best.

"They posted Mikey outside to make sure he doesn't come in."

"Mikey's outside?" And I'm confused by the hope I hear in my voice, because I'm supposed to hate him.

"Yeah. But he's not allowed to see you."

"Sandra says?"

"Kane says."

"Fuck."

Ashlyn giggles at that. "Potty mouth." For a moment, I entirely forgot she was eleven.

Smiling against the sheets, I ask, "How did you get so close to Sandra?"

Ashlyn doesn't answer at first. Instead, she edges off of the bed and stands. For the first time, I'm able to get a complete picture. She looks bigger than I remember, more meaty. Fuller than the flesh and bone she was when I pulled her out of that cage.

"I'm supposed to change the bandages on the bullet hole in your shoulder. You got lucky. The bullet went in and out. At least, that's what Sandra says."

I raise a single eyebrow at her and she pouts, "I got into a fight." She holds out her right hand and I can see nearly healed scrapes shimmering across the backs of her knuckles.

"You're lying." I gawk.

She stamps her foot and rolls her eyes. "Okay, fine. I got into three fights."

"*Three* fights? Are you crazy? What were you thinking? If I could, I would slap you upside the head. What were you doing fighting?"

She pulls on the bottom of her shirt, stretching it out. It looks slightly too small for her and I'm surprised. In the past months, she's grown so much. "When me and the other girls got back, we met the other kids. They haven't been out in Population."

Her voice drops and she stares at me, willing me to understand. I do. She doesn't need to say more.

I nod.

"One of the guys tried to touch Judith. I stopped him. She doesn't like when boys touch her. They just don't understand," she repeats, looking away as if ashamed, or as if recalling a memory I wished I could incinerate.

She comes close enough to touch and I take her hurt hand in my left one. My fingers don't move like they should beneath the splint, but it's enough to be able to touch her.

"But I do." I give her a light squeeze. "I'm sorry for what happened to you."

She shakes her head. "You came for us. All the girls think you're a superhero." She smiles then. "Me too."

I smile back. "I think superheroes usually heal faster than this."

Ashlyn shrugs. "Maybe." But her smile fades. "At least you're still alive."

She looks at me then and I know she's thinking of Becks. "Oh shit, Ashlyn, I'm so sorry," I sputter, remembering that Ashlyn has no idea because the last time she saw her mother, they were both alive.

She shakes her head and I can tell she's fighting to keep it together. Her voice trembles as she says, "How did she die?"

"She died fighting for you."

"Actually," Ashlyn says, eyes steely in their determination. "How did she die?"

Her voice is severe and I can't deny it. I tell her the truth that no eleven-year-old should have to hear as I recount to her the final stand Becks and I made for her.

"She didn't feel pain," I lie, and as I do, vow that it's the only lie I'll ever tell her. "Her last thoughts were of you. She'd be so proud to see you now."

Ashlyn sniffles and wipes her cheeks fiercely, but she isn't quick enough to catch the tears that fall. I take her hand in mine and grip it firmly. Too quickly, she calms.

"You can cry, Ashlyn."

"You don't cry." She shakes her head.

I tense. "It's normal to cry."

"You aren't normal?"

I smile at her, albeit weakly. "Have I ever been?"

Sniffling, she laughs ever so slightly and rubs her nose with the back of her hand. I imagine that if it were light —

or if I had Kane's vision — I'd see it was bright pink and slightly swollen.

"No, I guess not. And now you're the queen."

That takes me aback. "How do you know about that?"

"Everybody's talking about it. Maggie is freaking out, trying to prepare everything already. She's already got a guest list that's like a mile long, but Kane says she can't send anything out until after he deals with Elise."

"Do you know what he means to do with Elise?"

Ashlyn shrugs and shivers, returning to the task at hand. "I don't know. I'm only eleven," she teases.

"I forget all the time." I smile at her and hope that in the darkness she can see it.

"All I know is that somebody called the Lahve is supposed to come in a few weeks."

"A few weeks?"

Ashlyn must catch the skepticism in my tone because she says, "Yeah, I don't know. You'll have to ask Kane." She chews on her bottom lip. "Kane told me you killed Memnoch."

"I did."

"Good."

I want to know what happened to her, too, but I don't want to know, if that makes sense. I'm a coward with a ruthless imagination, so I tell her a truth, one that won't change the past but that is something we can both cling to,

"Nobody's going to hurt you again, not while I'm still alive," I say.

"I know," she sighs. "I love you, Abel."

My heart beats hard, just once. "I love you too."

She leans down and kisses my cheek and as her hands flutter over the gauze wraps, my gaze drifts back to the cuts on her hands. I'm no Becks. What she's dealt with is too hard for me to help her through. I hope she'll talk to Maggie about it, or someone more able to.

But for now, I say, "So now you work with Sandra? I still don't get the link."

Ashlyn shrugs. "After I punched Martin, she asked me if I'd help her out instead of going to Maggie's class."

"You like it?"

"Yeah." Ashlyn grins. "I do. Sandra says I'm good at it."

I exhale and make a mental note to thank Sandra next time I see her. "I'm so proud of you."

"I'm proud of you, too."

Ashlyn changes all my bandages and just as she applies the last piece of medical tape, she stiffens. Whatever she hears, I don't, as my busted ear is facing up, good ear pressed to the mattress.

"What is it?"

She grabs a scalpel lying on the bedside table and I tense. "Ashlyn, is everything…"

It's only then that I hear the voices. "…in my own house…let me…you fucking…" A roar and then a huge weight slams into my bedroom door.

Kane bursts through it shouting, "I want to see her."

Mikey is beneath him when they hit the hardwood, splinters of wood showering the Oriental runner that leads to the bed.

"Kane?" I say, distracting Kane long enough for Mikey to shove his shoulder under Kane's, flip him onto his stomach and wrench his arms behind his back. Kane strains his neck to look up at me and Ashlyn throws a sheet over my body before he catches sight of the carnage.

Kane speaks into the floor. "I want to see her." But Mikey has him safely pinned. Kane roars and throws his full weight back, lifting his brother off of the carpet and slamming him into the dresser. Mikey wraps his thick arm around Kane's throat, but it's Ashlyn, of all people, who quiets him. She quiets them both.

"You're scaring her," she shouts, voice shrill in an eleven-year-old's pitch. "She's not supposed to have her heart rate elevated and you're messing everything up!"

Kane's eyes hit mine, and though the muscles in his neck strain, he lets Mikey wrestle him out of the room. The door slams and it takes time for the commotion in the hall to subside. The moment it does, Calvin raps his knuckles on the back of my door before stepping through it.

"Christ." I cough. "What happened to you?"

Calvin edges into the room, rubbing his jaw. "Kane's in a particularly…explosive mood." He's got a welt on his jaw and a shallow scrape above his left eye.

"And Mikey's the worst person to be watching him. I wish Tasha was back." He ruffles Ashlyn's hair as he moves past her. "Mind if I sit for a while?"

Ashlyn blushes and tucks her hair behind her ears. "I guess so." And when she stares at him as she exits the room, I know just what to make fun of her for later: Ashlyn's got a crush.

I laugh as Calvin pulls up a chair beside the bed.

He asks me what's wrong but I change the subject. "Where's Tasha?"

"Ironically, she's at the Lahve's estate in the Diera. She's persuaded him to investigate the disappearance of her Notare and his Sistana, and last I heard, they were working on convening all of the Council *in person* by next week."

"How?"

"Apparently there's a couple working planes still, and the one coming up from South America will get here by boat." He shrugs. "Just glad to see you alive and well, *Sistana.*" He smirks.

I glare.

Calvin laughs and bows to me deeply before plopping into a chair. "I do believe congratulations are in order, by the way."

"Not funny."

435 ❯

"You really didn't know?"

"No idea."

He laughs. "That's rich. You deserve it though."

I don't know what to say to that and shiver.

"You need more blankets?" he says, noticing.

I shake my head. "No, I'm okay. Just a little itchy. Nice haircut though, by the way."

"What do you think?" He cocks his head and pretends to flip long locks.

I laugh and cough simultaneously. "It's a good look for you. Makes you look older than twelve, for once."

Calvin bites his bottom lip and leans forward onto his elbows. "If you weren't looking so corpsey right now, I'd go a few rounds with you."

"You know you'd never win."

"I know," he concedes, rubbing his nose. "But you make losing fun."

Laughing lightly, we lapse into a pleasant sort of silence before both speaking at once. "So I just wanted to say thank you..." "Look, Abel, I'm sorry..."

I laugh through my nose. Calvin's cheeks brighten with soft pink swirls.

"You first," he says.

I clear my throat. "I just wanted to thank you for what you did with those girls."

"Are you kidding me?" His jaw drops. "I didn't think you'd even want to see me after that."

"What? Why? You did amazing. You got them all back here, didn't you? Alive, at that."

Calvin concedes, then stutters, "B-but you. I left you. I should have sent the girls ahead and gone back."

I sigh against the sheets and sink even deeper into the bed. I'm surprised I haven't melted in with the fabric. "If you had left them alone I'd *never* have forgiven you."

Calvin shakes his head and breathes air through the side of his mouth. "Well, for a married couple, you and Kane certainly seem to have different priorities. He nearly crucified me when I came back without you. I had bruises for almost a week."

He's in a short-sleeved tee shirt and I see that the freckles on his arms match the ones on his rubicund cheeks. "I think the only person Kane hates more than me right now is his own brother. Crazy after all the guy did to get him back."

I shift uncomfortably, wincing when I stretch the new sutures winding across my back.

"The whole thing was pretty crazy," I say dryly.

"What happened?"

I shake my head. To reveal anything would be to condemn him. "What happens in Population, dies in Population."

Calvin's face falls. "That bad, huh?" His gaze sweep the gauze covering my back from neck to pelvis. "But why would…What did Mikey have to do with it?"

I close my eyes. "I really don't want to talk about it."

"Sorry," he whispers.

I shake my head again. "It's alright."

"I'll let you sleep, Abel," he says, rising to his feet.

"You sick of me already?"

He shakes his head, looking quite serious for once. "You need to get some rest. Sandra says you're not looking so good."

"Damn that woman. She seems to be spreading lies all over the place." I'm trying to make a joke, but I don't laugh and neither does Calvin.

Instead, he stares down at the sheet covering me and traces its shortest edge with his pointer finger. "Can I take a look?"

"Only if you do me a favor."

"Anything."

"There should be a mirror on the vanity." He nods. "Bring it over. I want to see for myself." I regret having asked the moment Calvin pulls the gauze away in one big sheet and engineers a couple mirrors so that I can see, too.

It looks like a map of downtown Seattle, lines forming in a checkerboard pattern, a few thicker stitches slashing sideways across it as they vainly work to hold the little skin there is together.

"You can put the mirror down now," I whisper.

"What in the world happened?" Calvin says a few painful seconds later.

"Mikey didn't tell you any of it?"

He shakes his head. "Mikael hasn't said much of anything except that he doesn't like being called Mikey."

"Of course not. Big stubborn oaf."

"He says you're the only one."

"The only one what?"

"That can call him that. Mikey."

"Oh." I quickly change the subject. "Do you have water?"

Calvin jumps to his feet, exits the room, and returns from the hallway carrying a cup, a pitcher, and a straw. He helps me drink, because in neither hand can I hold a cup without it falling. And when I'm finished with half the pitcher, he presses a small pill to my lips. It's only after I swallow that I bother to ask what it is.

"When I was out there, Sandra told me to give it to you. Morphine tablet. Apparently you're running them out of the good stuff." He flicks the IV line.

My head flops down onto the pillow beneath it and I close my eyes. It's hard to keep them open.

Calvin touches my right wrist, gives it a little squeeze. "I'm really glad you're back."

"Me too," I breathe.

"I'll leave you alone. Get some rest."

"I'm supposed to be bedridden for the next couple days. Will you come back?"

"Yes, ma'am. Or should I say, Your Highness."

"Don't you fucking start."

Calvin gives me a short salute from the open doorway. "Whatever you say, My Lady." I mean to make another jab as he steps out into the hall, but I'm asleep before I even hear the door shut.

I wake what would have felt like minutes later had the world not been shrouded in total darkness. My eyes open and my senses are alert and on the defensive, because I know I'm not alone.

"Who's there?"

A light flicks on and for a moment I don't quite make sense of the world in front of me. There's a sheet hanging a foot away from my bed that spans the full length of the room, dividing it. The light is on the other side. It's soft and orange, and illuminates a silhouette against the dark fabric.

"I didn't mean to frighten you." Kane's deep voice hits me like a bucket of ice water. It's shocking in its submersion. "I'm sorry."

"Kane," I exhale, "I missed you."

Kane doesn't answer right away and I start to breathe faster, harder.

"Kane?"

"I missed you too," he says brutally. "So badly everything fucking hurts. And these pesky humans that I afford so much power succeeded in keeping me from you for hours."

"It's only so you don't worry," I whisper. "At least that's what they tell me."

"They say many things," he breathes and he sounds exhausted. If he is, I feel him. Seriously. "They say I would not like what I would see if I looked at you." He pauses long enough to take another breath, this one even deeper. "Are they…correct?"

"It's just a few scratches."

"Are you lying to me?"

"Yes."

Kane snarls, the sound ripping from the back of his throat and making me flinch. "Don't do it again."

"I'm sorry," I whisper. "It is bad. You know the worst part was that the guy that did it — Jack — he looked just like you. And the guy that saved me — Diego — he looked just like my brother."

Kane doesn't speak again for some time, but I can hear him subtly shuffling, shifting, like he's trying to get comfortable, but can't.

"I want to see you," he says.

"I want to see you, too." I answer. "Please take the curtain down."

As if he'd been waiting for me to ask, Kane rips the curtain free of its staples and wrenches his chair closer by three feet. I gasp when he appears at the edge of the bed, face lowered so that we're eye-level and separated by an arm's length.

I don't miss the way he hisses, or the way his hand shakes. There are deep, plum bags beneath his eyes and though he's clean-shaven and his hair has been cut, it's sticking up all over the place. His body glows between us and a gold shimmer refracts off of his emerald eyes, filling them with intensity and with light.

His lips part and they look warm and supple, blood red as they had been, before Elise. I notice all this and more in the second before he kisses me.

He crushes his mouth to mine, like he's trying to pull the last breath from my lungs. His tongue invades me, meeting mine and tangling. Heat shoots through my body and my toes curl. I try to lift up, but he holds me where I am, breaking our kiss but only so he can kiss the edge of my jaw and trace the outline of my ear with his tongue.

"Mmm," I moan. "Kane…" I reach for him and grab whatever I find — I meet beard. It's trimmed now, shorter than it was and just a shadow lining his jaw and hollow cheeks.

"God, you're beautiful," I whisper in the space between us.

Kane sucks in a breath. He seems to be struggling with something. Finally, he bows his head and settles back in his seat. Looking back up at me, he traces his fingers gently across my swollen cheek.

"I told you once before, Abel, that I am a selfish male. When I felt your pleasure while Elise was busy draining the blood from my body, I have never known such rage..."

"I'm so sorry," I start, but Kane shushes me. He places a single finger on my lower lip, then slides it into my mouth past my teeth. I bite down, sucking on it, while the pleasure tethering us together swells in me.

He shifts where he sits, but doesn't bother to hide his erection. In just those damn silk pants again, it's obvious. And I want him. If I could take him like this, I would.

"When I felt your pleasure a second time, I was so angry that I..." He chokes and struggles to speak. "I wanted to see you punished for it. It was all I could think. I knew I was wrong and so I pulled away, severing the connection we share." He looks me over, and slowly shakes his head. "But I never could have imagined you in pain like this."

I bite my swollen lips together, unsure of what to say. I'm not good at this stuff. All I can feel is a mounting panic as he pulls away.

"No. Please. Kane I...you're not...are you done with me? You can punish me, if you want..."

I close my eyes, knowing I can take it and that it would be worth it not to lose *this*, but Kane only laughs humorlessly in a way that makes the hairs stand up on the back of my neck.

"You are a fool."

"I know."

"Mikael told me how he stole my sword from you, *hit* you, and forced himself on you. He also told me that you single-handedly rescued him and countless other Heztoichen from Crestor's clutches. And he credits you entirely with my rescue."

His voice trails off before picking back up with poorly restrained violence. "He loves you."

Kane growls and I hear a piece of metal clink as it hits the ground. I wonder what he's bent, or broken.

"Mikael has never made any effort to protect anyone other than himself, and yet now, every word out of his treacherous mouth is to protect you. He's protecting you from me and what he thinks will be my fury."

"No, that isn't…"

"Do you love him?"

"What?"

"Do you love him?" he repeats.

"What? No! Oh my gosh, of course not! I love *you*."

"Did he rape you?"

"Kane," I choke. "*No.*"

"Did you invite him to pleasure you, then?"

"No! I would never…" I'm too flustered to marshal my answer and immediately after, I realize my mistake.

"Then what difference does it make?" Kane roars.

He surges onto his feet, grabs the standing floor lamp and throws it across the room where it shatters against a painting. I can still see in the light of his chest, but only in that. I'm a little scared now by the way he paces, and scared to interrupt him when he's like this. I've never seen him like this.

"My brother took permissions with you that were not given. And I know already of your history with assault. You gave me this information in *confidence*. I know that you have never had a male worship you as I did and I was so ruthlessly jealous when I realized you were receiving pleasure that I wished you *ill*. I wished you pain when I *knew* that you were inexperienced. When it is possible that you do not even understand the concept of permission. Do you even know how to rebuff a male's advances?"

"I…" No. I don't. "Fight? Probably fight…"

Kane crosses the room, grabs the dresser and tosses it like it weighs nothing. I squirm, squeal and close my eyes. My heart is pounding as I hear his footsteps come closer.

When he touches my hair, his hands shake with a quiet rage betrayed by his gravelly pitch. "I left you in a position where you could only think to fight and it was with my own goddamn kin."

And then he quiets and his tone grows dangerously soft. "I will kill him for this."

"No, Kane. Please don't. I know that what he did was wrong. That what *we* did was wrong. I asked him for help when I got my period — I never had a period before and I was scared…"

"You got your period for the first time and my brother assaulted you?"

More things shatter. Wood this time. When I blink my eyes open, I see what got got. There goes his chair…

The bed dips beside me and I see him sliding beneath the covers. He lowers himself down so that we're eye-to-eye. He doesn't look like him, though. He looks like Jack. Too much like Jack. I close my eyes against the image. Against the rage. Against the memory.

I try three times to formulate coherent words but only manage a strained grunt, a swallowed mumble. My face floods with heat and I begin to feel sick to my stomach.

"Kane," I murmur when he still doesn't say anything. "I don't mean that what he did was right, or that what we did together was intentionally wrong. It just all happened so fast. He'd been in prison for years and hadn't had blood in months. I never had a man down there but you…"

Kane closes his eyes, face appearing stoic and still in a way that frightens me far more than his fury. "And now you're making excuses for him too."

"They're not excuses. They're just reasons not to tighten the noose. If I can forgive him, then you can forgive him, too. Just…so long as…you can forgive me."

Kane keeps his eyes closed and exhales deeply, then inhales in equal pulls.

Tears prick the backs of my eyes as I whisper, "I felt like I betrayed you when it was happening. I never felt anything like that before. I didn't know…don't know about this stuff. But I understand if you don't want me to be your Sistana anymore. I don't know how to break a blood bond, but I will if you want me to."

A tear trickles down my cheek. Kane flinches. "Is that what you want?" He opens his eyes and they heat as they track the tear all the way down to the sheets.

"God, no," I blurt out. "I love you." My stomach hollows. I can't swallow or breathe or blink. "I love you so damn much."

Kane looks at me in the quiet dark before scanning the rest of my body. I'm grateful for the blankets separating us. I don't want him to see the rest…

"Please, Kane," I whisper, watching as his large fingers trace the shape of my left hand down to the wrist until it disappears beneath gauze and plaster. "Say something."

He back teeth clench and his warm, rough hand tightens around my palm. My fingers twitch in discomfort and he releases me. He flips onto his back and massages his eyelids.

"I have been in love with you from the moment you challenged me for the key that opened Mikael's crypt — perhaps even before that. Seeing Memnoch and his minions go after you in that alleyway, I assumed it would be a quick death for you humans. But when you emerged, still breathing, and dragged me off into that disgusting store to *save my life*, I knew I'd met my match."

A smile appears then at the corner of Kane's mouth. "And then later, when you finally found me in Elise's torture chamber and pressed your wrist to my lips, I knew I was wrong to hate you. I knew with absolute certainty that I didn't. That I was weak. That I was jealous," he exhales, like a great weight is lifted.

He breathes out again, "I was jealous. Jealous to the point that I nearly killed you." Kane's fists clench, as does his jaw. He looks directly at me and his green eyes glow. "I wanted your blood in me so no one else could have it. All of it. And when Mikael offered you his blood to save your life, I denied you that."

He exhales, and his breath smells like peppermint. Just like he tastes. "So when you ask if I still want you, you fail to realize that it is I who should be asking that of *you*. You were taken advantage of by *my* brother, and I almost killed you."

Licking my lips, I try to speak. My heartbeat is firm and even and, if I concentrate just hard enough, I can feel his, firm and even, fluttering in my rib cage alongside it.

"There is nothing to forgive," I say. "I still want you."

"And I, you." He smiles at me, though it's a starved thing. Full of hope, yet still seeking salvation. "The blood bond will only break between us with my death."

"Or mine. Which is probably more likely at this point."

Kane doesn't laugh at my joke. He just shakes his head. "Not even then, Abel. You are mine for the rest of my life and I am only yours. I'd like to ask you a question I should have asked you weeks ago. Before the ball."

"I...okay," I grunt, struggling to clear my throat.

He reaches beneath the blankets, presumably into his pocket, and withdraws two long, delicate strands made of rose gold. Small sigils hang from the end of each, and when he tilts them to the light of his chest, I see that they are two intricately woven knots that have no ending.

"Would you honor me by becoming my Sistana?" Color rises to tint to his hollow cheeks and I grin outright. He's *nervous*. I didn't think such a thing was possible.

"Yes," I say, bellowing out a shaky laugh. "Of course I'll be your Sistana."

He exhales as if I might have given some other answer, and I laugh again, even if it makes my back ache and causes me to wince.

I cough. "I sort of thought I already was."

"There's a ceremony and mountains of paperwork — more so because I'm one of the Notare and you're a human. It'll be a huge affair. A ball. The Chancellor will need to be present, and wherever the Chancellor goes, hordes of sycophants follow. You'll be required to dance for hours."

Laughing, I try not to let signs of pain play out along my face, but I can feel the stitching acutely and every time I become aware of it, I'm revisited by the pain of the whip.

"Sounds like fun," I say.

Kane laughs quietly under his breath and drapes the heavier of the two chains around his neck. The finer one he reaches over me to lay on my bedside table, next to emptying jars of antiseptic and unused gauze pads.

"For when you're on your feet again. It was my mother's. The symbol is that of the blood bond, though each pair varies so as to be unique." Kane shakes his head quickly and chews on his bottom lip, looking suddenly concerned.

"Though if there is some token, or some way I might appeal to your human traditions, please tell me what you need. Anything within my reach is yours."

I smile. "I don't have any traditions." Pausing, my nerves flare unexpectedly. I lick my lips. "Kiss me?"

Kane hesitates, looking my face over, and for a moment I think he just might deny my request. But then he edges forward, moving more slowly than I otherwise would have thought possible, and very tenderly brushes the hair from my cheek. His lips meet mine and my whole body stirs. All I feel is pleasure and a numbing intensity.

He pulls back too soon and I whisper between his lips. "Do you forgive me?"

He closes his eyes, then opens them, and around the back of my head I feel his fingers curl into the hairs at the nape of my neck. "I can't go through that pain again, Abel. I won't."

"Nothing like that will ever happen again."

"And I vow that no one again shall ever put you in that position. From this moment forward, we shall not part."

I smile, feeling a tension leave my body like a bird taking flight. "I'm okay with that."

He kisses me again, more deeply this time, but it's still not enough. I want more. More and forever. Kane draws back with a slight hiss and tucks my hair behind my ear. His entire face is flushed.

"Have I hurt you?"

"No," I exhale.

He clears his throat and everything about him softens. "Your face is swollen. You have a cut here." His finger moves from beneath my eye halfway down my cheek. "And here."

I don't feel the pain, but I still shudder. "That's the least of it."

Kane curses. "I don't understand how this could have happened. Why was my brother not more severely injured?"

My mouth parts but I blank entirely on what to say. "He didn't... He didn't tell you what happened?" Calvin I understand, but Kane? How does this fall to me, now?

"I learned only that you were separated and that he found you like this. That, in the time you were apart, you were discovered by a gang which *tortured* you."

My heart beats harder at the memory, which I actively work to repress. It's easier with Kane watching me as he is. Around Kane I've always felt safe, even back at the beginning when I thought he was my worst enemy, and not the future love of my life.

I choose my next words carefully. "We got separated after I broke him out of Crestor's place. It was chaos with the survivors fighting the guards. I got chased by an alien called Trocker. We fought in the car, and then the gang caused us to have an accident. Our car crashed. I tried to escape, but they got us in the end."

I exhale, "They burned Trocker alive and told me that I had to watch. That they'd whip me unless I could keep my reactions in check."

"And you did not."

I shake my head. "No. I threw up." I couldn't stop throwing up.

My stomach gurgles audibly at the memory and Kane closes his eyes again and clasps the back of my neck. He rolls onto his side to face me and leans in again and kisses me more deeply this time. Pulling back, he just holds us close like this.

"I'm sorry I didn't kill him when I had the chance," Kane whispers. "If I had done what the Council suggested, then Crestor would not have slowed you down. You would not have been separated. Mikael could have protected you."

Crestor wasn't the problem with Mikey. But I don't tell him that.

"Why was Mikael not with you in the car when this Trocker hunted you and you were taken by the gang?"

"Good thing he wasn't. He'd have probably gotten drained and burned along with Trocker."

"You did not answer my question."

And I don't want to. I shake my head. "We just got separated."

"Abel..."

"What good is the truth," I whisper, "when all it can cause is pain?"

Kane doesn't respond, but his face takes on a distinctly murderous glint. "What did Mikael do?"

"Nothing."

"Mikael told me that he offered you myhr. Myhr is only offered between loved ones as an act of redemption for an egregious wrong. I thought he offered it to you for taking your sweetest blood against your will, but you're telling me that that wasn't even the worst of it? That he did something more to wrong you?"

I hesitate. I don't know what to say. "Mikey should be telling you this."

"*Mikey* should stay far away from me if he values his life. I want to hear from you what happened. Why did he offer you myhr, Abel?"

I close my eyes, clenching them tight. I feel so weepy and weak these days. Maybe I deserve them — these tears. Maybe here, out of Population, I'm safe.

"He left me." The words come before I can stop them.

Kane doesn't speak. I don't want to open my eyes to see how he reacts to this. "Why?" His voice is stone and hoarse.

"He wanted to go back for our…packs. I didn't want to."

"Do not tell me, Abel, that this has something to do with alcohol or drugs."

I don't answer. He told me not to.

Kane flips back the sheets and stalks towards the door. I see him reach it and he's holding the doorknob in a shaking fist. He's fighting to calm down. I can hear it in his labored breath.

"I'd like to see."

"What?"

"I'd like to see your back."

My fingers curl into the sheets. I try to sit up, but don't make it very far. Fresh pains light up all over my body. "I don't think that's a good idea. Sandra said that the cuts will leave scars, even with your blood, because the wounds have already started to heal."

Kane looks so tenuously stitched together, all it would take is a single pull. "I know. I hate that my blood isn't strong enough to heal you now. I'm not as old as Elise. A few drops of her blood kept you from dying. If I'd had a few drops more, you wouldn't be here, in pain."

"Sandra and Ashlyn are keeping me pretty hopped up on morphine." I smile. Kane doesn't. Instead, he turns and takes a brutal step towards me.

"Don't," I say. "You'll be angry." Angrier than he already is. "And maybe you'll decide to take back that necklace. Not sure I'll actually look the part of a queen after this." My voice is light, though it fails to mask a very real concern.

I get the impression that Kane senses it because all at once he comes towards me and presses his forehead to mine. He kisses it. Then kisses my nose, my lips, each of my cheeks.

"You have never been more beautiful than you are now. You're *alive*. You're with me." His hand clenches around the back of my head. "But I need a distraction right now. Give me a reason not to hunt down my brother and kill him in cold blood."

"Don't say stuff like that. He's your brother."

"Let me see, Abel. I will need to see, eventually."

I nod just once, too tangled in the sound of his voice and the tenderness of his touch. I don't stop him when he takes the soft edge of the medical tape and peels it back.

Cold air sweeps against my wounds and I struggle to look over my shoulder at his face. It's expressionless, and that frightens me.

"Pretty, ain't it?" My toes twitch as I wait for him to react.

For a long moment, Kane doesn't speak. When he does, his voice is hoarse. "Where is the man that did this to you?"

I shrug. "I don't know. Mikey didn't come across him, so he's probably still out there somewhere."

Another protracted silence. "How did you survive this?"

"Your blood is my best guess."

"You had so little of it. This should have killed you."

"When I was dying, I could feel you in my chest."

Kane replaces the bandages with care and draws the covers over me. He slides back into bed and brings himself as close to me as he can, but doesn't touch me. His hand hovers near me, but doesn't light down.

"I could feel you slipping away from me and had never felt more powerless. I couldn't move. I failed you."

"You did nothing of the sort."

Kane gulps audibly, though he keeps his eyes closed. "I let you down when I told you I never would."

"You didn't."

"How can I say it will never happen again when I could not prevent it this once?"

"Kane. Look at me and hear the words I'm telling you."

He opens his eyes and this time, I touch his face with my bandaged palm. His skin is so smooth. He doesn't look quite human like this…but he still looks so wounded.

"You don't get to play hero all the time. Sometimes, I get to be the hero, too."

"Never again," he growls, narrowing his eyes. "Next time, you'll leave me behind."

"Never." I shake my head, and close my eyes. "Never."

He leans in towards me and brushes my lips with his and wrapped together in him, I sleep as I never have before: unafraid of the darkness.

Because in Kane's light, there never is.

Chapter Twenty-Two

The next day, more visitors come and go. Gabe, Maggie, Calvin, Sandra, Ashlyn, Judith, Rebecca and a couple of the other girls. They clamor around me until a particular point midday when they all disappear at once.

I hear a banging that sounds very much like thunder and tell Ashlyn to go out and investigate. She's halfway to the door when it opens.

Tasha enters with purpose. Her tan silk shirt flutters in the wind her body creates. It's the first time I've ever seen her in pants, and like everything else she wears, it's a good look for her. She looks like she just got off a horse.

"Pardon me, Sistana, for not having come to see you sooner. I arrived this morning and have been struggling to navigate the murky waters between Kane and Mikael. As you can see, I didn't even have time to compose myself."

She swats at the flyaways that have escaped from her soft bun, perched so precariously on the top of her head. Her cheeks are flushed, as if she's been caught in a full out sprint, though I can't imagine her running for or from anything.

"Good to see you too, Tasha." I laugh. In her presence, I just can't help it. Tasha straightens. "Well, yes. It is a pleasure." When I roll my eyes, she smiles a little more fully. "I *am* glad you're alright."

"Alright is relative, I'd say," I groan, twisting to the side in a fruitless attempt to get more comfortable.

I've been on my stomach like this for a week now? I glance at the necklace Kane left there the night before. Lord, has it really only been two days?

"Truly, Sistana, what you have done is incredible. You saved Kane in the time it took for me to even open an investigation with the Lahve. He is so damn slow."

I laugh. "Wow. Why don't you tell me how you really feel?"

She gives me an annoyed look before her gaze pans out to the sheet draped over me. Without asking for permission, she takes hold of the sheet, pulls it down, then reaches for the gauze and peels it back.

"Hey!" Ashlyn chides. "I just taped all that back."

"Wow. Thanks, Tasha," I mutter, getting the chills.

Tasha gasps and she whispers a series of alien words that, together, might have been either a curse or a plea.

I grunt, "Now is that any way to treat your damn queen?"

Tasha blinks at me several times, but doesn't replace the covers. She bows and looks down at her feet. "I'm sorry, Your Grace."

"Seriously, Tasha. If you don't cut the name-calling out I'm going to sic Ashlyn on you."

Tasha takes a seat on the edge of the bed and looks at Ashlyn fondly. "It's good to see you again, little warrior."

Ashlyn's cheeks turn pink. "You too."

"Is it safe to move Her Highness?"

I'm shocked by the question — first because Ashlyn is being spoken to with such a degree of respect, and second, because it's Tasha. I never thought Tasha liked humans very much.

Ashlyn wrinkles her nose and crosses her arms over another too-small tee, orange this time. "Why?"

"Good question, Ashlyn," I grunt, letting my head fall back against the mattress below. I'm tired of trying to see stuff. "Tasha, as much as I love you, I don't think I'm up for a leisurely stroll."

Tasha clears her throat daintily into her fist. "Unfortunately, you don't have much choice in the matter. Mikael has gone and made a mess." She pauses. "Another mess."

Her fingers flit over my wounds and she asks Ashlyn to bandage me. Single-handedly, she lifts me into a seated position, and I don't try to help her. All the energy I have goes into listening.

"The myhr Mikael offered Kane took place this morning, at Kane's behest. He wanted it to take place before he gave you his blood, lest you should attempt to watch."

"Bastard," I grumble. "Did you see it?" I wince as Ashlyn smoothes another piece of tape over my shoulder.

Tasha nods. "I did. My presence was required."

"What for? We didn't need a witness when Mikey gave me myhr."

Groaning, I stretch out my legs. The hinges need oil. My right knee pops half a dozen times before I manage to straighten it.

Tasha stands and paces abruptly to the door. Opening it, she stares out into the hall. "Witnesses are not required for myhr. I insisted on being present for other reasons."

"What were those?"

"To ensure Mikael's survival. Technically, a myhr can result in death. The accused cannot fight back and any weapon may be used. That's why to offer myhr is such a sacrifice."

She returns to me when I reach my toes for the ground and try to stand. With a hand on my shoulder, she keeps me seated.

"Don't get up. Sandra should be arriving shortly with a wheelchair."

"Thank freaking God," I mutter under my breath.

Ignoring me, Tasha moves to a stack of clothes I hadn't noticed piled on top of the dresser. Well, the thing that used to be the dresser. It's missing a couple drawers, but Calvin did manage to get the thing into some kind of a square-ish shape. I told Kane I probably could use a replacement, but he just said that I didn't need it, or anything in this room anymore, reminding me that my room was now his.

"In the meantime, try this on, Sistana."

She picks a floor-length peach-colored gown from the top of the pile and pulls it over my head while I protest.

"Christ, Tasha, I look like an idiot. I'm a cripple with a half-swollen face and I haven't showered in a week. This dress is not…"

"Is not up for discussion, Your Grace."

She smiles at me in a clenched sort of way and stabs her fingers into my curls. As she pulls them away from my face, I wince and curse. Ashlyn admonishes her, but she doesn't listen and comes at me with a bag of makeup.

We argue for a few seconds before I drop the bomb. The big one.

"Tasha, I *order* you to put that shit away."

Her lips twist up, but I'm pleasantly surprised that this new tactic works. I grin, she stomps her foot, and Sandra enters.

Just before they help me into the wheelchair, Tasha lowers the chain over my neck that Kane gave me. "Thank you," I tell her.

"It suits you beautifully, Abel," she says. "Kane's mother, Arianna, would have been so pleased to see you wear it." She's got tears in her eyes that bring tears to mine.

I punch her in the arm. "Stop that."

"Apologies." She sniffs, then fans her cheeks.

I laugh and turn towards Sandra, hoping to keep the emotion monster from yanking my restraint away. "Let's get this show on the road."

As Sandra rolls me down the hall, Tasha leads the way, looking more annoyed than usual. Maybe annoyed isn't the right word either. *Anxious.* She looks increasingly more anxious...

"So why exactly did I have to get out of bed and put on this ridiculous outfit?"

"I beg your pardon?" Tasha shoots me her fiercest glare.

"I mean, why did I have to get out of bed and put on this *gorgeous* outfit?"

It's Sandra, above me who says, "Mikael has requested a Tentalin."

"What's that?" Ashlyn asks, jogging to catch up to my side. We're moving quickly, an urgency I don't understand in Sandra's stride.

"Nothing good, judging by the way Kane almost leveled the house."

"No. It isn't," Tasha says, rounding the next corner. "I'll explain when we arrive in the ballroom." We walk for a few more minutes in silence before the grand ballroom opens up before us.

The room is surprisingly full. Most of this little village's occupants line the room's walls. There are also a few aliens present standing just apart from the rest of the rabble.

"Who are they?" I say to Tasha, not bothering to whisper. I know they can hear me.

"The Lahve sent guards, upon my request," Tasha answers.

"Good work," I say as Tasha moves to my side.

In the gap her body's created, I get my first glimpse of Mikey kneeling in the center of the huge room where Calvin once taught me to waltz.

He's kneeling in a pool of his own goddamn blood!

"Holy hell! What happened?"

I try to stand, but my legs wobble and I collapse back into the wheelchair at the same time that Kane appears in front of me wearing a white tee shirt covered in blood spatter.

He doesn't speak, though the blood stains on his knuckles do. "Remain seated. You feel feverish." He stretches his hand towards me, but jerks back at the last second in a way that is very atypical.

"What..." I start to say, then redirect. "What weapon did you choose?"

"I didn't."

"And it wasn't a pretty sight," Calvin says approaching our group.

Kane doesn't contradict him and I gawk, waiting for an explanation that doesn't come. I don't really need one, do I? I know why he did what he did.

Pushing through the wall of Kane's body, I reach for Ashlyn's shoulder and use it as a crutch. Hobbling awkwardly to my feet, I plod barefoot over the parquet until Mikey's easily within earshot.

I can still feel Kane right behind me as I walk.

"Christ, man, you look terrible."

His whole face is a mess, with a cut on his mouth, blood streaming from his nose and both of his ears. His arms haven't fared much better and I can only imagine what the rest of him looks like underneath his black tee shirt and shredded jeans.

Mikey grins up at me and blood seeps out from between his teeth. He rises to standing and I see that he favors his right leg.

"Could have been worse," he hacks. "I could look like you."

I chuckle, even as Kane spits out a curse behind me — a threat. I feel strangely self-conscious standing between them in the way that I am, especially with the wide room around us completely silent. Everyone's watching.

Everyone.

"Yeah," I say as quietly as I can. "You could have died."

"But he didn't kill me."

"I should have," Kane snarls at my back, and though I want to reprimand him, I distinctly remember shooting Mikey a few days ago. Apparently he inspires similar emotions in everyone.

I turn to face Kane and see Tasha standing at his side. She's whispering in his ear, talking him off the ledge. I know that. I can see it in the fury in his face, the swelling and tightening of his shoulders. It seems to be working, until Mikey says at my back, "Abel, you have to take it off."

Kane roars and Tasha's heels slide towards me over the floor as she uses her whole body to block him. Two of the other aliens peel apart from their comrades and approach Tasha, and help her restrain their Notare.

"You selfish bastard," he shouts.

"Kane, no," Tasha grunts while the Others — a male and a female, both dressed in gear that makes me think military — push Kane back towards the door.

Tasha rounds on Mikael, even as she takes me by the shoulder and guides me away from him. "Mikael, control yourself."

As Kane reluctantly yields, he paces away from Mikey and me, moving into the center of the room. He laces his fingers over his crown and takes jerky, shallow breaths. I don't know if I've ever seen him so angry.

I turn and watch the room's occupants watch me. I've never felt more exposed as they follow me wordlessly with their eyes but don't speak. The entire room seems to be waiting for something.

"Your Grace, please have a seat." Tasha smoothes down her hair, then gestures for Sandra to bring the wheelchair.

I take a seat and let Sandra push me to a point near Calvin at the entrance while Kane and Mikey move into the center of the hall and square up against one another. "There's gonna be a fight? But I thought they did myhr?"

Tasha clenches her teeth. "They did, but Mikael has demanded a Tentalin be held today."

Maggie comes to stand beside me and lays her hand on my shoulder, and I get the very distinct impression that something terrible is about to happen. Sandra takes the place to my left and Ashlyn sits cross-legged at my feet.

"A Tentalin," Tasha explains while Kane and Mikey each drop to one knee in mirrored acts of genuflection, "is an ancient tribunal whose outcomes are to be respected by all parties involved." She licks her lips, and swallows hard.

"You are called forward as a witness to this Tentalin, which has been called in your honor."

"In my honor?" I mouth, searching her face for answers.

Tasha only nods. "Mikael has challenged Notare Kane in a Tentalin for the right to your...*bond*." Her voice breaks. "Should the Notare prevail, preparations for your joining will continue as planned. Should Mikael prove the victor, then he will have the right to blood bond with you."

"No!" I shout, rising up out of my chair, only to drop back down again when it wobbles.

Tasha's face turns bright red and she holds up a hand. "You dishonor them *both* by declining."

My mouth hangs open as vocabulary eludes me. Mikey's gone too fucking far. Does he expect to win? What does he hope to get out of it if he does? He feels guilty — I get that — but he doesn't even like me. Is this about Kane and his deep, deep envy? Or is this about my sweetest blood and his addiction to it, like his addiction to everything?

"Sistana," Tasha says. I snap back to attention. "You must honor the results of the Tentalin." There's fire in her eyes as she mouths a series of words, expecting me to repeat them.

"Fuck. Fine," I say.

She reddens even further and nods just once. "I am sorry, but you will need to remove the knot until after the Tentalin concludes. You may put it back on again should Kane prove the victor."

She doesn't meet my gaze as she steps up behind me, lifts the strand over my head and tucks it away. I'm not a sentimental girl, but when I touch my chest, I still feel loss.

"The Tentalin can begin Mikael, Notare Kane, whenever you are ready."

My stomach pitches as Kane and Mikael come together in the center of the room all at once, moving with all the speed of fire, and its destruction.

The battle seems to last hours and I refuse to watch. I don't care who it shames. I can't watch brother pitted against brother in my name. Even if I've got nothing to do with it.

But I can still hear it. The crack of bone. The slippery smacking sound their bodies make as they slide over blood. Muted thumps and growled grunts. Cries of rage and of pain.

"It's over," Tasha whispers in my ear some indeterminate amount of time later. "You can wear the knot again, Sistana."

I feel the weight of it slide over my neck and I reach down and grip the metal. I hold it, letting it fortify me, before I open my eyes.

Kane is all I can see. Everywhere. There's black blood smeared across his sweaty chest. His pants are ripped. His shirt is gone except for the top half. I try to look around him, but he grips the back of my head and rips open his wrist with his teeth.

"Drink," he says to me, and I don't know this tone and I don't dare deny him.

I press my mouth to his open wound and I drink. I drink and drink until Kane wavers where he stands and Tasha tells him to stop. She hands him a towel and as he takes it from her, she loops his knot over his neck.

"Notare," she says with a small bow.

"Clean up this mess," Kane snarls. "I will be with my *wife* in our quarters. Unless the world is ending, we aren't to be disturbed."

He slips his arms beneath me and even though I can feel my wounds healing themselves whole — the map on my back wiping itself clean, the bullet wound in my shoulder filling itself in, the bite in my leg erasing itself like it never was — and I'm pretty sure I can walk now, I still don't deny him this.

It seems like he needs it.

He carries me from the room, and even though people have started to move back and forth, I still catch one quick glimpse of Mikey in the center of the dance hall — the coliseum — as he's lifted onto a stretcher.

From head to toe, he's covered in blood.

I don't know what's broken or what's whole, because everything looks broken.

Sandra cuts off my line of sight as she hurries towards Mikey. Calvin and another three humans trail slightly behind her, each carrying a bucket and a mop.

Chapter Twenty-Three

"Kane?"

"No. No talking." He charges up the stairs like he's late for something and if he weren't tearing apart the dress Tasha put me, I'd be confused as to what was going on.

We make it to the hall his room is in but my legs are around his hips and I can feel his erection through his jeans and am rubbing myself against it.

"I'm still on my period," I tell him, panting.

Kane growls against my throat. "Good."

He lowers my feet to the ground and before I know what's happening, he drops to his knees and slips under the skirt of my dress. He pulls down my panties and the blood stained rag there and covers my core with his mouth.

My eyes roll back and pleasure pricks the top of my tongue, like I'm tasting something sweet and savory all at once. I might have Kane's blood in me, but Kane didn't even have a lot of Kane's blood in him, so I'm still woozy where I stand.

I reach out and catch myself on a painting and clumsily knock it down. It starts to fall over me and I fall and with Kane trapped under my skirt he falls too, and we land together, tangled underneath the painting and maybe we needed it because we both burst out laughing.

I burst into tears, too.

Kane crawls up my body over my dress, but under the painting, so we're still hidden in its shadow. He kisses the underside of my jaw and I can feel him fiddling with something below his waist.

I feel his erection press against my wet entrance a second later, but when I expect him to push forward, he hesitates.

"Do I have your permission?" he says, voice catching.

His eyes are worried, even though I'm completely wrapped around him — well, as wrapped around him as I can be with canvas pressing against my arms.

I smile and trace the outline of his face with my middle finger. I brush my thumbs under the bags under his eyes. I scratch his stubble.

"You always have my permission. Forever. Even if I'm asleep."

He barks out laughter at that, but still doesn't come forward. He kisses me sweetly at first, and something *changes* in the kiss. It's no longer so desperate, so feverish, so mad.

His tongue lavishes mine in stong strokes and when the weight of his hips sink onto mine and his cock slips past my lower lips, his gaze never leaves mine.

"I adore you," he says and his voice breaks as he enters me, seating himself fully inside.

And it's so full, it's like the very first time. I blink quickly, trying to lift my hips so he'll go faster, but he doesn't break his impossible tempo.

"You're still hurt," he says, as if that explains it.

"I'm healed. I drank from you."

He shakes his head. "I can feel your stitches like individual heartbreaks." His fingers brush over my shoulder and he slows even more.

Our tangled gazes and our tangled legs make me feel like I'm losing my grip on time and space. The painting shadows us like a veil. Like we don't exist in the rest of the world.

"It's just us," he breathes and his breath still smells like peppermint. Mine probably smells like blood. I don't care.

I stretch up and kiss his chin. He holds the side of my face. Our hips push and pull together in a choreographed movement. Tears. They come to my eyes like I'm suddenly releasing everything Population never let me release before.

For my brother.

For my parents.

For Becks.

For everyone who's ever died at my hand to live.

For the four men who I killed in that grocery store.

"I'm not a savage," I say and I don't know why.

Kane slows even more and I'm caught in the brilliance of his smile. "No. You're a perfect creation."

"No, *you* are," I blabber.

Kane refuses to relinquish the vice he's got around my heart. I try, but can't look away from him.

He grinds harder against my clit, knowing what I need and I can feel myself building towards something, but it's different than it was in the kitchens. Not an explosion, and not an arrival, but a release on top of so many other releases. Everything just goes.

It's like he unzips my soul.

I step out and I'm lighter than I was. My eyelids flutter, but I don't let go. Can't let go.

My mouth opens and I struggle to exhale my next breath as Kane grinds so, so slow.

"Oh…"

It comes and pulls me apart at the seams.

I'm only distantly aware that Kane is whispering words in an alien language to me as he straightens and falls forward. His mouth finds my neck, but he doesn't break the skin there as he comes inside me.

His ass clenches under my fingers and I hold onto his abs as he jerks, jolting my whole body forward. His pleasure becomes mine and I don't try to fight it.

I let myself get caught up in the rip tide as our emotions ebb and crest, lap and recede.

It takes a while for the purity of such overwhelming pleasure to release me from its grip. When it does, sweat and blood coat both our bodies and my back is starting to hurt me again. I still don't move right away, but I hold back from reentering the cycle as Kane collapses more of his weight onto me.

He pulls up just enough to be able to look into my eyes. He looks drunk and beautiful at the same time.

"This painting is scratching my ass."

I crack, laughing so hard my whole body shakes. Kane laughs into my neck, brushing little kisses across my sweat-slicked skin.

"There's also a fat baby staring at me," I chuckle.

Kane looks over his shoulder at the cherub painted there and grunts. "Revolting little thing. Does this creature exist on your planet?"

I laugh again and shake my head while he slowly slides out of me. We both groan as his softening cock slips free of my entrance.

"Not that I know of," I sigh, looping my arms around his neck.

"What is it? You just made a face," he says.

"I think I'm probably bleeding all over your floor."

"Good. You can bleed anywhere you need." He slips his hand down my body and his fingers trace over my lower lips in a way that makes my back arch in a natural desire.

He pulls them back and his fingers are covered in faint traces of pink. He sucks them clean and freezes, shakes his head, exhales shakily.

"Have I thanked your gods for creating you, yet?"

"Yes," I say smiling. "I think you already did."

"Well, my Sistana. Let me return with you to our room where I can worship their most magical creation properly."

He kisses me softly, and then he does just what he says he will.

Again and again and again.

Chapter Twenty-Four

"There. All done." Sandra brushes off her hands and leaves the room and it's only then that the tension Kane carried with him releases, just a little.

It releases a little more when he draws us a bath and sets me in it. He straddles me, like he once did, only this time, he's massaging my back so gently I can hardly feel it.

"Any harder and I could cause you pain," he says when I complain.

"You're not going to hurt me."

He doesn't answer, just keeps rubbing soap into my skin. "You would perhaps change your tone, if you could see what I'm seeing."

I don't have anything to say to that. "How are the scars? Hideous?"

He doesn't answer. I poke his calf.

"Way to make me feel better."

He huffs, "They look painful. I don't like that they look like they're hurting you."

"They don't hurt."

"You asked for my opinion."

"Yeah, I just wish you had a different one."

I reach for his knee and try to tickle the back of it. He doesn't so much as flinch. "Boring," I mutter.

He wraps his arms around me at that and drags me into his chest. "Boring?" he says, chowing at my neck.

I squeal and pretend to fight him off. Really, I just sink deeper into his lap, rubbing the curve of my ass against his erection. "I didn't mean it!"

"You better not have. If you think I'm boring already, what will you think of me in two hundred years?"

"You know humans don't live that long, right?" I say, turning around in his arms so I can straddle him properly.

"With my blood in your system, you never know. You could live as long as I do."

"Well, whatever happens, I want to die in the bath." I love the bath, I decide then.

He freezes. "What?"

"This bath. I want to die in it." I sit back with a splash and kick bubbles in Kane's direction. "Sitting here with you is what I think about every time the pain gets too much. It's my happy place."

Kane's voice gets soft. "Do you want to know mine?"

I nod.

"The first time you came for me and you looked so lost. So surprised. It was the first time I ever truly felt like a king."

I blush and look away from him, but I can't get anywhere, not when he has hold of both my feet. We lapse into a pleasant sort of silence while my mind wanders. I think at some point, I even manage to sleep.

"Let's go to bed," Kane whispers. Once there, he says to me, "What are you thinking?"

"Nothing."

"Tell me." He takes my hand in his and kisses the tips of all my fingers.

"I don't understand. Why would Mikey do that?"

Kane closes his eyes, lips moving over the large scar on my arm from one or both times my wrist was broken. It's a darker brown strip about six inches long, but still manages to look like it's decades old, and not just a few days.

"Mikael has not had much happiness in his life. You make him happy."

"I don't think it has anything to do with me," I say.

Kane doesn't answer.

I elaborate. "I think it's just envy. He doesn't like that you have something he doesn't, because you already have everything he doesn't. He wants to be you."

"Perhaps," Kane says softly, tucking my damp curls behind my ear. "But his envying me does not explain his selflessness towards you."

"Selflessness? Or guilt?" He almost got me killed — a couple times.

"It could be both."

"Whatever it is, I'm glad it's over. No more fighting between the two of you, got it? You're family. I'd kill to have mine back so I'm not going to let you or him or me destroy yours."

"Ours," he whispers. "He is our family. And I will do my best to be on good behavior, unless I am provoked."

"Good lord."

"He is untrustworthy."

I nod, considering. "Maybe. But it doesn't matter now. We're all here and I'm yours and everything's fine. We're safe."

But Kane doesn't agree with me.

"Right, Kane?"

He sighs, "Can we not have a few moments of peace before we reenter the fray?"

"Fray? Oh lord, what do you mean?"

"I mean Elise. She's still out there and now that I have been recovered, I can speak directly to the Lahve and he can kill her."

"Just like that?"

"For her crimes?" Kane nods. "Just like that."

"Where is he now, the Lahve?"

"The Lahve has gone to Crestor's estate in the hopes of finding and rescuing any of his Heztoichen victims. After he has put Crestor to death, he will come here and together we will discuss what to do about Elise.

"She is still Notare, so the same rules do not apply to her. He can't just have her executed, so she must be captured before she can be imprisoned. It won't be easy and I won't have you involved. My quarrel is with Elise, alone."

I push myself up on his shoulder and stab my finger to the center of his chest. "The hell it is. I'm not sending you back into the salt land after that wackjob nearly killed you. No way."

"And I won't have you anywhere near her either. The Lahve and his guard will handle Elise. Likely, we won't even have to leave this house. Or this bed." He flicks my chin, and draws me down for a kiss.

"This Lahve guy better be all you've cracked him up to be," I say, speaking against his lips.

Kane smiles and I can tell that he's exhausted by the way that he groans. "The Lahve is the last of an ancient bloodline, a species not entirely like our own. His senses are faster, sharper. He would argue that his higher level of intelligence makes him more capable of impartiality and leads him to have full command of his emotions."

Kane yawns and the last of the tension deflates from his neck and shoulders. "He's over three thousand years old. You will not be disappointed."

Seeing him exhausted makes me exhausted, and we sleep soundly through the next day and night. A blood-soaked honeymoon, I wouldn't trade it for any other life.

The days leading up to the Chancellor's arrival are filled with a ridiculous amount of Tasha fittings, checkups by Sandra, midnight poker with Calvin, Gabe, and Kane, lightning-round catch-up sessions with Ashlyn, and therapy with Maggie, Sandra, Ashlyn, Judith and the other girls that came from Memnoch's cave.

I don't see Mikey once, or rather, he won't see me. He keeps his door locked, and when I knock, doesn't respond, even though I can hear the distinct sounds of a body moving on the other side of the door.

I move on, taking a tour of the house, stopping by that cherub painting which has been rehung where it was, even if there's an ass-shaped dip in the canvas now.

I find Kane in his den arguing with a big guy called Far, head of the Lahve's security. Silent and clad all in black, they patrol the house relentlessly. I can feel one following me now, but don't bother acknowledging him.

"Knock, knock," I say aloud as my knuckles rap against the wood.

Both males turn when I enter. Far bows at the waist. "Sistana."

Far's face is almost perfect, with no lines or wrinkles or age marks. His eyes are two small beads of coal, as hard as diamonds, and like diamonds, they glitter as they canvass the room, gaze passing over everything with a hunter's precision. Kane tells me it's because the Lahve keeps only older Heztoichen for his guards. Far is nearly twice as old as Kane is.

I awkwardly salute. "At ease," I joke. Kane is the only one who laughs between them. "How are things going?"

"Well," Far says, though his face is drawn in a severe expression that contradicts it.

"Yeah?" I wade further into the room, moving to Kane's side when he lifts his arm.

He circles my waist and drags me in to meet his kiss, gripping me with the same ferocity with which I grip him. I slide my fingers through his hair, cupping his neck with my hands until he yields into my kiss, letting it wander.

Wavering on my feet, I allow my full bodyweight to rest against him until he releases a short, brutish laugh between my lips and severs the contact.

Pulling back, he snorts, "Far does have a way with words. We're unable to come to a compromise on the number of guards needed to prepare for the Lahve's arrival. I found twenty to be a bit excessive."

"Twenty doesn't sound too crazy," I say, trying to regain my footing. Far is staring off into space as if there's something particularly important on the bookshelf lining the wall. I laugh lightly.

Kane lifts a brow. "Twenty in addition to the fifteen already present and the ten that make up the Lahve's personal escort."

I whistle. "Damn."

Far clears his throat. "I would like to remind Your Graces that these guards will constitute the party sent to retrieve and detain Notare Elise."

"Fifty aliens just to take down one?"

Far doesn't flinch at my nomenclature. "Any fewer would be insufficient and would present a risk to the Lahve and to Notare Kane."

The lazy way I feel before drops like a blanket at my feet. "Kane, you're *going*?" My pitch rises and breaks as I glare at him, making me sound less condemning than I would have liked. I punch him in the arm. "But you said…"

"I have to."

I move from his side to stand directly in front of him. Placing my hands on each of his shoulders I push his torso back, forcing him to look at me. "Why?"

He grimaces. "You wouldn't understand."

"Help me, then. You said neither of us would have to leave this house and yet you're off talking to Robocop about a battle strategy that you're fully intending to be a part of. So again, let me ask you why you *lied* to me?"

Kane shakes his head, hair sticking out in every direction. "You don't know..."

"You're right." I throw my arms out to the sides. "I don't know, so enlighten me."

"You can't imagine what it was like with her...being tortured..."

"So that's what this is? Settling a score? A vendetta?" I punch my fingers back through my curls and huff, cheeks billowing out like small balloons. "I can't believe you're doing this. You're putting your life at risk because she wounded your pride and you don't even give a thought to *us*. To how I might feel if you..."

"That's *all* I'm thinking about," Kane snarls and I forget how tall he is until he comes at me like this.

He grabs my hips and pulls me under the arc of his body. He holds me tight and his voice shakes with rage as he roars, *"I gave you her blood."*

The words fly from his lips and hit me in the face with the force of a fist even though his touch is soft against my face. He traces the line of the scar there, which drips like a pale brown teardrop down the curve of my cheek.

"So?"

Kane sighs and the tension seems to have deflated from his shoulders. He looks defeated for reasons I don't fully understand. "Her blood is powerful. Far too powerful. I can smell it on your skin. Not even half the blood in my body was enough to overcome the scent of five fucking droplets."

"I still don't understand," I confess. "Why does it matter?"

"It just does." He stands abruptly and for a moment I think he might say more. Instead, he kisses my cheek tersely before moving away from me to the door. "I'm sorry, but I must see this through."

I'm pissed when he leaves me like that, and Far doesn't stick around to offer an explanation. I'm left to try to run through the house in search of him, but instead, I run into the other brother.

"Hey!" I jump. My voice is much louder than I'd meant for it to be. Clearing my throat, I try again. "Hey, Mikey. Wait up."

Mikey's shoulders are bunched by his ears and he hesitates before coming to a stop. I jog over the carpet, hoping to reach him before he changes his mind and runs. It looks like he wants to. He doesn't turn to face me and I don't touch him, though I want to force him to meet my gaze. A warmth hits my cheeks as I move to stand before him, and now that I'm here, I don't know what to say. He's wearing a white tee shirt and black basketball shorts. His hair is washed and cut, and when he turns, I see that he's shaved his beard.

"Wow." I hide my grin with my hand. "Somebody cleans up nice." It's true. His brother might prowl my dreams, but Mikey's a hot piece of ass.

When his mouth's shut and he doesn't have a bottle of booze in his hand.

I glance down and feel heat and anger light up my cheeks. "What's that?"

Barefoot, he shuffles uncomfortably from one edge of the carpet to the other while his upper lip curls into a cruel snarl. It's almost enough to make me want to put space between us, but I hold my ground.

"Nothing," he says, lowering the bottle in his hand. Bourbon, I think, but I can't be sure. It's missing a label.

"Wow. You get thirsty on the walk upstairs?"

"Fuck you."

"Okay, then." Annoyed that I'm the one being nice when I should be punching the shit out of him for *daring* to bring a bottle of booze anywhere near me — despite the fact that I ran into him — I roll my eyes, cross my arms and head towards the door to my and Kane's room, which is right in front of us.

My hand is on the knob when he groans, "Wait." I turn and he holds the base of the bottle towards me. "It's for you."

Confusion mingles with my anger enough to curb the bite of the blow. "Don't you remember my last little encounter with that poison?"

Mikey smiles, and with his clean clothes on, I can smell peppermint and fresh cut grass. "You couldn't walk straight. I thought I was going to have to carry you the rest of the way to Seattle."

I start to smile until I refocus on the bottle. "That stuff really is poison, so I think I'll pass."

He doesn't lower his hand, but instead moves a half a step closer. "It's not to drink. It's a symbol." His bottom teeth worry his lower lip. It's crimson and full, rather than split down the middle as I'd last seen it. There's not a scratch on him from what I can tell.

"There was one other bottle in my pack that I didn't tell you about. I tried to drink it when you were out, in pain, but I couldn't. The taste in my mouth…" He sighs through his teeth. "It tasted like shame.

"I vowed that it would be my last drink, and so far it has been. I mean, that isn't saying much. It's been…" He pauses, then, "Ten days. Ten days sober." His gaze meets mine and there's a hopefulness in the darkness that makes my eyes burn unexpectedly.

A lump forms in my throat as I take the bottle from him. "Eleven, I think."

He smiles and turns bright red. "Eleven, then." He nods and without warning, turns and starts walking away.

"Mikey, wait." He flinches as I blurt, "Why did you do it?"

"Do what?" But I can see his back muscles bunch together beneath the thin fabric of his tee shirt.

"You know what. Why did you request the Tantalin? Why on earth did you try to fight your brother for me? You don't even like me."

"I like you."

I balk. "You don't love me though."

He opens his mouth, then frowns.

"I like you, but I love your brother. Even if you had won, did you expect I'd just let go of him?"

Mikey closes his eyes. His breathing is hard. "No."

"Then why?"

"Because it isn't…"

A long pause, and I push, "Because it isn't what, Mikey?"

"Because it isn't fair. He shouldn't get everything good. He shouldn't…" He covers his eyes with his hands.

I step forward and take one of his big mitts in both of mine. I clasp it to my chest fiercely. "I know you don't want to hear this right now, but your brother isn't a bad guy. But he also isn't the only guy in the whole damn world. Heck — I know some people don't even find him that interesting. I was just telling him last night how boring he is."

Mikey shakes his head at his feet. "I'm sure that's how the conversation went."

"Of course it is." I let go of his hand and cup his cheek. "My point is that you need to stop looking at Kane and look at you. Because you're interesting too. And funny and witty and kind and even hot under the right circumstances?"

"You mean after a shower?"

I slip the bottle free of his fingers and hold it up. "I mean when you're sober." I pull back. "I'll take this for now and when you can look after it yourself, I'll give it back to you."

"I don't need it back."

"Fine," I say opening my bedroom door. "Then I'll give it to someone who can look after it for you when and only when you find someone up to the task."

"What is that supposed to mean?" he says as I shut the door between us.

"If you have to ask, then you're definitely not ready yet."
I close the door and leave him glaring after me.
Still barefoot.

Chapter Twenty-Five

"What are you wearing?" Ashlyn scrunches up her nose as she tries not to laugh.

I roll my eyes. "One of Tasha's contraptions. Now, shush. He can hear us from the driveway."

Kane's standing to my right, Ashlyn to my left, while a whole host of humans is spread out along the wall beside her. Mikey stands to Kane's other side, Tasha to his right. We look ridiculous, sixty plus people and aliens clustered in the freaking foyer, waiting for the Lahve and his goons.

Ashlyn gives my skirt a tug and I rip the material free of her grip, feeling annoyed. Not at her though. Once again Tasha has poured me into a garment that's two sizes too small. Long, it trails on the floor when I walk, or would have had I not been in nine-inch platform heels that bring me up to Kane's earlobe.

I might be Sistana now, but I don't have the patience to stand up to Tasha when she traps me in these garments, and from the corner of my eye I can see her glaring at me. At my side, I see Kane fighting back laughter.

The tall, double doors swing open in tandem and fifteen aliens dressed in maroon uniforms walking in five rows of three move into the already crowded space.

This is utter nonsense.

I make a mental note to give the Lahve a piece of my mind when I see him. And then I see him, and quickly lose the impulse.

He carries a cane, though he doesn't need it. It's thin and black, decorated with a silver handle that matches his fitted grey suit. His leather shoes click against the tiles as he walks and somehow that's all I can hear as I watch him. There is nothing else.

There's something sinuous in the way he moves, and something sinister in the way he stares. His skin is onyx and immaculately smooth, like petrified wood, and the bright whites of his eyes surround an even brighter amber.

Orange irises studded with two pinpricks of black, they land on me first and hit like a bludgeon before settling on Kane. I don't realize I've taken half a step back until Kane's hand on my wrist squeezes, trying to subtly hold me in place.

"Lahve," Kane says, releasing me and taking a single step forward to meet the presence that just entered.

There's no other way to describe him.

Not a man.

Not an alien.

Not an Other.

A *presence*.

He moves like he's dragging an imagined world with him and like that world's history is written in the margins of his coat and in the long, locked tendrils of his hair.

Kane holds out his hand and the Lahve suddenly appears before him. He doesn't move *fast*. I've seen bodies that move fast. He just *is*.

Not a man. Not an Other.

A presence.

I waver again, and this time I do take a half step back. The Lahve notices and his bright orange gaze slides slowly to meet mine.

I just about shit myself.

I don't understand how anyone can have a conversation with him, let alone a debate. A Notare is supposed to hold sway over this guy? How can they? He's not a guy. Not an alien.

A presence.

"Shit," I say out loud.

Kane speaks louder than I do as he clears his throat. "Greetings, Lahve," he says and I think he might be laughing at me somewhere in those gruff undertones.

The Lahve nods, thin, tightly-knotted locks falling over his shoulder, just as dark an ebony as his skin. "Greetings to you, Notare."

His voice is soft, and yet the overlapping chords of at least three other voices can be heard when he speaks. Did he eat people? Are they somewhere in there still breathing?

The Lahve still hasn't looked away from me and I don't introduce myself. I can't talk to this people-eating presence.

Kane takes my hand and tries to gracefully drag me forward, but there's nothing graceful about it. I stagger forward one unwilling step.

"This is my Sistana, Abel."

"Sistana."

He inclines his head towards me and straightens, movements all slow and smooth. He extends his free hand towards me and I take it and it feels like I'm touching marble. Stone and hard and cool. Though his face isn't a day over thirty-five, there's something ancient in his aura.

"I have heard tales of your resilience. I believe you were recently involved in a brutal attack? This was just before you rescued Notare Kane from Notare Elise's illegal settlement?"

The words come at me three times, hitting me like fists from three different angles. I can't ward off the overlapping blows, and I grab Kane's arm so as not to stagger. I nod.

"Yeah." And then I shake my head. "No. I mean, yeah, but it was before Mikey and I rescued Kane."

The Lahve's orange gaze glows like the surface of the sun as it flashes momentarily to Mikey. "It is a wonder that he was not injured." His tone is filled with implication.

Kane must hear it as well, because he stiffens at my side and says, "Mikael has offered myhr both to myself and to the Sistana for his failure to protect her."

"Not a failure to protect. A total abandonment." He pauses. It takes too long. Way too long. Then he says, "I saw how he glutted himself on wine at Crestor's table and allowed himself to be dragged away while the Sistana was released."

He tilts his head from the right to the left as his gaze switches back to me, landing like a spotlight. "They thought you would leave, the guards. They prepared to hunt you when Crestor slept."

I can feel Kane tense at my side and it's my turn to grab his wrist this time.

Not sensing the danger, or unconcerned by it, the Lahve continues. "You were very clever," he whispers and it sends chills crawling like ants up my back. Like termites, they burrow.

"You distracted them with your sweetest blood, and then you freed the mutilated ones, even though it came at great cost. I watched you fight them. You were magnificent. I had not believed humans to be capable of such things."

He pauses again and even though the time stretches on forever, there's still no opening for anyone else to speak.

No one would dare cut off a presence.

"I watched you escape with Mikael and I saw as you attempted to persuade him to follow you to retrieve the Notare. I saw as he turned his back on you. His own Sistana. He ran through the woods away from you and when he found what it was he sought, he drank an entire bottle before thinking to go back for you. For a moment, it did not look like he would."

He straightens and suddenly everything shifts. He looks a little bit more like a person, like he had to remind himself to be less of a presence.

"Apologies, it would appear this information has upset you, Sistana. Would you prefer not to have known?"

"Yes," I blurt, tears on my tongue. I look past him at Mikey and try to remember that we're here and now and that it's all over, but it's hard.

I suck in a shaky breath and look away from Mikey's face. He says nothing. He just stares at me in a shock and horror true enough for me to know he did everything the Lahve accused him of.

"You saw all of this?" I say, feeling anger on the heels of this fresh betrayal. Anger at *him*. The presence who saw too much and flung it all across my foyer.

He nods. "I see much."

"How?"

"The Lahve has a gift," Kane says and he chokes and I can tell he's trying to keep it together just as much as I am. "He can read memories, among other things."

"It is well put, Notare." The Lahve speaks slowly, like he's got all the time in the world. "I read the memories of the survivors we found near Crestor's estate. A surprising number of accounts depicted yours and Mikael's movements, up until you were delivered into the hands of this human gang. I was not able to source them."

The Lahve's body shifts ever so subtly and I can't get out what I was going to say next. He takes a step towards me until we're less than an arm's distance apart and I don't miss the way Kane angles his body in front of mine.

The Lahve looks to Kane first, then says to me, "May I see your injuries, Sistana?"

"You want to see my scars?"

He nods. "It has come to my attention, during your wait for Kane's blood, your wounds left scars. I would like to see the extent of the damage."

"Why?" I say rudely and I can tell it's rude by the way everyone in the whole room stiffens — the mulberry guard in particular.

The Lahve doesn't answer right away and I wonder if he's waiting for an apology. If he is, he can keep waiting. Finally, he says, "I would like to fill in the rest of the gaps so that I may have a complete and detailed history of our Sistana. I will write these down in the books so that nothing is forgotten. No successes, and no failures." His gaze slides towards Mikey and I feel the irrational desire to protect him, even though he wouldn't do the same for me.

Not wouldn't.

Didn't.

Not when it counted.

"Fine," I blurt, hoping to hold his attention and spare Mikey the grief. I start to turn and raise my hands to the clasp at the back of my neck, but Kane grabs my shoulder.

"Apologies, Lahve. I require that this conversation take place somewhere more private."

The Lahve bows again. "Apologies, Notare, please lead the way."

Kane nods and looks out at the overfull room. "You all are dismissed."

He turns on his heel and I follow closely behind, gesturing for Ashlyn to join me. She gives me strength as she grips my hand, the clamminess of our palms acting as adhesive between us.

I can feel the Lahve at my heels, following in long strides, each of which covers at least two of my own. I'm chased by the click-click-click of his leather-soled shoes on the marble tiles, and then off of the dark wood floor of the den.

Tucking his cane inside of his long cloak, the Lahve steps up in front of me as I stand in the center of the room. He lowers his gaze to Ashlyn beside me and I tense, fearing what he'll see about her too.

"I do not intend to offend, Sistana, but not even my guards have been permitted to enter the room."

"She stays. She's family."

The Lahve waits. He doesn't move. He doesn't blink. He doesn't look like he's breathing, either. "Very well, then," he says rapidly.

"You wanted to see the damage?" I say.

"If it would not trouble you."

"No trouble. Ashlyn, would you mind?"

She unfastens the clasp at the back of my neck, then brings the zipper all the way down. With her delicate hands she pushes the sides of my dress apart and I don't miss the way she gasps. I imagine I would gasp if I saw me, too. Every time.

I can hear the Lahve approach, but before I know what he's done, a tremor ripples through me as his fingers touch my left shoulder.

His hand is ice and my body freezes over while I'm throttled back into the past. Into memories I never wanted to see again — memories I would unsee if I could.

Mikey in the woods, staring at me with one eye swollen shut, telling me he'll come back for me. The sickening sense of abandonment that grips me as I'm all alone, running for my life, away from Mikey. The first time I saw Jack and felt hope. The last time I saw Jack and felt hopeless.

Diego's hollow eyes, so full of pain.

I wish I knew where he was…

"Lahve." Kane's voice snaps through the space like the tail end of a whip. With whips, I am all too familiar. "With great respect, you are in my house, in my territory, and while my Sistana may be generous enough to allow you the grace of touching her injuries, I am not."

Kane's face is blood red, though I'm distracted from the severity of his expression by Mikey at his side. Mikey's pale.

Ghost white. His gaze pans to mine and he clenches his fists. His eyes genuflect, dropping to the carpet between us.

"Apologies, Notare. Curiosity led me to overstep," he says, without sounding sorry at all.

"I see now what caused the marks and I am sorry for what you endured, Sistana." When he says this, it actually sounds like there's some truth to it.

I turn and see him wiping sweat from his brow and wonder…he said *saw*, but did he *feel* it, too?

Quickly, he says, "These marks are unusual, even for a human." Ashlyn zips me back up, and I turn to see the Lahve watching me with his head tilted askew.

"With your blood loss, I'd have assumed the marks to be more severe. You had little blood in your system and you were bled nearly dry. How did you survive?"

I look to Kane. "Kane gave me…"

Kane clears his throat, face betraying a nervousness that his tone doesn't. "I gave her blood from Notare Elise's lab."

The Lahve doesn't move, not even on the inhale. *Is he even breathing?* "Do you know whose?"

A long silence lingers. Painful this time. Kane takes a few steps forward, coming close enough to take my hand. His fingers are so warm and familiar, his lips soft as he brushes his mouth across the backs of my knuckles.

"It is the Notare's," he finally says. "I gave her five drops of Elise's blood."

"And it was enough to save her?"

Kane nods and the Lahve drags in a loud breath all at once, and I imagine that he's sucked all the air out of the room. I curl one arm around Kane's waist and drape the other over Ashlyn's shoulder. While Ashlyn takes my hand, Kane kneads the back of my neck as if to keep himself present, or to let me know I'm safe.

I wonder what he's feeling and what his thoughts are, because mine are entirely blank. I'm a goon now too, waiting for instruction, though the Lahve doesn't seem to be in any particular hurry himself. Then again, he's lived three thousand years. What's another five minutes?

"Interesting," he says.

"Lahve." Kane's voice is both a command and a question.

The Lahve nods and takes a slow turn around the room, unnaturally long fingers trailing the backs of the chairs and sofa as he walks.

"Crestor was not difficult to locate following the sacking of his estate by your hand, Sistana. My guards were able to effectively rescue those in his vault and those who wished to reintegrate into society are being rehabilitated, while those who requested release, were granted it."

I tense and Kane squeezes my neck reassuringly. I do the same to Ashlyn. While it hurts to hear that even those that escape may not have survived, it makes me feel better to know that some at least were able to live or die on their own terms. That they had a choice. That's all any of us can hope for in Population.

"Elise, however, has been more of a challenge."

Standing directly across from me, he grips the back of the armchair in front of him. His orange eyes glow fiercely against his skin and the even darker charcoal outline of the sky visible through the high arching window at his back.

"She is aware she is being hunted. Her compounds in the Saltlands where you were held, Notare, have been burned beyond recognition. There is no memory there. She razed it out and surprisingly, I have not been able to locate her since."

"She must be brought to justice for her crimes," Kane bellows, taking a step towards him. "Have your troops been sent to Brianna? Root her out. She must have returned to her own territory."

The Lahve waits to speak long after Kane has quieted. I can tell Kane has displeased him by the way the corners of his mouth twitch down, but that is the only reaction Kane wins from him.

"I understand your grief, Notare, but her territory has been thoroughly investigated and there is much terrain in this world — too much for my troops to cover inch by inch. It would be impossible, and Notare Elise is far too clever. But…"

He shifts and the light hits the hard angles of his face. He's built like a cut diamond. High cheekbones, pointed chin, straight nose leading to a broad, flat forehead. Only his mouth is human, and it's very human. Lips full and rounded, black on the outsides, but when they part I get intermittent hints of pink.

"There is another way."

"No," Kane says before the Lahve even finishes.

"I am relatively unfamiliar with the customs of humans, however, in our own culture, the Sistana has the right to speak for herself."

"You dare," Kane seethes, light flaring in his chest so bright it's visible through his blue shirt. "I could expel you now."

Quietly, the Lahve says, "And neither of us would ever find the Notare or bring her to justice, and perhaps she would grow just clever enough to realize what a position those five little drops have put her in. Perhaps she would come to reclaim what is rightfully hers." His eyes move over me, and Kane positions his body squarely between us.

"I'm confused," I say, stepping around Kane. "How could Elise possibly know that Kane gave me her blood? And even if she did, why would her blood matter?"

The Lahve tilts his head and stares at me like I'm half idiot. "It's not her blood that matters, Sistana. It's yours."

And then the wheels click all together now.

"Oh." I look up at Kane and he blushes. *Blushes.* "You don't mean that…it was just five drops."

"The quantity does not matter, Sistana. What matters is the effect. Five droplets of a human's blood would likely do little to a Heztoichen. Five droplets of my blood might, in fact, kill one of them.

"You received enough blood from her to affect your physiology," he says, sounding impressed. "You healed faster. You remained alive.

"Kane had much of your blood in his system when he was taken by Elise. I do not doubt that you are just as bonded to her as you are to him."

Silence.

Nobody says anything. Not Kane, not Mikey, not the Lahve and not Ashlyn. I moan and sag onto the sofa. "I thought this was over, but you want to use me to find her."

"It *is* over. For you," Kane simmers. "I won't allow you to be a part of this."

"I'm already a part of this." In a moment, my life flashes in crisp images against the blackness of my eyelids, and I wonder how I got to this point. I went from a scavenger trying to rescue my best friend's sister from the Others to so deeply involved in their world that I'm a queen, attached to two of the most powerful amongst them. What fucking luck.

"We need you, Sistana," the Lahve says, voice neither imploring nor desperate. He is simply stating a fact, and I can't shy away from it. "You have a blood bond with Notare Elise."

"We will find another way," Kane growls.

I shake my head. "Even if we could, she'd find me before we came up with a plan B and kill me. I put her at risk, don't I?"

Instead of answering my question, Kane says, "I will not allow that."

I look up at Kane and shake my head. "This is why you were so pissed? Why it was so personal?"

He doesn't answer.

I blow breath out of the corner of my mouth. "I'm sorry, Kane, but I've seen what she can do and I'm not interested in a plan B if plan A will do."

I look back to the Lahve, whose face is stretched in what I think might be a grin. It's a grim thing, slightly softer than skeletal.

"What do you need me to do?"

The Lahve quickly maps out a short-term plan which ends, rather than begins, with my locating Elise through our blood bond. The fear is that she'll be able to sense if I latch onto her location, and we'll lose our leverage.

He also forbids Kane from drinking any blood from me that isn't my sweetest blood. Blood from my veins has Elise's in it. He could bond with her, too, and if, for whatever reason, he drops dead and nobody else catches the Tare, then Elise could challenge me for his territory.

And I'd be doomed.

I don't know how many hours we're stuck in that room, but Ashlyn goes to get us all food *twice* and I couldn't say how many pots of coffee we finish. Ashlyn's asleep on the couch we share, her head in my lap. I don't blame her and could kiss Kane on the mouth when he suggests we get some sleep and finish going over the details in the morning.

"Do we have a strategy for transport?" Tasha says, entirely ignoring him.

She's joined us now along with several of the other Others and speaks says from her position at the brightly lit desk against the back wall.

Her hair has come undone from the braid it was in and falls around her shoulders in waves. She's been using her jade pin to point at everyone threateningly.

"If we aren't able to locate the Notare until the final hour then we'll need to have helicopters and cars ready so that we can access her location at a moment's notice. I mean, what if she's all the way in Tanen's territory? We'll never find her then."

"Tasha," Kane says gently, standing up. The Lahve stands with him, and Tasha, flushing, rises, too.

"We can discuss transport in the morning." He looks to the Lahve for confirmation.

He nods, face betraying not an ounce of tiredness. "There will be more than enough transportation options. Two of the Council members have even arrived by plane."

"Is Tanen coming?" Tasha says.

He shakes his head. "He will not attend, but this is not necessary. He has given me his proxy in this matter."

Kane sneers and shakes his head. "I'm glad they'll all be here, and that you have Tanen's proxy. It is imperative that we hold Elise for as little time as possible."

"Why?" I blurt, too sleepy to stop myself. "Worried she'll make a break for it?"

Everyone in the room looks at me like that's *exactly* the issue.

"I see," I whisper and when I stand, I drag Ashlyn up with me.

I'm almost at the door when a voice holds me in place. "Sorry. Kane, Abel, would you wait a second?"

I turn and rub my eyes at the sight of Mikey standing by the windowledge where he'd been sitting quietly this whole time.

"Sure. What's up?" I say as Kane slips an arm around me and holds me to his side.

"Though I have no right to speak here, I would formally request to be a member of the party that hunts down Elise. I was kept prisoner by her and her lackey, Memnoch, for over three years, and though my actions in Population towards the Sistana were criminal and wound me even now to think about," he says, gaze flashing to me and only me. It makes me feel good. Like he's learning to see past his brother.

"I'd like to help seek revenge against the one who threatens my Sistana." He bows to me and I feel totally weirded out by the gesture, more so than when Tasha or the others call me weird names.

To normalize the whole moment, I cast my vote right away. "That's fine by me. We'll need as many hands as we can get to take down Elise."

Mikey looks up at me and smiles a little when he sees me smiling. I give Kane a little nudge, hoping for him to respond, but he stays quiet.

It's the Lahve who answers. "Mikael must carry out his sentence and that may prevent him from functioning properly in battle."

"What sentence?"

"Mikael has offered you myhr as recompense for his moral failings, however his criminal charges must be dealt with by our Council."

I feel sick as I ask a question I don't actually want answered. "What's the punishment?"

"For drinking the blood of a Sistana, we will drain your blood from his system. To the drop. And for abandoning you in Population, he will receive one lash for each of yours. Salt will be rubbed into his wounds so that he does not forget what he has done."

"No fucking way."

"Sistana," the Lahve tries. Even Kane says my name. Even Mikey. Tasha, too.

I don't hear any of them. I don't have to. "Am I the fucking Sistana or not?" I shout. "Then let me speak."

I wait for the room to quiet. I wait beyond that, dragging time out in that horrible way the Lahve does, while I collect my thoughts.

"I don't know your laws. All I know is that it would hurt me to watch anyone go through what I went through. Is that your intent here? To torture me further after I've already been tortured, Lahve?"

The Lahve's expression betrays nothing. Time stands still. Then moves on.

"I have seen his crime, Sistana. I have felt it."

"Then you'll know how much it will hurt to watch it happen again. Every scar you saw on my back will reopen if you do this to him."

He tilts his head to the side and squints, as if trying to understand a very complex mathematical equation when one of the variables is wrong.

He clasps his fingers carefully before him and watches me with compassionless eyes. "I do not attempt to understand your meaning. My species does not have the ability to empathize in the way you speak of when we feel the emotions of others directly. However, if you feel that this is a burden too great to bear, I can bring your wisdom before the Council and they can decide there."

"I'm telling you, I won't allow it. You'll have to take him somewhere far away and do it there, because if not, I'll break him out, or I'll die trying."

The Lahve smiles with one corner of his mouth, and it's the most *tangible* he's ever looked. "That is a noble gesture, Sistana, yet perhaps less than prudent considering your… mortality."

"I've never considered it in the past. Not sure why I'd start now."

"Interesting," he says. And then he looks to Kane. "I believe that, for your Sistana, you have chosen well. I shall take my leave of you and discuss the…suggestions made by the Sistana on the subject of Mikael. For now, he may join us."

Excused by Kane, the room empties except for Mikey, who lingers at the door. "Thanks for that, Abel," he says.

"Sure."

"You didn't have to threaten the poor bastard," he laughs like he just can't believe it.

"I wasn't threatening anyone. I was just telling him what I'd do to stop this from happening to someone else. I'd do it for anyone."

"Would you die for them, too?"

I pause, consider. "I'd try for them, too."

Mikey's smile carries just a hint of sadness. He says, "One day, I want to grow up to be just like you."

I laugh and throw a couch pillow at him and he disappears, closing the door in his wake, while Kane angrily closes me in a rough embrace.

"You shouldn't have spoken for him like that."

"Why not?"

"Because the Lahve likely thinks you're insane."

"I am insane." I shrug.

Kane grunts, his lips coming very close to mine while the heat sparks in every direction between us. "Don't I know it."

He devours me and there's none of the same softness there was before. This is just heat and anger and fear and jealousy that moves us from the middle of the room to the bookshelves to the couch where I lower myself down onto my knees between his spread legs.

I grab his erection in my fist and watch precum bead along the slit. "You'll have to tell me what you like," I say. "I've never done this before."

Kane's jaw works, then clenches, as I lower my mouth over his straining cock. I lick and taste and suck, following the directions he gives until they become a stream of garbled nonsense and he's wrenching me up off my feet and lowering my body down onto the sofa beneath his.

"You better be careful with Tasha's dress."

I bury my hands in the thick mane of his hair, urging him to where he's headed.

He growls as his mouth works its way down my body, and the last thing I hear before my eyes shut to reveal an even deeper darkness is the sound of Tasha's dress tearing.

Chapter Twenty-Six

"It's time. Everyone out." Tasha claps her hands together and the room empties except for me.

The Lahve and me.

Kane is the last to leave. He hovers in the doorway in the same all-black outfit I'm wearing. It matches the combat gear the Lahve brought for us.

I'm not allowed to go after Elise myself — God knows I don't want to — but I'll still be joining the brigade and watching from the car with a satellite phone in case she moves and I'm able to sense it.

For now, we have to find her.

"No harm will come to your Sistana, Notare Kane," the Lahve says in that jarring, echoey voice he has. I don't think I'll ever get used to it.

"Kane," I say over my shoulder. "Really, I'm okay."

He grunts and doesn't respond, but grumbles as he finally closes the door, blocking out all sound so that the Lahve and I are in the den, alone.

I'm sitting on the couch and the Lahve is seated on the coffee table across from me. I have my hands on my knees and goosebumps prickle my arms and neck and calves. I curl my toes into my black boots. They're steel-toed and actually the right size for my feet.

"So um...how does this work?"

The Lahve is the only one *not* in combat gear. Somehow it's fitting that we're going into battle against a thousand-year-old psychopath and he's wearing a suit again, this one brown tweed.

Towering over me already, he scoots forward so that he's perched on the very edge of the table, his long, strong legs spread around mine, but not touching. He lifts his hand and traces the outline of my face, without touching. He's done this already three times.

"No distractions," he says finally, "There is not much of her blood to work with, so tracking her will be difficult."

"Okay," I say nervously when he lapses into another one of his impossible pauses.

His orange eyes flick to mine. "You were successful in reaching Kane when you had never seen the Saltlands before."

I nod. "Is this like that? I'm just supposed to like...search for her?"

He shakes his head no and his thin locks spill over his shoulders. Some locks hang even longer than his chest and stretch all the way to his stomach.

"I will search for her, but I will need your complete submission. Do not fight when I sift through your thoughts. You will need to give into the pain."

"Pain?"

He nods. "All of your thoughts are pain, short of a few."

I shiver. It freaks me out that he knows this. What's worse — or maybe better? — is that he's been with me there, in each of these moments, too. "You feel it, don't you?"

"Hm?"

"The pain."

His orange eyes blaze and shutter before I can read what lurks beneath. Emotion? He said he didn't have any of these. "All of it."

"But doesn't it hurt you?"

495 ◗

"Every time. That is the definition of pain, is it not?"

"But then…how can you stand it?"

"Because I must, just as you must, this time. Now, close your eyes," he says and I can feel the tender touch of his cool breath on my cheek.

My seat squeaks beneath me as my eyes shut and in that reverent darkness, I feel exposed. "What now?"

"Picture Notare Elise in the last moment you saw her."

Not a pleasant memory, I wince from it and nod. "I…I think I've got it."

His finger, just one, touches the space between my eyes and suddenly, I'm flying.

I'm in the cave and everything is dark and terrifying. The mountain is rumbling. My panic for Kane. The pressure of Mikey's mouth on mine keeping me alive — a moment he gets no credit for in any retelling of the stories. The light of her chest, winking out of existence.

Memnoch comes next and I hurtle backwards through memories and time until I start to make out the Lahve speaking to me.

"Picture her face and the light over her chest. Imagine you can feel the pulsation of that light in your own heart."

I'm sucked back down into the mouth of the mountain, rocks and boulders cascading, water and darkness consuming what is left, and yet just beneath the chaos I hear the thundering of two hearts. One of them glows fiercely, the other does not.

I shake my head, unable to place her. "I can't. Shit."

"Do not say can't. You do not know, Sistana, what it is that you cannot do."

And because I don't feel his presence shift in the slightest it scares the hell out of me when I feel his lips against my earlobe.

He brushes my hair off my shoulder and coos, "Elise… Elise…"

A wrenching on the front of my chest makes me waver wildly where I sit.

And still, he says, "*Tantena valys, Elise.*"

Boom. The sound isn't out loud. It isn't even in my head. It's in my body, in my chest, beneath my sternum hidden like a pebble. I look down and expect to see his hand striking my chest as if to reach the organ itself, but he isn't there and the clothes I'm wearing are no longer my own.

Panic grips me like a vice and I fly up onto my feet. Wait. I was already standing and when I move, all of my movements are filled with a strength that isn't mine. That isn't human.

I shriek words that I don't understand. I scream them at the top of my lungs. "Valyna Lahve estilnotam etes. Vie gurys Notare."

And in my ears, distant words ring and repeat, "Tantena valys, Elise…"

I start to shriek and suddenly I'm running, rushing towards a huge wall of glass. My heels are thundering over the carpet and I have no problem running in them at all even though they're higher than any Tasha's strapped me into before.

I reach the window and for a second, think about running straight through it, but I don't. *I can't lose.* Is the thought mine? Are they words? Did I say them out loud?

I press my palms to the glass and feel the chill beneath my fingertips. Heat forms around them like a fog.

And then there are words spoken in English — a language I only learned a decade ago. They belong to the Lahve, the miserable, ancient relic, and they echo against the glass and concrete walls surrounding me. Caging me.

"What do you see?" The Lahve breathes and I can feel his cool breath on my cheek, making my heart beat faster and faster and faster…

"No!" I unravel from the center and the thing in my chest that should bear the light pulses once, and then not again for several breaths. I cannot die.

I will not die.

My fist pounds into the glass, shattering it, and cold air caresses my face. I pull the largest shard of glass from the floor and see my own reflection inside. Eyes as dark as coal, skin as white as death. I blink and the black eyes are gone, replaced by eyes that are blue.

She screams again. I scream again. The sound is horrible and I fight to past it. I'm shouting words now. Shouting as many as I can. I don't know what they are, but I keep shouting them until she takes that sharp shard of glass, brings it to her own neck — brings it to my neck — and slices sideways.

I scream as I die. Blood explodes over my hands. My whole body throws itself forward off of the precipice. I fall into outstretched arms. Reality shatters over me.

The sound of a door slamming open makes me blink. I see the city. I blink again. I see the rug beneath me. I blink and see blood and then I blink and there are hands pushing me up into a seat.

"What have you done?" Kane roars.

"Dying…" I say, but when I grab at my own neck, there's no cut.

"Lahve!" A voice gasps.

One of his guards charges into the room — a female with pale skin and jet black hair that falls past her shoulders in a straight line — and she approaches the Lahve standing at the window ledge, but does not touch him.

"Do you need a moment?" she says.

He doesn't answer, but I can hear him gulping in the same little sips of air I am. Coughing bellows out of me and I clutch Kane to me and for a moment, I watch the Lahve and feel…*bad* for him.

He died too when he looked through me.

Only now, here, among the living, he has no ability to receive comfort.

He straightens and turns and he's again this *presence,* that ethereal being. He looks down at me and swallows many times. His hand flinches as he touches his throat.

"Follow my breaths," he tells me.

I don't dare disobey and between his calm and Kane's gentle hands on my hair, I finally find something like normalcy.

Kane gently coaxes me into a seated position and, when I'm finally vertical, takes my jaw between his hands and tilts it left and right, inspecting my neck for damage.

"She slit our throats," I tell him.

Kane's eyes flare and he inspects my skin with his fingers, finding it uninterrupted.

"Not *really,*" I say, pushing his hand away. I shake my head and struggle up to standing. I don't quite make it and sink back down on the couch while Tasha appears with a glass of water in front of me.

She hands one to the Lahve as well who surprises me by taking it. He drinks. I drink. We watch each other drink.

Kane says, "I don't want you reaching out to Elise, again."

"You know," I say, lowering my glass and breathing hard around it, "you're going to have to stop being so paranoid one of these days."

He doesn't smile. He sits down on the coffee table where the Lahve sat moments before and his fingers continue moving across my face as if searching for seams.

"Only when I figure out how to put a force field around you." His lips brush my forehead and his warmth eclipses mine. "Are you sure you're alright?"

"Yeah. I'm fine. I just..." My gaze switches away from Kane's face, past Mikey and Tasha and two more guards who have joined the first.

"That was crazy," I say on a laugh and I'm rewarded when the Lahve smiles with just one edge of his too-human mouth.

"Yes, it was."

"It really felt like she was killing me. Killing us. You felt it too?"

He bows his head forward. "All of it."

"How did she do that?"

"She is a powerful female, and now she knows where we are, so we need to move."

"But we don't know where she is," I say, but the moment I say it, my face scrunches up and my mind flashes and I remember all the words I shouted when I was her.

"Shit!" I jump to my feet, then fall into Kane's arms when all the blood rushes to my head at once. "I do know where she is. It worked."

"It did."

"So where is she?" Mikey says, looking like a menace with twin handguns already strapped to his either hip.

"She's in an apartment building between a...a movie theater and a super tall building with a green...greenish roof. It has a dome on the top." My gaze snaps to the Lahve's and I gasp as he lifts just one eyebrow higher than the other. "Holy fuck. She's in Vancouver. She's in the freaking Diera."

"Yes, she came back," he says slowly.

"But why? What for?" I gasp, so confused.

He smiles again and this time, it's a terrible, terrifying sight. He breathes, "Sistana, she came back for you."

Chapter Twenty-Seven

" "W hat did you tell her?"
"I told her to reveal herself."
"And what did she tell you?"
"That she is not afraid of you," the Lahve told me. *"It is her mistake, just as it was Crestor's."*
"What do you mean?"
"Underestimating you."

We drive in silence while I turn the Lahve's words over in my mind. Kane sits beside me, two guards in the front, two guards in the back. To my left, Sandra holds a bright blue box in her lap. She clutches it like a first-time father might hold a newborn.

I try to make conversation, but all the words are lodged deep in my lungs. Vocabulary ceases to exist as the bright green signs beckon us forward. Vancouver, B.C. eighty-five miles, then thirty-four, then suddenly six.

Bienvenue à and *welcome to* are stacked on top of faded ivory lettering that reads, 'VANCOUVER!'

We drive into the city limits and Kane has to remind me to breathe — twice — before we take the next left and pull onto West Pender Street.

West Pender and Abbott. Those are the cross-streets that I remember from a memory that isn't mine, but belongs to someone else.

Someone who wants to kill me. Or, at best, torture me and use me as leverage.

I inhale sharply and Kane asks me what's wrong. "I can feel her," I answer, clutching his hand when he offers it. "I couldn't before."

Kane nods solemnly and ducks his head, staring out of the window. "Good. Then she's still here. She wants to make her presence known to us."

"That's a good thing?"

He doesn't respond. We drive down the narrow city streets, and I imagine that at some point they had been broad. Now nature has overrun the city, brambles and overgrown tree roots preventing us from moving forward in places.

Where the debris can be cleared, it is, and where it can't we find alternate paths around.

We're a total of six huge SUVs and four pickup trucks. Seems like overkill for one woman...but I've been thinking about what the Lahve said and I know that the reverse should also be true.

We can't underestimate her either.

Power lines and bus cables drip from old utility poles, dangling in the wind. A building with a circular satellite tower passes on our left. It looks like the Space Needle I saw in Seattle.

Salt wounds heal, but they leave scars.

I can feel them on my back now, like nightmares glowing on my flesh, bright and luminous and a frightening reminder of all the places I have been. I get the feeling that we're nearing some kind of end when we pass by the broken sign for the Ramada — the RA and the final A are missing. I smirk at the remaining letters.

It's all gone mad, hasn't it? Me sitting with the enemy going to kill a shared one.

The enemy sitting with me going to kill one of his own because of the risk it places to me.

The love.

The car slows, and it isn't just because of the fallen tree branches that crunch beneath the tires, or on a cause of the roots as thick as steel that disrupt the asphalt.

"The movie theater." The one from my memories. From her memories.

Cineplex Odeon passes on our left. Its bottom floor has been decimated, windows all broken so that their frames hang like open mouths with shattered glass shards for teeth. But we slow nonetheless, because just across the street is our final destination: the apartment building.

It's abutted by the tower with the green dome on top. The air is cold when the car door opens and I shudder looking up, up, up. There's something menacing about that tower, even though it's the apartment building we're after.

Maybe when we're done here, we can just torch the whole block. Just for fun, you know?

Ducking my head, I glance past Sandra out of the window, scanning the apartment building in search of signs of life. I don't see any, but I feel them. One strong one that absolutely refuses to die. She isn't going down without a fight.

I guess she read the same rule book I did.

"Where the hell do you think you're going?" I grab Kane's arm when he starts to get out of the car, and feel the muscles in his bicep bulge beneath my hand.

His gaze is apologetic, though his words are pure heat, giving little in the way of concession. "I have to do this."

"We agreed that we would *both* stay in the car. Or did you lie to me again?"

"I never agreed to that," he says, and I think back to the whispered promises me made me while he was between my thighs, milking me for every ounce of pleasure he could.

Whatever he thinks he said, I heard something else.

"You're being an ass again. She could kill you."

The Lahve's guards have already exited the car and the trunk is open. I can hear them whispering in alien as they distribute weapons.

Kane's name is called, followed by, "Notare, we must go now. Her guards are on the move."

Kane nods, sparing them a glance over the backseat. He opens his door and I hit him as hard as I can in the thigh.

"You're going to get yourself killed."

When he dives back into the car, coiling his thick fingers through my hair and crushing his mouth to mine, his kiss is full of desperation. He knows I'm right. I can feel the thrumming of his heart beneath my bulletproof vest and I can barely breathe.

"Why are you doing this?" I gasp when he pulls back.

"Because I have to be sure."

"Have to be sure of what?"

"That she dies. Every second she's alive is a risk to the only thing I can't live without." His gaze flares and heats and I grab his bullet proof vest at the collar. I wrench him into me and bite his lower lip hard enough to draw blood.

I lick a droplet away greedily and he shudders in my arms.

"Come back to me. Or else."

He smiles at me very slightly while the wind whips his hair across his forehead in clean black lines. "For you, always." He begins to shut the car door, but hesitates and lifts a single brow. "I don't need to repeat myself, do I?"

I roll my eyes. "What trouble could I possibly get into staying here in the car?"

He narrows his eyes. "That wasn't what was promised."

I remember rolling him over and straddling his hips. Whatever he thinks I said, he must have heard something else.

"If you're in trouble I'll know."

"Abel," he growls.

"You're *coming* back. Even if I have to reach through the gates of hell and pull you out myself."

"Abel…"

"Notare," the Lahve's voice calls over the whipping wind.

I grab the car door handle and shut it between us. There's nothing left to say.

Kane glares at me through the tinted windows, but he doesn't try to argue with me.

The locks all click into place a moment later and half a dozen guards take up posts around the outside of the SUV. Beside me, Sandra sucks in a breath through her teeth. Her fingers are white around the edges of the box, but I don't offer her any encouragement.

Instead, I watch a line of guards move down the road, to the apartment building. Mikey, Kane and the Lahve jog after them in a second wave along with other guards.

The Lahve looks completely absurd in his suit and cane. Feels like he should have a top-hat or something. I snort at the image and Sandra jumps in her seat.

"Sorry," I whisper.

"None needed. Just jittery."

I nod. "Same."

This time, she snorts. "You hide it well."

"Saltlands isn't a place for nerves."

"This isn't Seattle," she tells me, but she's wrong.

I shake my head and touch the window. "Yes, it is. She brought it with her."

And even though another dozen guards hug tight to the Lahve, Kane and Mikey's backs, it still doesn't feel like enough. It feels, rather, like there's a picture in front of me, but it's turned down at one corner. There's something there and it's important, I just can't see it…

What don't you want me to see, Elise?

Low, imagined laughter floats through my thoughts as the contingent of warriors enter the apartment.

We wait.

The moments that follow drag on and I count the seconds in my head until I lose count and have to start over again. I do this a few times, the silence really grating. Sandra's breath sounds so loud. Or maybe it's mine. Or maybe it's someone else's.

I flex my one good ear forward, trying to hear... something. For now silence a good thing. Silence means no shots. No shots mean no deaths. I can track the pressure of Kane's pulse in my own wrist, though the other heartbeat that should exist right along there with it has flat lined again. But, like the stillness of the outside world beyond these windows, it feels forced.

I press my fingers to the cool windowpane and watch the moisture of my fingers form condensation against the glass. I breathe, and in the fog, draw a flower.

Sandra says my name, but her voice sounds like she's talking through water. Turning to face her, I feel my face scrunch up when I see that she's still sitting right next to me.

Her eyebrows knit together over her nose and she touches my arm. I can see her fingers on my skin but I feel nothing.

"Are you ready to watch him die, Sistana?"

The voice *consumes* me.

It's everything. Every sense. Every thought. Every feel.

I tighten, but I can't *find* her. I can't react. I can't move. It's like she reached in through the roof of the car and slipped into my skin without my permission.

Sandra's fingers press against my jugular, trying to get a pulse. Can she feel it? That third heartbeat pounding like a battering ram throughout my whole body?

Where did Elise go? Where was she before?

"What do you want?" I blurt out loud, unsure how she managed to communicate in intention, rather than in breath. She seems to be able to hear me nonetheless. Where is she?

"I want what everyone wants, little Sistana. I just want it more," Notare Elise's voice whispers through my thoughts, consuming me like a disease that corrupts the body from within. *"Immortality."*

I blink and see the city skyline, the grey looming so ominously above it, a blackened concrete building and a suite of cars parked just beside it. *Our* cars, from above. The top of the apartment building.

She can't be inside if she's looking down.

"So very clever you are, Sistana." Her voice fades to laughter and my hands fumble with the blocky yellow phone tucked into the back of the front seat.

I grab it and press the speaker button since it only connects to one other number.

"She's in the tower. Up in the green dome," I tell Kane on the other end of the line, but there's no answer. "Get out of the apartment. Get out of there!"

Sandra is panicking and the guards on the other side of the car door are shifting restlessly now. I bang on the window and a guard — the female with the dark hair from earlier — opens it just a crack.

"Why aren't they answering?" I shout.

"Why do you think? He's already with me. Why don't you join us, Sistana?"

Elise's voice grips my thoughts and makes it hard to think. I see images of Kane and he's hurting, but I don't know what's real. I picture his blood dripping into a drain… but that was from before. What's real? What's happening?

"She has Kane." Or she's pretending she does. "It could be a trap," I tell the guard. "But I'm sure of one thing. She's *not* in that apartment. She's in the building next to it. We need to go there and get her before she does something…"

And I can feel her doing something.

I just don't know what.

"If you're not going to do anything, then I am," I shout.

"I was ordered not to allow you to leave your vehicle, Sistana."

"And as your Sistana, I command you to open the door."

After a moment of uncertainty, the Other wrenches open the door and I stumble out into the cold. "She's up to something," I tell her and Far, who looms up behind her, looking concerned.

"You cannot trust what she tells you," the female says.

Far counters, "How much can be falsified through the blood bond, Laiya? I hear nothing from our guards when I reach out to them."

"We have orders to keep the Sistana safe, Far," the one called Laiya answers, but if she says anymore than that, I don't hear it.

I'm falling down, down, down until I'm hovering inches above my head.

I can see me up close even though I'm standing up above in the green dome, so far away.

I blink and then there's a second image. I'm back in that glass and concrete room again, only this time I'm focused on the wiring covering the ceiling, hard beige bricks being connected to timers and triggers and I understand. Finally.

"She wants me alone," I say, lurching out of Elise's mind. Out of her many, many wants.

"She wants me alone or she'll bring the building down on all of them. She wired the whole thing with explosives."

"Good girl," she whispers to me alone.

I glance up the length of the old building again, noting how it's managed to withstand the elements far better than the apartment next to it. The younger, newer, modern apartment.

Of course she'd want to finish things here.

"Now come and finish this."

"We should send someone in for the others," Laiya says.

I shake my head. "We don't have that kind of time and there are enough of us out here to be able to take her into custody. Aren't there?"

Inside, I feel rather than hear, as Elise laughs.

Laiya looks at Far. Far looks at me.

"Morithan," he barks and another guard jogs over to him. "Alert the Lahve that we have gone for Elise. The rest of you, prepare for war." As Morithan takes off, Far returns his gaze to me and as it settles, I feel sure.

We're going to take her ass down. I grin as the laughter dies in me.

"We look to you, Sistana," he says.

I reach, not for the gun strapped to my chest, but to Diego's knife in my pocket. I wish I had Kane's sword, but last I saw, Mikey had it. The dagger'll do for now.

I look at the aliens — the team — before me and nod once. "I guess we go through the front doors, then."

I look back at Sandra. "Stay here," I tell her. "And if Kane comes back, tell him where I went."

She nods, looking terrified, and I'm surprised when the female called Laiya unstraps one of the handguns on her belt and hands it to Sandra. "Take this," she says. "Stay safe."

Sandra's cheeks darken, her eyes widen, but she still nods.

I slam the car door shut and take off at a light jog, the pounding of feet echoing behind me. They sound like thunder, moving in unison in a way I find both soothing and frightening.

The glass doors are broken in and nip at my skin as I step through the open frame. A fire has claimed the lobby, though a single sign still hangs on the scorched walls. I'm still able to make out the words *Vancouver Sun Tower* in blackened flowery lettering covering the back wall.

"She's near the top floor. I can feel her." She's waiting. "We'll take the stairs."

When I take a step forward, Laiya pulls me back with a curt apology and heads towards the heavy wooden door first. Swinging her automatic rifle around, she places her hand on the knob. Black comes off on her fingers when she pulls it open, revealing bronze.

We step into a hollow stairwell, and a spiral staircase made of textured white marble leads in only one direction. Up. Black fissures run through it like life lines and I trace the crisscross patterns they make as we ascend.

We climb side-by-side until we reach the fourth floor and my legs start to tire and she starts to pull ahead.

She whistles through her front teeth and six of the twelve Others with us now surge ahead of me while the rest form a line at my back. When we take the next curve, I look back and see that Far and another male are actually climbing backwards, their hands on the triggers, ready.

They don't use them, though. Because no one attacks. In fact, the silence is pervasive, all but for the sounds of our boots on the dusty marble. The fire made it inside of the stairwell, and though the walls are charred, nothing burned but bodies. It must have happened a long time ago, because the smell is gone and all that remains is the dust they left behind.

We're on the fourteenth floor and my thighs are burning with the effort of keeping up when Laiya whistles again and all the soldiers around me come to an immediate stop. Must be another six or seven floors to go. We're most of the way there.

And then Laiya and Far and the soldiers at the top and bottom of the stairs turn in unison to face the doors in front of them. They start shooting just as the first bodies barrel through the wood and the abruptness of the attack and the roaring sound of bullets blazing leaves me stunned.

Laiya returns to my side while soldiers battle on the tenth floor and the twelfth.

Eleven.

This was Kane's floor.

And that's the last thought I have before the door in front of me flies open.

A soldier fires, but Laiya throws her body in front of mine and withdraws a short sword. In one swift motion, she decapitates the female warrior in front of her.

Far, below, shouts another order, which Laiya repeats and suddenly we're moving again, pushing and fighting our way up.

I try to find a target, but I'm a weak shot, and there are too many friendlies between me and the ones we're fighting. The Lahve's guards are also a formidable force. Shell casings twinkle against the marble far, far below as Laiya pushes me up, up, up.

I'm half-falling, half-walking. The heat from so many bodies is suffocating. When a door flies open to my right, the Other standing there levels her gun at my chest. I point my gun at her head and fire, taking the top half of it off before she manages to do whatever it was she was going to do.

She wasn't aiming for me, though. None of them are.

They want me alive.

Laiya grabs my arm. "Sistana, we cannot rise higher. There are too many of them."

She shoves me through the rusted metal door marked by blood spray and a faded number fifteen without waiting for my consent, and I stumble out onto hard concrete. In addition to Laiya, three Others from our side follow me.

Planting my feet firmly, I pivot, waiting for the first assault, but this floor is empty — under renovation, perhaps, and never completed. Now it's just desolate, full of an eerie silence that's broken up only by the sounds of the battle raging in the stairwell.

I can tell by the expression on Laiya's face as she moves past me that she's just as apprehensive as I am. Turning to face the Others that have followed us onto the empty floor, she rattles off a command and all four of them close in around me.

The door slams in its frame as bodies fall against it. Gunshots ring muted through the walls, and at the same time, a small earthquake shakes the foundations of the building.

"Kane," I breathe, taking off at a sprint to the east-facing windows, Laiya and the others holding that impenetrable square around me.

I press my face to the glass as I stare, horrified, at the demolition job happening next door. She said she wouldn't... if I came alone.

Grief grips my chest as chunks of concrete fly. The whole building collapses in its center, forming a black hole that sucks in everything. Would they have survived?

I feel Kane still there, but maybe I'm confused. Maybe it's Elise again trying to torment me...

"Sistana, do not panic," Laiya breathes into my ear. "Look."

She points towards the street and a subtle movement catches my eye. Black-clad guards move swiftly towards the tower. They hug the sides of the buildings, sticking to the shadows until they become mere shadows themselves.

"And there, Your Grace."

She points and I follow the line her finger creates. The Lahve in his stupid tweed suit is climbing in through one of the ground floor windows, and a swell of hope fills my chest when I see Kane with him. I smile down at him while the apartment building finally settles in a thick pall of dust and smoke. Looks like they were warned in time. Looks like Elise's leverage no longer exists.

"We should wait for them here, Sistana, before seeking out Notare Elise."

"It's a little late for that, don't you think?"

I blink and see me tucked safely within a ring of guards. I see my face, blood spatter on my cheek, gun clutched in my fist.

I blink and see her standing in the center of the empty room, dusty tarp billowing at her back like a curtain. She steps through it with her arms crossed wearing a dark and lovely blue.

Wordlessly, the guards create a triangle around me. Only Laiya remains at my side, gun trained on the Notare's chest, which glows so subtly I almost can't see it.

"You have something that belongs to me," she says, gaze locking with mine and making me feel small and stupid. She planned for this. Every move.

I knew that and I walked into it with more confidence than I had. Maybe I did underestimate her. Or maybe I overestimated me and the Lahve and Kane and everybody.

My mouth is dry but my hands are warm. I pull out Diego's dagger and hold it in my free hand. Her gaze flashes to it and she grins.

"You here to arrest me all by yourself, Sistana?"

"Yeah."

"Interesting."

"Yeah, I think so too. You ready to give up, yet?"

She actually manages to look surprised by that question. Surprised and annoyed. "You are a stupid human."

"Yeah. Definitely. But I've got your blood in me and rights to all your lands." Her face hardens. Her eyes narrow. "So if you want your blood back, you better come and get it."

Elise's chest pulses once with light before it fades and she moves and the guards begin firing as one.

I don't even get a shot off before Laiya grabs me and runs. The other guards stay behind — not to win, but to give us time. They're fighting though, holding their ground. I hear Elise hiss as bullets hit her stomach. She surges forward and a guard ends up fighting her hand-to-hand. The female falls and Elise reaches down and yanks her head off her neck while another guard stabs her in the back.

The door to this floor flies open and I'm shocked and thrilled to see Far standing there, Others I recognize behind him.

They start firing too, and soon Elise is surrounded.

But she's laughing. "Is this all you've got, Lahve?" she screeches, but I can't hear his answer if he gives one.

Instead, Laiya has my arm. She's pulling me across the room to the far wall and pushing me through the shattered opening of a window. I think she's killed me until my feet hit the unsteady foundation of a fire escape.

Holy freaking frick.

We're high up.

The tree house I fell from with Drago was nothing compared to this. This fall won't kill me, it'll *eviscerate* me. There won't be anything left but mush and blood.

I take an unsteady step down, but Laiya grabs me and shoves me up. "Up, Sistana." Her body presses against mine as she climbs after me, forcing me to go the opposite direction that all my instincts scream to move.

"Up?" I shout, but I've got no other choice with her boxing me in. "Up!"

Wind whips its ferocious fingers through the fabric of my shirt, though it doesn't manage to pierce my bulletproof vest. The vest insulates my heat and, with my adrenaline thickening the blood in my veins, I've begun to sweat. My feet hit the rusted stairs, but Laiya's still grabbing the back of my vest and shoving.

"Apologies, Sistana," she says, though she doesn't mean it at all.

"Don't think you can outrun your fate, little Sistana!" Elise's voice echoes up from three floors below.

My toe catches the bottom slat of the next step and I stumble while behind me gunfire reigns. I can feel Laiya's back press against mine as she urges me upwards until there's nowhere left to go. We've reached the dome and these stupid stairs just *stop* at a small, square window.

I grab hold of the open frame and am shocked that what I thought was a copper dome is actually just painted concrete. A prop masking something perfectly ordinary.

I smile just a little as hope flowers in my stomach. *Fitting that it should end here for her.*

"Move!"

I wriggle into the dome and Laiya falls into the space after me. Taller than I am, she has to duck low to avoid hitting her head on the yellow beams that crisscross overhead. Above us are a series of suspended metal walkways and in front of us is a bunch of industrial equipment. Large metal squares with cranks and dials and buttons, and beyond them a metal panel in the ground. Even though elevators haven't functioned in a decade, we've found the elevator room.

"Sistana, up." Laiya points to the metal stairs leading up to the very top of the dome.

I don't get this as an exit strategy, but I don't question her and move onto the scaffolding. I climb up the ladder and am halfway there when I feel it. No — when I smell it.

Her perfume.

"Laiya, behind you!"

Elise must have climbed around the dome like a spider because she's coming in through the oculus *behind* Laiya. I point and fire and even though I miss, the split second distraction is enough to pull Laiya — and the barrel of her gun — around.

She fires, missing nine times out of ten. The shot that meets its mark hits Elise in the leg and she staggers but only for a step. She reaches Laiya before I can get my second round off, and grabs her by the neck.

Laiya's body looks far too much like Becks's did as Elise throws her across the room and into the equipment against the far wall. She advances on Laiya while Laiya struggles to drag what looks like a shattered femur beneath her, and punches her fist through Laiya's stomach.

"No!" The word is mine, and I fire until my clip is empty, hitting Elise in the back twice. The force is enough to drop her to one knee, and she roars as she flips her hair back and turns to face me.

Sensing her intention, I stagger backwards as she jumps up onto the scaffolding in front of me. I fire, but my clip is empty. I chuck the gun at her and it hits her in the forehead and she gapes at me, like she's really shocked.

"Stupid human," she seethes.

I brandish my dagger at her and prepare for the end.

She raises one clawed hand, but it never falls, because as she focuses on me, a body slams into Elise sideways and with enough force to rip through the metal railings on either side of this narrow walkway.

Elise screeches as she plummets off of the scaffolding and lands at Laiya's side, Kane straddling her waist. He has his hands on her throat and I whoop with glee, but Elise isn't down like I'd hoped.

She releases a shriek and grabs Kane by the right shoulder and hip. She throws him into the concrete wall, which cracks dangerously beneath him.

She advances on him, but he's got blood on his mouth and determination in his eyes. He punches. She ducks. He kicks, nailing her in the chest and throwing her off her feet and into metal panel covering the elevator shaft. It buckles and starts to cave, but she manages to scramble off of it just before it gives completely.

It takes forever for the crash below and in that time, Elise staggers back to her feet. She dusts off her pants and sneers, "I was wondering how long it would take you to come for your queen. What did you do, scale the outside of the building?"

Kane doesn't contradict her. Nor does his gaze leave her face. As he rises to standing, he doesn't so much as blink.

"Very well, then. I can assume that reinforcements aren't far behind, giving me little time to savor this moment. Are you going to attack or should I?" She wipes the back of her wrist across her mouth, the crimson standing out vibrantly against her porcelain skin.

"Go up," Kane says, and it takes me a moment to realize he's talking to me as the two predators begin circling each other in that small, crowded space.

"Fuck that," I say, nearly shaking with rage. "I'm not leaving you alone with this crazy bitch."

"And I wasn't asking. I can't fight if I'm concerned for your life. You being here is a risk to us both." I've only ever heard Kane's voice like this once before. When we were in that cave and he was begging Mikey to save my life over his. Furious, I don't delay. I know we only have seconds as Elise's lips curl up.

She watches me run across the scaffolding, and as I reach the ladder, coos, "Fly, little bird, fly."

"Go!" Kane's voice is murderous and a very potent rage tickles the backs of my palms as I stow my dagger and climb the ladder up through a small opening in the concrete that leads into an even smaller concrete room, just big enough for a body or two.

Like mine and Mikey's.

I throw my arms around his neck and he hugs me back and lifts me all the way into the cupola. "Sorry I didn't give you this," he whispers against my throat at the same time that he presses my sword into my hand.

I zip Diego's dagger back into my pocket as I smile down at the sword, like I'm revisiting a familiar friend. "Thank frick. We have to go back and help him…"

He grabs my arm and shakes his head. He presses a single finger to his lips, then points that finger down. I follow the line it makes past the scaffolding, past Kane, past Elise to the broken opening of the elevator shaft just as the Lahve climbs through it.

He moves so quietly, I can't hear him at all. I wonder if the others can, but when Elise keeps her attention fixed on Kane, I feel the most overwhelming relief.

Mikey covers my mouth with my hand and pulls a pad out of his pocket. On it, I see words scribbled.

The Lahve planned it this way. The only ones who knew were Laiya, Far and him.

Bastard.

I laugh against his palm while tears prick the backs of my eyes. I remind myself that we are still in the Saltlands, so tears aren't yet allowed. But they feel imminent.

Just like the end.

He flips to the next page.

We never even went into that apartment building. The Lahve knew she'd try to get you alone and was waiting. Everything else was just a diversion. Not even Kane knew. And yes, he's pissed. I am too.

It suddenly feels like we're all pawns in an elaborate game of chess only the Lahve and Elise are playing. I shake my head, not caring at all if it means we win.

He flips to the next and final sheet.

He needed her to think she had the upper hand in order to beat her.

I nod, but as I listen to the silence radiating up from below, I can't help but think, How can we be sure that she doesn't?

We lower to our bellies now so we can peer out at the scene below and I pump my fist secretly as the Lahve launches himself at Elise in the same instant that she launches herself at Kane.

He reaches her first and tackles her to the far wall and a pained scream wrenches out of her.

"It's over, Notare," the Lahve says, easily holding her in place. "Yield."

She starts to thrash and cry and shriek and…and laugh.

She's laughing now and the sound is blood curdling. "Oh Lahve, I will admit, you did surprise me there. But did you truly think I wouldn't come with surprises of my own? Or that I would let you take me breathing?"

The floor beneath my belly begins to shake and I glance up at Mikey to see if he feels the same thing. His gaze meets mine and suddenly, he's got me in his grip, trying to wrap his whole body around me.

"Fuck!" He screams and it seems like he knows what's happening better than I do, because I'm still surprised when the concrete beneath our bodies is wrenched out from beneath us.

Smoke rises up and pulls me down into the elevator room below. I don't know what I hit, but it hurts *almost* as much as the concrete that falls onto my face and chest and tries to bury me alive.

Mikey's shouts are muffled and his arms are on my arms, but I'm being lifted through the rubble away from him. My whole body is in motion and I yelp in pain as I'm dragged from the aftermath by the hair.

I blink and gasp.

The entire roof of the dome has been blown open, bits and pieces of the cupola scattered in the wind. I'm freezing, even crushed against the warmth of a body...and it isn't Kane's...

"You think I didn't come with my own surprises?" Elise roars again.

She's got blood on her mouth and her right arm hangs at her side at the wrong angle. She keeps me trapped against her chest with her one good arm. Her hand cups my throat. She supports my entire weight as she edges back, my boots dragging limply against the rubble.

What happened?

Mikey roars, though he's buried in debris up to the waist. Most of the elevator room is too. Only Elise managed to escape it. She knew where to stand. Where to go. Where to duck.

The others didn't.

Kane is wedged between two huge machines. His eyes lock on me as he tries to free his legs from a mass of metal, and his eyes are screaming.

The Lahve stands from underneath some scaffolding that managed to stay put. He's got crimson on his knuckles but is otherwise untouched. He rises to his full height still holding his cane. He twists the handle and removes a thin sword, which he points at Elise.

"Elise, unhand the Sistana." The inflection he carries suggests the first hint of emotion I've heard from him. Irritation. Maybe also surprise.

Elise staggers to the left, edging her body behind some of the equipment, closer to where Laiya lies crumpled in half, knees tucked to her chest, black hair frayed.

She's still alive, though.

Her face tilts up to mine and I wonder if Elise notices the way her slanted eyes watch us with hate and promises of revenge.

I meet her gaze and hold it and without words, I try to say, *Take it.*

The dagger's still in my pocket, but I struggle with the zipper that I need to open to free it while Elise coils herself around me. She presses her face close to mine, silken tresses tickling my cheek as she uses me like a shield.

"That doesn't seem like a fair deal to me," she says, licking a line up my throat that makes me shudder. "I'm going to need something in return."

Kane roars, freeing himself from the metal caging him and staggering to Mikey's side. He slips his shoulder beneath Mikey's armpit and hauls him free of the rubble. Both of them are panting now.

"Release her and I will give you what it is you seek…"

The Lahve hisses in overlapping notes though when he speaks, his tone is even again. Even, but *loud*, like he's talking through a speaker.

"You dare make requests of the Notare? You dare blackmail me? You dare hold the Sistana captive? You will die for your crimes, Elise."

Elise's pitch rises to a shriek. "For all your glory, you cannot touch me! You are *just* the Lahve. I am a Notare. You do not hold the light…"

The Lahve tips the point of his blade to Elise's chest, only just visible around mine. I crane my neck so I can look down, but over the red and white swell of Elise's forearm, I don't see anything. Nothing at all.

And that's the point.

"Neither do you, Elise."

Elise's light is gone.

Elise screams and as she screams, her hold on me lets up just the inch I needed to reach my pocket, free the dagger, and toss it into Laiya's waiting fingers.

She jolts up without hesitating and plunges the dagger into Elise's back.

Elise falls forward, voice cutting off with an abrupt gurgle. She roars and it's a piercing blood-curdling sound that's equal parts maniacal, hysterical, and defeated.

Her hands clench around my arms and I'm suddenly sailing through the air. My shoulder hits a pile of concrete, spinning me around, but I don't stop.

My fingers can't seem to catch on anything as I skate over the dusty floor, which abruptly gives out.

Mikey yells. "No!"

Kane charges towards me.

The Lahve has Elise's hands pinned behind her back, her body pressed flush to what's left of the concrete wall. His orange eyes widen as they meet mine and without knowing him at all, I'm sure he's never been so surprised as this.

That can't be good.

I'm reaching up. Kane's so close to me now. His fingers touch my fingers but the slippery blood lubricates the contact between our hands. Our palms glance off of one another and then Kane's shouting and I'm falling backwards through the empty space of the elevator shaft.

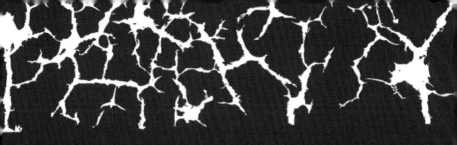

Chapter Twenty-Eight

I'm still falling.

It takes longer than it should.

Because while I fall, I panic, imagining what it'll feel like when I reach the bottom and what it'll sound like to Kane all the way up there at the top.

I'm pretty sure he wanted to jump after me, but I saw Mikey's body tackle him across the opening shortly after I started to fall.

Kane is screaming as if mortally wounded and Mikey is shouting and the Lahve is speaking and Elise is laughing until all at once, her laughter is cut short. A scream echoes down the hole that's taken me. Her scream. She sounds like she's in pain and a fleeting smile moves me.

One of the heartbeats I carried fades while the other continues to beat brutally in my ribcage willing *something* to happen that can't happen anymore. Because when I hit the bottom, there's no coming back.

It's just a split instant of pain. A jolt to the back of my head. My eyes close. My heartbeat jolts to a stop, and the last thing I feel is the will of a stronger heart.

And then not even that.

I die.

Almost…

Chapter Twenty-Nine

Waking up after I die is strange, and not just because I do. It's because of the smell. Blood and perfume.

My stomach lurches, but I don't retch. Instead, I just lay there, idling at the crossroads of life and death.

God?

There's wood at my back and against the outside of my arms that splinters my skin when I shift against it. My mind flutters and I recall some of my life's final events. In them, I was wearing a bullet proof vest and a shirt — two things I'm not wearing now — though I can feel the fabric of the same pants scratch my legs when pain shoots through them.

It ebbs and flows in time with the weird energy blowing through my bones like breath through a flute. I definitely feel like I'm being played.

For a fool, likely.

Because I'm *pretty* sure I died, and I'm a hundred percent sure that this is a coffin.

Fucking fantastic.

I wonder if they buried me alive, until I realize that doesn't make sense. I can't be buried when there's light and there *is* light. An intense radiance illuminates everything — the surface of the box inches away from my nose, the bloody fingerprints on the insides of the wood where hands closed the lid, sealing me in.

But why would they have left a light in here if they thought I was dead?

God? I ask myself again. But God doesn't answer either.

Instead, I look down, trying to root out the source of the light and gasp.

"Holy freaking crap."

The light is *me*. Am I on fire? No. There's warmth but it's the good kind, the bathtub kind. Not the Trocker kind. And there's light, but it's not the blinding kind that filtered in through the helicopter windows.

This light is like Kane's light, maybe even stronger. It blazes all the way across my chest, from nipple to nipple, collar bone to collar bone, all the way down to my ribs. coming from me.

I jolt back like I'll try to get away from it, but my feet kick the wood above me and I realize they're bare again when I stub my toe.

"Fuck!" I can't even move my fists up to touch my chest and investigate the light because the space is too narrow. "Fuck! Get me the fuck out of here!"

All at once my body slams into the wooden wall to my left. I hadn't realized I'd been in motion up until that point, but the stillness overtakes me as I keep kicking and fighting against my cage.

Sounds soon start to become more distinct. Voices are talking nearby and one's screaming louder than the rest. A female voice. I recognize it as Tasha seconds before talons dig through the center of the coffin, shredding the wood at the expense of slim fingers and manicured nails.

I see her face as she pulls the last board away. Her eyes are red like she's been crying, but right now she just looks stunned. She's staring at my chest.

"Howisthispossible…" The sentence comes out as a single word on her breath.

A voice behind her shouts, "Is it true? It can't be. She's dead!"

Tasha is immobile, and gargoyle isn't her best look. Clearing my throat, I have to swallow a couple times in order to remember how to talk.

"Get me the fuck out of this box!" I shout.

"Abel," she blurts, coming forward, but she seems hesitant to touch me. "Are you sure it's…safe to move you?"

"I don't want to be in here anymore. It's creepy. Get me out."

She grabs me and hauls me up into a seated position, and the moment I'm upright, I'm overwhelmed by the scent of clean air as much as I am by the reaction of so many beings — human and Other alike.

Calvin shouts my name, Sandra begins to sob uncontrollably, and the guards standing just behind them all take to one knee. They're standing beyond the edge of the open trunk, car tilted askew making it look like we've run off the highway or *been run* off the highway.

My legs fumble for the ground and I have a hard time walking for the first few seconds. Tasha holds my hand as I stretch out my legs and plant my bare feet on the cracked asphalt. I expect to feel chill in just a pair of pants, but all I feel is warmth.

"Stop that," I snap when I notice that even Calvin and Sandra are kneeling now. "Get up!"

They amble to their feet and I hug Sandra first, then Tasha, then go to Calvin, but he just stares at my chest — no, at my tits.

"Um…" He shoves his hand between us and I can't help it. I laugh and give his hand a shake.

"Where is everyone? Where's Kane?" I say, looking down the road towards the next SUV, but there's only the one.

Tasha's lips fumble and she seems to struggle to make sound as wind pulls her hair across her neck. "Notare," she says, as if testing the word on her tongue like a beginner taking a stab at a foreign language.

"You are Notare." This time she sounds sure, but I don't get how she can be.

"I...Notare? What? Where's Kane."

"You are a Notare now. You have the Tare," she says, voice getting louder and louder.

Sandra is either laughing or crying or both and Calvin's started clapping now. A couple of the other guards clap too, as if unsure about how to handle this.

Well, me too.

"Holy fuck," Calvin shouts, "Abel, how the fuck? We all watched you die. You were dead for more than three hours. You died...and now you're...you're a...I need to sit."

Calvin starts to sink down, but Tasha grabs his arm. "No time for that. We need to get you to Kane."

"Yeah. Where is he?" I say while she shoves me into the front seat of the SUV and gets behind the wheel. Sandra doesn't even have her door closed before she takes off, going zero to sixty in seconds.

The tires squeal. She keeps glancing over at me frantically.

"What happened, Tasha?"

I say, breathing hard as I try to keep my tits covered. Maybe some of the brightness, too. It doesn't help. I need a shirt. Or maybe a parka. The whole car is filled with my glow.

Tasha licks her lips and adjusts her rearview mirror so she can see me better. "You died and Kane killed Elise. The Council is trying to determine how to proceed. We haven't had murders like this between Notare in recorded history. But you get a vote, no matter what they decide."

She looks again to my chest. The light pulsates in time with my heartbeat, though I no longer feel Kane's.

I knead the skin of my pectoral and try to keep my voice steady as I say, "Why can't I feel him anymore? Is he okay?"

Tasha shudders. "He most certainly is not okay. He loves you and you died today. Blood bonds can be broken through death. And you died today," she repeats, "you died." She shakes her head and a smile plays out across her lips. "How many angels watch over you, Notare?"

We drive past that faded blue sign demarcating the entrance to Vancouver, race through the city block Elise leveled, and as we pass by that concrete tower, I think of Elise.

She spent hundreds of years trying to discover the key to Tare and died without knowing that she got something right.

How? I don't know. And I don't need to. I'm just a human with a serious mortality problem, but a knack for coming back.

The tires squeal as Tasha brings the car to a stop in front of a low building that might have, at one point, been a library. Calvin is outside wrenching my door open and pulling me out into the grey.

Tasha grabs my hand as we climb the concrete steps to meet a row of guards who don't even notice me. "Only Notare and the Lahve are permitted from this point forth," one of the guards says.

Tasha straightens, looking a little insane with her hair and clothes all disheveled and my blood covering most of her arms. Still, she's in fine form as she points to my chest. "You *dare* address a Notare like this? I could have you exiled, soldier."

The alien steps back, eyes widening as he finally registers me. I try to cover my chest, but Tasha holds my arms down and prods me in the back so I'm just standing there, tits out, proudly.

"I...you...you're human," the guard shouts as loud as he can.

"Uh yeah," I answer.

Tasha steps within an inch of the guard, eclipsing his height. "Escort the Notare inside at once or I will be forced to report your actions to the Lahve. Go!" She shouts when he still doesn't move.

The poor bastard jumps and bows to me deeply, so the others do, too. Tasha hangs back as they guide me inside through a set of heavy wooden doors, down a hallway lined in books.

The room opens up and there they are — the Council — looking rather unimpressive sitting in the middle of a rather immaculate library at a long wooden table.

Guess people didn't feel the need to loot books when the world ended.

The guard standing beside me clears his throat. "Uhm… I." He tries again while faces begin to turn in our direction. "The Notare is here?"

The Lahve sits at the head of the table facing me. His eyes find me and my chest and I reach up and cup my boobs and step forward.

Kane's sitting at the end of the table closest to me, but he still hasn't turned around. Can he feel my presence? Is he scared to look?

"Kane?" I say and he stiffens like he's been electrocuted.

"No," he whispers. "Kane, it's me."

One of the female Notare rises from her chair, looking lovely and ancient. "This is not possible," she says simply. She presses her fingertips into the table and looks to her left. "Lahve, please. An explanation for this."

He stands and when he moves, his chair thwacks to the floor. He holds his cane stiffly in his hand and takes one meaningful step forward.

"I have none, Morgana. It would appear that Kane's Sistana has been resurrected as Notare."

"That's not possible," Morgana repeats.

One of the males says, "Do you believe her capable of deception?" He smirks. "She does not appear it."

They launch into a debate after that, but Kane still hasn't spoken. I step forward over the faded dark blue carpet. It's hard and my toes curl up into it. I cover my boobs as I walk until I reach the back of his chair.

I place my hands on his either shoulder and I notice that the room has gone completely quiet around us.

Kane jolts under my touch, but his hand still reaches up to touch my fingers. He holds them in front of his eyes, looking at the blood crusted in the grooves of my palm and around my fingernails.

"Kane," I whisper. He shivers visibly and I step up behind him and press my lips to the top of his head. "This isn't a dream," I tell him.

He tilts his face back and up at the same time that he pulls me in front of him and onto his lap. His heat washes over me, and I notice that, at no point, does he look at my chest.

"Leave us," he whispers.

"We came all this way and now you're ordering us to leave?" The other female says. "I don't think so. We need to get to the bottom of this."

"Alright," Kane answers, voice deceptively even. "Then you can stay and watch."

"Watch?"

Kane stands, bringing me with him, throws back his chair and lowers my body down onto the table. He arches over my torso and kisses the light flaring between my breasts before his mouth works to the right, finds my nipple and sucks.

I yelp as excitement flashes through me, far hotter than any embarrassment I might have otherwise felt. I'm with Kane and he's here and we're both alive.

"I want to feel you," I gasp as his mouth moves up to my throat, biting and pulling at the skin there.

"I'm going to open you now," he snarls.

"Please." I grab his hair and yank his head into the curve of my throat, exposing it to him.

"First from me," he moans, and before I know what's happened, he's got a knife in his hand and he's dripping blood from his neck onto me.

The chairs at the table are all being pushed back now. I can hear voices arguing shrilly as Kane lowers his neck to my mouth and I suck while his hands move to the belt at my waist. He breaks it in a single pull and by the time I'm full on the taste of him, he's pushing me back onto the table and pushing himself into me.

He breaks the skin at my neck with his teeth at the same time that his erection plunges past my lower lips and fills me with a fullness that I hope to feel every day for the rest of forever.

His hips smack into mine with abandon and we find our first shared release on the table. But it isn't finished. Not by a long shot.

Kane carries me onto the floor where he turns me onto my hands and knees. I'm shaky and I feel strangely vulnerable in this position, not because I can't look into his eyes, but because of what he can see.

"Kane, are you sure? The scars…" I breathe.

He bends over and I see the glow of his chest burn a slightly darker orange than the lighter yellow of mine. Both just as intense. Both just as angry and consuming and tragic and whole and wonderful and, in this moment, one.

He kisses my shoulder. And then he kisses the back of my neck. And then he spends the next hours kissing every single scar Jack branded me with.

His cock lines up with my opening and as he kisses the side of my face, he enters me and moans my name. "I love your scars, because they are you."

He slows and I sit up and we somehow manage to have sex like this, front-to-back and seated. There are so many positions, so many possibilities for pleasure I would have never even thought of.

"I want you to show me," I whisper as I lean back and lick the blood from his cheek.

Misunderstanding my meaning — or maybe understanding it perfectly — he says, "I will show you everything."

He slides his hand between my breasts and my Tare shines around his fingers like a torch and in my ear, he whispers, "But you will never leave me again, and this is my command to you."

I nod as he picks up speed and the incredible pressure in my body builds as he pounds into me from below and my legs shake, fighting to keep up.

"I don't make a...a very good ghost."

"No, you don't." He barks out a desperate laugh and a moment later, he's releasing into me, and my insides are clamping around him.

I fall forward onto my hands and he falls on top of me, pressing me into the carpet so that I'll definitely get rug burn all over my elbows and knees.

As the tremors fade, I feel his lips on my scars again, then on my back of my head. He tilts my face to his and touches my chest, dragging just the tip of his finger through the light.

"You don't give up."

"Not even when I'm dead." I shake my head and laugh. "I think you're stuck with me, Kane."

"Good," he sighs, hanging his head forward and I get the feeling that I wasn't the only one who came back to life tonight. "Good."

"I love you forever," I say.

"And you might just get that chance, *Notare*..."

Chapter Thirty

Stepping through the front doors of Kane's house, I'm inundated by hugs and gasped congratulations. I guess because the Lahve and the Council voted that I get to keep Elise's lands? Or maybe simply because I lived.

Laiya survived too, and stands next to me now as the foyer fills with people. Well, she stands as next to me as she can given that Kane's still stalking me like a shadow.

Ashlyn bounds out of the hall and wraps me up in a hug that nearly takes me to the ground. I'm breathing hard when she makes room for others.

"Are you alright?" Kane says, for the hundredth time in the past twenty minutes.

I roll my eyes. "Feeling better than the average corpse."

Kane drags his heavy hand through my matted hair, fingers tangling in the knots he finds there. Abandoning the gesture altogether, he smirks. "Good."

Gabe and Calvin crack jokes in the open doorway with a couple of the alien guards. Sandra's managed to coax Laiya into a wheelchair and is determined to doctor her, despite her best efforts to resist. Sandra asks Ashlyn to get sutures and a first aid kit and Ashlyn's off again.

"Where's Mikey?" I ask when I don't see him in the crowd.

Kane grimaces. "He didn't take your death well. He ran."

"Ran where?"

"Here."

"Here? By himself? Where is he now?"

"I don't…" Kane cocks his head, then looks up at the stairs. "Here, it would seem. Your Sistana's gone and made herself a Notare now, brother. What do you think?"

I follow his gaze to see Mikey standing at the top of the staircase. He's got a bottle of booze trapped in each fist and both are nearing empty.

He doesn't react to anything Kane said, just stares like he's looking at the ghost of a lost relative. I guess, in a truer sense, that's exactly what he's looking at.

"You're *dead*."

He points one of the bottles at me and it falls from his grip onto the marble floor below, narrowly missing Tasha. She frowns up at him before rolling her eyes, and as she makes her way into the recesses of the house, she pulls the pins from her frazzled hair so that it tumbles around her shoulders.

"Animal!" She shouts over her shoulder.

"I was, but I decided I could do better than that," I answer.

Mikey shakes his head in shock, staggers, then runs. He takes the stairs two at a time, half-falling to arrive at my feet.

"You're drinking again," I say, reaching to take the remaining bottle from him. He gives it to me willingly while a blush ravages his already wind-chapped cheeks.

"You weren't supposed to die," he whispers, "that wasn't the plan."

"I don't think it was." I pull down on the collar of Kane's shirt and light spills out and over Mikey. "I don't think anybody could have planned this."

Mikey gawks, freezing in place.

"Easy, brother," Kane says, reaching around me to hold Mikey away from me by the shoulder.

"Easy?" Mikey doesn't seem to understand and scrunches up his bearded face. "Easy? How can I take this easy? She's a fucking Notare." I fleetingly expect anger — jealousy — but then a grin splits his face so wide, he looks a decade younger.

He grabs me away from Kane and wraps me up in one muscular arm. My feet leave the floor as Mikey tosses me over the shoulder and begins spinning wildly in the foyer.

"She's a fucking Notare!"

He shouts and I laugh and people are laughing and cheering and clapping, even as I drop the bottle of booze in my hand and Mikey slips on the spilled liquid.

I land with my knee on his neck and Kane scoops me up to stand before I can properly suffocate him.

"You did it," Mikey says, slowly staggering up after me. He grabs my head and gives me a noogie. "You beat Elise."

"*You* guys beat Elise," I counter, holding onto Kane's arms. I'm still dizzy from all the spinning.

"Mikael, for fuck's sake, be careful with her. She just *died*," Kane tries for light, but his voice breaks.

I grab his hands in both of mine and lean on his chest. There, together, he sighs.

Mikey's dizzy, too and Calvin jolts with laughter when Mikey trips and falls back on the stairs. He looks up at me grinning, still and then switches his gaze to his brother.

"So what now? Does she get Notare privileges and Elise's territory?"

Kane nods, but I'm the one who answers. "It looks like all of her territory passes to me."

"And?"

"And what?"

"What's the first order of business, captain? Or should I say, Notare Abel?"

Leaning forward, he props his elbows on his knees and looks up at me raptly. That's when I notice that the room is pretty much silent, bodies all leaning forward, listening to my answer.

I cling to Kane's hand in mine. He's my pillar of strength — one I'll need as I move forward with the crazy plan brewing inside me. "Elise's territory is now mine. It's called Brianna, with two Ns, I guess."

I inhale deeply as more than forty sets of eyes focus on me, waiting to hear what I'll do with this power, this responsibility.

"I've decided I'm going to try to rebuild. I want that land to be safe human territory. Others — Heztoichen — are welcome, of course, but there's not going to be any cannibal Saltlands gang crap anymore. It's gonna be safe.

"I want to canvas Population for survivors once I make sure basic things like infrastructure and water and all that are up and running."

Ashlyn is beaming at me from only a few feet away, on her knees in front of Laiya's wheelchair, and I can see Becks in her face, smiling too. Would she be proud? I think she she would.

Nerves make my stomach flutter as I continue. "The only thing is, I'll need some help. Kane said he'd help me get started, but he's got a lot on his plate, you know…running a seventh of the world. And I'll need humans of course to help me integrate the other humans from Population that haven't been as fortunate as we have.

"It's going to be dangerous. Really dangerous. And it won't be easy and it won't be comfortable. I know this isn't a great sales pitch and I don't know if now's the time to ask for volunteers, but I don't know what the hell I'm doing and I could really use your help."

The minute I stop talking, the chorus of competing voices that shouts back makes me laugh. My eyes blur but I blink the wetness away and focus on Calvin as he steps forward.

"No way in hell you could stop me from following your crazy ass across the continent."

Gabe, at his side, agrees. "I'm in, fearless leader."

"I'm coming too," Ashlyn chimes.

Sandra, still focused on the shears in her hand as she cuts through Laiya's pant leg, says, "And since there will be quite a number of humans, I think two doctors might be required." She shoots Ashlyn a conspiratorial wink.

Surprising me, Laiya places her hand on Sandra's and says, "And if you would need additional protection, Notare, I would be more than happy to join your guard."

Three of the other black-clad guards step in line beside her and, when she bows, they drop to one knee.

"And heaven forbid you should try to dress yourself on this voyage."

I turn and see Tasha reenter room, looking like she just got back from vacation. She's in an entirely new outfit, skin clear, hair braided like a zipper down the back of her head.

"I'll help as I can, Notare." She nods and I nod back.

I turn then to Mikey, but he just grins and shakes his head. "Don't insult me by asking if I'll come. You need all the help you can get with your mortality rate."

I grin and feel the reassuring pressure of Kane's hand on my waist as I glance around at my friends, my community, my family. A rush of warmth swells in me that has nothing at all to do with the bright flares of light that ripple across my skin, but everything to do with this newfound feeling of hope. I rub my cheeks roughly and laugh as a small chorus of cheers echo across the walls.

Cutting through them, I say loudly, "Well, then, it's settled. We are generation one."

~~Rules for the World After~~

Rule for the World After

Never give up, not even when you're dead.

MONSTER IN THE OASIS

POPULATION SERIES: BOOK TWO

Preview

Chapter One

Listening to the sound of voices, I wonder if I'm dead or asleep. It's the same question I've been asking myself for days now. Or has it been weeks? It doesn't much matter. Time doesn't exist. There's only pain. A bright, effulgent agony. It cuts across my skin, burrowing deep into my flesh, finding home near my brittle bones. The wind whistles through them these days, sounding like sand pattering against paper. I'm just dissolving away.

The hurt hurts worse against my face and chest...but also across my back and shoulders...and also, mostly my right leg, which has been partially flayed.

The bastard enjoyed doing this to me. I wonder if I was wrong in thinking that I'd escaped. Maybe Jack let me get away. Just so I could die like this. *Of course I did, Diego.* Fucker. His voice is all I can hear as I lay dying. That low, demonic chuckle.

My mouth is dry, lips cracked and bleeding, but I can't taste the blood. There's only ash as I lie on the side of the road like something discarded, the slow wheezing of my breath and Jack's ringing laughter keeping me conscious.

I wish I wasn't.

Wish I wasn't alive, either.

I want to die. I've wanted to die from the beginning, but instead, I clawed my way across this wasteland, moving from one water source to the next.

I thought finding the highway might lead me to some town where I could find medical supplies and recover but in the middle of the crumbling asphalt was where my body stopped working and I decided I'd rather let the crows and the carrion take whatever trash Jack left.

The brutal way my body was built was the only part of me with any purpose anyway, and there's no saving it. So there's no point to salvaging something worthless. Fuck it. Let the carrion creatures come out to hunt.

That's the spirit.

A sound in the distance grows louder as everything else begins to fade. Sounds like thunder. A lady once taught me about thunder. Said it was the cough of some great big man who lived up in the clouds. She called him The God. She also called herself mother. I didn't believe her when she said it, and I didn't believe her about that big man either. Nobody treats their kids like that.

Not her.

Not *him*.

How could you think that, my sweet, sweet Diego? I loved you. I love you still.

Another stretch of time passes before the coughing starts up again…then continues, pulling me out my drunken stupor and into the world of pain I thought I'd been lucky enough to leave behind.

The sound persists, forcing memories on me. Memories of big, fat trucks on heavily trafficked roads while me and the other kids running under Jack try to lift merch from them. We succeeded more than we didn't. Jack gave us each fat cuts. I was thirteen? Ten? Younger than that, maybe. But I was a prince to Jack's king. And he's right, I did love him. *Do, Diego, you* do *love me.*

Maybe he's right now, too.

But here and now, it's the sound that's wrong. I can't be hearing the groan of an exhaust pipe. The last time I heard that sound was a decade back, when eighteen-wheelers still ran. They're too big and too slow for Population though, because they present a moving target for gangs — gangs like Jack's. The one I joined sometime after the one called Mother.

When he found me, I'd been on the streets and I was convinced that he was The God she'd spoken about.

Shouting words sound over the thrum of the truck. Some of the voices are deep and distinctly male, but others are lighter, operating at too high a pitch. Kids or women? And that's surprise number two, because kids don't exist out here and the women that do wish they didn't.

I remember the last woman I'd seen on the road, strung up in a kill box. She'd been bloodied worse than anybody I'd seen in a long while, but she held out. She kept fighting. It'd been hard to watch — not the torture, but her spirit slowly evaporating into the sky. With those injuries, she wouldn't have lasted more than a few hours after I cut her down and let her loose. Whatever Jack didn't do, Population woulda done the rest. She'd a died just like I'm doing now. Broken and bloody and in pain. Alone on the side of the road. Road kill. Wearing her insides on the outsides.

Except I'm not alone. Not anymore. Because there are murmurs belonging to voices that belong to the people whispering them. Distinct words peel apart from the whooshing sound that's filled my ears. I hear "can't" and "Sandra" and "save him."

Don't, please don't.

Wishing I had enough strength left to slaughter one last person — whoever talking about trying to save my skin — I try moving my arms. My left hand twitches, but my right is numb, paralyzed up to the shoulder. It's been that way since I swallowed mud two days ago. The closest I could get to water. I'm just rotting now…rotting from within.

"Hey, hey!" Fingers slap my left cheek, the one that isn't a raw, pus filled lesion, then pull up on my eyelids.

Colors blur and swim, making it impossible for me to see the face looming above me as more than just a muddy smear against a darker light. The sky. It's hideous. But that doesn't matter, because I've seen the sky everyday, but I've only heard that voice twice.

"I know you," she shouts, voice too loud and too close and too fucking impossible. The woman from the kill box. The one who I cut down. The one who's dead.

"I know you and you saved my life. Remember? You fought your brothers for me."

I remember. How could I forget? The one halfway decent thing I've done in the past thirty-two years was what landed me here, strung out on the side of the road wearing my insides as a blanket. The irony is as tragic as it is hilarious.

Good men die in this world. Brutally. In piles of piss and shit and blood.

I'm a bad man, so how is it that I'm here, dying like one of the good ones?

My senses grow distant, numbing out into numbness, until I feel pressure on the open wound that rips down the right side of my neck. I hiss, my body writhing, trying to distance itself from the pain. I can't get up. I can't get away. My chest constricts as I push stale air out and I can tell this will be one of my last breaths. Finally.

"Hey!" The voice roars. "You're not allowed to die yet. I won't let my debt go unpaid. Just hold on. I've got a doctor here and she's going to work her magic. Isn't that right?"

I redirect the last seconds of willpower I've got to my eyelids and blink once to clear them. A brown woman sits at my right side, watching the dead one. Forehead wrinkled, lips turned down at the corners, her expression isn't one I've seen a lot, but I'm still human enough to understand it. She's sorry. She can't help me. Thank fuck.

"Abel," the woman speaks quietly, but I can hear her just fine. I'm dead, not deaf. "The most I can do for him is ease his transition."

"No no no no no." The dead one shakes her head, looking just as fierce as I remember. Just as obstinate, too. Her will to live must be stronger than mine because I don't understand how she could have survived the beating and the lashing and the smoke from the Other's immolation unless she had their blood in her system. A lot of it.

"There has to be something you can do," the corpse says to the breather. "You're a healer. *Heal* him."

The woman doesn't respond right away. After a moment, she coils a piece of rubber around my left bicep and inserts a needle somewhere in my arm. Not that I can feel it. I can't feel anything at all. "Ashlyn, bring me the morphine."

I feel her hand on my skin as if there are layers of dirt separating us. Rick told me that when you die, you hallucinate in your final seconds due to a lack of oxygen in the brain — that was a few days before I killed him. Is this an atrophy of the mind? Am I already six feet under?

A small blonde child comes up behind her, but the specter called Abel holds her back. "No! No, fuck that. Sandra, that's too much." Abel grabs the Sandra woman by the wrist. Clear globs of liquid drip from the needle's delicious tip.

Sandra meets my gaze. I stare up at her listlessly. She whispers, "I can end his suffering."

"No. Don't you fucking dare disobey me." Abel points a finger threateningly at Sandra's nose and shoves her shoulder. "I'm the *Notare*, goddamnit! If I can't exercise my power to save this one man then how am I supposed to save the rest of humanity?" A Notare? Sounds like Other speak. I wonder if I'm not hearing her incorrectly.

"Relinquish the few to save the many," Sandra counters diplomatically. But that's fine. I'm happy to be a statistic.

Abel surges forward when Sandra raises the needle a second time and shoves the woman's shoulder. Seated on top of her heels as she is, Sandra falls onto her ass. There are people — men *and* women — standing in the background, watching. None intervene.

"Don't give me that battlefield triage bullshit. I wouldn't be here right now if it weren't for him."

Sandra doesn't seem to rise to Abel's challenge, but instead retreats further into herself. Her hooded gaze looks off into the distance, anywhere but at my face. "If you had been as injured as he is now, then it is likely, Your Grace, that I wouldn't have been able to save you either. It was the blood."

My eyes close and open and behind Abel's frustrated expression I see the tops of heads and above them, spindly boughs crawling up the grey mist, looking like desiccated fingers desperately seeking salvation.

Abel turns to me, places her hand on my good cheek and says, "I'm going to give you my blood."

I gargle up blood and saliva when I mean to attack her. The hell she is. I've lived this long without their shitty alien blood in my body. I'm human. *All* human. One of the few left.

Her wrist comes towards me and I writhe — in my head — because outwardly, I'm not sure I move at all. Castrated by blood loss and incapable of rebelling, I'm grateful when a man steps up behind this dead bitch and grips her shoulders. For a moment I hallucinate Jack. How the fuck did Jack find me? But then I blink.

This guy's not Jack. He's bigger than Jack was — than Jack *is* because it's clear that fucker won't ever die. This guy's bigger than any human I've seen. He's got Jack's dark hair and Jack's green eyes but there's a slight orange pulse around the collar of his shirt that makes it look like he's smuggling a flashlight under his black tee. Huge? Glowing? Nah, he's definitely not human.

So he's a fucking alien Jack. How ironic. All of my favorite fucking things. *You know you could never get rid of me, sweetie.*

My outside shell is immobile though my insides scream as Abel says, "What's the point of *this*, if I can't save him?" She yanks down on the neck of her own black thermal and I see an orange glow pulsing in time to a quick, steady beat. I thought she was human. I was *sure* of it.

I must already be dead and already dreaming.

The other Jack — the Jack Other — shakes his head. "As my Sistana, I can't let you give him your blood. It puts us both at risk."

His voice is even though his eyebrows are pulled together, as if concerned. He watches the human with the glowing golden heart with a fondness that makes me think that he somehow *cares* for her. Jack would never wear an expression like that. He would slice that expression off of any of his dogs' faces if he saw it. He did once.

"Come, Abel. Let Sandra help him." He pulls Abel gently to her feet.

A second male that I recognize as equally inhuman steps into my line of sight. My optic nerve has all but incinerated with the effort it takes to keep my eyes open. I want to close them and fucking die, but curiosity holds my attention just enough to keep me anchored to the hard concrete at my back and the cold breeze nipping at my front like the cruel edges of small, sharp teeth.

"This is the guy?" The blonde Other says. His chest doesn't glow, or if it does, I can't see it underneath his sweatshirt. He's got on black basketball shorts and his hair is tied up in a knot on top of his head. He looks fucking stupid — aside from being nearly too big to take.

"Yes," Abel says, voice pleading and haunting. Not the melody I wanted to die to.

Her fists are wrapped in the glowing Jack Other's shirt. She's pulling. He's staring. They're all fucking staring. "He's the one who cut me down. I thought I was dying — hell, I thought I was already dead. But he fought off Jack's men — his war dogs, or whatever he called them. I was all by myself and *he* was the one who protected me before Mikey showed up." She looks to the blonde. "Before *you* showed up and carried me into the river."

But I'm still stuck — protected her? Is that what I did? Evidently in unknown coordination with this big, blood-sucking idiot.

Confusion puts a clamp on my throat. I'm not breathing. And then I'm seizing. My teeth clench together and my eyes roll back. Pain stabs its fingers into my wounds, whittling down through the diseased and rotten flesh until it scrapes bone with its nails. This is it.

I'm covered in pus and mud and blood and a shadow appears before my eyes where that fated fabled tunnel should have been. I'm dying until I feel a hard, warm object against my mouth and pungent heat dripping down the back of my throat that tastes like metal and eggs. A hand shifts behind my neck, tilting my head up at an angle and I cough as my tongue swells up in my mouth, fighting not to swallow.

"Come on man, you want to live or not?" The blonde fucker speaks to me in a low growl.

No, I don't. I really fucking don't.

But I can't speak and he doesn't hear me and the smell of piss is suffocating and the taste in my mouth is like sucking on pennies and shit. When he withdraws a few moments later, a tingling sensation sweeps my body and is followed closely by an unnatural euphoria. Drugs. Other blood and human drugs. They're working together to fuck me over by keeping me breathing.

Death was so close. I was almost there…

"Thank you, Mikey." Abel's voice whispers as sleep and I war with one another. Her low pitch and the Mikey Other's burn and blur together, becoming a thick haze. "Thank you so much."

"I owe him. The debt you sought to pay was mine."

I've never met the alien, but he sure as shit owes me now. He owes me a death. Because as air comes more easily to my scorched lungs, I understand that I'm not in hell but somewhere much worse. Instead of that easy slip into nothingness, I've been condemned to life.

Chapter Two

"Diego…Diego, can you hear me?" The words are faraway but coming closer, like a train from the World Before and I'm tied to the goddamn tracks. She calls me Diego. How in the hell does she know to call me that?

As if I asked the question out loud, she answers, "I remember your name from before. The murdering asswipe from your gang called you that, so I'm going to assume it's correct. You'll have to tell me if it isn't."

Her hand touches my forehead. I want to get out from under it. So hot and heavy and disgusting in the comfort it tries to provide. I don't need comfort. I don't need anything or anyone.

Suddenly another voice cuts in. I know it too. Sandy or Sana or Sancha something. "Diego, if you can hear me we've stopped moving for the night. I'm going to put you under again. I need to keep you sedated and tied down so that I can work on cutting out the scar tissue.

"Mikey's blood has rid your body of infection but the wounds were severe and, left to fester, his blood won't be able to heal your face so that it looks like it did before."

She doesn't apologize, but instead says stiffly, "I am going to see what I can do to minimize the damage."

I say nothing and relish in the numbness that creeps over me in the seconds before I pass out. It's as close to good as I've ever felt, so I take it without complaint once, twice, a dozen more times until finally I wake and somebody that isn't the blessed Sammy hovers over me.

The corpse is back.

The dead woman that is definitely no longer dead is sitting up, looking down her nose at me. Infrequent shafts of light hit the right side of her face. It's brown, like the skin on the backs of her hands and her throat. Darker than mine is. The same color as Santana but just…different.

Her hair is dark, maybe black, unlike the medium brown fuzz that grows out of my head and that I usually raze down to the root. Her hair is clean, too.

I don't see clean hair a lot in Population, so it distracts me. Little feathery wisps touch her jaw in curls. I think it might even be a little longer than it was the last time I saw her.

Now, definitely not dead, I find the way her dark blue eyes watch me annoying, but perhaps it's only because she reminds me of someone I knew once. Someone I liked. Or maybe hated. Is there a difference?

I think about Jack. I wanted him dead — to die suffering — but at the same time, I'd have done anything for him. I loved him with the entirety of my black, withering soul.

Corpse scoots towards me until I feel the warmth of her hip against mine. The first time I've been made aware of my own body in days. As she moves, something beneath her rattles. Metal on metal on wood. It takes me a second to understand, but I'm on a cot and there's another identical cot stacked on top of it. Above me, slats stare down. Bunks, but where?

The Other who gave me his blood sits on the cot across a short aisle, his sneakers propped up on the bunk I occupy. Abel pushes his shoe away when it brushes her other hip. It's a damn tight fit in here. Like army barracks. Except I can feel the rumbling beneath me and hear the humming of that fabled exhaust pipe and ever so often, the battering of the wind against whatever structure covers us.

So we're in some kind of moving army barracks. I'm alive. The corpse is alive. The Other who looks fucking stupid and stares at her like she's the sun to his universe isn't trying to kill me, but save my life. A blanket covers me. Beneath it, I'm naked. And Sansan's wonderful drugs are numbing me, but not enough.

"How do you feel?"

I don't want to feel. That's what I'd tell her if I could, but I lack the voice. Instead, I turn my head away and close my eyes and try to push back the sensation of sandpaper sheets rubbing like little razorblades against my too sensitive flesh. I focus on the sensation of air flowing in and out of my nostrils. The smell of a canvas tarpaulin. Grease. Metal. Human sweat.

"Diego, I don't know if you remember me, but my name is Abel. You met me a few weeks ago when you and the members of your gang trapped me and a Heztoichen named Trocker." I'd never fucking forget it. "You saved my life after Jack beat and whipped me. I can only assume that you got at least some of your injuries shortly after that."

She pauses again, as if waiting for me to say something. I don't and I won't.

I feel her shift on the cot beside me. I wish she'd just get the fuck off and go away. Die like she was supposed to.

"We found you on the side of the road five days ago and my friend Mikey gave you his blood to keep you alive. He's one of the Others. So is my husband, Kane, and so are my friends Tasha and Laiya and the Lahve.

"The Lahve isn't with us, but some of his troops are. They're here to protect us as we cross Population. The rest of us are human. There's a long story here that you probably aren't ready to hear now, but I'll give you the bullet points.

"The system of governance for the Others is based on which among them carry light, or glow in their chests, like Kane does and like I do now. These seven Notare have divided up the planet. They each rule a different region and the grey area we humans call Population is what was left to us."

Yes, I know Population. I know it well. My jaw ticks, and so do the muscles in my forearms as I remember years and years of pain and suffering. Not mine, but that which I delivered. So. Much. Pain.

"Through a series of events, I ended up bonding to another Notare when we swapped blood. She killed me and when she was killed in retaliation, her light passed on to me. That makes me one of the seven rulers of the world now, in the Others' eyes.

"I'm taking over her lands and making them a human sanctuary. Heztoichen won't be barred from joining us, but there won't be any more of this cannibalistic shit. There won't be any scavenging, no looting, no robbing, no rape, no killing. There won't be anymore gangs.

"It's going to be a helluva lot of work getting there and it's going to require a lot of man power and I know it's a lot to ask of you right now, but I'd love it if you stayed with us.

"I don't have a lot of warriors on my team and I could use someone with your skills. It's going to be at least another two months of hard, deep trekking across Population before we get there, and that's only if everything goes well. The plan is actually to try to find people on the road. We want to bring them with us, if they seem…amenable to it."

What a fucking joke. Jack laughs.

I agree with him. What a fucking joke.

Her tone is higher and more severe as she says, "We want to rehabilitate those that can be rehabilitated, both physically and mentally and we want to be able to give everyone we meet the same choice I'm giving you now. I've got Sandra and Ashlyn here as medics, and some of the humans who've spent more time out in Population can act as sort of... mediators. They'll try to help.

"But what I need now are contingencies. It's not going to be easy to convince people and it'll be harder to get gangs to disband and to absorb them. I want people on my team there for when things don't work out. I need warriors to defend us in case they attack and I've seen you in action."

Her voice trickles away as she asks me to give her something so many others have tried to take. That Jack took with love, with psychological fuckery, and with force.

My obedience. My free will.

"Would you consider it?"

"Because we could always just drop you off on the side of the road, like we found you," a hard male voice cracks. The blonde Other. The one with the stupid haircut. Mikey, she called him.

"Mikael," a deeper male voice reprimands. Who the fuck is this now? Fuck if it's that Fake Alien Jack.

You know you miss me with all your bloody soul.

My muscles twitch with an eagerness to smash my fist through Fake Jack's teeth in an attempt to reach the back of his skull. I'm weak though, arms too heavy to lift.

Of course they'd ask me now when I'm at their mercy, because that's what the hungry do when they finally achieve power. They make slaves. They devour.

I clench my teeth together and close my eyes, blocking out the light as I struggle to shut out the other sounds. Whispering nearby, loud talking just a few paces off.

In the seconds that I wonder what they're saying about me, my self-hatred grows. I don't give a fuck. I don't need this woman's protection. I don't need another Jack, even one with tits on her.

"Diego?"

I twist away from the sound of her voice until I feel the stitching on my neck begin to tear. Let it. Who fucking cares?

"Look, you don't have to answer now. I'm just excited to have you here and happy that you're better." I hear her rise to leave and the sound of heavy shoes hitting the ground beside her.

"Just to let you know, Sandra's managed to cut out most of the excess scar tissue. You'll still have some, but it's better than it was." Sandra. The docs name is Sandra. I hate myself for registering it. For caring.

"I'll get you some food and water. Sandra and Ashlyn have been keeping you on an IV but it'll be good to replenish the old fashioned way, chewing and swallowing and shitting. All that fun stuff."

She whistles, then shouts, "Calvin, would you bring Diego some grub?"

"Sure thing, boss," comes the faraway reply.

I wait for her to leave, but she doesn't. Instead the bitch fucking touches me again, this time my shoulder. I *hate* the feeling of it. I hate being touched. The stress of it brings a cold sweat to my armpits, my hairline and my crotch. It's a contrast to the ferocious and unwanted heat of her right hand on my exposed shoulder. My sternum shudders. I'd have broken her wrist with my own hands if they weren't under the drug-laced spell Sandra put them under.

So instead, I snarl up at her, "D-d-d-don't…fuck-fuck-fucking t-t-touch mmme."

It's been a long time since I've been forced to speak. A long time. Jack and his war dogs knew better than to try. The words come out more mangled than they usually do and I watch the frame of her eyes widen until I can see white on all sides of the iris. She sees me for what I am. Pathetic. And she pities me. And I hate her for it. She looks away and opens her mouth.

"D-d-d-d…" Don't. The word forms perfectly in my mind, repeating itself over and over. But the stutter is like a fucking intruder breaking into my home. I try to push him out the door, but the harder I push, the harder he digs his heels into the carpet. I'm sweating. Fucking convulsing. My face feels hot. My chest feels cold. My palms go clammy. And he's laughing the whole time.

"It's okay," Abel says without giving me a chance to speak. To try.

I'd cut the tongue out of her mouth for it. I've done it before. Jack approved. He held the boy down while I heated the knife, then whittled it in past the kid's teeth.

Jack wouldn't let anybody talk shit about my stutter. He never finished my sentences. He always waited. Patient. Tender. *Because I love you, Diego.* He did. And I worshiped him in return. Let him enslave me. It hurts knowing that he still does.

"Don't," I choke out, the word arriving minutes too late.

Abel nods once, hard, eyebrows knitting together severely over her well-shaped nose. "Calvin'll be over in a second with some food. Just rest up. You've got nothing to worry about while you're here — from any of us," she says, though both of the Others at her back look like they might disagree.

They follow her down the narrow walkway to a bunk bed three over where they whisper and throw uninhibited glances in my direction, judging me, debating their stupid decision to keep me alive and so close to the rest of the innocents.

Of the twenty some beds in the space, most are empty. A few aliens sit near the open entrance of the barracks looking old world stormtroopers, dressed all in black. They look lethal and are watching me like I'm a threat. *Let them come. Let them see what I made you.*

Only two humans sleep within one set of bunks from me. Sandra and, above her, a blonde woman. She doesn't seem to notice me, the blonde woman. The only one who looks over me and sometimes meets my gaze and no matter what, maintains her naive, stupid smile. I hate it. I hate her. I look away.

Coming towards me now is a blonde human man holding a plate and bottle of water. Like all the others *but the stupid, moron blonde chic* his grin fades when he looks at me. Probably because of the scarring, but maybe also because of the twisted expression on my ruined face — a face Jack ruined.

No, I didn't ruin you. You were born ruined.

I turn away from him and close my eyes, sparing him from the burden of having to look at me. Because I know the truth. I'm the most monstrous fucker here, alien or not. It's what Jack made me.

No, Diego. You were born a monster. I merely unlocked the cage and liberated you.

Continue reading anywhere print books are sold.

For more information on where to purchase and to stay up-to-date on new releases, visit
www.booksbyelizabeth.com.

All books by Elizabeth

Berserker Kings - Enemies to lovers. With magic.
Dark City Omega, Book 1 (Echo and Adam)
more to come!

Population - Battles and Heroes that Bite.
Lord of Population, Book 1 (Abel and Kane)
Monster in the Oasis, Book 2 (Diego and Pia)
Immortal with Scars, Book 3 (Lahve and Candy)
more to come!

Twisted Fates - Mafia. Brotherhood. Murder.
The Hunting Town, Book 1 (Knox and Mer, Dixon and Sara)
The Hunted Rise, Book 2 (Aiden and Alina, Gavriil and Ify)
The Hunt, Book 3 (Anatoly and Candy, Charlie and Molly)

Xiveri Mates - Aliens. Heat. New Worlds.
Taken to Voraxia, Book 1 (Miari and Raku)
Taken to Nobu, Book 2 (Kiki and Va'Raku)
Exiled from Nobu, Book 2.5, a Novella (Lisbel and Jaxal)
Taken to Sasor, Book 3 (Mian and Neheyuu) *standalone
Taken to Heimo, Book 4 (Svera and Krisxox)
A Very Xiveri Christmas, Book 4.5, A Novella (Svera and Krisxox)
Taken to Kor, Book 5 (Deena and Rhork)
Taken to Lemora, Book 6 (Essmira and Raingar)
Taken by the Pikosa Warlord, Book 7 (Halima and Ero) *standalone
Taken to Evernor, Book 8 (Nalia and Herannathon)
Taken to Sky, Book 9 (Ashmara and Jerrock)
Taken to Revatu, Book 10, A Novella (Latanya and Grizz) *standalone

64629578R00333